Statesmen   Soldiers   Just Friends

Three Kisses

Revised Edition

by

HEATH DANIELS

Copyright © 2016 Heath Daniels
All rights reserved.

ISBN: 1492153486
ISBN 13: 9781492153481

Photo credits:
The photo for the title page Book 1 "Desperation" was taken by Arvie Abanto, a professional photographer
The photo "Just Friends" on the title page and on page 549 "Brad and Frank say goodbye Arab Style" was arranged by Niklas Granroth and taken by Claus Ståhlberg.
All other photographs were taken by the author or downloaded from public domain locations.

Disclaimer: This is a work of fiction. Any resemblance to persons living or dead is entirely coincidental.

Book 1
DESPERATION

Chapter 1

Wednesday, April 12, 2006
Lattakia, Syria

Abdulrahman al Baladi leaned back in a swivel chair at his desk, legs crossed at the ankles, hands together smugly on his slight paunch. Balding darkish brown hair needing trimming belied his age of 36. A nondescript shirt with the tail outside of the pants strained at the buttonholes. A few days' growth of beard reflected sloppiness of many men in Syria.

Normally lifeless brown eyes gleamed with sinister pleasure; he had just received a coded text message to which he mused in Arabic: *Ali's in place. Soon I can prove to the Supreme Leader and Allah that I, Abdulrahman, the servant of God the Merciful, have served the great al Qaeda to slip someone into the Great Satan and obtain secrets of weapons destroying the noble freedom fighters in Iraq and Afghanistan. Now we can infiltrate many more servants of Allah to destroy their great mockery of symbols like we did on September 11, 2001.*

Allah must be smiling on me because I was alone when the message came from His loyal servants there. The news doesn't have to be shared just yet with that son of a dog Jihad who's surely Moukhabarat, the damned Syrian secret police. Syrians can't run their own country and even had to leave Lebanon in the hands of the infidel Christians, running like puppy dogs with tails tucked between their legs. His name is Jihad, but Syria doesn't know how to conduct a proper jihad in Lebanon. He's not even a true follower of the Prophet, but Alawite following the betrayer Ali. At least he's not one of the Shia scum who think they can remove us from our rightful place in Iraq.

The Great Satan destroyed the wonderful hospitals our beloved leader Saddam Hussein built for the glory of Allah in Iraq, including my hospital. Now only Syria has the medical facilities we need. Stupid Syrians need our money. The loss of Lebanon made them beggars and put them under our control; only the great al Qaeda has money the Assad leeches need. Allah, give me patience to tolerate this vermin who thinks Syria's so great.

Allah be praised; His servants over there found the young man who has one of our beautiful Arab bodies, but how can he be both Arab, the true children of Allah, and an infidel Christian? I'm just a simple man and follower of the Prophet; just a hospital administrator. I can't be expected to understand everything. At least we found another young man with a beautiful Arab body right here in our hospital to take the place of the infidel there with only a small amount of help from the surgeon's knives. He's also one of those Alawites and even has the name Ali, the great betrayer. At least he recanted and now follows the true Sunni path.

Allah, give me more patience. We must tolerate that despicable little Russian who stinks like tobacco and thinks he's a great physician. He's worse than the arrogant Iraqi doctors I had to deal with. He can't even speak the language of Allah and I must put up with Jihad who speaks that ugly coarse Russian and the detested English language of the Great Satan. Once our great Arab doctors, who gave medicine to the world, learn from the Russian, we can squash him like the cockroach he is.

Jihad Noussayri shuffled into the room wearing a non-descript light blue shirt wrinkled from a few days' wear, non-descript cotton-polyester black pants, and dull black shoes. His dark brown hair hung in waves almost to his ears and clearly had not been trimmed for several weeks; a few days' growth of beard completed his slovenly appearance along with dull listless brown eyes. Abdulrahman looked up but did not move or offer greetings, indicating Jihad's age of two additional years did not merit any sign of respect.

Jihad thought in Arabic: *The bastard didn't even stand to greet me much less give me three Arabic kisses. Couldn't call him Abed to his face;*

DESPERATION • CHAPTER 1

after all, Arabs must show respect to other Arabs no matter how stupid they are. To call him Abou Walid for his three-year-old brat of a son would show too much respect to both father and son. No, he's Abed like stupid bumbling Abou Abed in our Arabic jokes, especially with his stupid religious piety. He runs this project like a true Abou Abed; at least I'm here.

Soon we'll have enough good Syrian Ba'athists trained to take over the operation and send these zealot idiots back to Iraq. Let them harass their enemy occupiers who dare think they can take over an Arab land and bring in poison foreign ideas like democracy. They even tell us we have no right to be in our province of Lebanon with all of its capitalist pigs. Even Russians who gave us the socialist ideals of our great Ba'ath Socialist Party left us, but they still don't know when to stop meddling. At least we can use one of their supposedly great doctors. He too'll go, whether he likes it or not, once our surgeons are trained.

Abed's face is different; he's pleased about something, he thought and said in Arabic: "There must be good news."

"Yes," he replied in Arabic, "Ali's in place. Thanks be to Allah everything worked according to plan."

Here that religious idiot goes again, Jihad thought in Arabic. *He believes Allah did all of this. It's good Allah's the merciful one for him; we sure won't be.*

I'm the one who found the young medical student and convinced him with a few lies about his great future. I have to deal with that weasel of a Russian who made me remember Russian I learned years ago in the Soviet school. I have to deal in English with that Indonesian bitch, or is she Philippine? I had to smuggle things she got from Lebanon when they arrived by DHL. I had to arrange flights and go back and forth to the Beirut airport.

"Should we tell Viktor?" Abdulrahman asked in Arabic. "He's attached to Ali and worried about him. You have to tell him; he won't speak to me in the language of Allah and I can't speak the filthy languages he speaks."

Jihad replied in Arabic: "I'll tell him."

"Greetings Viktor Sergeyevich; I have good news," he said a few minutes later in Russian to the doctor who stood about five feet six inches with stringy mostly grey hair thinly covering his balding head reflecting his age somewhere between 55 and 65. He wore baggy gray cotton-polyester pants synched tightly with a narrow belt, a baggy light gray long sleeved shirt, and non-descript cloth slippers. Translucent white plastic rimmed glasses with extra-large square-ish lenses completed his appearance.

"Oh?" Viktor Sergeyevich replied showing tobacco-stained teeth thinking in Russian: *I wish the bastard'd speak English instead of his horrible Russian. We both speak English better than he speaks Russian or I speak Arabic, but he's such a stupid proud ass. A small thing among all the many I've had to tolerate on this project.*

"Ali's in place," Jihad continued in Russian. "I'm sure you'd want to know".

Viktor Sergeyevich smiled broadly and said in Russian: "Oh, wonderful. Thank you so much dear friend Jihad for telling me. I'm so relieved. Soon he'll be back and help me with our work here. With just a little more training, he'll be almost as good a surgeon as I am."

With visible relief he nodded goodbye and thought in Russian: *Now I can go to the hammam tonight and relax.*

Does this stupid arrogant ass of a doctor really think Ali's coming back? Jihad asked himself in Arabic walking to his office. *If he weren't so absorbed in himself, he'd realize we can never let Ali back in this country.*

CHAPTER 2

Wednesday, April 12, 2006
Fairborn, Ohio, USA

U.S. Army Captain Patrick Ferris, energized by the warm sunny spring day, smiled as he backed his few-months-old silver BMW 3 series out of his garage. His dark reddish-brown hair was closely trimmed military style; he wore a long-sleeved uniform shirt that does not require a jacket. Government-issue glasses for driving and sometimes reading covered his green-brown eyes.

PATRICK'S PRIDE AND JOY: A NEW 2006 BMW 3 SERIES MODEL

THREE KISSES

Driving through mostly empty streets in early morning his thoughts rambled: *It's spring; Elsie and I can take long drives and really put my baby through its paces. This's the first really nice car anyone in the family's owned. Mom and Dad had to be modest in car choices so customers wouldn't think they're making too much money charging high prices. Got grief from some fellow officers because I bought a German car after the way they acted towards us over Iraq. Am I too Lebanese? They sure love their status symbols.*

Now that we're living together we have more time to go driving. Maybe we'll settle down in one place someday. An Army career's been good, but we'd be moving every few years. Elsie's burning out with her long-haul travel schedule, especially now that AmericaWest bought the company and flight attendant schedules are screwed up.

PATRICK'S AND ELSIE'S RENTED HOUSE IN FAIRBORN, OHIO

Elsbieta Maryja Stankowski. With a name like that, she was teased by non-Polish kids in school. One day she announced that she would be Elise. A bratty girl said she should be Elsie, like Elsie the Contented Cow on Borden Milk. When they giggled, she stated she'd rather be Elsie the contented cow than Petunia the pudgy pig, poking her bratty classmate in her chubby middle. After that, she was Elsie except for her passport, driver's license, and company ID.

ELSIE THE CONTENTED COW

Elsie has a nickname. I've always been Patrick, not Pat, Patty, or Paddy. No one thinks I'm Lebanese. Mom was determined I have a good American name, but Grandmother Chemaly had to approve so I had to have good Lebanese name also. Lebanese Maronite Christians have given children French names, often saints, for generations. Mom's Nadine; Dad's Raymond. He even suggested Antoine or Pierre if I were a boy, but was overruled. I would be Patrick, Mom insisted, a great saint certainly known and respected in Lebanon, France, and the Christian world. Dad was delighted to be Abou Patrick for family and friends back in Lebanon. Mom insisted my second name be Nabil for her beloved father who was killed in the Lebanese civil war. 'Americans have two names', she insisted. Lebanese don't have middle names but merely take their father's name as a middle name when occasions require.

Our common distinguished Lebanese name is usually written 'Fares', but when passports were hastily issued under siege in Beirut, the *not-so-bright clerk wrote Ferris. Kids back home teased me about being a Ferris wheel, but it was fun to be the big wheel of Russellville, Alabama. Dad bought shirts for our soccer team that had a small Ferris wheel on them with the name Ferris Foodland. It's still a favorite store even with Super Walmart almost next door. Ferrises are among the town's most liked citizens even though we drove to the next town to go to a Roman Catholic Church. On Easter Sunday, I'll give a special prayer of thanks and light a candle at mass. Elsie promised to do the same in Munich.*

Why does she have to be away Easter weekend? She works Munich flights, but why this weekend? Felicia'll invite me for an Easter egg hunt with the kids. She always includes me and I do like being with them; makes me eager for Elsie and me to have our own kids. Elise's not jealous because she knows there's nothing between Felicia and me. She does think it's strange an attractive young Philippine widow is so attentive knowing I'm committed to someone else.

Wright Patterson Air Force Base, Ohio, USA

Patrick parked near the office of a joint armed forces task force for top secret small weapons development, asking himself: *Why's Felicia so early? That's her car. I hate traffic and I'm a morning person. Not Felicia. She has children to get to school and a single parent with no help.*

Felicia Cavanaugh was about five feet one inch with a petite well-proportioned figure. She had Asian features typical of Filipinas, and elliptical thin black framed glasses that highlighted her almond-shaped eyes. Her job title is 'cost analyst assistant'. She was an accountant in the Philippines, but because she could not get a full top secret security clearance, being a naturalized U.S. citizen with Philippine family ties, she could not advance to professional status. She had married Kevin Cavanaugh, an American helicopter pilot who was killed in the first Iraq war, settled in the U.S., and had two children. She became annoyed at having to spell and explain her given name, Khadija. Because she attended Catholic services

DESPERATION • CHAPTER 2

with Kevin and their children, she adopted Felicia, the name of a minor saint, so she said, that became her Christian name.

Patrick reflected as he bounded up the stairs: *She's a good colleague and does secretarial things just so long as it isn't expected of her, especially for me. She even takes my uniforms to be dry cleaned and really put up a fight to get a full refund for the uniform they lost. She was really helpful when I lost my wallet and drove me around to get things replaced, like a driver's license.*

Frank and Jen resent her attention to me, but he's so stand-offish with everyone except Jen; Marine Corps officer stiffness and Southern gentleman aloofness. Jen's bitchy like career women often are with each other, especially being a Navy officer who clawed her way up in a man's world. I haven't asked Felicia to pay so much attention to me, but it sure is nice.

He smiled thinking about unusual but fun things with Felicia and the children: *Goes out of her way to invite me for dinner when Elsie's away. I'm not much of a cook and wonderful Philippine food she prepares with so little effort's a nice change from meat-and-potatoes Elsie learned to cook from her Polish mother. Even trimmed my hair one night base barbershop was busy. Claimed she trimmed her husband's hair, but must've lost her touch. Wouldn't dare tell her I didn't like her haircut; Now I make sure hair's freshly trimmed when I visit. A model in one of the children's projects to make a complete plaster mold of my face, including the ears. Vaguely remember things like that in kindergarten, but cover the ears?*

He smiled and said to Felicia, who was sitting at her desk wearing pants with a simple complementary shirt-blouse and high-heeled shoes to give her height: "Good morning Sugarlump."

She barely said "hello."

"You ok?" he asked.

"Children kept me up late," she replied in fluent English, but with a detectable accent. Lots of work and I just didn't feel like fighting with them this morning; called the neighbor girl to come get them off to school."

She put her head down as if to start working causing Patrick to think: *Seems to be shuffling papers; best leave her alone. Coffee's made so I'll help myself and read the paper.*

THREE KISSES

"Good morning," Marine Corps Major Frank Reynolds said as he entered, took a cup of coffee, and went to his desk. He too wore a long-sleeved uniform shirt without a jacket that was clean, fresh, and pressed to a razor sharp edge; his shoes were shined so brightly the overhead light reflected. His medium brown hair, like Patrick's, was trimmed close; his green eyes intense as always.

Frank's never talkative in the morning, Patrick said to himself, *but why so reserved? Walks like he has a poker up his ass and uniform's all starch, spit, and polish. Only a couple of inches taller than I am, about five eleven, but you'd think over six feet the way he carries himself; always working out to keep slim and trim. Me? Just want to stay fit. Heaven knows I have a couple of extra pounds around the middle.*

Can't talk much about our work because it's highly classified; even though we have the same clearance, there's 'need to know'. He's friendly and talkative when groups are at lunch, but ignores me when we're in the gym. Doesn't even suggest we go together, although both go at the same time and sometimes goes with Jen who swims daily. Why doesn't he suggest we go to officer's club for a drink? We often see each other there. He and Jen are friendly with each other; sometimes see them together around town and at the club. Are they an item? Both're in their 30s, unmarried, and committed to careers, although Frank said he became a Marine Corps officer to command troops not procure weapons. They talk so little about their personal lives, while Felicia always talks about her children and dead husband, and I'm always happy to talk about Elsie.

U.S. Navy Lieutenant Commander Jennifer Lewis came in nodding hello, smiled at Frank while she got coffee, and sat at her desk.

Patrick continued observing: *She's dressed nice today, even wearing a skirt for a change, and she compliments her uniform well even though military uniforms and dress codes do little for femininity. Elsie's uniforms're different; make her look so sensual and elegant. Jen and Elsie are about the same height, about five eight, an inch shorter than me, but Elsie's so well-proportioned and has her shoulder-length blonde hair and baby blue eyes. Jen's, so, so military. I'm prejudiced. Jen's attractive, but who could compete with Elsie?*

DESPERATION • CHAPTER 2

He reflected on names again: *Frank stated he's Frank, not Francis or Franklin, and took his passport out of the readiness kit to show us. His full name, Frank Bartholomew Reynolds, is a curious combination, a simple first name that's usually a nick name and a long pretentious middle name. Told us about his family's southern aristocratic heritage, Marine Corps service, and attending The Citadel for generations. Reynolds have lived in Florida for a hundred or more years, long before it was fashionable to live there. I'm a southerner too and know what pompous asses they can be.*

He glanced at the clock thinking: *Time to put away the newspaper and get to work.*

Chapter 3

Wednesday, April 12, 2006
Fairborn, Ohio, USA

Ibrahim al Asadi woke up in a sleeping bag about 7:30 a.m., reached for his glasses, and said to himself: *Why the hell're we in a shitty dump like this sleeping on a dirty carpet? Screen door's broken. Our families' apartments are better'n this and they're damned bad. Adnan said we have to be close to where that Patrick guy lives and here he can pay cash. Anyone else awake yet? No, Boudi's asleep in his sleeping bag; Ali's on the couch. That asshole Adnan's in the bedroom; all that riding in the car and we sleep on the fuckin' floor while he sleeps in the bed.*

SHABBY APARTMENT IN FAIRBORN, OHIO,
WITH BROKEN SCREEN DOOR.

DESPERATION • CHAPTER 3

Brahim, as he was called by almost everyone, pulled on jeans over briefs wearing a t-shirt. He was slender with dark brown, almost black, slightly wavy neatly trimmed hair. With black wire-framed glasses that had round lenses, he looked studious or some would say geeky.

In the shabby kitchen he prepared instant coffee continuing to say to himself: *It was kinda fun driving the BMW, but all the time on my ass while Ali drove was too much. Stupid asses wanted us to steal a BMW. This's not Syria where you can steal anything and get away with it if you have connections. Mohammad convinced 'em if it was so damned important for Ali to drive a car like that guy's, they'd better come up with money. Besides they can sell it again and get most of it back. Bet he doesn't sell it.*

It wasn't so bad driving across New York to JFK Airport, except Boudi insisted on driving most of the time. A long wait for Ali because his flight was late. We thought he'd blown it and got caught with that guy's passport. Finally, he came through looking just like the photograph. He was dazzled and overwhelmed; a bit un-cool for an American Army officer coming home from a visit. We got him in the car fast and on the way. He had to drive all the way so he knows the car just like it's his own.

He was kind of nice to be with, but a little weird. Said he lived in New York City as a kid. He had to order at the fast food joints where to get used to this country. He also had to get us a room in the motel we stayed in. Finally, we got here and had to find this shitty apartment. Adnan said we couldn't call his cell phone for directions except in extreme emergency because someone might listen. The number'd been used for calls from Syria and maybe someone was monitoring it. If we did call, it had to be from a pay phone and we had to ask for Mr. Rodriguez.

He returned to the living room with the coffee saying to himself: *Nothing to read, can't watch TV, what the hell can I do? Makes me think how I hate this fuckin' country even though I was born here. My mother and father, Boudi's parents, and a few others from Yemen settled in Lackawanna where some Yemenis already lived. Life hasn't been bad for them; anything'd be better than being shot at back in Yemen. They have friends their age who speak Arabic and never leave their little circle. They don't know what kind of hell Boudi and me're in: not Yemeni, not American, not shit.*

THREE KISSES

Teachers never got our names right. Called me Abraham the fuckin' Jewish name. Don't they know Ibrahim was father of the Arabs as much as the Jews? They should read their own fuckin' bibles for God's sake. It says in Genesis God told Abraham, who we call Ibrahim, that Ishmael's also his son and his children'll be a great nation. Of course I've read the Christian bible. Why shouldn't I? I'll read almost anything. Jesus is the last great prophet before our blessed Prophet Mohammad, peace be upon him.

Boudi's teachers called him Abe or Abby. He wanted to scream at them 'it's Boudi you fuckin' bitch!' but how could he be disrespectful to a teacher? He just said Abdullah is Boudi just like James is Jimmy. Some finally got the message. Other Yemeni kids called him Boudi and me Bob like people back in Yemen call someone named Ibrahim. Now out in public, especially down south, we call each other Bud and Bob just like regular American guys and no one suspects a thing.

In high school some smart asses called us A-hab the A-rab. When a Yemeni guy beat up a kid screaming 'yeah, I'm Arab and damned proud of it', he got suspended, but no one called us A-rab again. Look at the bastards from Central America. They couldn't even speak English, but no one called José 'Josie'.

Why're we here setting things up to hurt the Americans? They don't give us any fuckin' choice. Damn it, we're Americans too, or so our birth certificates say, but they won't give us a chance. The great American dream. What fuckin' American dream? In high school I was on the honor roll and in the honor society. They'd barely talk to me although some teachers tried to be nice. When I wanted to go to college, they wouldn't give financial aid. They think my parents can afford it? Fuckin' black asshole bastards get financial aid, affirmative action. Said I'm not a minority who's entitled, but maybe I could get a student loan.

What's with blacks who think they deserve everything for nothing and treat us like shit? There're plenty of blacks in Yemen, or so we're told, and no race problems. Blacks think because they play good basketball they're hot shit. Boudi's a damned good athlete, but they teased him when he didn't want to take a shower and show his dick to everyone and coaches wouldn't do anything.

DESPERATION • CHAPTER 3

Damned bitches in this country won't even let us fuck 'em any more. Yeah, down south some of the girls still think we're different and cute with our dark skin and brown eyes, but they make us put those damned condoms on. They really like Boudi with his athletic body. I don't do so bad, but not like back in high school. Central American girls liked us to fuck 'em because we treated 'em decent and didn't hit them or beat them up. After 9/11 that sure changed. 'Oh, you might get us pregnant. You're terrorists'. One guy's girlfriend did get pregnant and they wanted to get married because they were in love. Her parents forced her to have an abortion because they didn't want a terrorist's kid in their family. Terrorist? They don't even know what a terrorist is.

That fuckin' Bill of Rights. History and government were my best subjects; straight A's. Freedom of religion, but we can't have a proper mosque because someone might vandalize it; have to hide it inside an old store front. Freedom of speech and a free press? They use that to defame our Prophet by publishing those cartoons. At least we're not protesting like in other countries. 'Cool it' our imam Mohammad says. We don't need to protest cartoons here; that's playing into their hands. Lay low. When the time comes we'll really show 'em. We made that World Trade Center collapse like Legos. Legos, ha, Danish; fuckin' Danes started this with cartoons.

America the great democracy where the people elect their leaders. Who do they elect? Fuckin' George W. fuckin' Bush who bombs Arabs and wants to destroy Islam. Who else could we vote for? John fuckin' Kerry who not once but two or three times went to Florida to tell the old blue-haired Jewish bitches that Israel's the greatest ally the U.S. has ever had and the Clinton cunt, our great Senator from New York who wants to be the next president? She goes to Jerusalem to the Wailing Wall and says she'll pick up a rifle herself to kill Palestinians. God, all Palestinians want is to protect themselves from an Israeli holocaust.

Damn, when're they going to wake up? Sitting here getting angry with nothing but coffee makes me sick at my stomach. Let's get on with this shit if we're going to do it. Today, Adnan says Ali has to get to know this neighborhood just like it's his own. We also have to dress him up in that Army uniform and make sure he looks like a real Army officer. Ha! Boudi and I thought about joining the Army after high school, but then we found out how they'd treat us. Another Yemeni kid joined; they really made it tough, but they couldn't keep him out for no good reason. After the USS Cole attack and 9/11, they made sure he was buried in some hell hole in Alaska. They say they have Muslim chaplains, but only those black bastards who call themselves Black Muslims. Our imam Mohammad is a true servant of the Prophet for whom he's named. He runs the business to get money for al Qaeda and pay us. I just wish he had someone better than this Saudi jerk Adnan to run this operation. Damn, it! When'll he wake up?

Some minutes later, Ali Salman stirred from deep, groggy sleep. *Where the hell am I?* he asked himself in English. *Oh, yeah, this crummy apartment where we wait 'til I go into action. Is this a dream? I woke up at 3 a.m. after a fitful sleep and tossed and turned at least an hour. Jet lag I guess, but I haven't traveled enough to know what jet lag is. Now I've been sleeping like I was drugged. Brahim's awake, but I don't want to talk to him just yet.*

Brahim and Boudi are OK and kinda good looking. All they talk about is sex, sex, sex, asking about my sex life too. There was that Swedish girl in high school just before we had to move to Aleppo. She came onto me saying she wanted a Syrian because she was tired of European guys. I was so nervous and didn't know what to do. I just put it in her and came right away. She wouldn't have anything to do with me after that, which was fine with me. I even worried I got her pregnant. Hey, there's Brahim going to the kitchen. Maybe I can run pee and shower.

Dressed only in boxer shorts and a t-shirt, he quickly but quietly walked through the bedroom and stepped into the shower continuing to think: *Oh, that feels good after a long trip, walking through hills across the border into Lebanon because I couldn't cross with that guy's passport, and had to leave my Syrian ID card behind. On the way to Beirut, stopping in his family village being careful not to talk to anyone; at least I can tell anyone who asks what the village is like. In the Beirut airport that jerk Jihad said he had to give me a hug and three Arab kisses. Yuck. Thankfully I won't see him again.*

Guess I wasn't too nervous going through Lebanese passport control pretending I don't speak Arabic; they let me through and didn't ask what I

DESPERATION • CHAPTER 3

was doing in Lebanon. Even in Prague they didn't ask many questions. It was smooth in New York too; just asked where I lived in the U.S. and how long I'd been gone. I have an Ohio driver's license in case I needed to prove anything.

I'm basically recovered from the surgery but it'd've been better to wait a few more days. They had to get me here before the American Easter holiday. Funny, the Christians in Syria have Easter a week later.

Adnan was still asleep when Ali came out of the shower, dried, and walked into the living room with a towel wrapped around him. He quickly dressed with the same clothes as the day before as he continued to say to himself: *Room's empty; I think I hear voices outside. I don't want to talk to them anyway. When they're not talking about sex, it's about how bad America is. They think I hate America like them. I liked America when I was a kid; they were nice to me, but I didn't go outside of New York City. Maybe things are different where they're from.*

I have to go along with them. What'd they do if they find out I just wanted to get out of Syria and this's the best way? When this is over, I'll run away and figure out something. I can't be Patrick, but I can be someone other than Ali Salman. I speak their language like a native and I'm a doctor. Maybe find some place that wants a doctor without proving who he is. Let me see if I can get coffee and something to eat.

In the kitchen, he fumbled with the stove looking for matches or a lighter, and asked himself: *how do I light this stove? I have to talk to them after all.*

He saw Brahim and Boudi talking outside the back door window. Abdullah Zakawi stood five feet 11 with a well-built athletic body. Like Brahim, he had neatly trimmed very dark brown hair and brown eyes.

Ali asked: "How do I light the stove?"

"It's a fuckin' electric stove, stupid," Brahim said.

Boudi showed him how to turn on the burner with a smile and pat on the shoulder.

Chapter 4

Wednesday, April 13, 2006
Lattakia, Syria

In evening, Viktor thought in Russian: *This's a crappy hammam, not a nice historical one like in Aleppo or Damascus. Better than nothing and haven't been in ages. Relax with a nice scrubbing and maybe see some things.*

He undressed, wrapped himself in the traditional long cloth, and lay on the big, low, smooth marble slab where a scrub 'boy' first scrubbed with a scratchy sponge, then soaped and rinsed his body and shampooed his hair.

He thought in Russian: *Old Ottomans knew it's healthy to remove dead skin; refreshing too. Strange to put dry saunas in these hammams, even old historic ones. Russians and Finns weren't here 700 years ago. He won't let me get a good look. Maybe in the steam room or sauna; sometimes guys'll spread their legs. In a way, this's more fun than Russian saunas where everyone's naked. Not a challenge to get a little peek.*

KGB had a double standard about homosexuality; lots of it, but could be used against you. Even recruited 'em as spies because experienced at living double lives. Always had something on everyone and homosexuality was just one. Couldn't be out, but sure had fun with guys in saunas.

When the scrub was finished, he wrapped the cloth around his middle and went to the steam room saying to himself in Russian: *Good to*

DESPERATION • CHAPTER 4

sweat after a good scrub. That guy over there; can I look without being too obvious? Which one is Moukhabarat? Surely figured me out. Want to get rid of me anyway once enough local doctors they trust. Ali's just an experiment to see if it can be done. I'll figure some way to get away. Got out of Afghanistan before Russians could kill me. I know too much about Russian guys' faces I fixed. They wouldn't let this kind of knowledge stay alive.

Had to stay in Kazakhstan longer than I wanted. Working on Asian faces is OK, but difficult to make duplicates of flat faces and high cheek bones. Then Tajikistan and Uzbekistan. At least their faces are better to work with. Back to Afghanistan; still had some old contacts. Taliban tolerated me. Found out about my experience making doubles, sent me to Syria where there's good hospitals and I could train people. A whole army of doubles of Americans sabotaging the whole country. What the hell do I care? I don't hate the Americans, but love my work.

Oh, he's moving his legs. Uncircumcised and a good size too; must be Christian.

Wait a minute! Wait, wait, wait! Ali's circumcised, pretty normal size; maybe a little smaller. What about the guy whose place he's taking? Is he bigger? Uncircumcised? He's Christian. Had to circumcise some doubles if going into Muslim areas; even some we infiltrated into Israel. Didn't worry about size. Americans are circumcised medical journals say and the guy was born there. What're their toilets like? What if he gets seen peeing?

Later in bed, Viktor tossed and turned thinking in Russian: *Should I tell them? Surely it's OK. Americans are circumcised, but what if he's bigger? If I don't tell them and he gets caught they'd blame me; who else? What if I tell them and nothing happens? They'd want to get rid of me as soon as they can. They're going to get rid of me anyway so it's just a matter of time. Can I take a risk with my dear Ali? All they have to do is tell him not to pee at a urinal.*

Chapter 5

Wednesday, April 12, 2006
Wright-Patterson Air Force Base, Ohio, USA

Felicia could think about nothing but Patrick as the afternoon went on: *They said they wouldn't kill him; what if something goes wrong? Have to make him breathe powder to give him a bad cold then sleeping medicine tomorrow. If I don't give him enough, maybe they'll kill him; if I give him too much, it'll kill him. Came early to rig up the thing on the lamp above his desk to drop powder, but what if someone notices? Think he noticed I'm not wearing a skirt. Had to come early to get his passport from them and put it back in the readiness kit. Cookies have powder; maybe Frank and Jen'll get a cold.*

When'll this be over? I just want to go somewhere and die. If Patrick dies, I'll kill myself like one of those Muslim girl suicide bombers, except I won't kill anyone else. Had enough of their orders. Steal his uniform. Steal his wallet. Steal his keys. Get his passport for them. Take videos making him think it was for fun. Make that stupid face mold. Even the kids suspicious about that. Go online logging onto Yahoo, MSN, and AOL messengers—all three going back and forth so there's nothing coherent on any one. Everything dropped off at very specific times. At least passport was waiting.

Send the kids away, leave, and never come back. Where? Kevin's parents love them, or I think they do, but would they like little half-Asian kids in a conservative city like Louisville?

DESPERATION • CHAPTER 5

How'd I get in this mess? Is Allah punishing me for letting infidels inside me and marrying one? What could I do? I was pregnant and knew it was his. Hadn't been with another guy in over a month and had a period since then. Kevin said he loved me and always treated me like he did. Bad enough when he was killed. Now they're forcing me to cooperate.

My mother called. Hurting her and would hurt her more if I didn't cooperate. Horrible voice speaking our language saying cooperate or they get hurt and have painful death.

Why'd my mother contact me after all this time? They disowned me when I married Kevin and moved to America. Probably would've killed me and the baby if I moved back. Dishonor to the family. Forced me to go to Luzon all the way from our Mindanao village. Work and send money. At least studied accounting and get a half-decent job. Kept needing more and had to pay for school. Had a pretty face and a nice body men would pay for. Then there was Kevin.

Called this morning; sister screaming she's being hurt down there unless I kept on doing what they said. Just want to tell them to go ahead after the way they treated me. They're my family; can't do that.

Frank sat daydreaming after his noon workout and lunch: *What's with Felicia? Looks terrible; trying to be all smiley and cheerful, almost forcing us to eat cookies. What's between her and Patrick? He screwing her? He just got engaged. Screw an Asian? Tried a couple of whores in Okinawa; Asian women didn't do it for me; no woman does. Thank god for finding The Serpent in Cincinnati. Damned good guys and friends; nurses, policemen, flight attendants. Better'n some asshole marine officers.*

Damn, why can't I forget that shit in Okinawa? My troops raped local girls. Reported them to military police like I was supposed to; wanted to court martial 'em and give 'em dishonorable discharges. No one deserves to be forced to have sex. CO reamed my ass saying 'boys will be boys'; Pacific commander supported him. Gave 'em a reprimand and let 'em go. Locals found out; all hell broke loose. Tried to make me the scapegoat, but I'd been around Marines long enough to know how to cover my ass. Bring me down and you go down with me. Forced the CO to retire and reassigned me first to headquarters and then here. Only thing I'll command is a desk. All I need is hang on for my 20.

Reynoldses have been Marine Corps officers for three generations; I'm not going to quit. This job's not so bad. Double life's driving me crazy. At least I can talk to Jen. Funny, figured her from the beginning, but why'd it take me so long to get courage to come out to her? Some of her girlfriends are pretty cool too.

Patrick thought: *Why'm I feeling tired? Maybe all the love making before Elsie left. Did it without condoms. Nothing like it! Forget rubber things that don't fit someone as long and thick as I am, and the long foreskin makes it worse.*

Back home got teased when we took showers after gym classes. What courage to finally ask Mom. Couldn't ask Dad; he's Lebanese after all! Explanation simple enough: some small emergency when I was born. I was whisked away and she barely got a glimpse of me. A couple of days later when the doctor mentioned circumcision, Grandmother Chemaly insisted little Lebanese Christian boys aren't cut on like Muslims; besides, they were paying the doctor enough. Dad didn't have insurance back then having just spent all his money to buy the store.

Oh well, back to work. Feels like I'm getting a cold.

Chapter 6

Wednesday, April 12, 2006
Fairborn, Ohio, USA

Adnan Mohamad Abdullah al Wahab rolled up his prayer mat after mid-afternoon prayer. He stood five feet eleven, was very slender, and wore blue jeans and a long-sleeved shirt; his black hair was slightly wavy and longish.

Dark brown eyes had a sinister gleam as he thought in Arabic: *Brahim and Boudi went shopping. We need food, but could've waited for prayers. They're almost wild to drive that fancy BMW. Why'd I have to get these two? Won't even pray like good Muslims. Reliable so far, but when this's finished strap 'em with explosives and send on a suicide mission; then they can have all the sex they want with the virgins in heaven. Brahim's bright enough, but Boudi's definitely suicide bomber type. Two more days and out of here. Where next? Hope not back to Lackawanna. But if Allah wills it....*

'Lay low, go sleep' they said; 'we'll find you'. Sent to Dallas, made into Eddie Rodriguez. I can be a good Mexican; look like one, dress like one, cut my hair like one. Talk like one too. Stupid infidels can't tell the difference between my accent and a Mexican one.

Back home they made me study molecular biology, but wouldn't give me a decent job; only those in the huge royal family get good jobs. Made me work in a hospital lab. Al Qaeda took me away from that. Sent me to Afghanistan. Made me a medic because I'd worked in a hospital. said I could go to medical school here. After 9/11, no more Saudi Arabians in school in the U.S.

Work construction, they said; you have a strong body even if you are skinny. Then a call to go to Lackawanna. Close to Canada. Lots of Yemenis there loyal to al Qaeda.

The Arab guy here is an infidel Christian who could be sacrificed to the glory of Allah, but we can't kill him; attract too much attention. A daughter of Allah working with him; Philippine, or is she Indonesian? Wouldn't keep quiet and do what she's told like a good Muslim woman.

Made me rent this awful apartment. Mr. Rodriguez just moved from Texas with ID to prove it. Can't communicate with Syria. No internet. Not safe to phone except in emergency; U.S. government monitors calls. Supposed to be stopped now, but who trusts them.

Ali lay on the couch in ordinary casual clothes, not daring to sleep, thinking in English: *If I sleep now, won't sleep tonight and'll be all messed up for tomorrow.*

So this is what the Great Satan of America's like. Have to pretend it's evil and that Bush has done horrible things, which he has. Any place'd be better than Syria. Anyone who dares speak is taken out by the Moukhabarat. Made a broken man of my father. A brilliant young law student from Lattakia, home of Haffaz Assad, played with the Assad boys as a child. All Alawite. Became a member of the Ba'ath party; had to in order to go anywhere. How old was I when he was to Syrian mission at the UN? Must've been a baby. In kindergarten and elementary school, I learned to talk and act like any American boy. Everyone treated me nice. Teased and called me 'fish boy' because my name's Salman. All in good fun.

Dad was transferred to Damascus to the foreign ministry. Up or out; couldn't stay in New York forever. Put me in the international school with diplomats' kids. Took a long time to realize Moukhabarat watched me.

Dad was really upset over massacre of ten thousand Islamists in Hama. Didn't censor the news that time. Lesson not lost on Dad even if no connections or sympathy with Islamists. Suddenly transferred to Aleppo as Americans call our second city Halab. Wouldn't it've been kinder to kill him. When are they kind? Wouldn't talk to me or anyone. Don't know if he talked to Mom. Moukhabarat turned sister against brother; daughter against father. For all he knew, I'm Moukhabarat.

Made me study medicine in Arabic language I spoke only on the streets. Finally, got them to send me to Lattakia for surgical residency. No pleasure being around family right in the Ba'ath homeland not knowing who's Moukhabarat. At least away from Aleppo with life of my own. Had to study with Viktor because I speak English and he speaks only Russian and English.

Finally, could do something that gives me pleasure. He's a master. Learned to restore broken damaged faces and bodies. Also had to deal with rich bitches who wanted nose jobs, but was tolerable. He's a nice man even though no one likes him. They wanted me to have surgery. Said I'm close enough to an Arab guy in America to make me look just like him. Take his place to get military secrets for al Qaeda. How could I cooperate with al Qaeda? Anything to get out of Syria.

Over a year hiding in the hospital so no one could see me as I was cut and healed. Work with Viktor in the operating room when patients anesthetized otherwise nothing but American television, American newspapers, American movies.

Now I'm transformed. Still call me Ali, but Ali's no more. Who'll I be next? Can't remain Patrick. They think they have me to use from now on. Sending me to Canada, Jihad said, to sleep until they need me. They can't keep me. Just slip away somewhere in Canada. Next week's worry. Work to do here tomorrow.

Chapter 7

Thursday, April 13, 2006
Fairborn, Ohio, USA

Patrick woke up thinking: *Damn, why do I have to have a cold now? Almost Easter; weather's nice. Elsie's not here but it'd've been nice to go for a drive. Can't go to Felicia's now; kids'll want to crawl all over me.*

In the shower, his mind meandered: *Where'll we go on our honeymoon? Elsie hasn't been to Russelville. She's met the folks here and Anna Marie came once too. What's to do there other than visit family?*

Mom and Dad went there because distant relatives were near; nowhere else good when they left Lebanon so fast. Alabama's good a place as any to blend in like Maronite Lebanese have done for a hundred years. Dad found the store for sale in Russellville and been there ever since. Had a little money and well educated like most Lebanese. Store does well, but a struggle at first. Had to work my ass off after school, weekends, summers. Fortunately, I'm bright and didn't have to study much.

Damn, I was mad at Dad because made me work so much. Was good too. Supported school activities; sponsored the soccer teams—football teams he said like back in Lebanon. We weren't rich, but could go to Auburn for engineering and got ROTC scholarship for MBA at Bama. Anna Marie had to work too; ran the cash register and worked in the office. Got mad at Dad and Mom too, but good to her too; sponsored cheerleaders. Went to Bama too. Fun having a little sister at the same school. Alabama's been good to us.

It's nice; lots of lakes and even beaches way down south. Not for a honeymoon.

On the way to the base daydreaming: *Maybe to Lebanon. That village Grandmother Chemaly's from, Harissa, is so beautiful with the view over Jounieh and Beirut. Two magnificent cathedrals, each so beautiful, but so different. Beino, the little village in that valley up north where the Ferrises, or Fareses, are from, was nice. Damascus, too: Christian quarter; Annanias's house on the wall that St. Paul climbed over to escape. No trips there now. Elsie and her family'd be scared to death. One day.*

Poland? Elsie said it's dismal when she was there. That can wait. Maybe never, unless she really wants to.

Wright-Patterson Air Force Base, Ohio, USA

In the office, Patrick made coffee and started reading his newspaper. Felicia arrived wearing a navy blue skirt with a frilly professional long-sleeved blouse and usual high-heels.

He thought: *She looks better than yesterday, but still haggard.* He said hoarsely with an obvious cold: "Hey Sugarlump; you seem better today."

"Yes, I slept better," she replied, "and the kids weren't as rambunctious. You don't seem so good, though."

"Gotta cold," Patrick said then sneezed. "Change of weather. Hope it doesn't get worse."

"Take care of yourself," she said. "If you need anything, let me know. I'll bring some of that hot spicy soup you like tonight. That'll clear anything."

"Thanks," he said, "but no need to go to such trouble."

"No trouble," she responded. "I make it all the time and you only live a couple of blocks away."

Frank and Jen came in, got coffee, and started working with only the usual pleasantries.

After lunch, Patrick slumped coughing, nose dripping, sniffling; Felicia said: "You should go home."

"Yeah, maybe I just need to sleep it off," he replied.

"I'll be over tonight with the soup," she said. "Do you need anything else?"

"Nahh, I'm pretty well stocked," he answered. "Wasn't doing anything special this weekend anyway with Elsie away. If I think of something, I'll call."

"What're you doing for Easter this weekend, Frank?" Felicia asked."

"Not much," Frank replied. "It's not a holiday from work. Getting a cold too; maybe stay home," thinking: *If they only knew the crucifixion party we're having at the Serpent on Friday night. Sacrilegious, I know.*

"What about you Jen?" Felicia continued.

"Oh, didn't you know?" Jen replied. "I'm taking the day off tomorrow and Monday to go home. Seems I'm getting a cold too; I'll let my mother take care of me."

Fairborn, Ohio, USA

All afternoon, Ali watched videos of Patrick, practicing moving and acting just like him. The rest of the time, into early evening, he watched television, one game show after another: Jeopardy, Wheel of Fortune, The Price is Right.

Adnan thought in Arabic: *Damn, this's boring. Has to listen and learn as much as he can to pick up the culture. Culture, ha! Assholes don't know what culture is; just stupid game shows. Uniform fits fine; practiced all day how to wear it, salute, and act military. Been over the route as much as he could and has detailed drawings to find the office. All we need is the signal from that woman.*

Felicia arrived at Patrick's house in the early evening. He was half-asleep on the couch watching TV in his robe. He stumbled to open the door, sniffling, barely able to say a hoarse 'hello', interrupted by a coughing fit and sneezing.

"Go back and lie down; don't try to talk," she said as she went to the kitchen to heat the soup. She looked for crackers, found none, so just brought it in a big mug.

DESPERATION • CHAPTER 7

"Hope it's not too hot for you," she said. "Don't talk. There's more in the kitchen"

When he finished, she took the dishes to the kitchen and returned saying she would see him tomorrow. He mumbled 'thanks' and began coughing and sneezing again.

On the way home, she almost hit a car thinking: *What can I do with the kids? Can't just leave them and kill myself. Maybe Kevin's parents would be forced to take them. Would they treat them well in Louisville? A couple of incidents here and this's a racially mixed community. Can't OD on pills and let kids find me. Fix it so police find me first. God, Allah, help me. Oh, have to call them from a pay phone.*

The call came to Adnan's cell phone: two rings, hang up, two more rings, hang up.

Give him an hour, Adnan said to himself in Arabic. After an hour, he dialed a number, waiting a few moments, saying to himself: *six rings on the land line, no answer.* He dialed again saying to himself: *ten on the cell phone; no answer. Another half hour and go into action.*

Half an hour later in Patrick's house, he said to himself: *There he is in the bedroom, sound asleep,* and signaled to Ali to inject him, whispering: "Do it in the back of the thighs just in case it leaves a bruise."

"OK," Adnan whispered.

Chapter 8

Friday, April 14, 2006
Lattakia, Syria

In early morning, Viktor tossed and turned in bed after two restless nights. He prepared coffee, looked for something to eat, and said to himself in Russian: *Have to tell them. Just feels right. After lunch. Give me time to get ready to go.*

He smoked his pipe continuing to think in Russian: *Likely won't come after me immediately, but gotta get out of here. Pack necessities so can get away quick. Done that enough times before.*

Maybe stay with Russians I sorta know in Aleppo. Stayed after Soviets stopped supporting Syria. KGB's gone; GRU taken some of its old duties, but not like KGB. Not like Moukhabarat who learned well from the KGB. That Putin bastard's KGB. If he ever finds out where I am, I'm dead. Probably worst they'd do in Aleppo is say I can't stay. May even hide me a day or two.

Where can I go? If I could get into Turkey, maybe keep going to Iran. Iranians might like to have me. If wrong people found out, they'd toss me to the Russians as a sop to get them off their back on nuclear issue. Turks might not like my fake Tajik passport; for sure would give me to the Russians if they caught me. Maybe Azerbaijan, but what the hell'd I do there? No way I could go to Lebanon and what'd I do there? Jordan? Imagine Jordanian border guards wondering what an old Russian's doing there and turn me over. Iraq and get my head blown off? Only ones I can trust are Americans.

DESPERATION • CHAPTER 8

Wouldn't they love to know all I know? Put me in prison the rest of my life; their prison's better'n what Russians would do to me. Walk up to their embassy in Damascus? Ha! Moukhabarat watches everyone walking up to the gate.

Going to Iraq's not so bad after all. Country's in such chaos I can hide somewhere. Better start packing.

Chapter 9

Friday, April 14, 2006
Wright-Patterson AFB, Ohio, USA

In early morning, Ali parked Patrick's BMW, nervous but feeling calmer, thinking in English: *Everything where they said it'd be and happened just like supposed to. Hey, I look good in this uniform. Maybe be a doctor in their army some day. Fat chance! The woman Felicia's supposed to be here. Had to breathe some of that powder to give me a cold too, but not as bad as him. Been around enough sick people; can pretend I have a worse cold than I really do.*

Felicia looked pale and distracted when Ali walked in thinking: *Thank God he's here. Looks just like Patrick!* She said: "Good morning, Patrick," doing her best to be cheerful and smile.

"Good morning," Ali nodded with a husky whisper. "Can't talk today."

"Oh, your cold is worse," she said. "You need to be in bed, not here."

"Can't; big meeting," he replied.

Oh, that's how it's going to happen, Felicia said to herself. *Pretend to go to a meeting* "Coffee's just been made," she said. "Do you want me to get you a cup or do you want to get it yourself **like you usually do**. Sit down and read your newspaper **like you usually do each morning**; I'll get it this time." *At least briefed him to bring the right newspaper*, she said to herself then to Ali: "You want sugar, two spoons **like you usually do**? You must not feel well; you didn't even call me Sugarlump **like you usually do**."

DESPERATION • CHAPTER 9

Frank came in with preliminary 'good mornings', got his coffee, and sat down.

Ali mumbled hoarsely: "Morning. Can't talk."

After a moment, Felicia asked: "Are you going to church this afternoon, Patrick? Guess not the way you feel. Take care of yourself. Be sure you're well enough to go to mass on Sunday to light a candle just like Elsie will."

"Yeah," Ali said in the same gruff whisper.

He put away the newspaper and started shuffling papers on the desk as he pondered: *Why'd she say that? Must be setting it up to look good in front of Frank. They briefed me where to find the classified documents and CD with details about grenades they're developing. Felicia can't help; can't get in the safe. Gotta wait until Frank opens it. Office rules: once the classified safe's open, it isn't locked again so long as Frank, Jen, or Patrick's here. Wish he'd hurry up. Gotta pretend like I'm doing something important. What do I know about engineering stuff? I'm a medical doctor. Hope they don't ask me too many questions.*

"Patrick, do you want this last cup of coffee?" Felicia asked. "**You always drink a lot in the morning.**" She poured the coffee without stopping for an answer.

Frank grumbled to himself: *There she is being so damned attentive again. What about me? I could sure use more coffee, but now I have to wait for a fresh pot and get it myself. He really has a bad cold. Maybe that's why she's paying so much attention. But damn it, I have a cold too. Oh, well, better go open the safe while I wait.*

CHAPTER 10

Friday, April 14, 2006
Lattakia, Syria

In early afternoon, Viktor entered Jihad's office saying in Russian: "Good afternoon, Mr. Jihad, there's something I need to tell you."

"Good afternoon Viktor Sergeyevich," Jihad replied in Russian. "Have you had a good day? It's lovely outside."

Viktor said to himself in Russian: *Arabs are always polite no matter how they actually feel.* "Yes, Mr. Jihad. We might have a little problem," Viktor replied in Russian: "We went to great lengths as usual to make sure Ali's a complete duplicate of the American man, but there's, well, ummm, one part of the body we can't always duplicate."

"What's that?" Jihad asked roughly in Russian.

"Well, er, uhhh, it's his penis," Viktor said in Russian.

Jihad said roughly in Russian: "Why the hell're you telling me now? What difference does it make?"

"Well, er, Mr. Jihad," Viktor continued in Russian, "some men aren't circumcised like Muslims, like our Ali must be, and some men're, ummm, bigger than others."

"The American guy's Arab," Jihad spat out the words in Russian. "That's why they picked him."

"Er, Mr. Jihad, he's Christian," Viktor continued in Russian. "Almost all the Christians I see here when I make, er, certain examinations are uncircumcised".

"Who'd notice?" Jihad asked in Russian annoyed. "We made sure his girlfriend's gone."

"Mr. Jihad, it's America, the country of crude, disrespectful people," Viktor continued in Russian. "To them it may not be bad to look at other men's members."

"Where?" Jihad continued in Russian annoyed. "He has a bad cold. We made sure so he wouldn't go to a gym."

"Mr. Jihad, how can I put this?" Viktor continued in Russian with mock meekness. "Men do have to urinate. In most countries they use urinals that are not inside stalls."

"How can anyone see from one urinal to another?" Jihad asked in Russian.

"Well, er, not every country has the decency to put dividers between the urinals like here," Viktor continued in Russian. "Maybe they don't have them in America."

"But what man would look at another man peeing?" Jihad continued in Russian.

"Er, well Mr. Jihad," Viktor continued in Russian, we know how perverted Americans are."

Jihad asked angrily in Russian: "Why the hell didn't tell us before?"

"Our work before this was one Muslim man taking the place of another," Viktor replied meekly in Russian. "We didn't consider such a possibility. How could we have?"

"Oh my god, Viktor Sergeyevich," Jihad exclaimed angrily in Russian. "How could you have made such a stupid mistake? What the hell do we do now?"

"Maybe get a message to Ali to go inside a stall to urinate is all we need to do?" Viktor replied in Russian.

"We don't have contact except in emergency," Jihad spat the words out in Russian. "Is this an emergency?"

"If you like, Mr. Jihad," Viktor continued in Russian, "I can go to Damascus to the medical library and read more in medical books and journals. I was thinking about going there anyway this weekend. It's such a lovely old city."

"Go, Viktor Sergeyevich," Jihad shouted dismissively in Russian. "I need to think about this."

Viktor returned to his room and continued to think in Russian: *After dark I'll sneak out, get a taxi to the center, and one of those long-distance taxis to Aleppo. Better not get on a bus; they have them watched. Wander around Damascus buses first and be seen asking questions about times. They can't watch every taxi driver. I hear plenty go to Aleppo now that not many go to Lebanon.*

Jihad grumbled to himself in Arabic: *Damned Viktor, and he was supposed to be so good. We don't even know if we have a problem. Damn. Damn. Damn. Should I wait and tell Abed? Or just do it? Damn.*

Chapter 11

Friday, April 14, 2006
Fort Meade, Maryland, USA

Bradley Spencer parked his candy-apple red, year-old Mini Cooper in the National Security Administration parking lot just in time for his 8 a.m. shift. His slightly wavy, blonde-brown hair was trimmed and styled. Standing five feet ten with a medium build, his preppy clothes fit well: olive green corduroy slacks with socks to match, a blue oxford-cloth long-sleeved shirt, and cordovan penny loafers. At 23, his sparkling blue eyes and an engaging smile charmed men and women alike.

BRAD'S CANDY-APPLE RED MINI COOPER

THREE KISSES

EMPLOYEE PARKING LOT, NATIONAL SECURITY ADMINISTRATION, FORT MEADE, MARYLAND

He chatted flirtatiously with the attractive Marine security guards about his age then continued to his workplace in the Arabic language section thinking: *Tonight's big date with Jason. Easter so we'll do something special, maybe Rory's in DC instead of Baltimore. Is he the one? He's cute, fun to be with, and good in bed.*

Should I go to Good Friday services? Nahhh, not in the mood. Went to Maundy Thursday services last night and of course on Sunday; he said he'd come with me. Should ask him more about church things if we're getting serious. Good growing up in a gay-tolerant church; God doesn't hate me.

He greeted two colleagues drinking coffee in the anteroom. Drew Nelson was dressed in a similar preppy style; Paul McKenna was more geekish. Soon they were at work with headphones listening to cell phone conversations from Arabic speaking countries to the US.

Brad drifted into idle thoughts: *Another boring day. Listen enough to know if something affects security. Mostly relatives calling.*

Drew and Paul're language geeks like me; upper middle class families from New England, not Minnesota. Went to top schools; no pressure about what they studied. Don't seem to be gay. Don't talk much about private lives. Can't while working and breaks and lunch at different times. They date girls it seems. Didn't Paul say he's thinking about getting married? They hire only guys like us; can't trust Arab-Americans, I'm sure.

Drew startled Brad and Paul exclaiming as he turned on the loudspeaker: "Listen to this. Couple of gay guys talking about someone's dick."

"…You want someone to go look at his dick?" the voice asked in Arabic with a strange accent.

"No, damn it, look at his penis," another voice said in classic Arabic.

Brad asked himself: *Why does he want me to listen? Do they suspect me? … Wait a minute. They're not gay.* He said: "Turn on the recorder quick and trace the calls."

"What for?" Drew retorted. "Just Arab queers."

"Just do it," Brad said, his index finger to his lips.

"What? Why the hell you want to know that?" the voice with an unrecognized accent continued in Arabic.

"Maybe he's different from Ali and someone'd find out," the classic Arabic voice said. "Maybe he has that layer of skin on the end of it, or maybe he's really big."

"Yeah, like the Central American guys here they make us take showers with in public at school," the accented voice replied in Arabic. "This guy's American like us. Who the hell'd look at him and know?"

"What if someone sees him urinate?" the classic Arabic voice said. "What're the WCs like there? Are urinals separated like they are here?"

"Not all of them," The accented voice answered in Arabic. "You think they're decent about things here?"

"Tell Ali to urinate in a stall not in the open," the classic Arabic voice said. "Find out what both are like."

"What, we're supposed to look at their dicks?" the accented voice exclaimed in Arabic. "You think we're perverts or something?"

"No, find out what their penises are like," the classic Arabic speaker said. This could be serious; just go do it!"

"OK," the accented voice said in Arabic with resignation. "Adnan may have the phone off. He took mine and left his here just in case an emergency call comes in. Doesn't want anything to make noise to wake the guy."

"Hurry!" the classic Arabic speaker said disconnecting.

Brad thought: *How do I explain without giving away too much?* He said: "Arab guys don't talk like that when talking about sex, or not in Jordan. This's almost clinical. Would American guys talk about a tight vagina or big mammary glands? They're up to something."

"Yeah", Drew added. "Had different accents; can't place one of them. The one who said he's American was using pretty simple words."

"The one giving orders sounds Syrian, or they talked like that when I went to Damascus," Brad added.

"Definitely not Egyptian," Drew said. "Wait. I've got a trace on the phone. It originated in Syria; the number called is in New York, but with roaming's going to Ohio."

"Better keep monitoring both phones," Paul said.

"Wait," Drew said. "The American one's making a call to another New York number, but trace says it's roaming and both are in Ohio."

"We can't monitor domestic calls," Paul said.

"Who cares?" Drew said. "We can listen and record and then decide what to do later. This's in English!"

"Adnan, we've got a problem," a voice said in unaccented American English. "A guy named Jihad called; says he's in charge. We have to tell Ali not to pee at a urinal and we have to find out what their dicks are like."

"What?!" another voice exclaimed in accented English. "What do you mean, find out what their dicks are like? What does this have to do with Ali peeing?"

The American voice said: "Some guys have a layer of skin on their dick."

"Yeah, but it's cut off when they're babies," the accented voice said. "Why'd he have such a thing?"

"Not everywhere, Adnan," the American voice continued. "Someone might see Ali pee. You know here in this fuckin' country they shower out in the open and don't have dividers in the restrooms. If someone sees Ali's different, we've got trouble, he says."

"Ali's gone already," the accented voice said. "What th' hell am I supposed to do?"

"Go look at the guy and call back so we can tell him," the American voice said. "Ask Ali when he gets back."

"He's going to your place first; you have to ask him," the accented voice continued. "Damn those idiots. Maybe just say that the guy's like all good Arabs and leave it at that. I don't want to look at him. We didn't do that when we examined guys who were injured unless they actually had a wound there and then we wouldn't really look."

"What if something goes wrong?" the American voice continued. "I gotta call Jihad back or he'll call back here."

"Ok, damn it. I'll call you back," the accented voice said and disconnected.

"Weird," Paul said.

Brad thought: *They aren't gay or nothing like the few I met in Amman. Click off this call; some nephew's birthday.*

Jordan. Seems ages ago, but only two years. Mom was upset when I said I needed to study abroad in the Middle East. She panicked when I wanted to go to Lebanon. 'Bombs everywhere', she said; tourists were getting killed in Egypt. 'But Mom, I'm not a tourist'. She wouldn't listen. Finally, I convinced her Jordan's safe and also has Biblical sites. Jordan was good. Petra's amazing; nothing like it in the world. It seemed kind of eerie, spiritual, to be at the place where Jesus was baptized, the top of Mount Nebo where Moses looked over onto the Promised Land, wade in the River Jordan, bob up and down in the Dead Sea.

"Here's another call," Drew announced.

"You won't believe this," the voice said in accented English. "He does have that ugly skin and his penis is big."

"Like Central Americans," the American voice said.

"We might have to get out of here quick," the accented voice asked. "Have to wait until Ali comes to you with the CD and the papers. You ready to copy?"

"Yes, I have the computer set up and Boudi's set to rush to the copy center," the American voice replied. "I'd better call Jihad now."

"Be careful," The accented voice said. "Don't know if the phone's monitored or not."

"What CD? What papers?" Drew exclaimed. "This sounds serious. At least we're getting names and a trace. Roaming's relaying the call through Dayton, Ohio. Oh, here's the next call."

"Mr. Jihad," the voice said in accented Arabic, "he's got that skin and big. Ali's already gone. He's supposed to come back here in a couple hours."

THREE KISSES

"Damn Viktor," the voice shouted in classic Arabic.

"Who's Viktor?" the accented voice asked in Arabic.

"Forget I said it," he answered in classic Arabic. "Get out soon as you can."

"What do we do with the CD and the papers we're supposed to copy?" the accented voice persisted in Arabic.

"Throw them away," he blurted out in classic Arabic. "Wait. Can't do that. If they find them missing, we've got more problems. I don't know. Tell Ali to put 'em back and rush away. Tell Adnan to get on the computer as soon as he possibly can. I'll be here all night connected to the internet. What time is it there?"

"About 8:30 a.m.," the accented voice said in Arabic

"That's what I thought; 15:30 here," the classic Arabic voice said. "OK, go do it and get out!"

The call was disconnected and Drew said: "God, this's fuckin' weird. What the hell do we do with this? Turn over the tapes now? They have names on them: Ali, Jihad, Boudi, guess that's Abdullah, and someone called Viktor. That sure isn't an Arabic name. We know someone's Christian; only Christians left're in Syria and Lebanon."

"Let them catch us taping domestic conversations?" Paul asked. "We need to wait and think this through. We need more to go on than this. We don't want to get our asses reamed if it's nothing. What do you think, Brad?"

"You're right," Brad replied. "Let it sit, at least through the weekend. See what happens. There're Christians in Jordan and some in Iraq."

Brad continued to think: *Wonder what they'd do if they found out I'm gay? Need Arabic speakers so bad probably wouldn't fire me. Always possible some intelligence service'd try to blackmail me. I'm sure every intelligence service in DC knows I work here and what I do. I'm just not big enough for them to follow me around and see me go to gay places.*

So what if they try to blackmail me. I could come out. Family'd still love me. Being gay got me into this job; tried to hide my feelings by becoming a language geek like some guys become computer geeks. I'm damned good at languages and Arabic is fascinating.

DESPERATION • CHAPTER 11

God what a day. Really need to go out and get it out of my system on the dance floor tonight with Jason, but what can I tell him? He knows sort of what I do. He knows me well enough by now to know when I have something on my mind. Can't worry about that now.

Chapter 12

Friday, April 14, 2006
Wright-Patterson AFB, Ohio, USA

Ali sat at Patrick's desk thinking: *Can't keep pretending to be busy, looking at Frank to see what he's doing. Wait, he went to the room where the safe is and coming back with files; safe must be open. I can get coffee before I get the file. Wouldn't look right to go straight there.*

Soon he was rummaging through the safe, thinking: *Termite. Not in alphabetic order. Ah, here it is—CD and papers.* He went back to Patrick's desk, put the CD in the computer, and pretended to do something with it.

After several minutes, Frank asked: "Patrick, you said you'd help me analyze data. Any idea when?"

"Er, sorry, I forgot," Ali replied in a fake hoarse whisper. "Really busy right now. Early next week?"

Frank thought: *Doesn't sound like him. Even if he couldn't help now, wouldn't answer that way.* After some more minutes, he announced: "I'm going to the snack bar," and walked out of the room.

Why should we care where he's going? Ali asked himself. `*Oh, I'm the only one here and need to lock the classified safe if I go. Need to pee. He can't be gone too long. I'll hold it.*

After several minutes, he was more uncomfortable and said to himself: *Can't hold it any longer. Could lock the safe, but don't dare to put Termite back; may never get it out. I'll be quick; maybe no one'll notice.*

DESPERATION • CHAPTER 12

He left without saying anything to Felicia and almost ran the short distance to the small men's room which had one stall and two urinals.

He said to himself: *someone in the stall; can't wait.*

Moments later, Frank entered, went to the other urinal, and said: "Too much coffee for you too?"

Ali mumbled: "Yeah, you too?" as he tried to force himself to finish quickly, thinking: *Does he suspect asking me about too much coffee? Am I drinking more than Patrick?*

"Yeah," Frank replied. "When'll Elsie be back?"

Ali quickly finished saying to himself: *How the hell am I supposed to know?* He said in the same hoarse whisper: "Not sure, yet."

He left quickly left without washing his hands.

That sure isn't like Patrick, Frank thought as he finished. *He's so attached to Elsie he'd know to the minute when her plane's due to land ... and he bolted out of here without washing his hands.*

He washed his hands, returned to his desk, got a cup of coffee, and sat up suddenly with a jolt, spilling coffee.

"*Wait!*" he exclaimed to himself: *That wasn't Patrick. He covered his dick almost completely with his hand and Patrick couldn't do that as big as he is. He has so much foreskin it'd've been obvious.*

He became aware they were staring at him as Felicia asked: "What's wrong, Frank?"

He answered: "I just spilled coffee on my shirt, damn it. I'd better run wash it out before it stains."

He rushed back to the men's room saying to himself: *Can think here a few moments.* He pushed the liquid soap button, turned on the water, and began to wash the coffee stain with his fingers, thinking: *That's why answers don't sound like Patrick. Someone's taken his place and looks just like him. What's he doing here? We've got lots of classified cutting-edge weapons systems under development. Is he after something classified? Yes, of course; he was in the classified safe. Did he torture Patrick to get the combination? Wait. No. He didn't go until after I'd opened it. What's Patrick working on? Maybe Termite, the deep penetrating tiny grenade to be used in Iraq and Afghanistan.*

THREE KISSES

Wait. Iraq. Afghanistan. Insurgents. God, al Qaeda'd love to get this. Al Qaeda? Arabs? Patrick's Lebanese and Arab. They find some other Arab who looks like him? He can't be on his own. A terrorist cell behind him? There're sure enough activities on this base that lots of people'd like to get into. Foreign technology assessment unit's a prime target; fighter planes and weapons the U.S. is reverse-engineering.

What now? Turn it over to Security Police or the Inspector General? What reason do I give? Looked at his dick and it isn't Patrick's? Yeah, sure, how'n hell should I know, and how'd they know? Medical records don't give penis descriptions. Tell 'em he's acting funny and has classified material. Since when is it a security breach to act funny, especially if he has a cold?

Even if I'm right, Okinawa all over again. I report and I'm the one investigated. Didn't find anything about me there except maybe a Japanese whore. Here they'd find lots. Not ready for career suicide even if I am pissed off at the Marines. Damn it, this's a threat to the country; everything the family and I've stood for.

Won't know what he's up to unless I watch and follow, see where he goes. Wouldn't do anything on base; must be taking it off-base. Must be driving Patrick's car. Wouldn't know my car unless he forced Patrick to tell. What'd he do with Patrick? Kill him? Dump him in the Miami River?

Call Fred. He's a policeman. Take him out myself one-on-one if he's unarmed, but what if he has back up? Wonder if he's on duty today. Supposed to meet at the Serpent tonight, so not working then. Phone's on my desk and can't call from here. Find Patrick's car, wait for this guy, and follow.

As soon as he went back to the office, he said: "I've got a meeting this afternoon and can't go like this. I'll have to go home and change shirts. I'll take the things for the meeting and not come back until after, probably midafternoon."

Felicia said: "See you later then."

In the parking lot, Frank said to himself: *Patrick's car's right up front where he usually parks. See if I can get my car closer ready to follow him.*

After parking his two-year-old cream colored Mercury Mountaineer nearby, he called and said: "Hey Fred, Frank; you on duty?"

DESPERATION • CHAPTER 12

FRANK'S 2004 CREAM MERCURY MOUNTAINEER

pause

"Need your help if you're not too busy," he continued.

pause

"Someone's made a double of a guy in my office and he has classified information; may be a terrorist," he added.

pause

"I saw him piss," Frank replied and explained events.

pause

"Yeah, sure, turn him in to the Security Police or IG," Frank said with a smirk. "Might as well put on a pink uniform with a big sign saying I'm gay. Seriously, it'd be like Okinawa; the guy who reports gets in trouble."

pause

"In my car ready to follow him," Frank continued.

pause

He said. "Can you come quick? I may need back up."

pause

"Good," Frank said, "your unmarked cruiser. Take 675 around Dayton towards the base. I'll let you know where I am soon as something happens."

pause

"Great idea," Frank concurred. "Luie usually works only mornings at the bakery and Paco's off today I think."

pause

"See you soon!" Frank concluded.

Ali got up from Patrick's desk, put on his hat, put the classified CD and papers into a folder, and said without disguising his voice: "See you this afternoon, **Sugarlump**."

Felicia forced a smile but didn't know what to say.

Chapter 13

Friday, April 14, 2006
Middletown, Ohio, USA

Police Sergeant Frederick Watson disconnected Frank's call standing in his living room amid renovation clutter, wearing sloppy blue jeans and a paint-stained sweatshirt. He stood six feet tall with dark blonde buzz-cut hair; brown eyes sparkled with a charm that captured attention of both women and men, an advantage in police work.

FRED'S HOUSE MIDDLETOWN, OHIO

He said to himself: *Frank's voice has that reserve of a Marine Corps officer; knowing him and with a police background, he's scared.* He called on his cell phone: "Paco, Fred. Glad I got you."
pause

"Frank needs us," he said. "Found a terrorist who took out one of his work colleagues."
pause

"He can't," Fred continued. "Discovered him by looking at his dick; you know what he's like. No time to explain; gotta to get up there to help him quick. If anyone knows Frank, you do; wouldn't ask for help if he weren't near desperate. Can you and Luie go too?"
pause

"Ok, I'll tell him," Fred said. "Call if Luie can come."
pause

"Bye, and just hurry," Fred concluded.

Underneath his sweat shirt, a t-shirt read 'Middletown Police Department'.

Can't wear that, he said to himself as he pulled it off revealing his muscular body that men and women swoon over. He rummaged through a pile of clean unsorted laundry saying to himself: *Here's one someone brought me from New York City; NYPD. Nope. One I wear to the Serpent. Perfect.* He put on a black t-shirt with psychedelic caricatures of men in leather with chains, restraints, and whips.

Several minutes later on I-75 towards Dayton in a black unmarked police cruiser, his mind drifted: *Been a police officer how long now? Almost 11 years. Started here in Middletown after Ohio University. Folks would've liked me closer back home in Toledo, but Middletown's one of the most progressive places around. Knew I'm gay so close to home's no good. Here I can go to Cincinnati and come home where no one'd know what I do there. Gotta make sure no places police'd raid even if not doing anything illegal, but no risk of that in Cincinnati. Across the river in Kentucky maybe, but wouldn't go there anyway.*

DESPERATION • CHAPTER 13

Remember first night Frank came in, scared shitless, fascinated. Wasn't too far back I was the same. He didn't know how to dress; just jeans and regular shirt. Almost immediately latched onto me; short hair and police officer bearing didn't make him feel out of place. He was nice and good looking. Oh, boy has he changed. We all have. Hooked up with Paco and Luie and had pretty wild foursomes. Frank and Paco have something going now. Fine with me; It's good with Luie. Hope we can still get to the party tonight; maybe all back to my place afterwards.

His cell phone interrupted as he said: "What's up, Bud?"
pause
"Just passing Beavercreek on 675", he replied.
pause
"Ohio 235 exit and left on Xenia Drive," he repeated.
pause
"Paco and Luie are on their way in Luie's four-by-four. I'll let them know where to go," he added
pause
"Bye," he concluded.

Luis Mendoza was driving his ten-year-old navy blue Jeep Cherokee, his cousin Paco Mendoza in the passenger seat. Luie, as almost all called him, was five feet ten, had dark brown hair kept closely trimmed to make it easier to put on a hairnet in the bakery, brown eyes, and a slightly stocky body. Olive complexion and facial features suggested Hispanic heritage. Paco was at least six feet two inches with broad shoulders and a husky body. He was an imposing figure, but soft green eyes could neutralize the impact. Although he had the slightly darkish complexion of many Hispanics, he could easily pass as an Anglo-American. Dark brown hair was cut military style. Both wore blue jeans, sneakers, and sweat shirts over t-shirts.

THREE KISSES

LUIE'S TEN-YEAR-OLD JEEP CHEROKEE FOUR-BY-FOUR.

Paco's cell phone rang; he answered: "Hey, amigo."
pause
"OK. Got it," he said. "See ya."

Paco relayed directions to Luie and let his mind drift: *So Frank's got himself a little trouble. Fred didn't say much, but if Frank asks for help, it's damned sure he needs it. Luie's always up for a good adventure. Good thing he's part-owner of the bakery and can take off once baking's done. I have the long weekend off too.*

Look at us; two Mexican boys with these two guys, a police officer and a Marine Corps Major. Put on leather and restraints, who gives a damn?

We did all right for ourselves. Have green cards, no legal problems. Luie started working in the bakery in high school; taught them how to make Mexican pastries; now half of Hamilton buys there. Owns half the place now that the old guy who started it retired. I always liked looking at men's bodies, so went to community college to be a nurse's aide. In Mexico, not many men nurses; here, they beg for us and big guys like me, especially in veterans' homes....

Chapter 14

Friday, April 14, 2006
Fairborn, Ohio, USA

Frank quickly parked, called Fred saying where he would be standing, then said: "He's here. Bye."

Some minutes later, Fred parked close to Frank standing half-hidden behind a utility pole who explained that Patrick's double had gone into the apartment concluding: "A guy came out with a big envelope, got into a late model BMW like Patrick's there, and drove off."

"How old?" Fred asked.

"Maybe a year older, different color, green, and New York plates," Frank answered.

"No, the guy," Fred said.

"Early 20s, 25 max," Frank replied. "Didn't get a good look. Arab or Mexican. Husky-like."

Fred said: "Luie and Paco'll be here soon. Any idea how many inside?"

"Frank replied: "Don't think they'd leave the double alone. This guy must've rushed off to make copies of the classified. Don't know about copying CDs."

"Can burn a CD on just about any laptop," Fred said.

"Do we jump him when he comes back?" Frank asked.

"Nah;" Fred answered. "Where's he likely to park? That empty place across from the apartment door?"

"That's where he left from," Frank replied.

"Backed in or parked frontward?" Fred asked.

"Forward," Frank said.

"He'll probably park that way again," Fred said. "Park your car behind that spot. I'll move mine as close as I can. Stay in your car; better get that uniform shirt off with your name tag on it. When he parks, pull out as close behind him as you can. Stall your car and keep trying to start it again. I'll ask him a question, catch him off guard, and handcuff him. You grab him from behind, get his keys, wallet, and phone. Lock him inside his car."

"Gee, you thought of all that on the spur of the moment?" Frank stated amazed.

"You're trained to make spur-of-the-moment decisions on the battlefield; I'm trained in police action," Fred said.

After moving vehicles, Frank sat in his SUV; Fred stood half-hidden behind a utility pole. Boudi drove into the empty spot. Just as he stepped out of the car with a big envelope in his hand, Frank backed out and stalled his car.

"Hey, can you help me?" Fred said loudly to Boudi, walking rapidly towards him. "I'm looking for B 15."

"Sorry I can't help you, man...." Boudi started to say as Fred poked his pistol into Boudi's stomach whispering forcefully: "Put your hands on your chest."

Boudi dropped the envelope and raised his hands in the air; Fred said gruffly: "No, on your chest."

Fred put handcuffs on Boudi as Frank took his wallet out of a rear pocket and removed his telephone and car keys.

Fred poked a pocket-size pack of tissues into Boudi's mouth, pushed the pistol into his crotch, and said: "Get in."

Boudi moved to the front door of the green BMW but Fred said: "No, damn it, back seat, and quick before doors lock automatically."

Frank pulled Boudi backwards, opened the back door, shoved him inside, picked up the envelope, and climbed into the driver's seat. Fred

DESPERATION • CHAPTER 14

got into the front passenger seat while Frank pushed the button for the kiddie locks.

He opened Boudi's wallet and said: "New York driver's license, Abdullah Zakawi, $18, and a condom."

"Arab. You al Qaeda?" Fred asked as Boudi tried to speak. "Just shake your head yes or no," Fred commanded.

Frank, held up the envelope, asking: "Where'd you get this? You just got it copied, didn't you?"

"No response?" Fred said gruffly and poked the pistol into Boudi's crotch who let out a muffled scream. "Who you fucking with that condom? Or is he fucking you? That guy in the army uniform? He got a big dick you like up you?" He said to himself: *Arabs are rabid homophobes. Rile him up accusing him of gay sex and maybe get something out of him. Sometimes get more out of angry people after provoking 'em.*

Boudi tried to scream shaking his head side to side.

"Bet he'd like a billyclub up his ass if he likes to get fucked," Fred said and tossed his car keys to Frank. "Get it out of the car; I can take care of things here. Get the leg restraints just in case. ... OK, fuckin' al Qaeda shit. You want to get killed like a suicide bomber? You're not good enough to be a martyr. Cooperate with us or you get the stick up your ass." Boudi kept up muffled screams, thrashing around kicking his feet violently; Fred said: "Oh, you want leg restraints too."

Frank opened the back door, got in with the billyclub and leg restraints, and started unbuckling Boudi's belt while Fred said: "Better use leg restraints too".

Frank sat on Boudi's thighs facing his feet and clamped restraints on Boudi's ankles while Fred kept pushing the pistol into Boudi's crotch. Boudi thrashed his arms up and down trying to hit whomever was closest.

"Time to put cuffs on from behind," Fred said. "Climb on top and grab his left arm while I unlock 'em."

Frank pinned Boudi down with one knee in his lower belly, one knee squeezing hard into his crotch, and grabbed Boudi's right arm tightly.

THREE KISSES

Fred, climbing through the opening between the two front seats, unlocked the cuff on the right arm while Frank bent it around to Boudi's back, Fred yanked the left arm back, and got the cuffs back on the right arm again behind Boudi's back.

"OK, now let's see what his asshole's like," Fred said as he started to unzip Boudi's jeans. Boudi's muffled screams got more intense as he resisted the best he could. Frank stuck the small end of the club into the opened jeans.

Suddenly Boudi stopped moving, tears coming to his eyes, and made noises sounding like: "OK, OK, I'll cooperate. Don't hurt me."

"Back off," Fred said. "OK, fuckin' terrorist asshole, how many guys in the apartment other than one in uniform?"

Boudi tried to say something, but no words came out.

"One more?" Fred continued to ask.

No response.

"Ten or more?" Fred persisted. Boudi's head bobbed up and down.

"Asshole, you can't have ten guys in there," Fred spat out words. "Go ahead and give his ass a good go."

Boudi screamed again: "No," tears streaming.

Fred stared straight at Boudi. "We can take out ten of you and more. You want it bloody or clean?"

Boudi started crying with big wet tears.

"OK, is it two?" Fred asked.

Boudi's head gently moved side to side.

"OK, three then?" Fred said.

Boudi's head moved even more forcefully side to side.

"Less than two? Only one? The guy in the army uniform and one more?" Fred continued.

Boudi's head moved up and down.

"OK, zip up his pants for now," Fred said to Frank. "We'll wait for reinforcements and go after them."

Chapter 15

Friday, April 14, 2006
Fairborn, Ohio, USA

Fred ran to Luie's Jeep, his hand out to shake at arm's length, eyes twinkling conveying he'd rather exchange kisses.

"They're Arabs," he said in a low voice. "One's in that green BMW; others're inside. Sorry to be abrupt, but need to work fast. Guy with Frank says only the double and one more inside; not sure we believe him.

"Need your backup to smoke one of 'em out. I'm going to try to get one out, cuff and gag him, then you two grab him from the back, get his wallet, phone, and any weapon with as little commotion as possible. Put him into the back of Frank's Mountaineer. No, wait; too risky. Put him in the back of your four-by-four; it has tinted windows. You've got leg restraints, don't you?"

"Yeah, of course," Luie said. "Then what?"

"Let's see how this turns out," Fred continued. "We need to get the double and see if anyone else's there. Frank needs to be with me. One of you watch the other guy. Wait. Got to get him out of that green car. Maybe you get him into your four-by-four without a big commotion. For now, stand out of sight on the left side of the porch, ready to jump him from the back if I get him on the step. Pretend you're Arabs."

Fred pounded on the door.

THREE KISSES

BACK OF SHABBY APARTMENT, FAIRBORN, OHIO

"Who is it? What do you want?" Brahim asked.

"Your car's blocking me," Fred said loudly. "Move it."

"Not mine," Brahim replied.

"Sure the hell is. Saw you drive in and leave it," Fred continued forcefully. "Get the hell out here and move it or I'll call the police."

Hearing 'police', Brahim opened the door and started to step out. Fred poked the pistol in his gut, grabbed one of his arms, and pulled him out onto the step. "Hands on your chest," he said forcefully as he twisted Brahim's arm.

Paco grabbed Brahim from behind while Fred snapped handcuffs on his wrists and stuffed a handkerchief into his mouth almost knocking off his glasses. Brahim twisted himself free and started to run. Paco and Luie grabbed him as Fred stuck the pistol back in his gut.

"You ready to come quietly or do we need to persuade you?" Fred said as he started pulling him along.

Brahim mumbled something like: "OK, OK." Paco took his wallet and keys while Luie found his telephone and force-marched him to the back of the four-by-four.

DESPERATION • CHAPTER 15

"Up inside, quiet, and make it quick," Luie said tossing in wallet, keys, and phone.

"Hurry, put leg restraints on him," Fred said. "One of you cover the door if someone else comes out."

Paco held Brahim's thighs as Luie snapped the restraints on his ankles.

"Ibrahim Al Asadi, Lackawanna, New York," Fred read Brahim's driver's license, "and another condom. You guys must have fun fucking each other. Who gets it from whom? The big athletic guy have a big dick?"

"No!" a muffled scream said as Brahim began to cry.

"Oh, you're ready to cooperate," Fred said tauntingly.

He shook his head up and down with tears flowing.

"Who's inside?" Fred asked. "Just the guy in the Army uniform?" Fred asked. Brahim shook his head up and down.

"More?" he asked. Brahim shook his head side to side.

"Watch him," Fred said to Luie. "I don't think he'll give you any shit. See if you can get the other guy in here without making a big commotion."

"You must be one of those al Qaeda shits," Luie looked straight at Brahim. "Fucked up life for Arabs in this country. Ought to beat the shit out of you, but not here."

Brahim started crying, trying to scream, as Luie raised his clinched fist saying: "Shut the fuck up."

Fred walked to Paco standing by the back door of the apartment and said quietly: "Go take over from Frank. He needs to be with me when we go after the double. Watch that guy in the car. He's big and can be rough, not like the little geek you just got; probably not a match for you, but be careful. Get him into Luie's four-by-four if you can. Use the billyclub if he gets out of line."

Paco got in the back seat with Boudi saying: "You're some big tough Arab, crying like that, a disgrace to all Arabs. Bet you're al Qaeda. Screw up life for all the world then buckle under slightest pressure."

He used his thumb to flip his finger on Boudi's crotch through his jeans. Boudi cried hysterically.

Chapter 16

Friday, April 14, 2006
Fairborn, Ohio, USA

Fred said to Frank: "If they're right, only one inside, but can't take chances. Door must be unlocked; let's go."

Ali, screamed: "Frank!"

Fred, using a pistol, commanded: "Put out your hands."

He cuffed Ali's wrists as a half-eaten sandwich dropped to the floor; Frank pulled out a wallet and car keys.

"I won't do anything," Ali screamed.

"Take over while I search the place," Fred said.

"Patrick Nabil Ferris, …" Frank read the driver's license speaking an address nearby, "and Army ID card." Suddenly he remembered when Patrick lost his wallet and said: "Who the fucking hell **are** you?"

"Ali Salman," he said timidly. "How'd you find me?"

Frank asked: "What're you doing here with the classified material we found on your buddy?"

"I just wanted to get out of Syria," Ali said.

Frank persisted. "I asked what you're doing with classified; and where's the CD?"

"I was supposed to give it to them," Ali replied. "I don't know what it's about; I'm a medical doctor."

DESPERATION • CHAPTER 16

"Medical doctor?" Frank said with a smirk. "Hah, funny. What the hell kind of medical doctor are you?"

"A cosmetic surgeon," Ali answered.

"Yeah, right, a Syrian cosmetic surgeon," Frank said.

Meanwhile Fred slammed the kitchen door into the wall and would have seriously hurt anyone hiding behind it. Seeing it was empty, he went to the bedroom and slammed the bedroom door the same way. With one eye on the bathroom, he examined the closet with the pistol cocked. Then he walked to the bathroom and slammed the bathroom door that hit the commode and splintered from the force. With his pistol cocked, he peeked around the door. Satisfied no one was inside, he went back to the living room.

"He's Ali from Syria and a doctor; a cosmetic surgeon he says," Frank said skeptically.

"Yeah, right." Fred smirked. "We've gotta get going. Been here too long already."

"One minute," Frank said, "Keep your pistol on him; he might not like this."

He started unbuckling Ali's belt and unfastening his pants as Ali squirmed and screamed: "What the hell? I said I wouldn't do anything; now you're going to hurt me?"

"Calm down, Doc. Just need to check something," Frank said as he unzipped Ali's pants and pulled down his briefs. "Yeah, not Patrick, but like the guy I saw earlier."

Ali jumped and said "oh", suddenly realizing how he had been discovered.

Frank continued: "Fasten yourself up. You can use your hands well enough for that."

"He's got a dick like millions of guys in this country," Fred said. "but if you say he's not like your co-worker...."

"Where's Patrick? You guys kill him?" Frank asked.

"No," Ali blurted out.

"Where is he then?" Frank demanded.

"In bed asleep," Ali said again. "I gave him injections."

"**You** gave him injections?" Frank asked.

"Yes, I am a doctor!" Ali exclaimed.

"Who's with him?" Frank asked.

"Adnan. Another guy; one of them," Ali replied.

"We can continue later," Fred interrupted. "We have to get out of here now; go somewhere safe. Go to your place."

"It's on the other side of town," Frank replied. "Why not go to Patrick's? It's close; we need to go there anyway to get the other guy and check on Patrick."

"Hey, you're right." Fred said. "How far?"

"Just a few blocks," Frank replied. "Address on his driver's license the doc had on him."

"OK," Fred said. "You have to drive Patrick's car; looks like you have the keys. Others in the four-by-four and I'll take the **doctor** in my car. Need information from him."

"Hey, wait. I can't leave my car in a neighborhood like this," Frank objected.

"I sure as hell can't leave mine," Fred said. Frank gulped in acquiescence.

Where's that classified CD?" Frank asked Ali.

"In the computer, I think," Ali replied. "Brahim was working with it."

"Who's Brahim?" Frank asked as he found a CD.

"The guy who was just here," Ali replied.

"Oh, yes, Ibrahim," Fred said. "Let's get a move on. Doc you play it cool and get in the backseat of that black car over there and nothing'll happen to you. If you step one inch the wrong direction, you know I have this pistol."

"I understand," Ali replied nervously.

"We might need to hide those guys in the four-by-four under something," Fred looked at Frank. "Get as much bedding as you can find."

"What the hell?" Frank exclaimed as they walked out.

His Mountaineer was in a parking space and the Jeep behind the green BMW where the Mountaineer had been.

"You said to get him in the four-by-four," Luie said to Fred. "I clamped the geeky guy to a handles. Saw the keys still in the Mountaineer. Easy. My buddy's watching them.

Frank tossed the bedding to Luie, and got inside his car to get his uniform shirt and hat.

"We're going to Patrick's place," Fred said. "Follow Frank in that silver BMW over there. I'll follow the four-by-four. We have phones if something happens. The four-by-four should go into the garage if possible. Park Patrick's car in front if you have to; won't cause any suspicion with the neighbors. Here's the address if you get lost," Fred said showing Luie Patrick's driver's license.

"Got it. Vámonos," Luie said.

Chapter 17

Friday, April 14, 2006
Fairborn, Ohio, USA

"What the hell're you doing here and who are the other guys?" Fred asked Ali as they drove to Patrick's house.

"I just wanted to get out of Syria, be a doctor," Ali replied. "Help people who're injured and disfigured."

"What about the other guys?" Fred continued.

"The two with me're poor Yemeni kids who felt screwed by the system. Involved with an imam who gives them work driving between Canada and North Carolina. They're naïve; harmless. Turn right at the next corner."

Must be smuggling, Fred mumbled to himself. "What about the guy where we're going?" he asked.

"He's mean," Ali answered. "Skinny, but tough. Saudi Arabian who worked in Afghanistan with al Qaeda to treat wounded fighters. Gotta watch out for him."

"Is he armed?" Fred asked?

"Don't know," Ali replied. "Didn't see any, but I'd guess he has a gun. There, that's the house."

"Is there a garage door opener?" Fred asked.

"On the flap that pulls down," Ali answered.

Fred quickly called on his cell phone saying: "Drive up just past the driveway so you can push the garage opener. It's on the visor. Park and go in the garage."

Fred turned on the blinkers and pointed so Luie could know to drive into the garage then drove the cruiser into the driveway parking behind the four-by-four.

He asked Ali: "Is that car the other guy's?"

Ali nodded his head and said: "Yes".

Once inside the garage with the door closed, Fred said: "You're going in ahead of me gagged and cuffed like a hostage. He tries to kill me, you get killed."

"Won't make any difference," Ali said. "He'd kill me just as soon as he'd kill you. I'm sure they were going to try to kill me in Canada, making it look like suicide."

Once all were in the garage, Fred said: "The guy inside's tough, mean, and maybe armed, the doc says. We have only one pistol and that'll be in the doc's back. Someone stand in the door keeping an eye on the four-by-four, but ready to jump inside the house and help. Other two come with me."

"I'm going in with you," Frank said. "Got to see if Patrick's all right."

"I'm going in too," Paco said.

"Someone give me a handkerchief," Fred said. Luie stuck one in Fred's hand, which he promptly crammed into Ali's mouth, saying: "Gotta make it look good, Doc."

Fred pushed Ali ahead and walked quickly into the living room; Frank and Paco followed. Adnan jumped up from the couch, startled, half asleep watching a muted television program. He reached in his jeans for a gun that apparently was not there.

"Hands in the air or your buddy gets his brains blown out," Fred said.

Adnan leaped forward trying to grab Ali and the gun.

Fred shouted: "I said hands in the air, damn it," and pointed the gun into Adnan's face.

Paco moved behind, forced Adnan's hands behind his back, and attached cuffs while Adnan kicked and screamed.

"Put something in his mouth. Can't wake Patrick," Fred commanded.

Paco shoved in a small pack of tissues that he always carried out of habit from the nursing home.

"Don't worry; he's out like a light. I saw to that this morning," Ali tried to say with a handkerchief in his mouth.

Fred said: "Take him to the garage and search him good for concealed weapons; these guys keep things in their crotches and up their asses. Take his wallet and keys too."

"I'll help carry him but I've got to come back to check on Patrick," Frank said as they took Adnan, kicking and trying to scream to the garage.

"Ok, Doc, you're still my hostage," Fred said. "We'll see what's in the bathroom and bedrooms.

Meanwhile in the garage, Luie said: "Look, long and thin like a limp piece of spaghetti."

Adnan was naked with Paco sitting on his legs saying: "Let's see what he has hidden up his ass. I've given rectal exams, but with gloves."

"Think we have some in the four-by-four," Luie said.

"Nahh, I'm not going to stick a finger in that dirty Arab ass, even in a glove," Paco continued. "Dirty blot on all Arabs; bet his asshole's the same. Use the billyclub; shove anything way up inside."

Adnan kicked and moved violently, trying to scream.

"OK, you disgraceful piece of shit" Paco said; to Luie. "Get the leg restraints."

Luie applied leg restraints while Adnan continued to resist as violently as he could.

"Ok, you filthy piece of shit, up inside with your two scum-bag buddies," Paco said. Luie got Adnan's wallet and keys reading from the driver's license: "Edgardo Rodriguez, Mesquite, Texas. Guess he goes with the Texas plates on the old Toyota over there. Is he Mexican or Arab?"

"Don't you know Arabs and Mexicans look alike, at least to Anglos?" Paco said then suddenly realized he had used the word 'anglo' that could betray him.

Chapter 18

Friday, April 14, 2006
Fairborn, Ohio, USA

Frank came into Patrick's bedroom as Fred said: "Pulse and breathing seem strong enough."

Ali tried to speak; Frank asked: "Take his gag out?"

"Yeah, go ahead," Fred replied.

"I was very careful with the dose and timing," Ali said.

"What's this?" Fred asked. "Hypodermic syringe and two small bottles of something."

"That's how I administered medication," Ali said.

"Name I can't pronounce," Fred said as he looked at fine print on the bottles. "Pharmaceutical lab in Canada."

"That's what I told them to get," Ali said. "Safe and effective if used in the right dose over the right time period. Can't be detected in blood or urine after a short time."

Smuggling meds from Canada too, Fred thought and asked: "How long 'til he wakes up?"

"If Adnan didn't give another injection," Ali replied, "the one this morning should last a couple more hours."

"How can we know?" Fred asked.

"Hand me the bottle, please," Ali said. "Don't think it's gone down since I injected him, but I can't be completely sure," Ali said when Frank removed the handcuffs.

"OK," Fred said. "Hey, maybe we shouldn't let him wake up today and panic because he didn't go to work. He might get really suspicious then. Maybe he should sleep until tomorrow. What do you think Frank?"

"Maybe if we make him think he came to work this morning and left because he was so out of it," Frank replied. "It'd make it safer for all of us if we can convince him he didn't sleep all through the day. He was definitely seen at the office, but if he believes he wasn't there, it could lead to questions we wouldn't want to answer."

"Do you think you could actually make him believe this?" Fred asked.

"Maybe, especially if Felicia's in on it," Frank continued. "Patrick'd believe almost anything she said. She's in on this somehow; has to be."

"Who's Felicia?" Fred asked.

"Philippine woman who works in our office," Frank replied. "Real thick with Patrick. Must've been the one who stole his wallet the doc here had."

"She's in on it," Ali said. "Forced her to cooperate. Didn't tell me much."

"What do we have to lose?" Frank said. "How many more injections can we safely give him, Doc?"

Ali pondered and said: "At least one more, maybe one more after that, max."

"Doc'll give him one more under our supervision before we go," Fred said. "Hey, maybe your friend can give it."

"Just a moment," Frank said. "One more thing I need to do. Sorry, buddy, for your sake as well as mine, I need to do this. Hope he doesn't wake up."

He pulled off the blanket and pulled down Patrick's boxers. "That's Patrick. Let's go."

Chapter 19

Friday, April 14, 2006
Fairborn, Ohio, USA

Frank walked to the garage thinking: *Have to take charge now. Fred's a great buddy the way he took charge, but it's my ass in trouble if this's discovered. They can walk away now and no one'll know about them.* "OK, guys," he said, "you've been the best buddies a guy can have, but this is my problem. Patrick's OK. I've got the classified material. If you go now, no one'll know you're involved and you can't get in trouble."

"Wait a minute!" Paco exclaimed. "What're you going to do with these guys in Luie's four-by-four?"

"I'll figure something out," Frank said. "It's you I'm concerned about; get out before something happens to you."

Fred thought: *Frank's right, get Paco and Luie out. I could walk away, too. Dump the three in the four-by-four on any police station steps. Ali's our problem, or mine. He's smart; probably figure out my car's a police cruiser. No, I'm still in at least until we can do something about him.*

"What could they do to us?" Luie asked. "We're just a couple of dumb Mexicans."

"I thought we had something going," Paco said looking at Frank. "Now you want to dump me?"

Frank said: "We do have something going. That's why I want you out of this. Couldn't live with myself if something happens to you because of my problems."

"Well, Mr. Marine Corps big man, or should I say **Major**," Paco continued. "Y'ain't getting rid of **me** that easy. I'm not one of your troops to be protected so nobly."

"So what can happen to us if we stick with you?" Luie repeated. "Put me in prison? Send us back to Mexico?"

Frank, stunned with this show of loyalty, said: "We have to do something with the guys in the four-by-four and we can't let the doc stay within a thousand miles of Patrick. They have a connection with Canada. Take 'em there; let the Mounties find them."

"Not a bad idea," Fred said. "Get 'em out of this country. How'd we get 'em across the border? Have to use a tunnel or cross a bridge where there's border control."

"Get them on a boat to the Bahamas and dump them?" Frank asked. "We sure can't put 'em on an airplane."

"Too easy to be found on a small island; besides how do we get a boat?" Fred added.

"Hey, take 'em to Mexico?" Paco said. "Keep 'em in the four-by-four and take off. Dump 'em somewhere close where we go camping. It's in the mountains and close to our family; no one'd be suspicious if we're there."

"Bridge at the border, isn't there?" Fred asked.

"Piece of cake," Paco replied. "We cross every year or so anyway and know a couple of Mexican officials. Only thing they're worried about is firearms being brought in, not people. Give 'em a couple of dollars for *cerveza*."

Luie thought: *Paco's sure bold about volunteering my vehicle and me*, then said: "When're we doing this? Got to be in the bakery tomorrow; Easter's one of our busiest times."

"Come off it; the bakery can run without you," Paco retorted. "So what if a couple of customers get pissed off because they can't get all the Easter buns they want? You're the best bakery in town and the only one that makes Easter stuff. Nothing's going to happen."

Luie gulped in acquiescence saying to himself: *sounds like fun anyway. Haven't been away with Paco in ages. Mexico in April. Yeah.*

DESPERATION • CHAPTER 19

"OK, how're we going to do this?" Paco asked. "We need to knock them out somehow."

"We have stuff used on Patrick," Frank said. "How many doses left, Doc? Any more needles and syringes?"

"What'd you use on him?" Paco asked.

"We have a couple of extra needles and syringes," Ali answered. "I told them to get extras. I'll get them and the solution so you can see."

"I'm going with you," Fred said

When they returned, Ali said: "Enough for eight or ten doses; one extra syringe and a few needles."

"That's what we use," Paco said looking at the bottles, "except ours is made in the U.S. Should be enough. I'm damned hungry. It's way past lunch time and hard to think straight on an empty stomach. How can we get some food?"

Fred said: "The only car we can take without drawing attention is Patrick's. I could drive it somewhere while you plan this out. Where can I go?"

"You passed a Burger King on the way," Frank said.

"Yeah, I remember," Fred said. "Who wants what? Should I get something for the guys inside? You may be dumping them, but don't want to starve them to death."

"They're not going to starve to death, are they Doc?" Paco said. "If we feed 'em now, there'll be that much more shit to clean up later. Got to figure out some way to keep 'em from messing up the car anyway."

"I'll have a Whopper, fries, and coke," Frank said.

"Just bring enough Whoppers, fries and cokes for everyone including the doc," Paco said. "Make it easy."

Fred looked in his wallet and asked: "Who's got a little money? Not sure I have enough."

Frank got out his wallet and said: "Here's $30. That should be enough."

"I've got $16," Fred added. "That's enough."

Luie looked at Paco asking: "Who's paying for this trip? Not sure I have enough money. Not in my plans."

"Don't worry," Frank said as Fred drove away. "I'm not rich, but I can cover this. It's my problem."

Chapter 20

Friday, April 14, 2006
Fairborn, Ohio, USA

Paco said: "OK, knock 'em out and cover 'em with blankets and camping gear. Need to buy adult diapers and enemas. Doc, maybe not put you under until just before the border, but if you even bat your eyelash funny, down you go."

"Why at the border?" Ali asked. "I can just be quiet and get under the blankets. You know I'm cooperating with you. Can't I go somewhere else? I don't speak Spanish."

"Shut up, Doc!" Frank said angrily. "We said we can't go to Canada. We're giving you a fuckin' chance taking you to Mexico. You've impersonated a U.S. Army officer, assaulted him, and stolen classified material to give to a known enemy. You'd be put in prison the rest of your life or executed. Remember Moussaoui?"

"Doc, use your damned medical knowledge," Paco retorted. "You could sneeze or cough. Even if you're all covered up, a Mexican border guard could hear. You're going under the needle; only question is when."

"Maybe worry about these details later?" Frank said "What do we need to do now? I need to go to the base soon to return the classified and at least let Felicia see my face."

"Maybe buy diapers and enemas," Paco said. "We can stop at Walmart for rest of the stuff we need. Need to clean this place if you want it to look like no one was here. We'll do that while you're at the base. What're we going to do with the old Toyota? Can't leave it here."

"Maybe Fred'll have some ideas," Frank said. "Wouldn't want it found too close to Dayton. There's that green BMW too."

"What do we do with their clothes? Their wallets too?" Luie asked.

"Maybe a dumpster or Goodwill box," Paco suggested.

"Must be a dumpster somewhere, but wouldn't we attract attention if we're putting something in it?" Frank said. "Where's a Goodwill box?"

"What's a Goodwill box?" Ali asked. "Adnan complained about having to drop and pick up stuff at a Goodwill box early in the morning."

"It's a big box where people dump old clothes, toys, and things they don't want any more, like when they're moving," Luie explained. "Goodwill hires handicapped people to sort them out and resell them to poor people."

"Oh, you do things like that in this country? Thieves don't steal the stuff?" Ali asked in mild disbelief.

"If it's stolen, guess it's going to people who need it," Luie laughed.

Paco said: "Use Patrick's phone book to find Goodwill."

"Toss their wallets in the Mississippi River, hit a garbage barge like that Tom Hanks movie," Luie added.

Fred brought in food; all ate in silence until Paco said: "OK, Fred, here's where we are: Frank's going to the base with the classified and'll buy diapers and enemas."

"Diapers?" Fred asked surprised.

"Yeah, adult diapers like we use in the home for old guys who can't control it anymore," Paco explained. "Can't have 'em shitting and pissing all over the four-by-four."

Fred nodded, surprised he hadn't thought about that.

"We'll clean the house while he's gone," Paco continued. "I'll dose 'em up good and they'll be sound asleep by the time he gets back. Leave in a couple of hours, go load our camping gear, and take off before it's too dark."

Luie said to himself: *There he makes plans without consulting me. Sounds like he knows what he's doing so who am I to say anything? It's just my car. How does he think we can sleep? Can't drive straight through after a day like this.*

"Doc had Patrick's stolen wallet on him. What do we do with that?" Frank asked. "And the other wallets. Luie says throw into the Mississippi River.

Fred replied: "Stolen wallets get turned into police all the time, usually put in a mail box with valuables taken out. Give it to me; I'll find a mailbox; Fairborn police'll get it. The guy from Texas could have his wallet found there; you go through there just toss it somewhere it can be found. For the others, Mississippi River's as good a place as any."

"What do we do with his old Toyota? We thought you might have some ideas," Paco continued.

"And the green BMW?" Frank added.

"The ideal thing'd be to drive the Toyota to Texas and leave it so it doesn't get noticed with a bunch of other Texas license plates," Fred said. "I don't guess there's any way you could go in two cars? Don't worry about the BMW. I'll put it in my garage for now."

All were quiet for a moment; suddenly Paco blurted out: "Frank, you come with us. Three of us will switch off driving two cars while one sleeps. Come have fun with us in Mexico and see your buddies off too."

Frank thought a moment and said: "You know I've been wanting to go to Mexico with you, but authorities would have a record of me crossing the border. Don't know if that's a good idea right now. Besides, I've got to be at work on Monday when Patrick shows up. Could I drive down and fly back from Dallas or some place?"

Paco replied: "We cross the border at Eagle Pass. Go right through Dallas and San Antonio. You can fly from either place. Where should we dump the car, Fred?"

"I can run a check on the plates when I can get to my car and the radio and see where the car is registered," Fred replied. "They may want to know why I am doing an off-duty check, but I can deal with that."

"His driver's license said Mesquite," Luie said. "We go right by there. It's next to Dallas, isn't it?"

"He said he's from Dallas," Ali added.

"OK, done," Paco asserted. "We drive two cars to Dallas, leave the Toyota in Mesquite, and Frank flies from Dallas. We'll leave as soon as you get back with the stuff."

Frank said: "I'll take Patrick's car to the base; it has a sticker and I put the classified in it."

Fred said: "We'll figure out the logistics while you're gone. We need to go back to that apartment to see if there's incriminating evidence left. Must be some clothes there for Goodwill too. Don't need to clean it; places like that get trashed all the time."

"Here's a shopping list," Paco said.

"If you're going to Walmart, get a couple of Rand-McNallys too," Luie added. "One I have is a couple of years old and you need one too."

As Frank drove away, Fred said: "OK, Doc, let's go clean up. You've got to change clothes too. Oh, shit, we need to get rid of this uniform you're wearing. I'll find a place for that when I get home. You must have stuff for Goodwill too. Can't take clothes with you; just what you were wearing. Make sure that room is just like you found it. I'll look for a phone book".

Back in the garage, Paco and Luie started stripping the guys one by one as they kicked and tried to scream.

Paco told Luie: "You sit on them and hold them down while I take off the cuffs and restraints one at a time, strip them, and put the restraints back. Then I'll inject 'em.'

"You give enemas when they're asleep?" Luie asked.

"What do you mean 'you'?" Paco retorted. "We do this together. Carry 'em one by one to the bathroom and hope they don't make too big a mess to clean up. Better to clean it up in the bathroom than in a dirty diaper. Been in that situation many times."

Luie frowned, saying to himself: *He's right. Sure glad I don't have a job like that.*

Chapter 21

Friday, April 14, 2006
Wright-Patterson Air Force Base, Ohio, USA

Frank parked thinking: *Better park in the back in case someone notices it in front and thinks Patrick's here.*

When he opened the office door, Felicia jumped, and said: "Frank, you scared me to death!"

"All I did was walk through the door," He replied. "Hey, you don't look good at all."

He walked into the room with the classified safe thinking: *Have to tell her something and get her to convince Patrick he was actually in the office today. Learned from Okinawa don't tell lies; can catch up with you. Doesn't mean I can't throw in a few misleads.*

"It's tough being alone with the kids," Felicia replied, "trying to keep the house running without Kevin. Patrick helps a lot, especially at times like Easter, but it's not like having a real daddy around. I'm worried about him. He hasn't come back yet and it's been hours."

Frank said: "I'm listening, just putting away classified. He's OK, just really sick. I got his classified to put back. I'm not supposed to tell you; against rules and you know how he is about following rules. I don't think he'll be able to help you hunt Easter eggs this year unless he gets much better soon." He said to himself: *If she'd give me half a chance, I could help her with the kids; for sure not going to have any of my own.*

"He gave it to you? You saw him?" Felicia asked.

"Yeah, turns out we ended up at the same place; not the same meeting," Frank continued. "He's really out of it. You know he was feeling bad this morning. Other guys there were concerned too. In the end, I drove his car home and saw he was in bed. He was so out of it I had to bring the classified. Wouldn't surprise me if he forgets he even came to work today; we may have to remind him on Monday. You know he'd panic if he thought he slept all day. I contacted a friend to help with my car. I won't bother you with details."

He walked to his desk, turned on the computer to check email and rummage through things on his desk.

Felicia was almost beside herself thinking: *Is Frank in on this? He must be if he saw Patrick in bed. Doesn't look like he changed shirts, either. If he's in on this and taken classified from that guy, maybe he knows about me. Am I the next one to have something happen to me? But he said Patrick would come back to work on Monday.* She asked: "You're sure Patrick's OK?"

"I'm not a doctor," Frank said. "He's really sick, but not anything life-threatening. Maybe took too much cold medication that makes him drowsy. You said you're going to check on him tomorrow, didn't you? If he's still out of it, then maybe get him to a doctor."

He turned off his computer, straightened up the desk, and said on the way out: "Take care of yourself this weekend and take care of those kids. Patrick too. See you Monday."

"What'd you say you're going to do this weekend?" Felicia asked forcing herself to be casual and friendly.

He answered: "A couple of guys I know said they wanted to go to Texas. Lots of military flights going to Texas these days with the president there; on Easter weekend it might be possible to get space-available seats." He said to himself: *If someone sees me in the Dayton airport, I couldn't get a flight back so went commercial.*

"Have fun," Felicia said wanly as Frank walked out thinking: *Oh, God, Allah, now what'm I going to do? I'd jump into traffic on the interstate right now if it weren't for the kids; another foreign war bride widow who couldn't cope. Can't do anything 'til Monday. Kids're out of school.*

THREE KISSES

Today's Good Friday, Christian day of mourning; maybe I should go to church. Everyone thinks I'm Christian, but I just went to church with Kevin and pretended. Most Philippine people are Catholic anyway.

Chapter 22

Friday, April 14, 2006
Fairborn, Ohio, USA

While Frank was gone, Fred and Ali cleaned Patrick's house; Paco and Luie were in the utility room washing clothes before taking them to Goodwill.

Luie asked: "How long until they go under?"

"A good hour to go completely," Paco answered; "after 20 minutes or so they'll be so out of it we can start."

"Where're we going to do this?" Luie asked.

"In the bathroom in the bathtub, I guess," Paco answered. "Where else?"

"There's that little half-bath over there," Luie replied.

"You think we can make them sit on the toilet seat?" Paco smirked.

"Why not?" Luie asked. "Might not be easy, but there's a drain here in the floor. Use washing machine hoses to wash something away. Seems a hell of a lot easier than dragging them down the hall, maybe get the carpet dirty."

"You might be right," Paco said. "Maybe I should give Patrick that other shot to carry him through 'til morning."

When he returned, he asked Luie, who was taking a load of dry towels out of the dryer: "How're we going to go? If we go the way we usually do, we'll go right through the middle of Nashville and Memphis. Lots of traffic and lots of trucks to look into our windows."

"I'll get the old Rand-McNally," Luie said. He returned and said: "Here, we can take these parkways across Kentucky; interstate-type highways.

Then there're highways in Tennessee that'll take us to the bridge across the Mississippi River into Missouri, then to Arkansas, and down around Little Rock like we always do. Mostly small towns and open country. I'll check it out in the new atlas."

When Frank walked in with shopping bags and a big plastic gasoline can, Paco said: "Sit the can down beside the four-by-four. Need to keep the back clear and open to lift 'em out to give enemas. Suppose you can help me? Luie's squeamish. Don't want him with an upset tummy before a long drive. Maybe just have him lift and carry the guys."

"Yeah, sure; it's my problem," Frank answered with distinct lack of enthusiasm. "Can't say I've given enemas, but I've seen my share of shit."

"We're here so let's get one of 'em inside," Paco said. "Then strip so we don't get our clothes wet and dirty."

Boudi was nearest to the door. They dumped him on the floor next to the dryer while they stripped off their clothes. Hearing the commotion, Fred and Ali came to the door. Ali was noticeably startled and obviously staring at Frank's and Paco's naked bodies as they worked.

"Can you two bring another one," Paco asked, "so we can start right away when we finish this guy? Then carry him back to the four-by-four and wrap him in a blanket?"

When they finished with Boudi, Paco took a dry towel to dry both himself and Boudi, lay him on the floor, and put a big diaper on him.

"One down, two to go," he said.

Fred and Ali brought Adnan, then took Boudi back. The procedure was repeated for Adnan and Brahim.

"Done. Let's clean up," Paco said wiping the floor with the used towel. "We need to wash this. How can we get it dry so Patrick won't notice when he wakes up?" Paco asked.

Luie said: "I took dry towels out of the dryer. Apparently had left them to dry and didn't take them out unless you washed towels today."

Ali shook his head 'no'.

"OK, we wash dirty ones, put them and the dry ones in the dryer, turn the dryer on, and walk away," Luie said. "Did you two use any towels last night or today?"

"Just the ones hanging in the bathroom," Ali answered.

"Leave them," Fred said. "He probably won't notice anything unless you got them really dirty."

"Don't think so," Ali said.

"OK, here's what we do," Fred said. "Paco stays here and rests while watching the washer and dryer. Luie, Frank, and I go to the apartment along with the doc in my car. We check out the apartment to see that everything's OK and then drive to my place and wait for you to get there. Frank takes his car home and waits for Paco. There's a Goodwill box on Dayton-Yellow Springs Road right on the way. Paco drives the Toyota to Frank's place whenever things are done here. Luie drives the green BMW to my place. Paco and Frank come back here in the Toyota, give the place one last look over. Then Frank and Paco drive the Toyota and four-by-four to my place. You three take off for Hamilton with Doc.

"Oh, here I found his gun. Best thing would be to dump it in Texas or just leave it in the car."

Beavercreek, Ohio, USA

FRANK'S HOUSE IN BEAVERCREEK, OHIO

THREE KISSES

Paco drove the Toyota into Frank's driveway minutes after he had parked the Mountaineer in the garage and went inside. He opened the front door for Paco, walked down the hall to the bedroom, took off his shoes, and started undressing. Paco came into the bedroom, grabbed him roughly, pulling the clothes off, almost tearing buttons off.

"You asked for it!" he shouted and gave Frank a hard slap on the buttocks.

Frank forced his face into Paco's, kissed him deeply and passionately, and started to unbuckle Paco's belt.

Paco slapped him hard again saying: "You wait until I'm ready. You know better than that."

"Sorry," Frank said meekly as Paco stripped off his clothes and jerked Frank's boxers off.

After passionate activity, Frank slapped Paco saying: "See what you made me do? Now I've got to clean it up."

Chapter 23

Saturday, April 15, 2006
Lattakia, Syria

Abdulrahman paced the floor in midafternoon thinking in Arabic: *Why haven't they sent a signal? Maybe I should see that jerk Jihad and find out if he knows anything.* He shuffled down the corridor to Jihad's office, walked in without knocking; Jihad, startled said in Arabic: "Oh, Abou Walid."

"What've you heard from America?" Abdulrahman demanded in Arabic.

"Nothing," Jihad replied in Arabic, annoyed. "They're supposed to send you the signal."

"You have the phone to call Adnan," Abdulrahman stated in Arabic.

"He has strict orders not to call and I call only if there's something urgent like when that slimy Viktor screwed up," Jihad replied in Arabic.

"Speaking of Viktor, where is he?" Abdulrahman asked in Arabic. "We can usually smell his horrible pipe."

"He's been in his room all morning so far as I know," Jihad said in Arabic. "He often stays and reads on weekends. Oh, he said he might go to Damascus. I can check."

When Abdulrahman left, Jihad thought in Arabic: *I'd better call. It's about eight in the morning there. ... No answer. Maybe they have it on silent.*

When there was no answer to his pounding on Viktor's door, he said to himself in Arabic: *No answer. I'll get the key he's not supposed to know I have.* He returned saying: "Viktor Sergeyevich," and opened the door.

He exclaimed to himself: *Gone! No luggage. Where the hell could he have gone? Damascus? We've got people watching him.* He called his Moukhabarat contact asking in Arabic: "Where's the Russian?"
pause

"What? No trace?" Jihad exclaimed in Arabic. "You're supposed to be watching him."
pause

"Yes, I know," he said in Arabic. "Keep me informed." He disconnected then said to himself in Arabic: *Another time to America. ... Damn, still no answer. Better tell Abed. Maybe escape myself. If we've screwed this up, they'll turn on me and make me disappear. Where can I go? In this country, Moukhabarat everywhere and I can't trust all of them. Maybe to Lebanon; still have contacts there.*

He slowly walked to his office and said to himself in Arabic: *One more try on the phone.*

After no answer, he walked to Abdulrahman's office and said in Arabic: "Sit down, Abou Walid, no answer in America. It's early and they may have phones on silent. Viktor's gone."

"Gone?" Abdulrahman shouted in Arabic. "Gone where? When?"

"Not in his apartment," Jihad replied in Arabic. "Doesn't look like his bed was slept in. He can't get too far; we watch all buses leaving town." He suddenly realized he betrayed his Moukhabarat status then said to himself in Arabic: *He surely knows anyway and I'm already done for.*

He admits he's Moukhabarat, Abdulrahman said to himself then asked in Arabic: "What do we do now?"

"Wait and see what happens," Jihad replied in Arabic. "Someone'll call sometime. I'll keep checking."

"Keep me informed," Abdulrahman said in Arabic as Jihad walked away. He began mentally planning in Arabic: *If I get in my car now, I can be at the border crossing where recruits cross to join the great soldiers of*

DESPERATION • CHAPTER 23

Allah fighting for the liberation of our country and preservation of Islam. I'll blend in with them and find a place in Baghdad to hide.

Jihad began thinking in Arabic: *Cross at El Arida; Moukhabarat have Tartous sewed up and too far to other safe border crossings. One more try to call Adnan.*

Chapter 24

Saturday, April 15, 2006
Fort Meade, Maryland, USA

Shortly before 8 a.m., Brad parked yawning. He was dressed preppy style like the day before, but wore faux tortoise-shell brown plastic rim glasses rather than usual contact lenses. He had not shaved.

My luck, he thought as he walked into the building, not stopping to flirt with the Marine guards. *Be here early to orient new guys while Jason's sleeping away. New employees start Saturday shifts and someone has to orient them. Same happened for me. My turn for Saturday duty so can't complain, but damn why'd we stay up so late? He'll be fresh and ready to go when I get home. Just going to have to entertain himself while I take a nap.*

He found three eager new employees, two young men about his age and a similar aged young woman, all dressed preppy style. He showed them how to make coffee. They waited briefly until persons they replaced turned over headphones. They had been trained on the equipment and needed only orientation for their first day of work. Brad was giving a description when a noise signaled a call coming in.

He said: "That's a signal for numbers we marked for monitoring. Hey, it's the same numbers as yesterday." He signaled them to watch and turned on loudspeakers to hear the ringing sounds as he continued: "Yesterday, we set both of these numbers to be monitored and traced. See, it shows the call originates in Syria and going to a number in Buffalo but with roaming forwarded to Ohio. Today it's Middletown. Person called is moving around. Someone isn't answering."

He gave more explanations and guided them as they listened briefly and then disconnected from conversations between mothers and daughters, brothers and fathers.

"Here it is again," he said. "We'll make a note. When it's repeated that soon, there may be some urgency that helps interpret what it's about."

He drifted off to daydreams while the newcomers continued to monitor calls: *Jason wants to go to church tomorrow, especially being Easter. He misses church from growing up, but doesn't miss homophobia and gay bashing. Didn't talk about which church; guess to UCC where I've gone a couple of times but didn't really like it. Not enough time to find that gay church, the Metropolitan Community Church. He might like it. From what I've heard, it appeals to people from an evangelical background.*

Gee, there's that buzzer again for that phone in Syria. Someone really wants to get through bad.

He drifted off into more daydreams.

Chapter 25

Saturday, April 15, 2006
Dyersburg, Tennessee, USA

Just past dawn, Paco drove the four-by-four with Frank in the passenger seat, having passed Dyersburg going westward on Interstate Highway 155.

He squeezed Frank's thigh, saying with a big grin: "Nice to be with you all alone, except for those assholes in the back."

"We're making good time," Frank commented. "Might be in Dallas in late afternoon."

Paco asked: What's it like to drive with the doc?"

"OK," Frank replied. "He was amazed at big city lights of Cincinnati and Louisville and our highways; says they have something like interstates in Syria. Mostly slept. Not too happy I made him pee in a dark place by the road and stand close enough to grab him if he ran. One time had to find an empty lonely rest area for him to take a shit with me standing just in front of the stall door."

"Luie and I got worried if Mexican customs see an open box of adult diapers," Paco said. "We should buy a few more full new boxes so we can say we're taking them to Luie's aunt. Next time you're driving the Toyota, we put the doc with us and you stop at Walmart. He looked in the road atlas and said there're Super Walmart's right on the interstate in just about every town. We need other things too."

DESPERATION • CHAPTER 25

"Poor doc," Frank said in mock sympathy. "He gets shuttled back and forth. Good thing you remembered to tell me to buy that gas can. Sure not a good idea to park this four-by-four next to a big well-lit gas pump where anyone can look in. It's too early to go shopping. It's only 7 a.m."

"Walmart's open 24/7, remember?" Paco said.

"Oh, yeah, forgot," Frank said. "I shop mostly at the Base Exchange and don't pay much attention to when Walmart's open. Hey, that's the Mississippi River Bridge. We're supposed to throw the wallets in here aren't we?"

APPROACHING BRIDGE FROM
DYERSBURG, TENNESSEE

ENTERING MISSOURI FROM
TENNESSEE

"That's what Luie said," Paco replied. "We can do it if we can stop without drawing attention to ourselves."

"Where's your camera?" Frank asked. "Stop in the emergency lane and I'll take a picture of sunrise over the Mississippi like some gawking tourist.?"

"In that bag on top of the bodies," Paco answered, "both the camera and the wallets."

"Stop here," Frank said. "No one'll notice wallets going over."

He stepped out of the car and while taking snap shots, quickly hurled two wallets into the water.

Paco said: "Maybe you drive a while; I need to get in back and give them injections. When we see a rest area, we'll stop. Really need to do it before traffic picks up."

Chapter 26

Saturday, April 15, 2006
Fairborn, Ohio, USA

A ringing cell phone jolted Felicia from deep sleep; she said to herself: *Damn, finally got to sleep after taking Nytol, but it **is** almost nine.*

She disconnected the call in disgust and near panic, saying to herself: *that ugly voice saying get on the computer.*

She groggily put on a satin-type light blue robe that had seen many washings over her feminine gown, put on her glasses, wearily walked to the family room, connected with all the messengers on the computer, and waited.

"Where is he?" words on the screen asked.

"Where's who?" she typed back on another messenger.

"The guy supposed to go to your office yesterday. He show up?" a third messenger read.

"Yes." Felicia typed.

"When you see him last?" the words continued.

"Before noon," she typed.

"What about guy you give sleeping medicine?" the words came on the screen again.

"Gave it," she typed.

"He go to sleep?" the words asked her.

"Don't know," she replied.

"Contact him." the typed words demanded.

DESPERATION • CHAPTER 26

"How?" Felicia asked typing.

"Call on phone, damn it," angry words read.

She called on her cell phone and after a few moments typed: "No answer,"

"Keep trying. Remember old mother back home," the words read and all messengers disconnected.

What'm I going to do now? Felicia thought in anguish: *Both of them must be dead. Mother back in the Philippines. That's what I'll do. Go to the Philippines, or pretend to, and not come back. Leave children with Kevin's parents.*

"Good morning, Denise," she said forcing a smile to her eight-year old daughter who came into the family room several minutes later wearing a girl's light weight fleece gown. "Come give me a kiss."

"What're we going to do today, Mommy?" she asked.

"I don't know yet," Felicia answered. "We should call Grandmother and Granddaddy Cavanaugh so you can wish them happy Easter. Maybe you and Timmy can go visit them; just you two alone. You're a big girl now; why don't you call yourself? I'll give you their phone number and you can write it down. Get a pencil and paper from your room."

When Denise returned, Felicia gave her the number; Denise dialed and said into the phone: "Good morning grandmother. This is Denise."
pause

"Mommy said to wish you happy Easter," she said.
pause

"We dyed lots of Easter eggs and made lots of things in school," she continued.
pause

"Timmy's just fine," Denise replied. "He's still in bed. I'll get him. Mommy says we might visit you, just Timmy and me alone."
pause

Felicia said: "Happy Easter, Mother Cavanaugh."
pause

"Oh, I need to go see my mother," Felicia replied. "She's really bad. I thought the children would be OK with you for a little while. It won't hurt them to miss school. Timmy's only in kindergarten and Denise is a good student."

pause

Timmy entered wearing little boy's pajamas with designs of soccer balls and players.

"Here's Timmy," Felicia said into the phone.

She doesn't seem enthusiastic, Felicia thought. *Still better to have the children with them.*

Timmy said a few things in his five-year old voice ending with: "Good bye, Grandmother. Here's Mommy."

Felicia spoke into the telephone again: "I'll let you know about the children. Goodbye now. Please wish Father Cavanaugh Happy Easter too."

After giving the children breakfast and cleaning up the kitchen, Felicia called to the children: "How'd you like to go to King's Island? It opens today."

"Oh, yes, mommy," both responded enthusiastically.

King's Island on opening day is the last place I'd want to go, Felicia said to herself. *Maybe the hassle will keep my mind off other things.*

Later that night she fell in bed exhausted after putting the children to bed, not bothering to look at the caller ID on her fixed-line phone nor missed calls on her cell phone.

CHAPTER 27

Saturday, April 15, 2006
El Arida, Lebanon

Jihad drove to the Lebanese border station thinking in Arabic: *Strange crossing legitimately after all the times I snuck across. Easy on the Syrian side. Obviously recognized I'm Moukhabarat. Didn't even charge the 200 lira exit tax. Of course had to give baksheesh.*

He produced his ID card and automobile documents and waited while his mind wandered in Arabic: *Have to do something with this car. A late model Dacia'd really stick out; Don't import them into Lebanon. In Syria one of the few cars we can afford with all the taxes. Romania's one of the few countries that still does business with us. No one in Lebanon'd buy one of these when they can get nice new cars from all over the world for good prices. Get it back to Syria, sell it, and buy a nice new car here.*

Fadi Haddad, a sergeant in the Lebanese military police who monitored the border, wore a freshly clean, starched, and pressed grey camouflage uniform with brightly shined black boots and a red beret smartly on his head. He was clean shaven, indicating pride in both his uniform and personal appearance. Black rimmed glasses with rectangular lenses complimented his closely trimmed dark brown, almost black, slightly wavy hair.

He thought in Arabic: *Something's not right*, then said in Arabic: "Please park your car over there while you go into the building for passport control."

THREE KISSES

Sergeant Haddad gave an eye signal to another sergeant, walked to the passport control building, and gave Jihad's Syrian ID card to Captain Elias Khoury, who was in charge.

Jihad entered the station going to the window for other Arab nationals where the well-groomed military police corporal, dressed like Sergeant Haddad but without a beret, said in Arabic: "Your passport please."

"Passport?" Jihad said in Arabic. "I don't need a passport to enter Lebanon. You have my ID card; you're supposed to be holding it here for me."

"All nationalities, including Syrian, must now have a passport and visa," the corporal stated in Arabic.

"Since when?" Jihad asked in Arabic.

"Since Lebanon was liberated from Syrian occupation and Syria started requiring passports and visas of Lebanese," the corporal responded calmly and professionally in Arabic.

"One moment," Jihad grumbled as he turned his back, rummaged through papers, and slipped a U.S. $20 bill inside one of the folded papers. He thought in Arabic: *Good the government now lets us have dollars legitimately; that's the main money they use in Lebanon; $20 should be enough.*

Jihad handed the paper with $20 inside to the corporal who motioned to the sergeant who was supervising. He gave the paper with the money to the sergeant without comment.

"Please come this way," the sergeant said to Jihad in Arabic as he pointed to a sign posted prominently on the wall written in three languages, Arabic, French, and English: 'Offering a bribe is a crime and will be prosecuted.'

Jihad hesitated and the sergeant walked to his side taking him by the elbow to lead him into Captain Khoury's office. The sergeant handed the paper with the $20 to the captain and walked back to the door blocking any exit.

Captain Khoury, who stood about six feet and had neatly trimmed dark brown hair with faint hints of gray suggesting an age of about 50, said to Jihad in Arabic: "Major Jihad Noussayri, what brings you to Lebanon today? Stealing more television sets and stereos? My mother-in-law sure did miss that nice TV you took the last time. We know all about you. Now you violate our laws offering a bribe. You were untouchable until now. The Gendarmerie in Halba wants you to visit them. Step over there with the sergeant."

Jihad bolted away attempting to run past the sergeant at the door who grabbed and handcuffed him.

"We can use leg restraints if you make it necessary," Captain Khoury stated in Arabic. "The sergeant will empty your pockets and take your car keys. Someone will drive it back to the Syrian side. We'll keep your telephone; you won't have any use for it."

Jihad said to himself in Arabic: *Who do these fucking Lebanese think they are treating us like this? We Syrians saved them from self-destruction during the civil war and kept them from being occupied by Israel. Some gratitude. As soon as Moukhabarat find out, I'll get out. They may think we left this country, but we'll show 'em. Wait? I need to get those papers from the car.*

The sergeant led him to a waiting pick-up truck saying in Arabic: "Hurry, get in the truck."

Jihad walked to the passenger side and attempted to open the door with his handcuffed hands.

"No," the sergeant scowled in Arabic. "In the back."

The sergeant pushed Jihad to the back of the pickup truck, roughly pushed him up into the cargo area, and then attached his legs to a ring on the floor.

Chapter 28

Saturday, April 15, 2006
Qaim, Iraq

Well after dark, Viktor stumbled to the Iraqi border post carrying a heavy vinyl plastic bag, exhausted from walking a long way to avoid the Syrian border post.

"Halt!" an Iraqi soldier said in Arabic, pointing a rifle.

"Inglisi! Amerikani!," Viktor screamed.

"Go in that compound; take your clothes off and empty your bag," the Iraqi soldier commanded in Arabic.

Viktor stood stupefied, not understanding a word, wailing: "Inglisi. Amerikani."

The soldier angrily used his rifle tip to motion the direction Victor must go where suicide bombers could be searched and defused or blow themselves up away from the main station. *He keeps saying English and American,* he said to himself in Arabic. *I should get an American soldier.*

Viktor went into the compound and stood in a trance.

An American voice came over a loudspeaker: "Strip. Take your clothes off and dump your bag on the ground."

Viktor complied.

"Turn around," the voice commanded.

He turned, terrified as dogs sniffed his belongings.

DESPERATION • CHAPTER 28

"Get dressed and come over here. Bring your passport if you have one," the voice continued commanding.

Viktor hastily rummaged through his bag and walked to the border station holding out his fake passport.

"What the hell kind of a passport is this?" the American soldier asked noting Cyrillic characters.

"It's from Tajikistan," Viktor replied in heavily accented English. "I'm Russian. I worked there as a doctor. Take me to your commander. Please."

"What're you doing here, then?" the soldier asked.

"They forced me to work for them. I'm a doctor; take me to your commander. PLEASE!" he pleaded.

"Who forced you to work?" The soldier asked.

"Al Qaeda," Viktor answered in a very low voice.

"Al Qaeda?" the American soldier exclaimed, saying to himself: *Is this guy a nut case?* He said: "You expect me to believe that? We'll take you to Baghdad and turn you over to the Russians."

"No!" Viktor screamed pleadingly. "Put me in your prison. Russians'll torture and kill me."

Jesus Christ, he IS a nut case, the American soldier exclaimed to himself. *We can't deal with this out here.* "Lock him in the bus," he said to the Iraqi soldier. "Baghdad can figure out what to do."

Once he was seated on the bus, he worried in Russian: *What'll they do with me now? Couldn't be as bad as what I left. Taxi driver was suspicious all the way to Aleppo. Dumped me and demanded double fare. Had to take another taxi to the Armenian quarter where Vladimir Alexandrovich lives with his Syrian-Armenian wife. Wouldn't even let me in his house; said his wife's been co-opted by the Moukhabarat.*

No taxi'd take me to the border. Finally, one said he'd do it for 10,000 lira; really needed money. Even then wouldn't take me all the way; walk at least two kilometers. Rest of my life in an American prison's better than anything in Syria.

Meanwhile, five kilometers to the south, Abdulrahman quietly walked across the border thinking in Arabic: *A little way to a farm trail, left and walk 5 kilometers to the main road,* repeating instructions he had been given.

"Halt!" a voice said in English in the darkness. Abdulrahman dropped his bag and started running.

"Halt!" another voice said in Arabic as a shot was fired over his head.

"Ask what he's doing here," the American soldier told the Iraqi soldier who was also a translator.

Hearing the question in Arabic, he replied in Arabic, trembling, trying to mimic a Kurdish accent: "I'm just a poor guy who's been struggling to earn money in Syria. My poor mother in Mosul's sick; I need to go see her."

"Why're you crossing here and not at the main crossing?" the question was translated into Arabic.

"Lost my ID card," he replied. "Stole it from me. Couldn't cross there."

"Who are you?" the questions continued.

"Zozan Bedirkhan," he lied, giving a Kurdish name.

"Doesn't speak like a Kurd," the Iraqi soldier said then shouted: "Strip!"

"Walk over there and dump your bag," the American soldier said in English using a flashlight to indicate where.

Abdulrahman hesitated and the Iraqi solder repeated in Arabic: "Strip! Everything."

"For the sake of Allah, you want me to expose myself?" Abdulrahman replied in Arabic.

"Where the hell do you think al Qaeda hide explosives and weapons?" The Iraqi soldier said in Arabic. "Do what I say or I'll shoot you on the spot and no one'll know any difference; just killing an infiltrator."

Abdulrahman stripped to all but his underwear and emptied his bag on the ground.

The American soldier said in English: "He seems clean unless you really want to make him take off his underwear. Let's cuff him, put him in the jeep, take him up to the border post, and put him on the bus. Let people in Baghdad figure out who he really is."

DESPERATION • CHAPTER 28

"Viktor!" Abdulrahman exclaimed several minutes later as he climbed on the bus stumbling with his bag.

"Abdulrahman!" Viktor shouted waked from sleep.

Chapter 29

Saturday, April 15, 2006
Mesquite, Texas, USA

In late afternoon, Luie was driving the four-by-four on I-30 westbound while Ali rode in the Toyota with Frank; Paco said to Frank on his cell phone: "We're about to get onto 635 south. How far back're you?"
pause

"Address on his driver's license is Belt Line Road," Paco said. "Can take the U.S. 80 East exit off 635 and almost immediately an exit for Belt Line Road."
pause

He said, "give you a few minutes to park. Walk to the street and stand on the curb. We drive by and you hop in.
pause

The disconnected and a few minutes later, Frank got in the Jeep saying: "Gee, another dump; not as bad as in Fairborn. Straight to DFW airport I guess?"

"Map shows road to the airport's a toll road," Luie said. "Don't think we should drive through toll booths."

"Oh, yeah, think I remember couple of times I've been to DFW," Frank said. "Let me off at a big hotel. Get a taxi or shuttle. I saw a Fairfield Inn when we took an exit. Go back there, drop me off; you can get on 635 again. Give me his wallet," Frank said. When the hotel was in sight, he said: "Drop me anywhere you find a place to stop and I'll walk."

DESPERATION • CHAPTER 29

After stopping, Frank gave Paco a big hug and kiss. Frank and Luie strained to give each other a kiss from their awkward positions.

Frank turned to Ali not knowing whether to give him a pat on the back, a hug, or a punch in the nose, and said: "Take care of yourself, Doc. Remember, come back to this country and your ass is fried just like Moussaoui's'll be."

Before Ali could reply, Frank got out of the car with his bag and walked back towards the street and to the hotel.

Book 2
DISCOVERIES

CHAPTER 1

Sunday, April 16, 2006
Fairborn, Ohio, USA

Denise and Timmy ran ahead of their mother out of Mary, Help of Christians Roman Catholic Church at the end of early mass eager to get candy eggs given to the children. Denise was wearing a new frilly pale yellow and blue Easter dress and white grown-up style pump shoes. Timmy had new khaki pants and a red and white horizontal-striped shirt, along with a new pair of shoes.

MARY, HELP OF CHRISTIANS ROMAN CATHOLIC
CHURCH, FAIRBORN, OHIO

THREE KISSES

Oh, God, last thing I want today is to mingle with people, Felicia thought standing away from the crowd having coffee and tea. She wore one of her nicest pale blue dresses from last season, was well groomed as always, but her face showed fatigue and her body stood limp as she thought: *The priest had to preach on resurrection; all I want is to die and never resurrect. Allah, where are you? Why's this happening to me?*

Both children screamed with delight: "Patrick!" "Patrick!" as they ran to put candy-stained hands on his smart new outfit of Polo Ralph Lauren khakis and shamrock green polo shirt Elsie gave him to remind him of St. Patrick's day.

"Hey there, you two!" Patrick shouted as he embraced both at once. "Was the Easter Bunny good to you?"

Felicia saw the children with Patrick, stopped short, turned white, and almost fainted as if seeing a ghost, exclaiming: "Patrick!?!?! What're you doing here?"

He let go of the children and stammered: "I always go to this mass; you see me here all the time. You know Elsie and I promised we'd each light a candle for Easter."

Felicia, shaken, thought: *It's Patrick; it's his voice.* She said: "Oh, er, you were so sick Friday at the office; I'm surprised you're able to be out of bed so soon."

"I tried to call you yesterday," Patrick replied, "but you didn't answer on either your regular phone or your cell."

"Oh, er, we went to King's Island all day. I knew I wouldn't hear the cell phone in all that commotion so I just left it at home. How are you? You look OK."

"Still have a little runny nose and cough, but fine," Patrick said. "I just needed a good sleep. Wait. You said you saw me **Friday**? The reason I called yesterday was to say I'm sorry I slept through work on Friday. I hope it didn't cause any problems. Did you cover for me? Why didn't you call? I saw a missed call from you but it was on Saturday. I was in the shower."

She replied hesitatingly: "You were in the office on Friday; Frank saw you there. He said he had to help you home because you were so sick."

DISCOVERIES • CHAPTER 1

"Huh???" Patrick exclaimed perplexed. "Frank helped me home on Friday?"

"Ask him tomorrow if you don't believe me," she said.

"Hey, kids, you going to invite me to hunt Easter eggs?" Patrick asked.

"Yes, Patrick, please come. He can come can't he Mommy?" Denise said.

Felicia, embarrassed, replied: "You were so sick Friday I couldn't imagine you'd be up to it. We don't have Easter dinner; we were at King's Island all day yesterday."

"Ahhh, who cares about Easter dinner," Patrick said surprised, thinking: *That isn't like Felicia, not making Easter dinner.* "We can just have deviled eggs. You did dye a big bunch this year didn't you?"

Felicia gulped saying to herself: *At least I pulled myself together enough to do that. I'm not ready to handle this. I was resigned, looking forward to killing myself; now what?*

Patrick misinterpreted her silence as embarrassment over not having food and said: "This time it's my treat. I'll stop at Boston Market and pick up lots of good things. I know you like mashed potatoes and corn on the cob."

"Oh, yes, oh, yes," Timmy said. "Can I ride with you?"

"I'm bigger; I get to ride with Patrick," Denise retorted.

"No fighting now," Patrick scolded smiling. "You both ride with me, but Denise rides in the front because she's bigger. Young kids have to ride in back, or so the base safety authorities say. Fasten your seat belts too. Hear?!"

He thought: *Take our slow, sweet, easy time so Felicia can go straighten up if she needs to. She sure looks like she needs time alone. If any good movies're showing, maybe take the kids and let her be alone a while.*

Beavercreek, Ohio, USA

"Haaarrrrow. Frank Reynolds," Frank spoke into his cell phone groggily waked from a very deep sleep about 9 a.m.

pause

"It's OK, Fred," Frank said.

pause

"Got in late," he continued. "Managed to get a flight; had to change in Nashville. Cost a fortune; only business class from Dallas to Nashville."

pause

"Yeah, everything went off without a hitch," he continued. "Nothing much really to tell."

pause

"Hey, when you off duty?" Frank asked. "Want to come up and get Easter dinner and talk more?"

pause

"Oh, ok. I understand," Frank said.

pause

"Nope, haven't heard a word from them," Frank said.

pause

"Huh? Next weekend you say?" Frank asked.

pause

"Yeah, you have to get it out of your garage soon," Frank said. "Let's wait 'til we hear from them."

pause

"Love ya," Frank said and disconnected, rolled over and soon was back into his deep slumber.

Chapter 2

Sunday, April 16, 2006
San Juan de Sabinas, Coahuila, Mexico

Luie rolled out of his sleeping bag and walked out of the tent in boxer shorts singing under his breath: 'Oh, what a beauuu-tiii-ful moooor-ning, oh what a beauuuu-tiii-ful daaay', thinking: *This is Coahuila not Oklahoma and that's a pretty corny song, but fun when we did it for the high school play. God, I'm tired and stiff. Got to unpack the four-by-four. I need coffee and something to eat.*

He opened the Jeep saying to himself: *Camp stove, grill, charcoal, matches, pots, dishes. Didn't look at that last batch Frank bought. Instant coffee, good; powdered milk; sugar; breakfast bars, granola bars, muesli bars, Rice Krispies bars. Hey, we'll have cereal coming out our ears and asses. Canned corn, pork and beans. These Muslim boys'll love that. Aren't we supposed to be Arabs too? Put the pork and beans back. Canned luncheon meat. Hey, it's Spam; that's pork too.*

What's this? Trying to be funny, is he? Refried beans, tamales, canned tortillas, and salsa. What do the English say: 'taking coals to Newcastle'? We'll get him for that.

Portable shower. Lots of bodies to clean. Get water boiling. Water from the creek should be clean; fresh melt from snow on the mountains, but Moctezuma's revenge is the last thing we need. Let's see if he bought water. Yeah, some; at least enough for coffee.

About an hour later, Paco walked out groggily.

"Got coffee for you," Luie said. "Plenty to eat if you like all that healthy granola and muesli stuff."

"Thanks. Gimme a minute," Paco said. "You know it takes me a while to wake up."

"Water's ready for a shower soon," Luie continued. "Any of the others awake yet?"

"Doc may be stirring," Paco replied. "Didn't have as much of the knock-out drops. Take others longer."

"Good," Luie said. "Things'll be hectic when they're all up. We need to make decisions while things're calm."

"I've already figured out lots of things," Paco said. "Couldn't tell you too much with Doc in the car with us."

Yeah, right, typical, Luie grumbled to himself. *He makes all the damned decisions without consulting me. Guess I love him too much to make a fuss about it.* He said: "Hey, are we still Arabs?"

"Haven't thought," Paco answered. "Yeah, let's still make 'em think we're Arabs. 'Course the doc knows we're not; gotta keep him from telling them. We might need to keep 'em way apart anyway; if they know special treatment he's gotten, might gang up on him."

"They all start speaking Arabic to each other, we won't have any idea what they're plotting," Luie said. "Have to keep our clothes on too; Arab men don't expose themselves to other men. What're we going to do today once they all get up? Someone's got to go to town and do things even if it is Easter Sunday. Have to wait at least 'til tomorrow to get clothes for them; everything's closed today."

"Yeah, for sure I gotta go into town," Paco said. "See family; call others.

"By the time we get 'em out of diapers and clean, it'll be afternoon," Luie added. "Gotta find places to dump 'em, too. Not so far they can't get to a town before they die of exposure and hunger, but far enough to give us time to get away. Can't drop 'em all in the same place either."

"Water's probably hot enough," Luie said. "You want a shower now? Oh, forgot to get the soap from the four-by-four. You fill the shower while I get it."

Luie returned to find Paco naked holding the shower nozzle. He quickly removed his boxers and shoes, walked up behind Paco, and slapped his buttocks hard.

DISCOVERIES • CHAPTER 2

"Oh, you want to get rough, do you?" Paco said as he gave Luie's buttocks a hard swat with the nozzle tube.

"You asked for it, now!" Luie said, twisting Paco's arm, forcing him to drop the nozzle, and proceeded with intense rough intimacy.

"Aghhhhhh." Paco screamed in both pain and pleasure. "You damned bastard. You'll pay for this!" Paco shouted as he slapped Luie hard on the face and buttocks and proceeded to do the same to him.

Paco glanced at the tent opening, saw Ali, watching and said: "Come here."

Ali shook his head side to side stammering: "I can't."

"Why can't you?" Paco demanded. "Oh, that's why," he said seeing his erect penis ejaculating. "Want to join in?"

"No, no," Ali screamed.

"You liked that, didn't you?" Luie asked. "Got you excited. As much as we might like to or you might like to, don't worry; not a good idea to diddle the captives."

Paco said: "It's going to be a big mess cleaning them. We'll need all the help we can get, Doc."

"Yeah, sure," Ali gulped reluctantly.

Paco said: "Doc, we've got to make it look like you're not helping us voluntarily. You've been good and we're not going to hurt you on purpose, but if those guys know you're getting favored treatment, they might try to kill you. We're going to restrain you and maybe slap you around, but it's mostly for show. You play along with us and we'll do our best to protect you from them. We won't make you touch their bodies so they won't get the idea that you're looking at their private parts. You do the dirty work picking up the diapers and things like that. OK?"

"OK," Ali mumbled.

"Now let's get cleaned up and get to work unloading," Paco said. "Go inside the tent and get towels, Doc."

"OK," Ali said meekly, "but can I have something to eat and take a shower?"

CHAPTER 3

Sunday, April 16, 2006
Baghdad International Airport, Iraq

U.S. Army Reserve Corporal Lindsay Myers got off the bus inside the U.S. Forces prison area in late morning thinking: *these trips from the border are killers. Watching for bombs, snipers, potholes, road hazards. Thank goodness I don't have to drive the bus.* He asked the private at the gate: "The CO around? Got a couple of real nut cases."

"Probably at the church service the chaplain organized," the private answered. "It is Easter Sunday and he's a deacon in the Baptist church back home."

"Oh, yeah, it's Easter, isn't it?" Corporal Myers said. "Out here it's easy to forget."

"Got'ya man. Forgot it myself until I heard something this morning," the private replied.

"Any idea when service'll be over?" Corporal Myers asked. "Got to sort out these prisoners and get most of them over to the Iraqi prison at Abou Ghraib."

"No idea," the private answered. "Best you go see. I can't leave this post and no phones here."

"Walk'll do me good anyway," Corporal Myers said. "Been sitting on my ass for too many hours."

He was 20 years old, 5 feet 10 inches, had medium brown closely trimmed hair and green eyes, stereotypical Midwestern reflecting his

DISCOVERIES • CHAPTER 3

Nebraska origins. After a few minutes, he entered the mess hall and gently put his hand on the shoulder of U.S. Army Reserve Colonel Albert Jones, the prison commander, who at first was annoyed at being disturbed, but walked out with Corporal Myers. Colonel Jones stood 5 feet 10 inches, had neatly trimmed dark brown hair with faint touches of gray reflecting his mid-40s age, and was clean shaven. He wore gray light-weight wool-polyester pants and a muted blue plaid short-sleeved sport shirt tucked into the slacks. Black wire rim glasses had rectangular lenses rounded at the corners. He presented a conservative appearance typical of a small businessman, a funeral director, back in Lincoln.

Outside, Corporal Myers said: "Sorry to bother you, sir. I didn't know if this's important enough, but decided it's best to make a mistake by disturbing rather than waiting."

"It's ok, son," Colonel Jones replied as he thought: *He's a good kid; he wouldn't disturb me if he didn't think it's important. Besides, the sermon was getting to me. What can he say about resurrection and new life here with people getting shot at and killed?*"

"We just came from the border at Qaim," the corporal replied. "We've got lots that'll go to the Iraqis as usual, but there're two really strange ones. One shriveled up old man claims he's a Russian doctor who escaped from al Qaeda and begging to be kept in an American prison and see you."

"That IS weird," Colonel Jones said. "Begging to be in our prison after publicity over Abou Ghraib."

"The other's Iraqi, or speaks like an Iraqi, the interpreter says," Corporal Myers continued. "Claimed he's Kurdish from Mosul and needs to visit his mother, but when the Iraqi Security Force guy with me said they'd turn him over to the ISF in Baghdad to be turned over to the Kurds, he begged to be brought to Americans. Said he's a hospital administrator and has a story to tell. Absolutely terrified over being in ISF hands; in a state of panic all the way here."

Colonel Jones said: "Sounds like a Ba'athist who escaped and tried to slip back in. We turn him over to the ISF and they'll hang him by his toenails and feed him to the dogs. We're catching enough grief for turning guys over to the Iraqis only to have the Shiite militias torture them. Thanks for telling me. Take them to clinic for their check-up; the doctor's in the service, but it'll be over by the time they're ready. You must need a shower and a nap. Take the rest of the day off."

"Yes sir. Thank you, sir." Corporal Myers saluted sharply and walked away.

Several minutes later, Army Reserve Captain Robert Sensenberg, MD, walked into the clinic thinking: *What now on Easter Sunday? Of course Easter Sunday, or any Sunday, doesn't mean anything to the Iraqis. Gives me something to do today. This sure is some way for a pediatrician to spend time called to active duty. At least I get to go out into the villages and treat children. Army Reserve is the price I pay for them paying my way through medical school.*

"Two new prisoners," the medical orderly said to Dr. Sensenberg as he walked in. "Two weirdoes; both almost begging to be put in prison here. One claims he's a doctor; he speaks English. The other says he's a hospital administrator; doesn't speak English. The CO wants you to find out anything you can about them."

The doctor, who was six feet two inches with light brown hair and blue eyes, gave a professional appearance at all times. He put on a white physician's smock over his uniform and walked to an examining room where a slightly built, frail-looking old man was sitting in boxer shorts.

He said: "I'm Dr. Sensenberg. You are Viktor Il-ar-i-o-nov?" stumbling over each syllable.

"Yes, Dr. Viktor Ilarionov," he answered in guttural-accented English, holding out his hand.

Dr. Sensenberg shook his hand and asked: "What kind of a doctor are you?" thinking: *Maybe I can trip him up.* "Open your mouth wide." *Ooooh, tobacco stained teeth; bad breath,* he thought. *But he hasn't had a chance to brush his teeth or do anything hygienic.*

"A cosmetic surgeon," Viktor replied.

"Oh, what kind of cosmetic work do you do?" Dr. Sensenberg asked. "Open your eyes wide, then turn your head so I can look at your ears."

Viktor moved his head to facilitate the examination saying: "The past few years, I mostly repaired facial damage of persons injured by bomb blasts and other war injuries. Most of my career, I made persons to take a different identity." *He's testing me,* he thought in Russian.

DISCOVERIES • CHAPTER 3

"Where'd you study and where'd you practice?" Dr. Sensenberg asked. "Sit up and take deep breaths."

He put the stethoscope to Viktor's chest and back while he answered: "The Medical School of Moscow University; top medical school in Russia. I worked mostly in Central Asian republics and stayed after we lost Afghanistan and the Soviet Union broke up."

Some loss of lung function, Dr. Sensenberg made a note on the chart thinking: *He smokes so makes sense.* He continued asking: "How'd you get here? What have you been doing recently?"

He listened to Viktor's heart who answered: "Al Qaeda forced me to work on a project. Do I have to talk about it now? Shouldn't I tell your commander first?"

Heart seems OK, Dr. Sensenberg thought and said: "Oh, OK. What're some of the most recent developments in your field?" *Maybe I can trip him up on that,* he said to himself then said: "Stand and cough when I put my hands on you. You know what to do in a hernia test."

Viktor coughed and said: "Recently there was an article in the *British Medical Society Journal,* or maybe the *New England Journal of Medicine,* about advances in repairing children's faces and bodies while bone structures are still growing and changing. All those articles think everyone has access to the latest microsurgery. There's not much written for us who work with old-fashioned scalpels."

What?! Does he know I'm a pediatrician? Dr. Sensenberg said to himself. *I recall that article myself. Maybe he's legit.* To Viktor: "OK, you know we have to test for penile infections and venereal diseases. Do you want to insert the swab yourself?"

"No, you can do it. I don't mind," Viktor replied as he thought in Russian: *No more questions to test me, I hope. Wonder if I've convinced him?*

Afterwards, Dr. Sensenberg said: "Get dressed. Maybe we can talk more about your medical experience later."

Several minutes later, he went to Colonel Jones's office, who said: "Come in, Bob, and sit down."

"Thanks Bert," Dr. Sensenberg said then continued: "The Russian doctor seems legitimate. Says he's a cosmetic surgeon, something I haven't seen since medical school. May be putting something over on me, but don't think so. Wouldn't say much about what he's been doing before; says he wants to talk to you. How'd he get here?"

"Turned himself in crossing the border from Syria," Colonel Jones replied and explained details he had been told. "What about the other guy?"

"Big bluff," Dr. Sensenberg answered. "Knows a little about a hospital, but not like any real hospital administrator. Maybe like one of those county hospital administrators back home: a politician's cousin is appointed to collect a pay check and stay out of the way while an assistant administrator is hired who knows how to run a hospital. All answers were through an interpreter. He was scared of the interpreter, asking him where he's from, and trying to find out if he's Sunni, Shia, or Kurd. For sure he's not Kurdish; didn't understand a word, only Arabic."

"Are they healthy?" Colonel Jones asked.

"Enough we can keep them around other prisoners," Dr. Sensenberg replied. "We can't test for everything and won't know until we get lab test results."

"Let's go. This's Easter Sunday," Colonel Jones said. I'm sure we'll be in touch on this issue later."

Chapter 4

Sunday, April 16, 2006
San Juan de Sabinas, Coahuila, Mexico

Luie and Ali sat talking, Luie in jeans and t-shirt, Ali in a blanket; Ali asked: "Do you always do it that way?"

"What way?" Luie asked.

"Hitting, slapping, hurting, screaming," Ali said.

"No, not always," Luie said. "It's role play; makes sex more exciting. You never heard of S&M?"

"S&M?" Ali asked.

"Sadism and masochism," Luie explained. "Sexual pleasure from getting and giving pain. Straights do it too."

"Oh," Ali said surprised.

They heard a vehicle and soon Paco walked up, hands full of bags, and asked: "What're you two up to? I stopped by Paloma's place. Of course, she wanted me to stay for Easter lunch, but I said I had to get back. She gave me all this food, some of her special *tortitas de camarones*."

"We're talking about what it's like being gay," Luie commented. "How's Palomita? She's a dear soul."

"Chubby and sweet as ever," Paco answered.

"Now that you're back," Luie said, "the doc needs to get dressed or at least put on underwear."

Paco said, "help me and we'll get his clothes."

Out of Ali's earshot, Paco said: "I found an internet café and looked up phone numbers, fax numbers, and email addresses for the *secretarías* in Mexico City to notify them."

Luie asked: "Notify 'em of what?"

"Oh, guess I didn't tell you," Paco said, "Frank and I decided we should contact places that handle foreign affairs, police, and defense just before we leave Mexico and say Arab terrorists're loose in Coahuila. I have an idea what we can do with Doc so we don't leave him with the others."

Luie grumbled: "What's that? Another thing you and Frank decided?"

"No, I got the idea on the phone with some relatives," Paco replied. "A little out of our way, but we can leave him with Uncle Gonzo in Monclova. Call and ask tomorrow."

"Uncle Gonzo? Who's uncle Gonzo?" Luie asked.

"MY Uncle Gonzo, not yours. Mami's brother, Gonzalo Guzmán" Paco explained. "When we were young, us kids called him GG, you know like 'hey hey' in Spanish, like we were laughing at him. He's old now, lives alone. Never married. Owns a small store in Monclova."

"Oh, yeah, think I remember some of your mami's family," Luie said. "Is he gay?"

"Yeah, pretty sure," Paco replied. "Never tried anything with me when I was young; too decent and nice, but pretty sure he'd've liked to when I got older. Don't think I'd've minded, but you and I were doing it regular by then. Besides we came down here only every couple of years and when we did, always big crowds of people."

"You think he'd do something with Doc?" Luie asked.

Paco answered: "Pretty sure he wouldn't do anything Doc wouldn't want. Keep him a day and put him on a bus to Saltillo. All likely end up in Saltillo in the state prison."

When they returned to the campsite, Ali had laid out the food and said: "Hope it's OK to get the food ready."

"Oh, sure, thanks, but you likely wouldn't be able to eat much of it," Paco said.

"Hope I can eat something," Ali said. "Why wouldn't I be able to eat it?"

DISCOVERIES • CHAPTER 4

"You're Muslim; there's ham, sausages, and pork things" Paco said. "You likely can't get it in Syria."

"First, I'm not Muslim," Ali replied, "and yes we get it where I'm from; about half the people are Christian. We had ham, sausages, and salami until last month when the government stopped importing Danish products because of those cartoons."

"What are you? Not Christian it seems," Luie asked.

"Alawite," Ali replied.

"What the hell's that?" Luie asked again.

"Group that broke away from the main body of Muslims over a thousand years ago," Ali said. "Followers of the true heir to the Prophet named Ali. That's why my name's Ali. Lots of Alawites have his name."

"Oh, like Shiites who run Iran and're trying to take over Iraq?" Luie continued to ask.

"No, different from Shiites except both come from Ali," he continued. "Don't ask me about religion; I'm not religious at all. You guys sure don't know much. You're like all westerners. You think you know so much about Arabs and the Middle East. You've been good to me and I don't want to offend, but thought you'd like me to be honest. You pretend to be Arabs. You've got to be a lot more careful about making assumptions and using stereotypes."

"Yes be honest," Paco said.

Luie grunted: "Yeah."

"Alawites aren't supposed to eat pork, but ones like me who aren't religious do," Ali said. "Sometimes I had a ham sandwich, but mostly I eat at the hospital and no pork there."

"Dig in," Luie said. "It's getting cold."

Several minutes later Paco, Luie, and Ali were basking in the warm sun, dressed, half asleep.

"I hear someone stirring," Paco commented, looking in the tent. "It's the muscular one."

"Oh, Boudi," Ali said.

"Boudi? I thought he's Abdullah," Luie said.

"Boudi's what we call someone whose name is Abdullah," Ali said. "The other guy's Brahim or sometimes a person named Ibrahim's called Bob."

Paco brought Boudi out, laying him on the ground while Luie removed tape from his mouth.

"Huh? Where are we?" he asked groggily. "Did you bring us to Yemen? Looks like it from pictures."

"Shut up," Paco commanded. "You talk only when you're spoken to. Understand?!"

He removed the diaper, tossed it towards Ali, and said: "Now sit down."

Paco scrubbed Boudi's upper body, face, and hair, demonstrating his nursing skill, and said to Luie: "unfasten the handcuffs and be ready to fasten them back quickly."

He washed Boudi's arm pits and back, and said: "We can put the handcuffs on from the front now. Time to remove the leg shackles. Watch out he doesn't kick you." He scrubbed his mid-section not dwelling on it like in the nursing home, then said: "Now turn him over."

With Luie sitting on his legs, Paco cleaned Boudi's rear end area thoroughly and rinsed it well, then said: "Put the restraints back on his legs. ... Now stand up and get dried. We need towels and blankets. Go get 'em, Doc."

When Ali returned, Paco grabbed towels and blankets brusquely, then said to Boudi: "You get covered in a blanket; no clothes until tomorrow."

"Brahim's awake," Ali said, and Paco brought him out.

"Hey, Bob!" Boudi greeted Brahim. "Looks like they brought us to Yemen."

"Shut up filthy disgrace of Arabs," Paco shouted. "You speak when given permission. Didn't you hear me?"

"Can't see a damn thing," Brahim said groggily, "Where're my glasses?"

DISCOVERIES • CHAPTER 4

Luie thought: *Oh, glasses. Put 'em somewhere in the four-by-four. Get 'em later; can't have him stumbling around getting lost after we dump him.* He said to Brahim: "What the hell do you need glasses for? So you can concoct terrorist plots to get Arabs in trouble again? You can just be blind for all we care."

The same procedure was repeated to wash Brahim and wrap him in a blanket. All sat in silence with Boudi and Brahim as far apart as possible but still in eyesight.

Soon Paco said: "Other guy's stirring. Let's get him."

Paco removed the diaper and tape, then Adnan exclaimed: "Where the hell did you bastards take me? We're back in the Middle East!"

"Shut the fuck up!" Paco shouted. "You don't talk until you're spoken to, you fuckin' terrorist scum of the Arabs."

"What're you doing just sitting there?" Adnan shouted in Arabic. "Let's take 'em out! four of us and two of them."

"I told you to shut up," Paco exclaimed as he forced a paper towel dirty from lunch into Adnan's mouth. "One more word out of you in Arabic, the tape goes back on. Where'd you put the duct tape?" asked Luie.

"I'll get it after we get him cleaned up," Luie said.

"Why's it called duck tape?" Ali asked.

"Who the hell said you can talk, you terrorist shit?!" Luie shouted at Ali. "One more word out of you and you get your mouth taped too. It's duct tape you stupid asshole of a doctor who thinks he knows it all. Now get rid of those shitty diapers, or get one of 'em crammed in your mouth."

Ali winced, shocked, almost crying, then suddenly realized: *Yeah, they said they'd pretend to treat me bad.* He gathered dirty diapers and put them in the fire.

"Should I cuff his hands to something while you wash him? He's a violent one," Luie asked.

"Take it slow, step by step, and see," Paco replied. "One funny move, wrap the cuffs around his neck."

Adnan thrashed around, but didn't cause trouble. Luie spread his legs as far apart as he could, sat on them, and removed the restraints.

"If he pulls and stretches your dick, will it get longer and thinner like vermicelli?" Paco taunted. To Luie: "We've got to turn him over. It may take both of us."

Luie said: "Let's get these things back on his legs. OK, Dr. Frankestein, clean up the trash and come with me."

When out of earshot of the others, Luie said: "Sorry about that but you know what we're doing."

Ali nodded 'yes'.

"It's duct tape, d-u-c-t," Luie explained. "Made to seal air ducts. That's why it's a grey metal color. It has many other uses, as you see. But damn it, you've got to be careful. Not a word! Understand?"

Ali mumbled "yes" sheepishly.

When Luie and Ali returned, Paco put the tape over Adnan's mouth, leaving the paper towel inside, as Adnan tried to resist as much as he could.

Paco said to Brahim and Boudi: "You haven't eaten in a couple of days; your digestive system needs to adjust. We'll give you soft food and not very much. He parceled out the remainder of Paloma's *tortitas de camarones*.

Chapter 5

Monday, April 17, 2006
Baghdad International Airport, Iraq

In midafternoon, U. S. Army Major Joshua Armstrong of the Defense Intelligence Agency saluted Colonel Jones in his office. In his early 30s, standing five feet ten inches tall, he had military bearing with neatly trimmed very slightly wavy medium brown hair. The colonel returned the salute, stood, and shook hands.

Major Armstrong thought: *He seems pleasant and hopefully easy to work with.* He said: "Good afternoon, sir. Maybe you know we brief prison commanders on our interrogations as courtesies; we haven't had a reason to meet you yet, but today as you know there are two new prisoners with whom we had preliminary interrogations."

Colonel Jones replied: "Please have a seat. Thank you for the courtesy. What do you have?"

Major Armstrong began: "The Russian doctor's telling a bizarre tale. It must be generally true; no one could concoct something like that. He says he was forced by al Qaeda to go to Syria to make a double of someone in a western country. If he didn't cooperate, he and the double would've been killed or tortured, or both. If he did a poor job, the double'd suffer. He has no idea who was being duplicated or where he is. Something went wrong. He didn't say what, but he had to flee or be eliminated.

"He says the other person we have is Iraqi and in charge of the project, had some kind of a hospital background, and is stupid as well as being a strict Muslim. Someone from the Syrian Moukhabarat was actually running things. He has no idea where the Syrian is and was shocked to see Abdulrahman, the Iraqi, here. We don't think he's telling the full truth, but we didn't press more today."

"Our local doctor talked to him quite a bit and is convinced he's a real doctor who knows his stuff, but can't evaluate his cosmetic surgery skills," Colonel Jones said.

"The one the doctor says is stupid isn't completely stupid," Major Armstrong continued. "He refuses to talk to interpreters; keeps asking their names, family background, where they're from, and then refuses to talk like he's really afraid. Interpreters think it's because they're Shia. They think he's really trying to figure out if they're associated with the radical imam Muqtada al-Sadr."

"Our doctor said essentially the same thing," Colonel Jones added. "He thinks he's a political hack who actually did work in a hospital, but as a figurehead."

"He's likely a Ba'athist who fled after Saddam Hussein was toppled and joined al Qaeda," Major Armstrong continued. "We have our ways to get cooperation."

"Wait a minute," Colonel Jones said. "We need to avoid that. You know what happened when a reserve unit was in charge of Abou Ghraib and certain interrogation techniques were used. The unit in charge of the prison was blamed and I will not allow that here.

"We might possibly have a solution for you. We have a young guy here who speaks a little Arabic; learned it from his grandmother. Not enough for us to use him as a translator or interpreter and he doesn't like the idea either. He might find out enough to give some idea. You want to try?"

"Why not?" Major Armstrong replied, "doesn't hurt."

"Make sure he knows it's strictly voluntary and nothing'll happen if he can't talk to him," Colonel Jones said. "It's bad enough he was taken out of master's studies at the University of Nebraska when we were called to active duty. Morale can be a problem. I'll get him to report to you."

DISCOVERIES • CHAPTER 5

Soon, Army Reserve First Lieutenant Anthony Gorani saluted Major Armstrong in an interrogation room, saying: "The commander said to see you."

He was in his early 20s, stood five feet nine inches, had brown eyes, very dark brown slightly wavy hair that was well trimmed, and was clean shaven. He wore stylish rimless glasses. His summer uniform was clean and well pressed.

"Hello, at ease," Major Armstrong said as he held out his hand. "Please sit down. Colonel Jones said you speak a little Arabic you learned from your grandparents and might help us. He says you don't know enough to be an interpreter and we don't want you to be an interpreter, but even if you understand a little, it might help. If it doesn't work, don't worry about it."

"Actually it was my grandmother, Dad's mother," Lieutenant Gorani said. "Granddad spoke English and Mom's parents were too far away to talk to them regularly."

"Oh, are you Lebanese?" Major Armstrong asked.

"No, Egyptian," Lieutenant Gorani replied. "Granddad and Grandmother were Egyptian Christians who fled in the early '50's when Christians were being harassed. Granddad was an experienced agriculture engineer, educated in the US, so it was easy for him to get a job here."

"Ah, I hadn't thought about Egyptian," Major Armstrong commented.

"It's interesting you think I might be Lebanese," Lieutenant Gorani continued. "Most think I'm Italian. My last name Gorani sounds Italian and everyone calls me Tony. Mom named me for St. Anthony. Grandmother wanted to name me Antoine because the French were good to Egyptian Christians, but Mom held her ground saying I needed an American name."

"If you're Christian, then you've been celebrating Easter," Major Armstrong said.

"We're Coptic and similar to Orthodox. Easter's next week. Most Iraqi Christians are Orthodox, but I don't think I'll go to a church here. Mom, Dad, and the rest of the family will be at church then; I'll just be there in spirit."

Major Armstrong said: "Here's the situation. There's an Iraqi guy, or we think he's Iraqi, who was caught trying to slip in from Syria. When we said we'd send him to the ISF prison at Abou Ghraib, he became panic-stricken and says he has something to tell Americans. When we used interpreters, he always asks the interpreter's name, home town, and other personal things, and then refuses to talk more. We're getting the idea he's refusing to talk to Shiites out of fear. We'd like to find out who he will talk to. You don't need to find out his story, just how we can get it."

"I could try," Lieutenant Gorani said, "I don't speak Arabic well; I always understood better than I could speak."

"Do the best you can," Major Armstrong said. "It won't be held against you if you can't. I'll send for him now. You two can have those arm chairs there and I'll sit in the background. I can sit behind a screen if that helps."

While Lieutenant Gorani and the prisoner talked, Major Armstrong observed body language and heard tones of voices. It was obviously a tedious conversation.

Finally, Lieutenant Gorani stood, saying something sounding like 'shu-krawn', then said: "I have an idea now."

Major Armstrong said: "Please tell him he'll be taken back to his cell until we need to talk to him again."

Lieutenant Gorani spoke a few words in Arabic, then Abdulrahman left with a guard.

Lieutenant Gorani began: "He won't talk to a Shiite under any circumstances; he'd rather have Americans torture him and be locked up forever than have things he says taken to Shiite militias. He says they would track him and his family down eventually, torture them, and likely kill them. He'll talk with someone he can trust, like Sunnis or possibly one of the small minority sects like Christians or Turkmen."

"Thanks a lot, Lieutenant," Major Armstrong said enthusiastically. "You've been a big help. I'll put in a good word to the commander for you."

"Thank you, sir," Lieutenant Gorani said as he stood.

Shortly, Major Armstrong entered Colonel Jones's office without sitting and said: "Your Lieutenant Gorani's really a good man and he's probably saved us a lot of effort and hassle. We need to find interpreters who

DISCOVERIES • CHAPTER 5

aren't Shia and who can convince the prisoner he won't fall into the hands of Shiite militias. One of us will be back in a couple of days. Thanks for your cooperation."

"Yes, he's a good young officer," Colonel Jones concurred. "He'll go far in the Reserve if he wants to. We'll expect to hear from you soon, then."

Colonel Jones held out his hand to shake with a friendly professional smile typical of a funeral director.

Chapter 6

Monday, April 17, 2006
Wright-Patterson Air Force Base, Ohio, USA

Patrick was drinking coffee, reading a newspaper as usual, when Felicia came into the office wearing one of her usual stylish business-like dresses.

He said cheerfully: "Good morning, Sugarlump. Thanks again for yesterday."

She replied: "You're the one to thank. You bought lunch and took the kids to a movie."

"My pleasure," Patrick replied. "Did they like it? It might've been too mature, especially for Timmy."

"Oh, Timmy was pleased to be out with you," Felicia said. "It's really hard on him not having a daddy."

"How are you?" Patrick asked. "You still don't look like your old self."

"I'm OK I guess," Felicia answered sighing. "I get depressed at times like this not having Kevin around." She thought: *I was set to kill myself and felt good about it then he shows up. Of course I'm glad he's alive and can't blame him, but ups and down of feelings're more than I want to deal with.*

Frank came in looking more alert than usual and said: "Good morning," poured coffee, and sat.

Patrick folded the newspaper and said: "Hey, Frank. Felicia tells me you had to take me home Friday."

Frank replied: "Don't you remember?"

DISCOVERIES • CHAPTER 6

"No, don't remember a thing," Patrick said.

Frank thought; *No lies, but something he'll believe*, then said: "You were faint and pale. You needed to be home in bed for sure and didn't put up resistance."

"Did you come inside?" Patrick asked.

Frank replied: "Yes; I thought I'd see you made it to bed OK and I had to pee."

"Maybe that's why the towels in the utility room bath weren't where I usually leave them," Patrick said. "I didn't think I'd been in there and Elsie's been gone a few days."

"Oh, sorry if I messed up the towels," Frank said. "Yes, I was in that bathroom. Just before I left, I saw you in bed and said 'sweet dreams' or something. You didn't respond so I just went on."

"Oh, the towels weren't messed up, just not where I keep them," Patrick said. "This's weird. I don't remember a thing. Thanks, even if I don't remember."

"Think nothing of it; pleased to help," Frank said.

Felicia thought: *OK. Frank dealt with that. Why's it so important to Frank that Patrick believes he was here? He's in on this some way, but what? Did he do something with that other guy? I can't deal with this.*

Several minutes went by and Frank said: "Hey Patrick, you remember you said you'd help me analyze data for my project? Any idea when?"

"Yeah, sure, whenever you want," Patrick replied. "We can just dump the data into the SAS program on my computer, or, if you like, we can install it on your computer and I can show you how to use it. Piece of cake."

"Thanks," Frank replied. "Let me see if I can pull it together. Maybe this afternoon. Say, are you going to the gym today? Want to go together and then grab lunch?"

Patrick, surprised a moment, replied: "Sure, yeah, I think I'll go. I'm still not feeling the best, but can have a light workout. Do me good."

Chapter 7

Monday, April 17, 2006
San Juan de Sabinas, Coahuila, Mexico

Paco and the four captives in restraints sat outside the tent. Paco was dressed, Ali in underwear, others in blankets.

God, we've got to get this over with; can't stand much more, Paco said to himself. *Sitting doing nothing. Packed everything that can be packed. Take the tent down? Nah, might need to put someone inside. Nothing to read. Can't talk. Sat staring at the stars last night until we went to sleep. Had to put them in corners with Luie and me right by the opening in case they tried something. Couldn't sleep. Would be good to talk to Doc just to have something to do, but can't let others see he's treated differently. Hope Uncle Gonzo'll take him, otherwise where'll we leave him? Oh, maybe that's Luie.*

Luie walked up carrying bundles and said to Paco: "I'll dump this and you can help bring more."

"I'll put stuff in the four-by-four, too," Paco said.

Out of earshot of the others, Luie continued: "Found a Caritas shop and got used clothes for them. They'll look like poor Mexicans. Got underwear and socks around the market. They were curious I was buying adult shoes based on drawings, but smiled and ignored them. Oh, got your Uncle Gonzo on the phone. He was surprised, but said he remembered me. Said you're going to visit him. He'll be in his shop all day and gave me his phone number."

DISCOVERIES • CHAPTER 7

When they were back with the others, Paco took charge: "OK, we take cuffs and leg restraints off one at a time to dress you. Any funny stuff, you know what happens."

"This flowered shirt with pink in it's perfect for Spaghetti. Dress him first," Luie said.

Adnan started thrashing his arms trying to hit Paco and Luie as they put the shirt on.

"You terrorist asshole," Paco said as he slapped him hard across the face. "At least we got you clothes so you don't get sunburned."

"You want vermicelli after all," Luie exclaimed.

Adnan screamed as his hands were cuffed behind him.

"Your shirt gets buttoned wrong so locals can see what a stupid Arab you are," Paco laughed.

Adnan tried to kick both of them when the leg restraints were removed.

"You damned son of a bitch, you asked for it now," Luie shouted as he kicked Adnan's knees from behind forcing him to buckle over and fall on his buttocks.

"Legs in the air," Luie commanded as Paco had one foot on Adnan's stomach putting as much weight as he dared.

After struggling to get the underwear and pants on, Luie commanded: "Sit up and stick your right foot out. Got to dress you like a baby."

When shoes and socks were on and leg restraints reapplied, Paco shouted: "Stand up!" yanking him by an arm.

Luie inserted a belt, tightening it as much as possible as Adnan gasped for breath.

Having watched Adnan's treatment, Boudi and Brahim allowed themselves to be dressed with no resistance.

"Button your own damned shirts," Paco said. To Ali: "OK quack of a doc, your turn."

"Can I **please** dress myself?" Ali pleaded.

"What the hell," Paco replied, "guess you're not going to blow us up here and now. Still we unfasten hands and feet separately; any funny stuff, you know what happens."

Ali dressed himself while Paco dismantled the tent.

As Paco and Luie carried the tent and other things to the four-by-four, out of ear shot, Paco told Luie his plans about where to leave Brahim, Boudi, and Adnan.

"You've thought it all out as usual," Luie said. "What about Doc? What if your Uncle Gonzo doesn't take him?"

Paco answered: "If he doesn't, we dump him on the streets of Monclova. Did you put money in their pockets?

"Yep, one 20-peso bill each," Luie said, "and I got 'em a bottle of water."

Back at the empty campsite, Paco continued: "OK, idiot terrorist brains, here's what happens: You get blindfolded. We dump you one by one; you're on your own from there. If you're as smart as you thought you were when you tried to terrorize the world, you can figure out how to save your asses. Otherwise, you can die a worse death than the innocent persons you bombed in Madrid and London. If you have any stupid ass notions that you're going to get back into the United States, ever, just remember what's happening with Moussaoui who's on his way to get executed."

Let them discover for themselves that they have money in their pockets, he thought.

Chapter 8

Monday, April 17, 2006
Monclova, Coahuila, Mexico

In late afternoon, Luie drove while Paco said to Ali: "Doc. We're leaving you with someone we think'll keep you and put you on a bus to Saltillo. Learn that. Saul-**tee**-yoh."

"Yes, Saltillo," Ali said. "What'll I do there?"

"Turn yourself in to police," Paco replied. "Mexican police may not treat you nice, but won't hurt you. Things go like we expect, you'll hook up with your buddies, but you'll be in custody so they probably won't gang up on you." To Luie: "Right at the next signal 'til you see the big church."

Back to Ali: "No names. You don't know who he is; he doesn't know who you are. You don't know our names. Don't ask and he'll be instructed not to tell. We're keeping you safe; now you have to keep him and us safe. You say absolutely nothing to him about where you're from, what you're doing here, or anything else. Understand?! If he doesn't know, he can't tell if by chance someone finds out you were here. He doesn't speak English anyway and you don't speak Spanish. Maybe you'll find out the name of this town, maybe not. If you have to tell how you got to Saltillo, you came on a bus from Torreón. Learn that one too. Toe-ree-**own.** Got it?"

"Yes, Torreón," Ali repeated.

"Left in front of the church to the next main street, then right," Paco said to Luie, then to Ali: "We could've dumped you on the road like the others. We don't want to see you killed or hurt. Don't EVER try to find us again. Understand?!"

"Er…yes, sure," Ali stammered.

"On the left; you'll see his store," Paco said.

Luie parked across the street from a shop in a slightly shabby lower-middle class neighborhood; Paco said: "Stay here until I motion you to come in."

In the small general-purpose store, Uncle Gonzo gave him a big hug saying in Spanish: "Paquito! How are you? It's been so long since I've seen you."

Uncle Gonzo was short and stocky in his 60s, about five feet six, and had thin graying hair and brown eyes.

"Yes, I'm sorry," Paco replied in Spanish. "I promise I'll come more often to see my favorite Uncle Gonzo."

He replied in Spanish: "Let's have a *café* or *coca*."

"Not just yet," Paco said in Spanish. "There're some people outside. We need a big favor of you, Uncle Gonzo."

"Oh, what's that?" he asked in Spanish.

"A young man's with us," Paco explained in Spanish. "He's a nice man, but got mixed up with the wrong crowd. He needs to stay tonight and you put him on a bus to Saltillo."

"What? Who is he? Where's he from? What'd he do?" he continued asking in Spanish, perplexed.

"We're not going to tell you for your own protection," Paco continued in Spanish. "If you don't know anything you can't be forced to tell. I promise on my honor, your favorite nephew Paquito, he's not a bad man, he won't do anything bad; he won't hurt you. Doesn't speak Spanish."

"Where'll he sleep?" he asked in Spanish. "I only have one bed in the back room."

"I don't think that will be a problem," Paco said in Spanish with a small grin and wink. "He's from another country and hasn't been out in the world much. You wouldn't do anything he doesn't want to do except he must get on the bus to Saltillo."

DISCOVERIES • CHAPTER 8

"What if someone sees him here?" Uncle Gonzo protested in Spanish. "Business is bad enough. People go to the big *supermercados*. I can't lose any more business."

"Don't worry," Paco said convincingly in Spanish. "Just keep him in the back room. Get him a book to read in English. Here's money to pay for his food and pay for his bus ticket, and here's $100 for you when you go to Eagle Pass shopping the next time."

Paco gave him double the amount of pesos he would need along with five $20 bills and continued in Spanish: "I'll get him. Luisito's here too. OK?"

"I guess so," he said hesitatingly in Spanish.

"Remember, **no names**, not even Luisito when you see him," Paco said in Spanish as he waved from the door.

When Luie and Ali came in, Uncle Gonzo gave Luie a big hug, remembering just in time not to say his name saying in Spanish: "Oh, how are you. I haven't seen you since you were a little boy, about ten I guess."

"Nice to see you again," Luie replied in Spanish returning the hug warmly. "Wow, about 25 years ago."

"This man will stay with you," Paco said in Spanish.

"You'll stay with him," he said to Ali in English.

Ali said: "Hello" awkwardly.

"Oh, what a nice young man," Uncle Gonzo exclaimed in Spanish offering his hand to shake. "Come let's sit down. *Café, cerveza, tequila, whisky, coca,* something else?"

"He's offering us something to drink," Paco said in English. "What'd you like?"

"Coffee and some water," Luie said in Spanish.

"Also for me," Paco said in Spanish.

"you're having coffee," Ali said. "I'll have the same."

"*Lo mismo para él,*" Paco translated for Uncle Gonzo.

"He likes you and you can stay," Paco said. "He's a nice man and won't make you do anything you don't want, except you must get on that bus. You're free now. You could walk away, but you'd soon end up in the hands of the local police and be cold and hungry. We'll stay long enough to be polite."

Conversation over coffee was strained, then Paco said in Spanish: "Thank you so much. It's been great to see you. Wish we could stay longer, but we need to go home. I promise I'll come again, just for you, the next time we're here. Before we go, we have something you might be able to sell in the shop." To Luie and Ali in English: "Get the diapers and unopened food."

Paco and Uncle Gonzo chatted a few minutes in Spanish about cousins, aunts, uncles, nieces, and the like until the others came in, giving bags to Uncle Gonzo.

"What's this?" he asked in Spanish.

"Diapers for adults," Paco said in Spanish.

"Diapers? For adults? What adult'd want diapers?" he asked in Spanish.

"Someone who's old and sick and can't hold it very well anymore," Paco replied in Spanish. "Remember Graciela before she died?"

"Oh, yes, I remember her very well, bless her soul," Uncle Gonzo said in Spanish as he made the sign of the cross. "It would've been nice if she had something like that. But who'd buy them in my little store?"

"Put them out and see," Paco said in Spanish. "If they don't sell, donate them to the nursing home."

Paco then gave Uncle Gonzo a very strong warm hug and took a few steps away.

Luie also gave him a hug saying: "*Muchas gracias.*"

Paco and Luie looked at Ali as Paco said to himself: *We have to hug him Mexican style or it won't look right.*

He gave Ali a hug saying: "Take care of yourself."

Luie said: "*Adios,*" and gave Ali a hug and a slight pat on the buttocks out of sight of the others.

They left without looking back to see Ali's sad and bewildered look.

Soon Luie was driving northward saying: "If no traffic, we cross the border tonight. Sooner I get home the better; now all I want is a proper bed. Did we dispose of everything that might cause a problem at the border? Needles and syringes?"

"Find a trash can somewhere along the road," Paco replied. "Also need to send the fax and email and make a phone call. If we sent 'em from Monclova, could bring someone here and find Uncle Gonzo."

Paco was trying to write on a pad of paper he had taken from Uncle Gonzo's store, but without much luck because of bumpy streets, stopping and going.

"We can stop in Sabinas or Nueva Rosita and find an internet café," he said. "Most of them have fax too."

"What're you going to say?" Luie asked.

"That's what I'm trying to compose now. Something like …," he spoke Spanish.

"Guess that's good enough." Luie said. "God, let's just get this over with. I've had enough adventure for a while."

Chapter 9

Tuesday, April 18, 2006
Eagle Pass, Texas, USA

Luie stirred in bed in the Hillcrest Motel, saying to himself: *I should get up. Is Paco asleep? Dead to the world. Finally got to bed about 11. More hassle at the border. Found this motel; at least it's clean. Let me see if there's a place for breakfast. Hey! There's a sign that says* Panadería *right over there.*

In the bakery, he said to himself: *They have* conchas. *Wonder if they're as good as ours.* To a woman who took his order: "*Dos de éstos y un café.*" To himself: *Likely speak Spanish more than English here on the border,* but held up two fingers and pointed, just in case.

In a booth, he examined the pastry carefully, taking a bite, and said to himself: *Good. Not as good as ours, but very good. A bit heavier. Maybe talk to the baker on the way out. Grab* bolillos *for sandwiches later.*

Several minutes later after a conversation with the baker, he returned to the motel room saying to himself: *Paco's still sound asleep. I can catch a shower.*

Moments later, under the shower spray, Luie felt cooler air and the shower curtain moving as Paco stepped into the tub behind him, slapping his buttocks hard. Soon they finished, dried, and dressed.

Paco said: "Time to call Frank," then said into the phone: "Hey, love, we're in Texas."

pause

"Oh, sorry if we disturbed you," Paco said.

pause

"OK, later," Paco said as he disconnected.

"Gee, Frank was short, like he's really pissed off," Paco said. "He did say he's in his office and would call later. I'll go look for breakfast. You coming along?"

"No, go ahead," Luie said. "I've already eaten at that bakery across the street. I'll put things in the four-by-four."

A few minutes later in the bakery, Paco ordered *conchas* and coffee and sat when his phone rang.

"Hey, love," he almost shouted with delight.

pause

"Yeah, that's what I thought," he said, "but damn you were cold like you were in Iceland. Hang on just a second. I'll go to a table outside where I can talk."

pause

"We're in Eagle Pass," he continued, "Crossed the border last night and nearly died in bed from exhaustion."

pause

"Everything fine, considering," he said and briefly described events.

pause

"Huh???? He wants us all to go to Florida this coming weekend?" Paco asked.

pause

"Yeah, he needs to get it out of his garage, but why Florida and why all of us?" Paco continued to ask.

pause

"Yeah, it'd be fun at a bar there, 'specially if it's like the Serpent," Paco said. "Change of scene's always nice. Don't know. Don't remember my work schedule.

pause

"We'll let you know when we get home," Paco said. "Probably tomorrow. Luie really wants to get back."

pause

"Love ya doll," he said and disconnected.

He returned to the motel to find Luie had everything ready to go. He was about to climb into the passenger seat, but Luie gave him the keys.

"You're driving!" he said. "Had enough of that steering wheel. Going to get a newspaper and maybe a book in San Antonio and just relax on the way home."

Paco filled Luie in on the conversation with Frank as they drove away.

"What? Drive all the way to Florida this coming weekend?" Luie exclaimed. "No fuckin' way! It'll take my ass months to recover from this trip."

Chapter 10

Tuesday, April 18, 2006
Beavercreek, Ohio, USA

Shortly after work, Frank carried shopping bags into his house, thinking: *Fred sure is keen on going to Florida this weekend. I just got back from a long drive. Can imagine how Paco and Luie feel. Might be a good to visit the folks. Go now; won't be pressure to go in summer when so damned hot and oppressive. Maybe take Paco and introduce him. No, would raise too many questions. They wouldn't treat him very well; he'd be uncomfortable too.*

The doorbell rang. Frank and Fred exchanged deep wet kisses and rubbed each other's bodies. Fred was wearing a dark blue t-shirt with a suggestive Polish sausage on it and writing about a local Polish festival.

"Hey, guy, it's been ages since you were up here alone," Frank said. "Good to have you. What'd you like to drink? Got beer and wine and you know what liquor I have. Thought we might go to a new Italian place in that old strip mall where the pizza joint was. Haven't been there yet. If we have wine there, we can start with a glass now."

"Sounds good," Fred replied. "Don't mix our poison."

Frank served wine and tossed a bag to Fred saying: "Here Mr. t-shirt man."

Fred took out a navy blue t-shirt with an angry longhorn bull with nostrils flared and red letters outlined in white that read: 'DON'T MESS WITH TEXAS'.

"Hey, thanks, man," Fred said and gave Frank a kiss.

"My pleasure," Frank said. "Got it in the airport shop where I left the guy's wallet."

Fred asked: "What'd you hear from Paco? All I got was a text that they're in the U.S."

"Talked to him this morning," Frank replied. "Went well; said Doc's gay." He recounted what Paco had told him then said: "Hey, what's this about going to Florida? He wasn't enthusiastic and said for sure Luie wouldn't go."

"Car's been in my garage four days now," Fred began. "Sooner or later it's going to be reported stolen. If it's found around here, could draw attention to this area. So far hasn't been reported, but can't press our luck."

"Yeah, but why Florida?" Frank asked.

"Long ways from here," Fred said. "Long ways from the other car in Texas. Lots of crime in South Florida and lots of cars with New York plates. I looked on the internet and found what looks like a good leather resort and a bar in Ft. Lauderdale, The Ramrod. Thought it might be fun."

"Yeah," Frank said, "a foursome road trip could be great. But now? Let's see what Paco and Luie say and I'm not all that keen after my drive to Texas."

"OK, but what're our alternatives?" Fred persisted.

"Weren't they running cigarettes from North Carolina?" Frank asked. "That's closer then Florida."

"Might be a possibility," Fred continued, "but it might stick out with New York plates. If worse comes to worse, we could take it there."

"We took the Toyota to Texas to hide it among cars with Texas plates; why not take it to New York?"

"We could do that too," Fred replied "but far from Lackawanna like out on Long Island. That's a long drive; might as well take it to Florida and have some fun."

"I could visit my folks," Frank said, "but don't know about driving a car that could be reported stolen."

"I can check stolen car reports regularly and call you the moment it's reported, if it is," Fred continued. "You can abandon it and get a rental car."

DISCOVERIES • CHAPTER 10

"Maybe tell the folks I got a hop to Homestead," Frank said. "Then leave the car in Fort Lauderdale, take a commercial flight to Daytona Beach, and then here. I'll tell the office I may be on leave next week."

"Don't forget we have those cell phones," Fred added. "I was going to mail them to Homeland Security from around Atlanta just to put them off track with a note to taunt them about terrorists slipping through their fingers."

"Oh, I didn't tell you Patrick was back in the office yesterday as though nothing had happened," Frank said. "Felicia and I convinced him he was there Friday. He's a nice guy and trusting. Maybe too trusting for his own good.

"Let's go eat," Fred said. "I had an early lunch."

After dinner, Frank got out brandy snifters and said: "You know I have to get up early to go to work tomorrow. I didn't say anything in the office about coming in late."

"That's what I thought," Fred said. "Doesn't hurt me to get up early and get moving. I have lots of things to do at home before going on my shift."

"Well maybe we need to go to bed early, then; drink up," Frank said with a smile.

Chapter 11

Sunday, April 23, 2006
Baghdad International Airport, Iraq

Major Armstrong arrived at Colonel Jones's office after worship services saying: "Sorry to bother you on Sunday. We have to work on Iraqi time. We found a Sunni and a Christian interpreter we used yesterday. The Christian didn't want to work today, the Orthodox Easter.

"The prisoner's Iraqi like we were almost certain and Sunni; Ba'athist who fled. Apparently the Sunni interpreter's background was safe enough and he didn't have any problem with the Christian interpreter. They reminded me later that Christians came to terms with Saddam Hussein; his chief deputy was a Christian."

"Yes, Tarek Asiz," Colonel Jones added.

"His story's very similar to the Russian's," Major Armstrong continued. "It must be true; they couldn't make up the same bizarre tale when they don't speak same language. They don't coincide exactly and details are incomplete. Both said something went wrong and they fled in fear of reprisal from the Moukhabarat. They wouldn't say what, but the Iraqi blames it on the Russian doctor. The doctor said they'd blame him no matter what. They both talk about a Syrian assistant director who was Moukhabarat. We don't have good sources in Syria to follow through and it may not be that important."

"What'll we do with him now?" Colonel Jones asked. "Send him to the Iraqis at Abou Ghraib?"

DISCOVERIES • CHAPTER 11

"No, I don't think so," Major Armstrong replied. "He's terrified at the idea of going there; he'd rather stay here and be tortured by us or locked up forever, he says. He might even commit suicide if we send him there, and the Iraqis might let him if they don't kill him first. There's still some useful information we might get out of him."

"How're you going to get information out of him here?" Colonel Jones asked. "I hope you're not going to use techniques that were used at Abou Ghraib."

"Oh, no," Major Armstrong answered. To tell the truth, we don't have a lot of leverage over him. He has a wife and son who he took to Syria with him. He doesn't seem to care about his wife, but he's concerned about his son. Typical of Middle Eastern arranged marriages. He knows it's not safe to have his son back here, but he's worried his wife doesn't have money for food for the kid. We told him as a reward for cooperating today we'd try to get money to his wife.

"We can't do too much in Syria these days. We might get the wife and son to Lebanon. The tricky part's getting them out of Syria, not into Lebanon. We can work on these things and maybe use it to get him to talk more.

"That leaves the Russian doctor. We have no leverage over him. No family, nothing we could threaten him with other than turning him over to the Russians. He's not hostile, but cautious."

"We might have something you can use," Colonel Jones offered. "He's been bugging our doctor to let him come to the clinic and hang out, maybe work with him. Claims he's bored out of his mind and making up ailments just to be able to talk to our doctor. He's also begging for medical journals. He seems to read them like you and I might read *Time*, *Economist*, or *Forbes*. He must be a real workaholic. He's offered to let himself be restrained or kept under guard just to be able to be around medical stuff.

"Our doctor wouldn't mind having him there if it can be done within protocol. He'd like someone to talk to also. There's not a whole lot of work except when someone really gets sick or we get new people. He goes out in the villages to treat children, but that doesn't occupy all his spare time. I'd probably agree to let the Russian stay in the clinic because we have a guard there. Maybe let him spend time in the clinic in exchange for more information."

"That might work; wouldn't hurt to try anyway," Major Armstrong said. "I might have some medical journals sent from Washington or maybe Germany, and parcel them out as rewards. Could I go talk to him now?"

"Yes, sure," Colonel Jones replied.

Major Armstrong walked to the interrogation area thinking: *This commander and his operation are the best we've had in the reserve units they rotate through here. He does his job well, is helpful and offers good suggestions, but knows his place. Others are worse than incompetent, like the Abou Ghraib group that was a disgrace to their uniform and country. Or else they think they're in charge and try to order us around. We need to put in a good word in Washington; let the Nebraska senators and congressmen know what a good job their reservists are doing.*

Several minutes later, Major Armstrong stopped by Colonel Jones's quarters again saying: "That was a brilliant idea; the Russian doctor accepted it. We even went to the clinic area right away. When he could see we're true to our word, he told us more. He confirmed what we suspected, the double was sent to the U.S. He still wouldn't or couldn't tell us where in the U.S., who was being duplicated, and who the double is. Maybe we can go back and forth between the two of them to piece together information."

"Glad to be of help," Colonel Jones said. "Let us know if we can do something else.

Chapter 12

Sunday, April 23, 2006
Ft. Lauderdale, Florida, USA

Paco and Frank tossed and turned in the bed they were sharing in the Inn Leather gay guest house, not having another choice of where to sleep. They had gone to bed in silence a few hours earlier following a big fight. Frank got out of bed when it was apparent both were awake.

INN LEATHER GUEST HOUSE, FORT LAUDERDALE, FLORIDA.

He said, still angry that Paco had ignored him at the Ramrod, but played with others: "Do you want to have a cup of coffee before we ditch the car and go to the airport?"

"Why'd I want to go have a cup of coffee with you?" Paco answered, still angry.

"You used to want to be with me," Frank said.

"That was when we were together a few hours at a time, not two fuckin' days and nights," Paco said tersely.

"Why does that make a difference?" Frank asked upset.

"You treat me like a fuckin' object!" Paco exclaimed. "Like some dumb Mexican who doesn't know shit."

"Oh, come now!" Frank replied angrily. "You know I'm not the slightest bit prejudiced against Mexicans. Had lots of Mexican-American troops, even some officers."

"That's the point," Paco exclaimed. "Someone you work with, not someone you care about. I busted my ass with Luie saving your ass taking those guys to Mexico. To you I was just some underling doing my job."

"Lighten up," Frank shouted angrily. "I said thanks and how much I appreciated it. What more do you want?"

"Yeah, with a pat on the back and an 'attaboy' just like one of your troops," Paco said tersely. "What do I want? Warmth and feeling like I'm part of your life."

"You sure don't complain about warmth when we're getting it on," Frank said bitterly.

"That's part of the whole damn thing," Paco said. "You're a machine, a robot with a switch that's on in the sex mode, like a robotic doll to be used and abused like you're automatically programmed. Then switched to the other mode programmed to take charge and show no feelings. It's this part I hadn't seen before. I may be a hot blooded Latino who expects too much, but man I can't handle the two extremes."

Frank immediately retorted: "I guess you can't understand what it's like to be in the military.…"

"Don't give me that shit," Paco interrupted, "I work with veterans all the time, or did you forget? Maybe you think they suddenly got mellow and sweet in their old years before they came to our nursing home. Some of 'em are senile, crotchety, not that nice to be around, but most are nice old men and a pleasure to be with and take care of. You don't need or want

DISCOVERIES • CHAPTER 12

anything except when you want to 'do it'. You wouldn't know what to do if someone showed you a bit of kindness and wanted to do something to care for you."

"Guess I hadn't thought about your working with veterans," Frank said a bit more softly.

Paco interrupted again: "That's another point in the whole damned situation. You don't know how to put yourself in someone else's position to know how they might feel and think. It's all you, your own fucking damned self. How do you think we managed to get along with Doc? We put ourselves in his position: he's desperate and'll do anything, even have himself cut on, just to get out of Syria and have a new life. On top of that, thinks he might be gay. We didn't make a conscious decision to put ourselves in his position; just did it. Doesn't mean we approve of what he did. Doesn't mean we like him that much. At least we could sense what was going on and make life easier for him and for us. We can do that with someone like Doc who's a stranger and a foreigner. You can't even do it for someone you care about."

"Hey, that's not fair," Frank said angrily. "You know I was taking care of Patrick, keeping him from getting hurt."

"Big fuckin' deal!" Paco exclaimed. "You were saving your ass and doing your duty to your country like you're programmed to do. Nothing wrong with that, but don't be so damned noble and show some feelings!"

"You ever read *The Great Santini*?" Frank asked.

"No, what's that?" Paco asked.

"That book's about me, or close to it," Frank answered. "Pat Conroy, the guy who wrote it, writes about a guy growing up in a Marine Corps family with a father who treats his kids like shit, only he's writing about himself and his own father. His mother was nicer than mine and he had brothers and sisters. Read that and maybe see why I don't go to see them any more than I have to, and didn't want to take you there. And while you're at it, read *Lords of Discipline*, also by Conroy. It's about being a cadet at the Citadel like I was. Terrified at anything that might make someone think I'm gay. Terrified about admitting to myself I am gay."

Paco said: "What's that got to do with me now?"

"Damn it!" Frank exclaimed. "You just excoriated me for not putting myself in someone else's position and telling me how great you are doing it. Go read the damn books and put yourself in my position and what I've had to deal with. I didn't have the guts to break away like Conroy. I was the dutiful son who kept the family tradition. It wasn't until I met you guys that I began to have any kind of a life. I have my hang ups, but damn it, I'm not Attila the Hun or Genghis Kahn like you want to make me."

"I don't know what the hell 'excoriated' means and I'm not sure I know who Attila-the-whomever or Genji Kahn are," Paco continued; "maybe you have a point. I'm not much of a reader; Luie's the reader. We've got to go if you're going to catch your plane. Mine isn't 'til later. You'd better shower too unless you want your folks to smell the things from the Ramrod last night."

"OK," Frank replied more softly. "Do I dare ask if you want to take a shower with me?"

"No, not now. I need more time," Paco said. "All I want is to get to Cincinnati quick as I can, see Luie at the airport, and get some TLC for a change."

"Does that mean we're through?" Frank asked.

"I don't know what the fuck it means," Paco exclaimed. "All I know is I loved you more than I loved any other human being, 'cept maybe Luie and I love him in a different way. All the love in the world's not enough to put up with a robot with no damned feelings."

Chapter 13

Monday, April 24, 2006
Mexico City, D.F., Mexico

Representatives from the *Secretaría de la Defensa Nacional*, *Secretaría de Relaciones Exteriores*, and *Procuraduría General de la República* met in a conference room of the *Secretaría de Seguridad Pública*, all dressed in the 'uniforms' of their jobs, navy blue or charcoal gray designer suits, some solid, some pin-striped, with stiffly starched dress shirts, and silk conservative ties.

After pleasantries, the Deputy Secretary for Police, an executive in the host organization, opened the meeting with all dialogue in Spanish: "We've been talking to each other for the past few days, except the *Procuraduría*. We agreed it's time to be together to decide what to do next. What we thought was a crank message like we get all the time now has the potential to be a major international incident. The *Procuraduría* was invited because it's involved in major intelligence-gathering."

"I'm not sure of our role here," the *Defensa* representative said. We've checked our installations and there's been no apparent effort to infiltrate any of them. We agree there're serious potential problems, but how do they involve us?"

"Maybe the prisoners were caught before they actually infiltrated," the police representative offered. "If you don't feel you're using your time well, we won't keep you. It may be useful if you stay and give us your opinions. In a situation like this, every informed opinion is useful.

THREE KISSES

"If we may, let's review to make sure we're all up to date: Last Tuesday, all of us except *Procuraduría* got a message about four escaped Arab terrorists loose in Coahuila. Before dismissing this as a prank, we contacted Coahuila police, especially when the message said one might be heading for a remote point on the U.S. border. Coahuila police had heard nothing and wanted to dismiss it as a prank also. After we mentioned the possible border problem, they agreed to send an officer down the road that leads to the *Río Bravo* where it's possible to cross the border by boat, swimming, or wading to Big Bend National Park on the U.S. side. Because there's friction between the U.S. and us now, we decided it'd be best to be cautious and go look.

"That's where we found the first one. We've given them nicknames because we don't know their actual names. The Coahuila policeman found the one we call *Flaco* because he's tall and skinny. He was wandering along the road, almost delirious from exposure and lack of water and food, dressed in weird clothes. He had been caught trying to steal food in the little village of La Babia. Local men beat him and chased him out of town taking the small amount of money and bottle of water he had. He attacked the policeman as well.

"He's been belligerent the entire time and has to be restrained. When the others were put in the same cell with him in Saltillo, they soon started beating him up so we had to separate him. We don't care much about his wellbeing the way he acts, but if indeed he's Arab, we don't want a major international incident if he were killed in our prison.

"When Coahuila investigators tried to get information out of him, he shouted in English, defiantly, that they had no right to keep him. He gave a name, Edgardo Rodríguez; said he's from Dallas. Said he had been abducted at gunpoint by Arab terrorists, had his car stolen, was bound and gagged, and brought to Mexico. He doesn't understand Spanish, or at least didn't respond to Spanish. His English seems accented. We have police contacts with the U.S., but don't want to use them in a case like this. There are lots of Rodríguezes in the U.S. with the name Edgardo. There's no way to know if he's from Dallas or even from Texas.

"We have very good reason we'll get to in a minute to believe he's Arab for sure. If indeed he was in the U.S., he must've tried to avoid detection as an Arab by claiming to be Mexican-American. Many in the U.S. think Arabs and Latinos look alike, but most Mexicans, especially up north in Coahuila, would know the difference, or at least be suspicious. He's the oldest of the group; seems in his mid-30s. Here's a picture.

"A few hours later, the other two showed up, one in each of two smaller cities up there, Sabinas and Nueva Rosita. The local police called Saltillo because they'd received a bulletin to lookout for strangers behaving strangely. Each one was wandering around confused, almost out of money and water, hungry, and with no identification. Both wore ordinary clothes like poor Mexicans so didn't attract attention at first. Both seem in their mid-20s and the youngest of the group.

"We call one *Mamado* because he's athletic-looking and the other *Gafas* because he wears glasses. They don't understand Spanish, but it seems they speak English like natives of the U.S. They say they're from New York.

"They said they were abducted by Arabs just outside their car, knocked out by injection, and brought to Mexico. They imply car theft was the motive. Their story is like *Flaco*'s and they obviously know him. They won't give names except Bud for *Mamado* and Bob for *Gafas*.

"They didn't resist being restrained, were taken to Saltillo, and didn't cause any trouble until they were put in the same cell with *Flaco* and started beating him up. The guards were not watching closely, but think *Flaco* provoked them. The guards said they all were shouting in a language they couldn't understand and they didn't think it was English, but prison guards are not well educated and may not recognize English. We have good reason that we'll get to in a moment to believe that they too are Arab, or at least Americans of Arab descent, and the language they were speaking was Arabic."

The *Relaciones Exteriores* representative said: "Maybe it isn't one of our defense installations that was being infiltrated. So far three of these guys say they're from the U.S. and there are U.S. defense installations all along the border, aren't there? There are different groups of Arab terrorists in the U.S. and maybe one or more of them are watching U.S. defense installations. When they find some rival group trying to infiltrate the base, they abduct them and try to get rid of them by dumping them in Mexico."

"Yes," the *Defensa* representative replied, "there're big installations in El Paso and Del Rio and several not far from the border in places like San Antonio. We have only minimal contacts with the U.S. Department of Defense as you in *Relaciones Exteriores* know. If there's any contact, it'd have to be through your *Secretaría*. Why bring them to Mexico and how'd they get them across the border?"

"It's easy to get them across the border; everyone's looking for smugglers taking people into the U.S., not out of the U.S. into Mexico," the Deputy for Police replied. "If a group of Arabs were found killed near a military installation in the U.S., all hell would break loose. In their mind, it might be best to dump them in Mexico and hope they'll die from exposure or thirst.

"The last one, who we call *Doctor* because he claims he's a medical doctor, turned himself into police in Saltillo. He claimed he'd ridden the bus from Torreón. That doesn't make sense because Torreón is far to the west and the abductors obviously came from the north, probably crossing the border at Piedras Negras. Insists the abductors drove him to Torreón, arranged a place for him to stay overnight, and told him he must take a bus to Saltillo and turn himself in, or face prosecution and execution in the U.S.

"Says he had to leave Syria for political reasons, and the other three prisoners were supposed to meet him in the U.S. and take him to Canada. Instead, a group of Arabs abducted all of them and brought them to Mexico.

"The prisoners must have had some falling out because *Doctor* says the reason he was taken to Torreón was to keep him separate for fear the others would beat him up or kill him. That doesn't make sense considering they ganged up on *Flaco* when they were in the same cell; we're not sure whether he participated or was trying to break it up.

"He seems definitely above the others in social status, which is consistent with being a medical doctor. He's mild-mannered, not resistant at all, and doesn't refuse to answer, but gives vague answers. Says all he wants to do is get on with his life and practice medicine. Told us one of his names, Ali. He might be more forthcoming if we handle him right, but so far we're not sure he'd have any more information that'd help us make the decisions we need to make now. He's the only one of them who openly admits he's Arab, but doesn't fit any terrorist profile we can imagine. Here's his picture."

"It seems they were abducted and brought to Mexico, so they must have been in some vehicle," the *Defensa* representative said. "Any lead on the type of vehicle?"

"We asked," the Deputy for Police replied. "They said they were blindfolded or unconscious most of the time. It was a big vehicle, like a Jeep, maybe navy blue. That's not much to go on but we checked records of SUVs crossing borders, especially at Piedras Negras. There were several and no one stuck out as suspicious. As we'll see, I'm not sure this information would do us much good.

"Let me wrap this up. We gave them a physical exam at the prison here. They all seem healthy and *Flaco* seems to have recovered from exposure and dehydration. We also ran their fingerprints through Interpol and a couple of other sources; no match. Because of evidence building up that they're Arabs, we notified *Procuraduría*. Their representative is here to give a report.

Before that, maybe we should take a short break and digest all of this; give you a chance to ask questions."

Chapter 14

Monday, April 24, 2006
Mexico City, D.F., Mexico

The meeting began again when the Deputy for Police of *Secretaría de Seguridad Pública* said, all dialogue in Spanish: "Because they're likely Arab, we notified the *Procuraduría*. Their representative will report."

"After 9/11," he began, "we suggested and the government concurred that we need to develop Arabic-language intelligence activity. We didn't have much direct contact with Arabic-speaking people, except indirectly through OPEC, and Pemex handled that. Whether we like it or not, being next to the U.S., something's bound to spill over.

"We've had a fair number of Arab immigrants through the years, mostly Christians from Syria and Lebanon; Carlos Slim is a prominent example. Some are in the second and third generation; that's where we've recruited and are training translators, interpreters, and intelligence agents. They're young and have almost no experience so this event was an opportunity for them to get experience, if nothing else.

"We used young men and women as interpreters for our regular interrogators. They speak English, but we did not tell the subjects. *Flaco* was first and we had a young woman interpreter. He refused to answer, saying in English he wouldn't talk to a woman who's an infidel and a stranger. We didn't let him know we understood English and kept trying. Finally, we gave up. We returned a few hours later with a male interpreter. From faint body language, facial expressions, and looks in his eyes that interrogators are trained to observe we detected understood Arabic. He wouldn't respond and repeated in English that we had no right to detain him.

"Next we went to *Mamado* and then to *Gafas*. Both said to speak in English because they don't speak Arabic very well and they don't have anything else to tell us. By chance, we had female interpreters because more young women than men want this kind of work. The interrogator noticed a certain type of eye movement which gave us the idea for the next round that I'll get to in a minute.

"*Doctor*, we'll call him Ali now, responded readily to Arabic and replied in Arabic. He said he wouldn't tell us more until he knew his status, what would become of him, and get assurances. He didn't say what assurances.

"For our last round, we used young female agents we've been training to use their, er, seductive charms to elicit information. We decided to develop this capacity because Arab men are notorious womanizers. When the interrogator noticed eye moments of *Mamado and Gafas*, we thought this was a good time to test our capabilities."

"What? You use them like prostitutes?" the *Defensa* representative interrupted. "That sounds like old spy movies. Doesn't the government have any moral qualms about forcing or at least encouraging agents to have sex? Think of the disease issues, if nothing else. We have enough problems with STDs in the defense forces."

"Well, yes, this's a bit like old movies, but with one exception," the *Procuraduría* representative continued. "These women do not go, er, 'all the way', but they can use the prospect of full intercourse to encourage the men to talk. The moral and ethical issues are something we can discuss another time, but this type of intelligence gathering has been widely used as an effective means to get information since the beginning of time and is still common in most countries.

"The women wore hidden microphones, which is a bit of a challenge when or if they undress so we make sure they have long hair to conceal them. Sound quality isn't great, but we can listen and record. We used private rooms on the pretext we needed to give additional medical examinations. They were dressed as nurses and spoke only Arabic.

"Ali saw through the ruse. He gently resisted seductive moves and did not become physically aroused, which the agent verified, er, manually. He spoke with her in very good Arabic saying he understands what she's trying to do and he will not give any more information until he knows more and is given assurances. She finally gave up and left.

"*Mamado* and *Gafas* reacted in similar ways, although *Mamado* got aggressive and, er, 'touchy feely'. Both were physically aroused and would've been willing to continue. It was as if they were sex-starved, which was likely.

"We got different bits of information from each one. They're from western New York where there are lots of immigrants from Yemen. They work in a wholesale distribution business for cigarettes and gasoline, traveling up and down the east coast of the U.S and into Canada.

"The final and by far worst situation was *Flaco*. First he sat in stoic silence while the agent became more and more seductive. When she became more, er, manually assertive, he grabbed her by her hair, slapped her face, and shouted in Arabic that she's an infidel whore, that no decent Arab woman would ever behave this way, that Allah will punish her severely, and she deserves to be killed to restore the honor of her family. Fortunately, he didn't disturb the microphone. She was able to extricate herself using her fingernails and a knee to the groin.

"In a perverse way, it's good she got this experience. If she continues this type of work, she needs to get used to the bad along with the good. We immediately restrained him, put him in solitary confinement with minimal rations, and said he'd be charged with assault and punished as severely as the law allows. We'll likely do nothing because a public trial, even of a prisoner, would expose too much.

"Moving to language analysis: we do not have good Arabic language analysis capability, although we're working to develop it through professors at the National University. Our main contact there listened to recordings and drew tentative conclusions. He said he'd like outside verification and he has a good rapport with linguistic professors in other countries, especially the U.S. In the end, we contacted a specialist in the U.K., not wanting to involve anyone in the U.S. We involved you in *Relaciones*

Exteriores. Someone from our embassy in London met a British professor and offered a small honorarium.

"The British expert confirmed what our professor suspected: Ali speaks cultured, classical Arabic with a Syrian accent typical of educated, upper middle class professionals in the Levant region of Syria, Lebanon, Palestine, and Jordan.

"*Flaco* speaks with an accent of the Arabian Peninsula, most likely Saudi Arabia. Because Saudi Arabians and others in the smaller countries on the peninsula were relatively poor peasant-type people about 70 years ago before oil was discovered, there's not much to distinguish accents by socio-economic level. The same is true of many Mexicans who've risen socially and economically without losing their accent. The choice of words often reflects education and culture. This seems to be the case with *Flaco*. The British expert said he could have used cruder terms to describe his perception of our agent and her, er, perceived sexual propensities. The conclusion is he's a reasonably well educated Saudi Arabian.

"*Mamado* and *Gafas* have an accent that is almost certainly from Yemen. Part of what is now Yemen was a British colony so there has been interaction through the years that allows British linguists to draw conclusions.

"Even though they speak like native speakers, their vocabulary is limited and simple, much like a child and someone who did not have much formal education in the Arabic language. The British expert said it was consistent with British-Arabs who learned the language from their parents or grandparents, but had no formal education in the language. It would be consistent with their claim they're from the U.S. The fact that they talk to each other in unaccented American English further confirms this fact."

"But they would not necessarily be U.S. citizens," the *Relaciones Exteriores* person commented. "They could've come to the U.S. as infants or small children."

"You're right," the Deputy for Police stated, "Now we can get to the reason we called this meeting, deciding what to do with them, but maybe we should take another short break."

Chapter 15

Monday, April 24, 2006
Mexico City, D.F., Mexico

The Deputy for Police from the *Secretaría de Seguridad Pública* began the meeting again with all dialogue in Spanish: "With the information from *Procuraduría*, we talked again with the prisoners briefly and very guardedly.

"We mentioned repatriation to Syria to *Doctor*; he immediately rejected the idea firmly and forcefully. He said he'd be abused maybe killed by the Moukhabarat, the Syrian secret police, who are indeed infamous in international police circles. We very tentatively asked if he were considering asking for asylum in Mexico, implying we really would not like to have him and he'd have to fight for asylum here. He reverted to his usual comment that he wouldn't say any more without knowing where he stands and having much more information. We decided we don't want to notify the Syrian embassy and *Relaciones Exteriores* concurs.

"When we mentioned notifying the Saudi Arabian embassy to *Flaco*, we got an even more intense reaction from him as he screamed 'No! You have no proof I'm Saudi Arabian'. Indeed, we have no proof and again *Relaciones Exteriores* concurs it'd be premature to notify the Saudi Arabian Embassy. With the sensitive issues over oil, we'd rather not raise too many additional issues unless it were absolutely necessary. We've always had good relations with them and we want to keep it that way.

DISCOVERIES • CHAPTER 15

"Finally there're the two supposed Americans, who may or may not be citizens, but could conceivably be from Canada. When we cautiously suggested turning them over to the Americans, they panicked and said they'd be arrested and could be executed. This was an extreme reaction for someone who's so far claimed no wrongdoing; at worst they've been smuggling cigarettes and gasoline. There's obviously something else here we might possibly pursue, but whether we want to is the issue.

"Now that you've heard the details, the overriding issue is what to do with them. We can't keep them in our prison much longer. None, except *Flaco,* has committed a crime in Mexico soil and his crimes are not serious enough to warrant a public trial. Most important, keeping them any longer than absolutely necessary risks nasty international incidents. We're in the middle of a presidential election campaign and do not want even the faintest bad press."

"We in *Relaciones Exteriores* concur wholeheartedly," their representative said.

"Why not just send them back to the U.S., maybe even dump them like they were dumped here?" The *Defensa* representative asked.

"If we could readily without causing a scandal, we would," the Deputy for Police replied. "Turning them over to the Americans would be the best solution we can think of, but how? It's virtually certain Americans would not take them back voluntarily. We have no proof they came into Mexico from the U.S. Furthermore, none of them, including the two who might be U.S. citizens, wants to go back.

"Even if by some miracle Americans would agree to take them back, actually getting them back would lead to publicity that neither we nor the U.S. would want right now. We could possibly fly them in on one of your planes to a U.S. military installation, but that requires lots of persons knowing you were landing and an idea of what you're doing.

"Using a land border is out of the question because of all the people around. As for dumping them, we'd have to use some place like Boquillas on the *Río Bravo* or maybe a fishing boat to dump them on *Isla de Padre*. The U.S. watches the borders much more carefully now. Even if we could just dump them, there's the risk they'd be discovered dead or dying from exposure, creating all sorts of human rights scandals.

"If you like, we can go over each and every possibility we thought of for dumping them, but none was feasible. The only thing we in *Seguridad Pública* have come up with is to use a third country to make the transfer to U.S. authorities under circumstances in which the U.S. would have no choice but to take them. For that we need the guidance and help of *Relaciones Exteriores*, and possibly *Procuraduría*, which is the main reason we're all here."

"We have agents and resources in some countries that could possibly help," the *Procuraduría* representative said, "but mostly in Latin America. We don't have an extensive network because Mexico isn't involved in major international intrigues and we don't need them to protect our interests. The countries where we do have them are not ones where the U.S. has much of a presence outside of normal diplomatic relations, but I would just as soon not say publicly right now what we have and where."

"Mexico has good relations with the NATO countries, but not military relations, and the NATO countries obviously have relations with the U.S." the *Relaciones Exteriores* representative added. "I'm thinking out loud because we obviously haven't had a chance to think this through in our *Secretaría*. Using a NATO country would be problematic. I can't imagine any of them, even countries like Spain, Italy, or Germany that're not pleased with U.S. foreign policy in Iraq would take our prisoners without knowing for sure the U.S. would accept them voluntarily."

"What about countries like Kuwait, Bahrain, Qatar, and the U.A.E. that all have good military relationships with the U.S. and even have U.S. military bases?" The *Defensa* representative offered. "The prisoners are Arabs; let the Arab countries take responsibility."

"We do have good relationships with these countries, but mostly related to oil and OPEC issues," the *Relaciones Exteriores* person said. "We've not been in a position to ask for favors or provide favors in a *quid pro quo*. I don't know if now's the time to try. These countries might not want to antagonize the U.S. by making the U.S. take four Arab prisoners involuntarily. …Wait! I just got an idea. Why didn't we think of this before?! There's one country where there's a U.S. military presence. We have good relations with this country, it owes us a lot of favors, and it could almost certainly force the U.S. to accept these prisoners. I think you all know which country I'm talking about, but I won't say the name publicly now for the record."

All present had expressions of suddenly realizing what country he was talking about.

"We have agents and resources there who could help if needed," the *Procuraduría* representative offered.

"How do we get them there?" the *Defensa* representative asked. "The U.S. watches their airspace very carefully and the sea as well. If one of our military planes or naval ships were to go there, questions would be raised."

"The U.S. wouldn't be suspicious about our ambassador's plane landing, especially if she were on board," the *Relaciones Exteriores* representative added. "We would need to bring her to Mexico anyway to work out details. Their ambassador to Mexico is an idiot and we wouldn't want to involve him at all. Even if he gets upset with us when it's over, we have plenty of reasons to declare him *persona non grata* and send him home. We might consult with some of their lower-level diplomatic staff.

"Our ambassador there was selected carefully by our *Secretaría* for her diplomatic skills and she was politically acceptable to the President and others at the highest level. We can trust her to arrange this or tell us if we're way off base. She's definitely not a 'yes' person. We can put the prisoners on the plane with her when she returns. They aren't a threat to anyone on board, except maybe *Flaco*, and we have ways to deal with him if necessary."

"Brilliant!" the police representative said. "I need to run it by the Secretary, of course."

"Likewise," the *Defensa* representative said.

"I need to get approval of my Secretary as well," the *Relaciones Exteriores* representative said. Remember we're in the middle of an election campaign. It'll be a close election. All of our Secretaries are involved in the campaign and wouldn't want to be distracted. Let's get all the details worked out and just present it to them for 'yes' or 'no', but present it in such a way t they can't really say 'no'. After all, we're saving them from a major international scandal."

Chapter 16

Thursday, April 27, 2006
Fort Meade, Maryland, USA

In mid-morning, Brad sat at his station half daydreaming thinking: *Looks like Drew and Paul are bored as I am. Weekend's almost here. Jason's coming; need to go shopping.* A buzzer shook Brad out of his thoughts as he said: "Hey, Drew; isn't that the number you marked to be monitored that day we got the weird calls?"

"Yeah, I'll turn on the loudspeaker," Drew said.
click

"Now we're getting the trace on it," the voice came faintly through the speaker, apparently not talking directly into the phone. "Area code 716. That's New York.".

"Yes, Buffalo," another faint voice was heard. "Weird; the package was mailed from Georgia."

"Let's dial with the other one," the first voice said.

"Strange," Drew said. "These calls are going to a land-line number in DC, but the number's blocked."

"Blocked?" Paul said. "Our equipment's supposed to see blocked numbers."

"Not if they're sensitive U.S. Government numbers," Brad added.

"Wait. Here's another one causing the board to light up," Drew said.

"OK, I got a trace on that one," the first faint voice as before said in the background. "Same 716 area code."

"Yep, same place, but different phone company," the second voice said. "I'll start checking received and dialed calls while you check the third phone."

pause

The faint ringing of a phone in the background came over the loudspeaker.

"Guess that's not one of the phones we're monitoring," Drew said.

"There was one call to and one from the same foreign number on the call register," a faint voice said. "Country code 96 or maybe 963. Need to look that up."

"Like the others, area code 716," the first voice said.

"Looks like they have three phones," Drew said. "We're only monitoring two."

"Looks like calls are to and from Syria," the second voice was heard saying, "maybe some truth in that note that these are terrorists' phones. This is above us and our little lab. Better turn them over to the crime labs. Let's tell the boss and see what he wants to do."

click

click

"This is weird. First to and from Dayton, Ohio," Drew said. "Then a series of unanswered calls from Syria to Middletown, Ohio. Now going to a blocked number in DC."

"CIA?" Paul suggested.

"I think that's a Virginia number," Drew said.

"What about FBI or DIA?" Brad offered.

"Could be," Drew said. "For sure it's some super sensitive place or we'd be able to get the number. I think we need to turn this over to the chief and let her analyze it."

"We have those domestic calls we monitored," Paul stated. "Will we get in trouble for that?"

"Doubt it," Drew said, "not when they see the whole sequence and find out who's that last place getting the calls. Worst they'd do is slap our wrists. Better type up the translations."

DISCOVERIES • CHAPTER 16

Quiet resumed and Brad drifted off into his own thoughts: *Need something for tomorrow night and Saturday night. Maybe go out to dinner on Saturday. Nahh, want to fix Jason a special dinner at least one night, best Saturday. Something simple tomorrow, maybe sandwiches and beer. We'll likely go to bed early anyway. Steaks on the grill Saturday night? Weather's getting nice. No, too butch. Chicken? Takes a long time to cook. Lamb chops? Hey, that's a thought. Certainly out of the ordinary. Not too butch. Never cooked lamb chops, but sure I could.*

Baked potatoes? No, too ordinary and not about to clean and chop French fries. Rice? Maybe find a good rice recipe, but I need potatoes anyway for a big weekend breakfast like Mom does. Has to be on Saturday because we're going to try the MCC on Sunday. Just cereal and fruit or something Sunday. Need to have home fries, eggs, bacon—nahhh, ham for Saturday; fresh fruit and nice bread.

Wonder if there's good fresh asparagus to steam. Just have broccoli if need be. Salad greens too. Better check the balsamic vinegar. All good gay households have balsamic vinegar. Isn't that what Will said on 'Will and Grace'?

Gotta make a nice dessert. Cake baking's not my thing and don't want to spend the day in the kitchen. Pie? Yeah, a custard pie like Mom makes. Buy a frozen pie crust. Cook custard, chop fresh fruit and lots of whipped cream.

Wine of course. Nice California Cabernet Sauvignon'd go great with lamb. Hey, I'm an Arabic language expert; should look for Middle Eastern wine. Jordanian wine was good but not exported. Lebanese wine is very good. Wonder if it's sold here. Maybe a specialty shop in DC; I can make a few phone calls, but don't want to drive all over town. California wine's just fine and as good as Lebanese, but wouldn't it add atmosphere to serve Arab wine with a seductive Arabian Nights atmosphere?

Yeah! No lamb chops; we'll have lamb kebab. Wonder if I can get eggplant this time of year to grill. Would there be any place to get hummus and babaghanouche?

Chapter 17

Monday, May 1, 2006
Baghdad International Airport, Iraq

Viktor sat with Dr. Sensenberg wearing hospital-type scrubs instead of orange prison coveralls.

Most topics of conversation had been exhausted so they sat in silence as Viktor thought in Russian: *Wish I had medical journals to read.*

Need a good book to read, Dr. Sensenberg thought.

Suddenly an orderly came in excited and said: "One of our corporals, Myers who does the border runs, took shrapnel. Doesn't seem badly injured, but his face is pretty bad. We'll take him to the examining room."

Dr. Sensenberg hastily put on a white doctor's smock and went hurriedly to the examining room. Viktor walked along, not invited, but no objection was raised.

"Good, you're cleaning his wounds," Dr. Sensenberg said to Corporal Alex Lutkin, the nurse on duty. "Any internal injuries? Better take his clothes off."

He scrubbed his hands and put on examining gloves.

Corporal Lutkin was in his early 20s, stood five feet 11 inches with a physically fit body, light brown almost blonde hair typical of his Slavic background, and intense blue eyes. He wore the easily washable white uniforms of military nurses. He cut and removed Corporal Myers clothes.

Viktor quickly walked to the head of the examining table and said: "His face is badly injured. Can I examine?"

Dr. Sensenberg ignored Viktor's comment focusing on the now-exposed torso saying: "Superficial wounds on the thighs. He's lucky; nothing in the groin area. He can still have children," thinking about his first love in medicine.

"Please, let me look at his face," Viktor pleaded going to scrub his hands and put on gloves.

Dr. Sensenberg mumbled which Viktor took as assent.

While Viktor examined Corporal Myers's face, Dr. Sensenberg gently felt his body and said: "We need to get him to x-ray quick to look for internal injuries."

"He needs surgery on his face now," Viktor said. "If we act fastly, we can fix some damage now. If we wait 'til it starts healing, it'll be worse, lots of scar tissue."

Dr. Sensenberg observed the first time Viktor made a mistake in English, but quickly dismissed it saying: "What? We don't have facilities for cosmetic surgery here, only emergencies. We med-evac anything else to Germany."

"Don't need much," Viktor continued, almost pleading. "You have scalpels and sutures. Just need to do **emergency** things so his face won't be permanently disfigured; your specialists can take over when he's sent somewhere else."

"I, I don't know. I don't know if I can let you operate," Dr. Sensenberg said. "I can't supervise you properly; I'm not a surgeon much less a cosmetic surgeon."

"Please. I'm not going to hurt him," Viktor pleaded. "I wouldn't hurt anyone, and certainly not him. He was nice to me; treated me decently on the bus even if I was a prisoner. He even made the bus stop so I could pee when I couldn't hold it any more. I've done emergency surgery many times. That's about all we did in Afghanistan and places like that."

"OK, I'll think about it," Dr. Sensenberg replied. "First get him to x-ray."

"Yes, of course," Viktor replied. "I can get things ready while he's being x-rayed. In the battlefields, we had no x-ray and sometimes internal bleeding interfered; sometimes lost the patient before I could finish. Do you have blood here? We never had blood in the battlefields."

"Very little," Dr. Sensenberg replied. "In an extreme emergency, so I'm told, we look for a donor from the troops if it's one of our troops who's injured. Otherwise, we send them to Germany or an Iraqi hospital. Nothing serious has happened since I've been here. I'll send a note to the commander; he can object while he's in x-ray."

Chapter 18

Monday, May 1, 2006
Baghdad International Airport, Iraq

About two hours after surgery on Corporal Myers, Major Armstrong stopped in Colonel Jones's office saluting saying: "Good to see you again."

"Likewise," Colonel Jones replied returning the salute. You're always welcome. We had some excitement today I'll tell you about, but please tell me about our prisoner first."

"We talked to the Iraqi again;" Major Armstrong began, "we now have a name, Abdulrahman al Baladi. People who don't like him, and that seems a lot, call him Abed. It's a common Arab nickname. Abou Abed's a character in jokes who's stupid and bumbling so some call our prisoner Abed, including his wife; she thinks he's a stupid religious zealot. We brought him a note from her acknowledging the money to take care of his son. There's no love lost between them.

"She doesn't seem in need of money, but took what we offered. Seems to be living at least as well as upper middle class Syrians. The resource suggested she may be supported by other Ba'athists who also fled Iraq, maybe even have another man in her life, may have been recruited by the Moukhabarat, or all of those. If she's Moukhabarat, then we've likely compromised our resource.

"We told the wife we could arrange for her and her son to go to another country and work. The resource was very careful not to give the wife too many details and we didn't give the resource too many details for her protection. Some high government officials in Lebanon with whom we have a rapport said they'd be willing to have the wife on their staff in some capacity and take the little boy too. They probably wanted to keep an eye on her and control who she contacts and where she goes.

"The wife was indignant saying she was not a domestic servant and she would not be treated like one, although our resource hadn't said anything to suggest domestic service. The wife said that she's a graphic designer and architect and that's where she deserved to work. She wouldn't move anywhere or do anything until occupiers were forced to leave Iraq and the rightful people are back in power.

"We don't have much more leverage over the prisoner, and I don't think he knows all that much more anyway. He keeps insisting all details were carried out by his assistant, a Syrian named Jihad, an Alawite infidel and Moukhabarat. The Russian doctor told us the same.

"We got the prisoner to grudgingly give the double's first name, Ali. He said he had been Alawite, but had given up infidel beliefs, recognized the truth, and now follows the correct path of the Sunnis. He said he doesn't know Ali's family name. We suspect he does, but won't tell us. Ali's one of the most common given names in the Arab world, so he knows we can't trace him based only on that; by not giving the family name, he's protecting himself.

"Most Alawite family names are easily recognized. Alawites control the Syrian government, the Ba'ath party in Syria—which is different from the Ba'aths in Iraq—and the Moukhabarat, even though they're a small minority. It's not surprising Jihad would be Alawite and Lattakia, where the hospital's located, has a substantial Alawite population."

"What's this Alawite group?" Colonel Jones asked. "I don't think I've heard of them."

"A group that broke away from the main Muslims some thousand years ago," Major Armstrong explained. "Followed a leader named Ali just like the Shiites, but they're different. Some would say they're not even Muslim. I can give you things to read or have you briefed. Alawites are mostly in Syria, but a few Lebanon and other countries."

"Thanks," Colonel Jones said. "It's pretty boring here most of the time; it could be interesting to have something to read about them. What does this mean for us? Do we keep him or turn him over to the ISF at Abou Ghraib?"

"Good question," Major Armstrong replied. "I suspect Washington'll want to keep him here, at least for a while. You know Shia militias who've infiltrated the ISF would torture him and maybe kill him. We don't need that kind of publicity. There's always the hope we can get more out of him, especially if we go back and forth between him and the Russian. How's it working out with him being in the clinic?"

"That's what I have to tell you," Colonel Jones replied. "One of our corporals, Myers, I think you met him, was caught with a bomb blast today. No life-threatening injuries, but lots of shrapnel wounds on his face. The Russian doctor insisted he had to do surgery now to make it better for the cosmetic surgeons later or his face could be permanently disfigured. Our doctor sent a note saying they were going ahead with surgery, but didn't ask my permission. That's OK. I trust Bob's judgment with my own children; no reason not to trust him here. Bob said he was a master at his work."

"Oh, I was going to see the Russian doctor," Major Armstrong continued. "The hospital in Germany found a few old medical journals; I thought I'd give them to him and maybe get more information. If he just came from surgery, he may be too tired and not willing to talk now. I'll just leave them with you to give to him later."

"It might be just the opposite," Colonel Jones said. "He might be so happy to have been able to work that he'd be more inclined to talk. It wouldn't hurt to try. I'll ask someone to find out where he is."

CHAPTER 19

Monday, May 1, 2006
Guantanamo Bay, Cuba

In early afternoon, U.S. Marine Corps Corporals Gerardo Ramírez and Alejandro Palacios sat listlessly at the Northeast Gate of Guantanamo Naval Base. Their uniforms were wilted in the humid heat, but otherwise reflected the high standard demanded by the Marine Corps. Both were in their early 20s. Alejandro was tall and slender, five feet 11 inches, with medium dark complexion and wavy black hair that was well trimmed to military standards. Gerardo was two inches shorter, also had dark complexion typical of his Hispanic heritage, a more stocky build, and straight black hair also trimmed military style. Their normally bright, dark brown eyes were dull from boredom.

NORTHEAST GATE, GUANTANAMO BAY NAVAL BASE, CUBA

DISCOVERIES • CHAPTER 19

Because of the Cuban holiday, they did not expect traffic. Few people used this entrance, but it was necessary to guard the one remaining land entrance. For lack of anything better, they scanned television channels, bypassing May Day celebrations on Cuban channels, lingering sometimes on bland shows on Armed Forces TV.

They were startled by loud noises from the 'no-man's land' separating their guard post from the Cuban guard post. Four men dressed in sloppy clothes ran towards the gate, bleeding and screaming.

"They're killing us!" one screamed with glasses hanging on one ear, blood dripping from his head and face.

Another stumbled in shock, his face and scalp a bloody mess soaking his shirt covering up the bright colorful outrageous pattern. Yet another stopped to lift and drag him towards the gate.

A fourth, only slightly more composed, ran to the window screaming: "Open up, please! We need help."

Gerardo quickly opened the inner gate of the security hatch and closed it behind him, while Alejandro rushed to the window saying: "¿Qué pasa?"

Gerardo shouted: "¿Quién es?"

"¿Qué quieren?" Alejandro asked.

"English; Americans. Let us in!" One pleaded.

"We're badly injured and need help. I'm a doctor," the one at the window shouted.

Alejando rushed to guard the outer gate as Gerardo closed the inner one. When the outer gate was opened, the one with glasses rushed inside, dragging the tall skinny one. The one at the window rushed swiftly inside, pausing to help the one in traumatic shock.

Loud voices from the no-man's-land were heard: "*Lárguense, espías de mierda.*"

"*¿Qué coño hacen aquí?*"

"*¡Váyanse a la mierda, hijos de la gran puta!*"

When the outer gate was closed and all were in the security hatch, Alejandro asked again: "*¿Quiénes son? ¿Qué quieren? ¿Qué pasa?*"

"English, please; we're American," the one with glasses repeated panicked. "They raped us and beat us."

"Take us to a hospital quick; he could die," the last one said pointing to the traumatized one.

"Call the hospital and the command post," Gerardo told Alejandro in English. "I'll watch them. Bring the first aid kit and water." To the one who said he is a doctor: "Who are you and how'd you get here?"

"I'm a doctor from Syria," he answered. "We were abducted, taken to Mexico, flown here, and turned over to thugs who beat us up and raped us."

"That's too amazing," Gerardo said skeptically. "You're injured so I suppose we have to keep you. They're Americans?"

"They say they are," the doctor replied. "The unconscious guy is Saudi Arabian, they say."

"Too fucking much!" Gerardo exclaimed.

Alejandro arrived with the first aid kit and water, saying: "An ambulance is on the way. The command post said they'd send someone. I said best go to the hospital."

He opened the first aid kit to tend to the traumatized one while Gerardo was giving all sips of water.

When he started to give water to the traumatized person, the doctor half shouted to Gerardo: "No! Dangerous to give water to someone in shock." To Alejandro in a calmer voice: "Better let me do that," taking the first aid kit gently from him. "Tend to the other two."

Gerardo poured water on their wounds and asked: "What about your wounds?"

"Mine aren't life threatening; I can wait for the ambulance," he replied as he tried to feel pulse and breath of the one in shock. "Where're some blankets?"

"Blankets? In this heat? This is fuckin' Cuba in May," Alejandro exclaimed.

"He's in shock and needs as much warmth as he can get," the doctor said tearing off his shirt to cover him.

"I'll see if there are towels or something," Gerardo said as he went into the guard station. Within moments he came back empty handed and said: "I hear the ambulance coming."

Chapter 20

Monday, May 1, 2006
Baghdad International Airport, Iraq

Several minutes after he completed surgery and was relaxing, Viktor expressed his gratitude profusely to Major Armstrong for the medical journals.

Major Armstrong said: "I hear you did a very good job on the corporal's face."

"Oh, it was nothing," Viktor replied. "I've done things like that so many times. I hope the surgeons in America do a good job when they finish the process. He's a nice young man and deserves to have a nice face.

"The ones who did good work are Doctor Bob and Corporal Lutkin the nurse; Dr. Bob called him Alex, good Ukrainian names. He's a very nice young man. He loves his wife very much and misses her; they'd just gotten married before he had to come over here. I saw his wedding ring and asked him to remove it and about her."

"Let me ask you about two other young men," Major Armstrong said: "Who is Ali, the young Alawite man you made into a double at the hospital in Lattakia? And who's the young man in the United States you duplicated?"

Oh, he knows Ali's name; I know I didn't tell him, Viktor said to himself in Russian. *He knows he's Alawite, knows it was in Lattakia, and that it was the U.S. Maybe, I can find out more about Ali, dear Ali.*

"He was a student at the medical school who they arranged to help me," Viktor began. "He had basic medical training somewhere else, but was sent to Lattakia for advanced residency. They made him study with me and help me because he speaks English and I don't speak Arabic. He didn't have a choice, but discovered he likes cosmetic surgery and was eager to train with me.

"Jihad had been looking for a young Syrian man who he could trust to make into a double for an Arab man in America. He found a couple, but I didn't think they were good matches. Finally, he thought Ali might be good and convinced Ali to offer himself. It was a good match. Jihad trusted him because he's Alawite, but convinced him to pretend he's a good Sunni to please Abed. They promised he'd go to Canada after he'd finished his mission. Please tell me where he is. How he is. I've been so worried."

"Who is 'they' who were going to take him to Canada and what was his mission?" Major Armstrong continued.

"Al Qaeda of course," Viktor replied; "the ones who forced me to go to Syria and do this. Abed's part of them."

"What was the mission?" Major Armstrong persisted.

"They didn't tell me," Viktor answered. "It was non-violent. Ali refused to cooperate if he had to hurt someone."

"Why Canada?" Major Armstrong continued.

"He just wanted to get out of Syria," Viktor replied. "Canada's a good country."

"What's his family name?" Major Armstrong asked.

"I don't know," Viktor lied feigning annoyance.

I bet he's lying, Major Armstrong thought. *I won't press him right now and antagonize him so he won't talk any more. Maybe I can get it from Abed.* He then asked: "Who was the person who was duplicated? You must surely know something about him."

"No, they wouldn't tell me," Viktor replied. "I know a lot about him physically, of course. Another Arab. He had to be Arab for us to duplicate his facial features."

"Tell me about him physically," Major Armstrong demanded, "if you want to help your young friend"

DISCOVERIES • CHAPTER 20

Viktor thought: *If I lie and they find out, that could cause problems for Ali.* He said: "He's 177 centimeters tall, weighs 80 kilos, has dark red-brown hair and green eyes."

"Not too slender at 80 kilograms," Major Armstrong persisted. "How about his body type? Muscular? Chubby?"

"Just a little muscular and just one or two extra kilos in the middle," Viktor replied quickly. "Ali had to work out to duplicate the muscles and gain a little weight."

"How did you match things like arm length and leg length?" Major Armstrong asked.

"We had some of his clothes and knew how they fit," Viktor responded almost automatically.

"Ali's arms and legs were the same then?" Major Armstrong continued rapid-fire.

Viktor replied: "We thought we might have to lengthen his legs, but we built up his shoes. Most people won't notice slight differences in arm length."

"What kind of clothes?" Major Armstrong persisted. "Clothes can fit loosely or be form-fitting?"

"These were form fitting," Viktor replied quickly.

"How do you know?" Major Armstrong asked.

Viktor said: "It was a military uniform and the person was known to have well-fitting uniforms."

Now we're getting somewhere, the major said to himself and asked: "What kind of uniform? What color?"

"Kind of green, or olive like we say in Russian," Viktor replied. "Usually for the Army."

"What about foot size?" Major Armstrong asked.

"Foot size is not a big issue unless one or the other is unusually large or small," Viktor replied. "Most persons won't notice. I was told his shoe size; Ali was close enough. Ethnic groups have similar foot sizes. Arabs tend to be slightly smaller than average so two Arab men of the same height and weight would have similar size feet."

He's thorough, Major Armstrong thought. *Has a ready answer for everything.* He continued: "What about hair color. There can be lots of shades of red-brown."

"He kept his hair cut very short," Viktor said. "Ali was close enough. We could've used hair coloring if necessary."

"And eyes? Green covers a big spectrum," Major Armstrong asked.

"We decided Ali's are close enough," Viktor replied. "We could've used contact lenses. The man used glasses to drive and read and they would detract attention from the eyes. We had Ali wear identical glasses."

"And voice?" Major Armstrong persisted.

"He had a bad cold," Viktor instantly replied.

Now I'm satisfying my own curiosity, Major Armstrong said to himself. *Better not push much more, but he's sure proud of his work.* He changed topics and asked: "Where in the U.S. did they send him?"

"They didn't tell me things like that," Viktor answered.

"You said there was a big mistake and that you'd be blamed," Major Armstrong continued. "What mistake? You sound so thorough I can't imagine you made a mistake."

"Please, Mr. Major; I'm very tired now," Viktor pleaded. "I didn't make a mistake, but they'd blame me. I think you say 'make me the scapegoat'?"

I've pushed him as much as I can today, Major Armstrong said to himself. *We can get more, I'm sure, if we handle him right.* Then he said: "We're trying to get you some more medical journals from the United States."

"Oh, thank you so much," Viktor said.

Major Armstrong stopped briefly by Colonel Jones's office to say goodbye and give a brief summary: "You were right. He was in a good mood and talkative until I asked about the mistake that was made. The duplicated guy's in the Army and Arab. Must be Arab-American like your Lieutenant Gorani. There'd be hundreds if not thousands of them. Military records don't show ethnic background and looking for names can be tricky and unreliable, just like 'Gorani'. We got a good physical description. The double was going to be sent or taken to Canada, so the person doubled may have been stationed in the North. There aren't many Army posts in the North so maybe we can narrow the search down a little."

He saluted and took his leave.

Chapter 21

Monday, May 1, 2006
Guantanamo Bay, Cuba

A few hours after the incident at the Northeast gate, Admiral Jeffery Crenshaw, commander of the Guantanamo Bay Naval Base, hastily called a meeting with Marine Corps Colonel Jeremy Walker, chief of security; Navy Commander Michael Goldberg with the Defense Intelligence Agency; and Lieutenant Commander Dr. Dale Fisher, M.D.

"It seems we had some excitement," Admiral Crenshaw said looking over his half glasses wearing a smartly hand-tailored uniform. "Guys stormed the gate and wanted in. Hundreds of Cubans would do that every day. What's different here?"

Were he standing, he would be six feet tall with light brown, slightly curly brown hair, graying at the temples reflecting his age in the mid-fifties.

"There were four," Colonel Walker began. "Badly injured; one barely pulled though. Said Cuban thugs beat and raped them, and chased them towards our gate. They don't act like Cubans. Don't understand Spanish or else they're putting on a damn good act. I asked the doctor to tell you more.

"It's not sure they were trying to get onto the base, but were being chased. Said their attackers were drinking and acted like they were going to kill them, but dumped them at the gate saying they were American

DISCOVERIES • CHAPTER 21

spies. Our guards at the gate understand Spanish and confirmed they heard voices accusing them of being spies for, er, the euphemism they use for the United States."

"So who the hell are they?" the admiral asked, "and how'd they get to Cuba in the first place?"

"From the little we've gotten out of them, two of them say they're American but have no proof," Colonel Walker continued. "The one who's least injured, or maybe I should say least traumatized, says he's a doctor who escaped Syria for political reasons and the two claiming to be Americans met him in the U.S. to take him to Canada. They say the other guy's Saudi Arabian. They don't seem to like him, but weren't going to leave him to die.

"They have a fantastic story about being abducted in the U.S. by Arab terrorists, taken to Mexico and abandoned, captured by Mexican police, then flown here, and turned over to soldiers and eventually thugs who put them in the back of a truck for a long trip, and attacked and chased them to our gate. When we heard two of them are Arabs, one by his own admission, and that Arab terrorists abducted them, we immediately called DIA".

"How do we know they're not just Cubans pulling an elaborate stunt to get us to give them asylum and get to the U.S.?" the admiral continued skeptically, scowling as he looked over his half-glasses again. "Maybe something went wrong so their smugglers beat them up."

Colonel Walker replied: "As you know, sir, Cubans'll do desperate things to get to the U.S., but we can't imagine a Cuban'd do anything this desperate to get onto our base. We're not sure they wanted to get on the base. The three who're conscious speak unaccented American English, including the one who claims to be Syrian."

The doctor added: "Another thing is they're all circumcised like almost all Americans and Arabs. Cubans would not likely be circumcised. We're expected to look for anomalies such as a new detainee being uncircumcised indicating he's not Muslim.

"The one who says he's a doctor seems to be genuine or has had substantial medical training. He anticipated everything when we examined him, answered questions before we asked them, telling us things we may not have asked about. He has facial lacerations, abrasions, and bruises, but not as severe as the others. He was telling us what to do to treat the other three to the point that people in the ER and I were annoyed. He was especially interested in facial injuries, telling us things to do to prevent scarring and disfigurement. Said he's a cosmetic surgeon.

"He didn't seem to be interested in his own face, which we thought strange. When we examined him, it looked like he has faint scars as though he had cosmetic surgery recently. The only cosmetic surgery I know is from medical school rotations a few years ago. I know enough from trauma medicine that he's right about needing to do certain things to facilitate cosmetic repair later. We dressed his wounds and put him in a regular ward on a normal diet because there's no apparent contagious disease or other conditions that need immediate treatment, although we need to wait for test results.

"The one they say is Saudi Arabian is critical, but stable and unconscious. His injuries are not extreme; the primary issue is traumatic shock. We put him on IV and examined him as best we could. He's in intensive care. He was bleeding from the rectum. Either objects were pushed up there or he was raped as the others claimed they'd been. The damage will probably heal on its own without surgery or sutures, but we need to watch things. I decided to test for semen residue as well as for anything else that might be there. We're not trained in criminology and I haven't seen anal rape cases since medical school rotations.

"While on the subject, the Syrian has rectal stretching but no apparent injury. The other two have minor damage, but no bleeding. I decided to test them all for semen residue, also test for HIV. If rape was very recent, which it seems to have been, HIV wouldn't show up for a while. I also decided to make their penile swabs before getting urine samples to see if semen residue was there.

"I've gotten ahead of myself. The two who claim to be Americans have severe lacerations, abrasions, and bruises, especially on the face and upper body, but nothing life-threatening. We dressed their wounds, and put them on IV for the rest of the day in intensive care just to be sure. Unless something shows up, we'll move them to a ward tomorrow."

DISCOVERIES • CHAPTER 21

"That's very impressive, doctor," the admiral commented. "You must have something from a DIA perspective, Mike."

"The security people are to be commended for bringing us in immediately," he said. "We notified headquarters. We weren't able to get much out of the subjects and medical people understandably don't want us interrogating right now. We can't imagine al Qaeda doing something so bizarre to infiltrate the base here. Still, we need to keep the victims separated from detainees and each other under close watch.

"It doesn't fit the profile of a medical doctor to use smugglers to enter the U.S. and then go to Canada, and the two younger guys don't fit the profile of people smugglers. If indeed the doctor's from Syria, there must've been some other way to get him into the U.S. and some other reason for his being there, if indeed he was in the U.S.

"We talked to the Syrian doctor and the other two briefly and they seem to speak American English, including with each other. We asked for and got finger prints and foot prints. One guy's unconscious, but we took his prints anyway. We're sending them off for analysis. Tomorrow, or whenever the medical people say we can, we'll send Arabic-speaking interrogators around. We'll also send an Arabic-speaking Muslim chaplain.

"My bosses at the Pentagon were so surprised they didn't respond much saying they'd get back to me. I'm not sure they're taking this all that seriously. Like you at first, sir, they may think these guys are just desperate Cubans trying to get asylum and to the U.S."

The admiral gravely shook his head from side to side and said: "They may not be taking it seriously, but you've convinced me I must. The whole world's looking at us under a microscope. Congressional investigators come in and out. The Red Cross demands access. We're required to report in detail who we have here and their nationality. If indeed those two are American citizens, or even legal residents, all hell can break loose. The Defense Department, and especially Donald Rumsfeld, have so little credibility we'd be raked over the coals and crucified for abducting them ourselves and bringing them here for torture.

"Then there are the supposed Syrian and Saudi Arabian. We're required to notify their governments of their presence. I need to get on the horn myself to Navy headquarters. I'm sure our headquarters will be in touch with yours. Our task now is to keep this quiet. If word leaks out, I don't even want to imagine what'd happen. How can we make sure the medical staff won't tell anyone?"

Dr. Fisher said: "I don't think we need to worry much there. The ER staff is used to having patients brought in not knowing or even wanting to know who they are. Some of them may have overheard the Syrian doctor, but knowing medical personnel, it would've gone in one ear and out the other. The ICU and ward nurses have lots more important things to worry about than listening to these kinds of details. Still, we can't blow it off. Shall I ask the hospital commander to come see you or will you do it yourself?"

"I'd better do it myself, but you can certainly give him a heads-up if you get to him before I can," the admiral replied. "I need to call the Pentagon first."

Turning to Colonel Walker: "What about the two Marine guards at the gate? Maybe they've already spread the word if they're off duty now."

"This is a tricky one, sir," Colonel Walker answered. "The two corporals are model guards, good loyal American Marine Corps corporals, both from Puerto Rico. You know we use Spanish-speakers at the gate. It was luck of the draw that they got sent there today on a Cuban holiday.

"You're right, they'll talk to their buddies; they'd have to brief their supervisor and replacements if they've gone off duty and make entries in logs. If we tell them to be quiet and not make log entries, we could have worse problems. If they think they're being made part of a cover-up, that could lead them to be whistleblowers. I'll get on this right now and find out as much as I can. I'll definitely keep you informed, sir."

The Admiral stood indicating the meeting was over.

Chapter 22

Friday, May 5, 2006
Guantanamo Bay, Cuba

Admiral Crenshaw opened a meeting in early afternoon with those from the previous meeting and Dr. Rhonda Philips, a political and foreign policy liaison specialist from DIA headquarters. She was smartly dressed in a simple emerald green sleeveless linen-cotton blend summer dress with a multicolored silk scarf that had green highlights and was large enough to spread over her shoulders in the well air conditioned room. Her graying brown hair was pulled back into a bun; she had brown plastic rimmed glasses hanging on a gold chain from her neck. She looked older than her actual 52 years. Had she been standing, she would be petite at five feet two inches. Off-white block-heeled shoes gave her height; she carried a large matching leather bag.

Admiral Crenshaw began: "Thank you, Dr. Philips, for coming down here. You, too, think this's serious and we need to get them out of here soon as we can."

"Yes, but we need to know a lot more about them than we know now," she replied. "The longer they stay here, the greater the risk of serious misunderstanding. They came onto the base voluntarily; we've never had a case like this before. U.S. military facilities do occasionally take people with medical emergencies for humanitarian reasons, and these were medical emergencies, but we've always had some place to send them once their medical conditions stabilize. Apparently you've talked to Navy headquarters and they told you to keep the lid on and wait for instructions."

"That's right," Admiral Crenshaw confirmed. "Let's review them one by one and you can give your assessment. Let's start with the troublemaker and with you, Dr. Fisher."

"We have a tentative name, Adnan," Dr. Fisher began. "When he regained consciousness in the ICU, he became wild, demanding to know where he was, tried to get out of bed, messed up the IV, and would have pulled it out if the pain weren't so great. In the end, we had to restrain him, fasten him to the bed, and sedate him. He urinated in the bed rather than ask for a urinal. We left him for a while so he'd understand such behavior won't get a response. Eventually, he let a male orderly, not female, clean the bed.

"After talking to security, we decided it was time to bring a chaplain. Security can tell you more about that. His behavior has improved, but far from ideal. We see this behavior from quite a few detainees, which suggests he's indeed Arab, but security will address that also. So far he's not gone on a hunger strike, but picks at his food. His wounds are healing, but there'll likely be scarring. Lab tests didn't reveal infectious disease, but he had semen in his rectum; actually all four of them did. There was none in the penis. The HIV test was negative. Because of the extent of rectal damage, he needs to be tested again after a while."

"Maybe we can get rid of him before any HIV appears," Admiral Crenshaw interrupted.

"The doctor stated: "We can't ethically send a potential HIV carrier without notifying the place he's going."

"He's right, Admiral," Rhonda Philips confirmed. "It would be a political and foreign policy disaster if we sent potential HIV positive cases somewhere else without at least notifying someone."

"Now from security," Admiral Crenshaw said.

"When we were able to interrogate him," Colonel Walker began, "he insisted on speaking English and wouldn't acknowledge he speaks Arabic. His English is fluent but accented and doesn't seem Hispanic. He first said he's Edgardo Rodriguez from Dallas and that we have no right to keep him here. He told a fantastic story that is essentially the same as the others told.

"When we asked him to prove his identity; he was vague and gave an address in a Dallas suburb. He said he was born in Dallas, gave a birthday, but was slow giving parents' names; we're sure he made them up. There were no matches on finger prints for him, or for any of them.

"Dr. Fisher mentioned a chaplain. We have a tenuous but workable relationship with the Islamic chaplains, and they speak Arabic. We insist to them that we respect clergy confidentiality and don't use them to get information. We brief them on patients' injuries and what we observe about their behavior in case that helps them, and chaplains report back to us anything they think would help us deal with a patient, or if the detainee wants him to tell us something. We didn't tell the chaplain about the apparent rape because Muslims have extreme views on male-to-male sex.

"The chaplain spoke with him in Arabic because his English is limited and Adnan responded. We didn't listen, but from a distance observed body language and facial gestures, on the chaplain that is; almost all of Adnan's face is bandaged. The chaplain didn't stay long, but Adnan became more calm and relaxed. The chaplain told us Adnan was indignant about being touched by a woman who's not his wife or mother and would refuse any form of care by a woman. We told the medical staff and they now use men. From all this, we're convinced he's Arab and certainly not Hispanic American. Over to the DIA."

Commander Goldberg began: "When the interrogator challenged him and said we could turn him over to Saudi Arabian authorities if he's innocent, he became almost panic-stricken saying we have no proof he's Saudi Arabian. When we pinned his companions down for proof, all they say is that's what he said. Each separately said he told them his name is Adnan; they can't remember his family name because he just mentioned it briefly. They don't like him and aren't trying to protect him, but they're not going to indict him either. Rhonda?"

"I didn't attempt to talk to him because being female would likely upset him even more," she began. "I can only give a second-hand analysis.

Our relations with Saudi Arabia have been tense, as you know, ever since it was obvious many nine-eleven attackers were Saudi Arabian citizens. Still, they help us and we help them with intelligence, and they face al Qaeda threats also. We can't afford to damage the intelligence relationship, not to mention political issues over oil, Iran, and several other things.

"As you also know, we won't release someone from here who we believe'll be a continued terrorism threat. We don't know whether he's a threat and, as we must remind ourselves, he's here voluntarily, not a detainee. If Saudi Arabia accepts him back, they'd unlikely put him in prison, unless he's committed a crime or terrorist act in Saudi Arabia. Even if they aren't the world's greatest respecters of human rights, they tend to comply with basics. They could watch him carefully to keep him from slipping back into terrorism, if indeed he is a terrorist, but what're we going to tell them? A fantastic story that he ran to our gate chased by Cubans soldiers after being abducted to Mexico?

"Then there's the policy of the U.S. that we won't release prisoners to a country that'll torture them or subject them to inhumane treatment. We usually don't worry about Saudi Arabia in this respect, but the political fallout just in case something happens wouldn't be easy to deal with. In short, he needs to stay put for the time being until we get more information; besides, it appears his medical condition isn't good enough to move him anyway."

"OK," the admiral grumbled. "Let's take a short break and let this sink in before we go to the others."

Chapter 23

Friday, May 5, 2006
Guantanamo Bay, Cuba

Admiral Crenshaw continued: "OK, who's next?"

"Ali, the Syrian doctor, has been annoying, but not a troublemaker," Dr. Fisher began. "He comes to the ER to talk about medical things, asks for medical journals to read. He has only limited interest in reading other things and is bored by television we have here. I'd be bored, too.

"He actually helped us a couple of times with detainees who needed medical attention, sometimes brought by guards against their will. Because he speaks Arabic, he calmed them down and got information we needed to treat them. On one occasion, we actually asked him to help. We can put up with him and he does know when to stay out of the way.

"We asked a chaplain to visit him. He thanked us and seemingly thanked the chaplain in Arabic, but said he's not Muslim. We offered to send a Christian chaplain; he said he's not Christian either."

"What is he then?" Admiral Crenshaw interrupted.

"He says he's Alawite, but not religious," Dr. Fisher replied. "Apparently the DIA knows more.

"Lab tests for infectious diseases, including HIV, were negative. As mentioned, he had semen residue in his rectum, but no serious damage. He also had semen residue in his penis. When we asked him about it, he became extremely embarrassed and his face turned as red as that wall-hanging over there." He gestured towards one of the Admiral's prized deep crimson kilims from when he was on a joint exercise with the Turkish navy in the Sea of Marmara. "He mumbled sheepishly with obvious discomfort it was a spontaneous ejaculation during the event."

"What? He enjoys being raped?" the admiral interrupted. "Is he gay or something? Maybe it wasn't so involuntary after all. Maybe it was him getting it on with the others. All the more reason to get rid of him."

"I'd hardly think so, sir," Dr. Fisher replied. "We could've done DNA matching to see if semen residue in his penis matched residue in rectums, but we're not trained in criminology and it didn't occur to us. Furthermore, even if that were true, I can't imagine what impact it'd have on us. A more logical explanation may be that he knows what happens to persons who resist violent rape, so he gave in to minimize physical damage to himself and nature took over.

"He said scars were from altering his appearance at a hospital in Syria. We asked who did it and what kind of facilities, but he became vague. Cosmetic surgery to alter one's appearance is a highly specialized area, far more than conventional cosmetic surgery. We can't imagine Syria's medically advanced enough.

"He's recovering well, doesn't need to be hospitalized, and we'd just as soon have the bed for someone else. Any remaining treatment could be outpatient. According to security and the DIA, we can't just release him; apparently he has no place to go."

Colonel Walker added: "He's given no indication he's a terrorism threat nor that he's committed a crime, so we have no reason to confine him. Even if we could manufacture reasons, it's not a good idea to have him with detainees. At the same time, we can't let him have the run of the base. We could possibly put him in a room at the Navy Lodge where Rhonda's staying, with guards around the clock. That'd use guards we'd rather use elsewhere, and is a form of detention that could cause political issues. The DIA has more to say."

DISCOVERIES • CHAPTER 23

NAVY LODGE, GUANTANAMO BAY NAVAL BASE, CUBA

Commander Goldberg began: "We suggested we notify the Syrian government to have him repatriated. He became tense, almost begging us not to because he and his family could have serious problems. When we pursued the topic, he wouldn't say more, wanting to know what'd happen to him here. He kept saying if he were going to be prosecuted and persecuted, it should just be him alone; he's not going to give information that could hurt others.

"The really strange thing for us, that makes no sense, is surgery to alter his appearance. It happened, he said, while he was in medical training to be a cosmetic surgeon himself—and all indications are he's genuinely trained in cosmetic surgery—but why go to that effort to have himself altered just to leave the country?

"Maybe he did something serious enough to cause the Syrian secret police to track him down and eliminate him, but he wouldn't've been able to attend medical school in the first place if he were in serious trouble with the government because all education is heavily state controlled. Also, Syrian hospitals are state run and the secret police surely know everything that goes on inside, especially altering one's appearance that takes a long time.

"Syria was virtually a Soviet satellite for many years, so medical interaction would've been with the Soviet Union or other satellites. The CIA might give insight.

"Another issue is being smuggled into the U.S., and these three helping him. Why the U.S.? Why not directly to Canada? It's hardly easier to get into the U.S. than to Canada. There's no organized people-smuggling out of Syria to the U.S. that we know about; the CIA may know more.

"Where'd the money come from to pay for this? There're wealthy families in Syria, but he doesn't want his family to know he fled. Changing identity's been known to happen. Soviets did it in the old days, we're fairly sure. We think Israelis do it. Rhonda has more."

"He's likely been duped, maybe by al Qaeda, and seized the opportunity to get out of Syria and into a country like Canada," Rhonda Philips began. "Medical doctors, even if they're well educated, are often naïve because of their humanitarian instincts and don't think of consequences. He doesn't remotely fit the profile of a terrorist.

"I talked to Ali myself. He's pleasant and has no issues with women. I picked up on his being Alawite because the ruling Ba'ath party and government in Syria are dominated by them. Maybe his family is, or at one time was, in the good graces of the party and government and that's why he thinks they could be hurt if he were forced to return to Syria.

"I convinced him that if we're going to find an alternative to repatriation, we must know more about his background. He reluctantly gave a family name, Salman, and admitted his father had been involved in the government, but was now out of favor. One reason is that his parents sent him to an English-speaking international high school.

"I picked up on English-speaking schools and flawless American English. After I pushed him, he admitted he lived in the U.S. as a boy and started to school there. This would be in the early 80s, and the only thing that makes sense is his father was at the U.N. Few Syrians would've been in the U.S. without diplomatic reasons. He admitted it'd been the U.N., and he spent his early years growing up in New York City. We can check this out.

DISCOVERIES • CHAPTER 23

"I tried to find out more about the physical alteration of his face. He was obviously emotionally and physically exhausted, and wouldn't say more without knowing what'd happen to him. I was tired too, so I brought things to a close.

"In conclusion, sorry to say Admiral, we need to keep him here a while longer. There's no serious short-term political fallout. There'd be much more fallout if we sent him back to Syria and he and his family were persecuted. As long as we don't actually lock him up, and have him here only for humanitarian reasons, there aren't going to be groups in the U.S. agitating politically. The greatest potential for political fallout by far would be if it were discovered that he was able to slip into the U.S. undetected. We have to know where he'd go next before we can get him out of here.

"Also, I wouldn't object to having him as a neighbor in the Navy Lodge. He's pleasant and inoffensive; others might be upset at round-the-clock security guards."

"Thanks, Dr. Philips," Admiral Crenshaw said. "This is taking forever, but it's necessary. Another short break."

Chapter 24

Friday, May 5, 2006
Guantanamo Bay, Cuba

"Let's keep on and see if we can end by a reasonable time," Admiral Crenshaw said. "Who's next?"

"The one in glasses," Dr. Fisher said. "His name is Brahim, for Ibrahim; Bob's a nickname too. He's been OK; always wants something to read and the selection in the hospital's not much. He doesn't have one cent so he can't buy anything. I'd give him money to buy a book or magazine, but that'd set a bad precedent.

"His test results were all negative. He had slight rectal damage which is healing and semen residue in his rectum, so more testing needed. No semen in his penis.

"We asked the chaplain to visit, again not mentioning the rape. Bob spoke to him in Arabic; there wasn't much communicated, and the chaplain left without saying anything to us. It seems clear he's Muslim and Arab. He's not confined to bed. There's no reason to keep him in the hospital; his wounds need only outpatient care."

Colonel Walker picked up the discussion: "Our interrogation's in English because he says that's the language he speaks and understands best. The interpreter said he spoke simple Arabic that sounds like a Yemeni dialect. He's bright, confused, and frightened; not belligerent or demanding, but expresses himself forcefully.

"He started with questions and comments about where he was, why he's being detained, he's American, etc. We said he's outside the U.S. so U.S. law and rights don't apply, but we're committed to standards of humane treatment. We informed him in no uncertain terms that he's not detained, he entered the base voluntarily and we have five witnesses that he was begging to enter the base. We accepted him on humanitarian grounds and he's free to return to Cuba any time he wishes. He cringed at that thought, almost in panic.

"We said we could return him to the U.S. if we can prove he's American, but we wouldn't just turn him loose to do as he pleases. He'd be screened by border patrol just like anyone entering the country. He hesitated and said Arabs have no rights in the U.S. so why'd he want to go there.

"We decided to get really rough and told him he'd better give information about who he is and details to prove his identity, or else we'd have no choice but to return him to Cuba. We gave another big push saying he might like to have some more good times with the man who left semen inside of him. This got the strongest reaction yet. He said forcefully: 'What do you think I am some f-ing gay fag?'

"When we repeated we'd send him back to Cuba if he didn't give us details, he finally gave his name, date of birth, place of birth in New York, parents' names, etc. His parents are immigrants from Yemen, confirming the Yemeni dialect. He and the other guy, Boudi, worked for a man who distributes Middle Eastern products, cigarettes, and other things to Arab-owned gasoline stations and small shops up and down the Appalachian Mountain area.

"When we tried to get information about the supposed abduction to Mexico, he said the abductors told them they'd be punished if they got back to the U.S. for being Arab terrorists, just like Moussaoui. Why should he give more information when Arabs have no rights in the U.S. and he's going to be treated the same way if he gives information or not? He looked and acted like he was exhausted. The only thing I can add is that the story of cigarette distribution really smells. At our bases in the states, we have to worry about tax-free cigarettes and liquor being smuggled off the base for resale. They may not be getting tax-free cigarettes on bases, but it's easy to get them in low tax states like North Carolina. Lackawanna's on the Canadian border. This isn't our concern, but we can inform the FBI. Let's hear what the DIA has."

"Our primary interest was the Yemen connection," Commander Goldberg said. "We have a fair number of Yemenis here and we're concerned these two were sent to contact them. As you likely know, there were the so-called Lackawanna Six, naturalized citizens who were accused of connections with al Qaeda. That doesn't explain the other two. A Saudi Arabian may be sent to contact detainees, but a Syrian doctor doesn't fit. It's a bizarre and convoluted way to get them here, involving cooperation of the Mexican government, if we're to believe what we're told.

"We pushed him on Yemen connections. He said his family and others fled Yemen before he was born because of tribal conflicts. We said he might be a dual citizen if his parents registered his birth with the Yemeni Embassy, and we could send him there. He can't imagine his parents would've bothered to register his birth as a Yemeni because they're glad to be away from there. We got the name of a home village. We have resources in Yemen so we can follow through. So far, we don't see any connection with the Lackawanna Six. Still we want to keep him and the other guy away from any contact with Yemenis here and separated from each other. Let's hear from Rhonda."

"I talked to Bob myself," Rhonda Philips began. "He's polite and respectful, although he did express himself forcefully. He must've been brought up to respect older women. I especially wanted to follow through on his comments about rights of Americans. I really pushed a button there. He gave a long discourse on the U.S. Constitution, the Bill of Rights, U.S. history, a land of immigrants, the Statue of Liberty, and how none of this means anything to Arabs trapped in the U.S. after nine-eleven. No access to higher education, no jobs, constant questioning because of their names and because they look Arab. Blacks get favored treatment and are arrogant about it. Illegal Central Americans get jobs, but Arabs work as hard.

"He's anti-Bush, anti-Clinton—Hillary that is—anti-Kerry, anti- some others, because of their blind support of Israel due to Jewish influence in the U.S. while there are just as many Arabs in the U.S. as Jews. I could go on and on. The point is not his opinions, but he's obviously well educated in American history, civics, and politics, and a keen observer of current events. It's almost certain he attended schools in the U.S. for most if not all his life, which would be the case if he were born in New York.

"His claim of U.S. citizenship is likely valid, although we need proof. The big inconsistency is he's been intimidated by his alleged Arab captors over the Moussaoui case. Someone as well informed as he is should recognize Moussaoui's case is different. Maybe the most recent details didn't come out soon enough for him to know them.

"He admitted it was the week before Easter when they went to New York City to pick up Ali, but he doesn't have a good sense of when they were abducted, taken to Mexico, and brought to Cuba. He said one day blended into the next, and they were unconscious a couple of days.

"We could have some potentially serious political problems if he and his cousin are U.S. citizens, which seems likely. Members of Congress from New York are not likely to make a big fuss about Arabs being detained, even if they are U.S. citizens; as he said, they're strongly influenced by the Jewish vote. Even if New York politicians wouldn't be upset, there're Arab-American politicians, including some in Congress, who could raise a big fuss. Some would be delighted to make certain New York members of Congress appear to be uncaring about their constituents.

"It's essential we keep the appearance that they are not detained and are here for humanitarian reasons. If you're trying to keep him separate from the others—and it's certainly a good idea—maybe take him to the base library and make him spend the day there. I can leave him the books I brought to read on the airplane, maybe as a reward for further cooperation and information."

While Rhonda got two books out of her ample bag, Admiral Crenshaw said: "Thank you; this **is** complex. You can check into the possibility of the library, Jeremy. This's really dragging out, but good we're getting all the details. Another short break before hopefully the last one."

Chapter 25

Friday, May 5, 2006
Guantanamo Bay, Cuba

"Admiral Crenshaw said: "Dr. Fisher."

"The final one's Abdullah; Boudi's a common nickname," Dr. Fisher began. "He causes no problems. He's restless; seems athletic and wants exercise. Again, negative test results, semen in the rectum, rectum healing, and more HIV tests needed. His wounds are healing. We could monitor him on an outpatient basis like the others."

Colonel Walker picked up the discussion: "He's not as bright as Bob; not stupid by any means, but more of a jock who'd rather be playing sports than reading. He spends his time watching sports on television. He and Bob have different last names, but're cousins. We asked the chaplain to visit with the same results as for Bob. We got full name, birth place, parents' names, etc.

"I pushed him about the car and smuggling. I grew up in South Carolina and know New York plates stick out, except on major highways. He said they use cars with New York plates because the same cars to go to Canada and other state's plates would stick out when they show ID crossing the border. They're careful about obeying traffic laws, sticking to major highways that have traffic to and from New York, and not parking where they'd attract attention.

"He says it was just before Easter, but a work day, when they were abducted in Ohio. He seemed to realize that he shouldn't have said Ohio;

this was the first clue where it happened. Ohio doesn't make sense if their objective was to smuggle Ali into Canada because Lackawanna's right on the Canadian border. He said they were released in Mexico after Easter because Easter decorations were being taken down; it was a holiday, but no one was going to church and some shops were open. They likely were abducted on Good Friday and released the Monday after. We pressed for more details and got more information for the FBI and DIA.

"We need to keep Boudi and Bob apart so they don't compare stories and make up new ones. It's probably best to keep all four separated, but the hospital's just so big and all but Adnan're free to walk about."

Commander Goldberg added: "Just now, it popped into my mind that there're military activities in Ohio, especially Wright-Patterson AFB, that could be of interest to al Qaeda for lots of reasons. Rhonda?"

"I decided to talk to Boudi, more as a formality, but didn't get much new," she began. "He, too, was polite and respectful, but not so forceful in his opinions. This is a big base, Admiral; surely you have several recreational facilities. Maybe have a guard take him to a different one each day until he finds one he likes. No basketball with the detainees, but a workout that doesn't interfere with his healing."

Admiral Crenshaw interrupted. "Can you look into that one also, Jeremy?"

"The final major concern is Mexico," she continued. "Boudi gave us more specific information there. More important, their stories are all very consistent and so bizarre they must be true. It's beyond credibility that three persons could independently come up with the same fantastic story. We don't have much interaction with Mexican intelligence officials because there's not much interaction on defense issues. Mexico does have reasonably well developed police and intelligence activities at the national level, although they seem to break down where drug trafficking is concerned. It wouldn't be surprising that Mexican officials picked up on the fact they're Arabs and wanted to get rid of them as quickly as possible. Why send them to Cuba is a question that needs thought and analysis, and we'd better turn that over to the CIA. Mexico has good relations with about every country, but maybe Cuba's the only one which Mexico had enough leverage over to convince it to take these four."

"Why can't we just send them back to Mexico, then?" Admiral Crenshaw interrupted.

"First, we don't have proof that they were in Mexico, only their comments and our speculation," she replied. "Also, if Cuba accepted them willingly, even if under pressure, they'd feel no obligation to take them back at our request. More importantly, Mexico's in the middle of a heated presidential election campaign and that's probably why they wanted to get rid of them quickly.

"Our relations with Mexico right now are a bit touchy. I can't imagine we'd want to do anything that could even remotely affect relations at the moment. Ultimately, that's a decision for the CIA. There's a major seminar and workshop on Tuesday at CIA for all intelligence agencies involved with terrorism, especially Arab terrorism. I'll be there.

"Thank you very much for your hospitality, Admiral," she concluded. "I have a flight to catch that's being held for me. Rest assured we understand your eagerness to have these four out of here as soon as possible."

"Thank all of you for coming. It's been a long afternoon. If you'd like, we can all go to the Officer's club," Admiral Crenshaw said as he closed the meeting.

Chapter 26

Saturday, May 6, 2006
Baghdad International Airport, Iraq

Major Armstrong stopped in Colonel Jones's office in late morning on his way out, saluting and saying: "Sorry to keep disturbing your weekends."

"No problem," Colonel Jones replied. "Weekends aren't much different than other days. Please sit; We're becoming old friends now. Coffee?"

"Thanks," Major Armstrong said as he sat.

Colonel Jones called, Carrie, an Army private in her early 20s, to order coffee, giving her enough money to get something for herself and the other assistant, Jimmy, a corporal only slightly older.

He asked: "How was your visit today? Productive?"

"Very," Major Armstrong replied. "We had uncovered information about Abed and wanted to see if we could use it to get more out of him. I also brought medical journals for Viktor. We went back and forth between the two. When subjects know that, they sometimes open up more."

"I was waiting to tell you that Corporal Myers arrived at a hospital in the States where they'll do facial repair," Colonel Jones said. "They sent word back that Viktor did a brilliant job and his face will be completely restorable. He's doing more things when prisoners come in with bad injuries and helps with general emergency care too. Both he and our doctor seem pleased with the situation. What about Abed?"

THREE KISSES

Major Armstrong began: "He comes from a middle class Sunni family; his parents were nominal members of the Ba'ath party. One of his uncles was active in the party and seemingly well off financially.

"The parents had a shop and other businesses and were doing well under the old regime, but are struggling now. They're living mostly off a fairly large dowry his wife's family paid when their daughter married because she was getting too old by their standards and apparently other men refused to marry her because of her personality, no matter how much they were paid. The uncle arranged the hospital administrator job as part of the deal so the wife wouldn't be seen marrying below her status.

"When the old regime fell, Abed, his wife, and child fled. The uncle went underground as many former Ba'athists did and seems to have enough to live comfortably. He recently re-surfaced and was elected to the parliament.

"The wife's family doesn't seem concerned about their daughter and grandson; apparently they're getting information from the Iraqi Ba'ath community in Syria. Maybe they're providing financial support through this network. They definitely don't want their daughter and grandson back with the sectarian violence now.

"None of them seems to know Abed is here; no one seems to care other than his parents. Because of the uncle's being in parliament, we'll have to keep him here until we see how things settle. It wouldn't be a wise idea to have a parliamentarian's relative in Abou Ghraib.

"We confronted him with this information and offered to get word to his parents. He told us why he fled Syria. He suspected he'd have been eliminated sooner or later and the project taken over by the Moukhabarat, so he decided to flee quickly. He didn't have proper travel documents, all neighboring countries would be hostile, so his only choice was return to Iraq."

After Carrie brought coffee, Major Armstrong continued: "It's almost certain this is an al Qaeda project, or al Qaeda's financing it; Syria doesn't have resources for anything like this on its own. Abed probably fell in with al Qaeda after fleeing Iraq, so they put him in charge, nominally.

They likely viewed him as loyal, stupid, and compliant enough to be a nominal figurehead.

"Syrians wouldn't allow al Qaeda complete control, so they made the Moukhabarat guy, Jihad, his assistant doing the work. We used what limited resources we have to find out about Jihad. He seems to have fallen off the Earth."

"What's the mistake the Russian made?" Colonel Jones asked. "It's none of my business, but I'm curious."

"That's interesting; bizarre," Major Armstrong began. "Abed was so embarrassed and ashamed I wish I could've videotaped his comments for you. I can't duplicate his words much less body language. It's amazing how many hang-ups grown Arab men have, especially stupid religious ones.

"He kept referring to the 'thing between the legs', not using the Arabic word for penis, much less slang, and 'a piece of skin that doesn't belong there' instead of 'foreskin'. According to him, the person duplicated is a filthy disgrace of an Arab who's infidel and still has this skin. He went on a tirade about the great father of all Arabs, Ibrahim, who started to sacrifice his son Ishmael to Allah, but Allah made him stop, and decreed all males must be circumcised as a symbol of faithfulness; my words; I'll spare you the tortured way he described it. Ishmael's offspring are Arabs, and all true sons of Allah must be circumcised to show their faithfulness. I'm not much of a church-goer. I vaguely recall a story about Abraham starting to sacrifice his son Isaac; God stopped him and showed him circumcision as a sign to show faith, and the descendants are Jews."

"Actually, Abraham had two sons, Ishmael and Isaac, from different mothers," Colonel Jones interjected. "God told Abraham to circumcise all his household, including both sons, and all of their descendants must be circumcised. Ishmael's mother and he were banished when Ishmael was a small boy, and almost died of hunger and thirst. God rescued them because Ishmael was to become the father of a great people, who indeed are the Arabs. Isaac also was the father of a great people, the Jews. Sorry, I don't mean to be giving you a bible lesson, but I'm a deacon in the church and know the story well. If you want to know more, I'll tell you, but maybe we should leave it at that now. How'd they find out about the guy being duplicated in the U.S.?"

Major Armstrong continued: "Jihad apparently called the double's handlers. They must've discovered his intimate details. Abed emphasized, without our asking, that they had never, nor would they ever go so far as to examine Ali's private parts, but because he was a good loyal follower of Allah, he must be clean before Allah like all Muslims."

"Weird," Colonel Jones responded, "but why was the Russian doctor blamed?"

Major Armstrong replied: "They needed to blame someone; certainly they wouldn't blame themselves. The Iraqi prisoner says the Russian doctor should've anticipated this situation and done something, or at least informed them before Ali went to the U.S., not after he got there.

"Viktor opened up when we confronted him. He says he anticipated the situation, of course; any one in his place would. Because Arabs have so many hang-ups about their sex organs, he couldn't approach the topic directly. Instead, he went about it indirectly and made sure the girlfriend of the person being duplicated would be away. They even had to move the date of Ali's travel forward because his girlfriend would be away for several days. They also made sure he had a bad cold so he couldn't go to public showers at a gym or swimming pool. He says he suddenly realized he hadn't taken the precaution to tell Ali not to urinate in an open place; he told Jihad they should get word to Ali to urinate in a stall."

"Who'd have ever thought of such a thing?" Colonel Jones commented. "I wouldn't, and I'm not Arab with these hang-ups. How would they know these things about a girlfriend being gone and his getting a cold? Had al Qaeda infiltrated the organization? If so, why go to this elaborate scheme to get a double there?"

"There're lots of unanswered questions," Major Armstrong replied; "there must've been someone feeding information, providing uniforms, face molds, and the like. The part about the person duplicated being an infidel of an Arab strongly indicates he's Christian, at least nominally. As you know from your Lieutenant Gorani, Arab Christians have been fleeing for several years; by far the largest number in the U.S. is Lebanese."

DISCOVERIES • CHAPTER 26

"Yes, almost everyone knows about Danny Thomas and some others," Colonel Jones added.

"Military records don't show a person's ethnicity," Major Armstrong continued, "so unless the official photograph shows a clue, like a person's being black or Asian, we don't have anything to go on; Lebanese wouldn't stick out in photographs. Names, as you know from Lieutenant Gorani, are unreliable, and who'd have thought Danny Thomas is his actual Lebanese name, although it's pronounced differently in Arabic. Records don't show details about penises either. We can't search to locate the guy who was duplicated. If we get clues from another place, we can use this as a means to confirm a likely identity."

"It sounds like progress," Colonel Jones stated. "So we keep Abed as our guest for a while. So far as prisoners go, he's a model. He reads the Koran. Muslim chaplains stop to visit often. Who knows what they might be cooking up, but of course we don't listen. It's always possible a chaplain can take information outside and bring it back. Anything else?"

"We asked Viktor where in the U.S.," Major Armstrong added. "He said they used a name that sounded like Daytona. That didn't make sense. There're no Army installations in that part of Florida. We pushed the Iraqi prisoner on this point. We finally got him to say Dayton, which makes more sense. There's a big Air Force base, Wright-Patterson, there and smaller Army installations around. There'd likely be Army personnel at Wright-Patterson as big and diverse as it is.

"Oh, Viktor keeps asking, almost begging us for more information about Ali. He's really worried, much more so than a doctor-patient relationship would suggest. He must've mentally and emotionally adopted this Ali as his son."

"Gee, what else?" Colonel Jones asked.

"You mean that's not enough?" Major Armstrong smiled chuckling. "We'll keep you informed if we need to come back. We now have a lot for Washington to digest. Take care and see you again. Thanks for the coffee."

Chapter 27

Tuesday, May 9, 2006
Langley, Virginia, USA

A few minutes past noon, analysts from the U.S. government's intelligence agencies filed through a CIA headquarters' cafeteria line during lunch break at a workshop on terrorism. Three of the men, who happened to be in line together, sat at the same table to eat; they were acquainted, but not close colleagues.

An FBI analyst said: "This terrorism stuff's getting weird. You're not going to believe what we got from the NSA last week. A caller from Syria was asking about some guy's dick, how big it was, whether it was circumcised, and the guy in the U.S. didn't know what circumcision is. He called back, said it was big and uncircumcised. The weirdest thing is the telephones in the U.S. were mailed to FBI headquarters with a note saying they're a gift for U.S. intelligence from terrorists who got away."

"What's that again?" asked a DIA analyst. After a brief repeat, he said: "This's too much of a coincidence. We've got a case from Iraq about two weirdoes who crossed the border from Syria into Iraq, asked to be locked up in our prison, and then told a story of having made a double of someone in the U.S. Army to send to the U.S. The project collapsed because they forgot to check the dick of the guy being doubled; it was big and uncircumcised."

"This is getting weirder by the minute," the third person, A CIA analyst, exclaimed. "I'm ready for early retirement, an appointment with the shrink, or both. We were just called in to collaborate on a DIA case from Guantanamo where four guys were chased onto the base from Cuba; one of them is a Syrian doctor who apparently had surgery to alter his appearance to look like someone in the U.S. He got caught because his dick was different from the guy who was duplicated. I think FBI was brought into the case too."

"This is definitely too much to be just a coincidence," the FBI analyst exclaimed. "This may be just the connection we need to get the ball rolling faster.

"There's Rhonda over there," the DIA analyst said. "She's the one pushing this, it seems. Let's go get her."

After the workshop, Rhonda Philips and the three analysts met briefly. She was dressed smartly and professionally in a short-sleeved dusky rose summer linen-cotton blend dress wearing a scarf with black and pale silver-gray patterns, a large pale silver gray designer leather bag, and matching medium-height block-heel shoes.

She said: "This's a lucky break. It likely would've taken weeks to put this all together otherwise. I've got it set up: we meet on Thursday afternoon at 2:00 at the FBI Operations Technology Center at Quantico."

Chapter 28

Thursday, May 11, 2006
Quantico, Virginia, USA

Promptly at 2 p.m., Roosevelt 'Rosie' Jordan, Chief of Operations of the FBI Operations Technology Center, opened a meeting of an ad hoc task force to investigate the apparent infiltration of an al Qaeda operative into the U.S. and the subsequent appearance of him and his handlers at Guantanamo Naval Base. He was a large, tall man with tightly curled black hair with tiny flecks of gray reflecting his age in the mid-50s; his dark skin revealed his African-American roots. Deep brown eyes were sparkling and kindly, belying his no-nonsense approach. He wore the FBI 'uniform' of a starched well-fitting white shirt and navy blue tie that went well with the well-made gray suit.

Others from the DIA and CIA sat around the table in shirt sleeves with suit jackets on the backs of their chairs, non-descript ties, solid colored skirts with plain blouses or summer dresses. Younger FBI agents sat away from the table wearing the FBI 'uniform' of gray suit pants, white shirts, and conservative ties, or similar skirts and blouses.

He began: "Welcome. I'm opening the meeting only because we're at our location and hosts, so to speak. Rhonda suggests the FBI take the lead role because our agency and other Homeland Security agencies like INS seem more directly involved. I can speak for my boss that we're willing to take charge if that's the collective decision. Like Rhonda, we feel this's a serious matter that needs to be resolved quickly as possible; we don't want jurisdictional issues in the way. We're willing to turn the lead over to whomever wants it, and we're willing to revisit the issue any time. What're your thoughts, Ralph?"

Rafael 'Ralph' D'Angelo, lead CIA representative on the project, was a high-level executive, a deputy undersecretary in the CIA director's office. He was in his mid-50s, average height with a slightly stocky build. He wore a navy blue pin-stripe suit consistent with his executive status, a white shirt, and navy blue tie with red stripes. He had 'gold'-rimmed glasses with rectangular lenses. His suit coat was on the back of his chair.

He replied: "We're pleased to have you take the lead. As you know, we have **just** gotten a new CIA director as of today. He can't give formal assent because he's not been informed of this issue, much less had an opportunity to make a decision. If we can get things resolved quickly enough, we may just inform him after the fact. Please go ahead, Rosie."

Rosie Jordan asked: "Do any of you have anything that's come up before we begin? Our agents are here to brief you on what the FBI's discovered so far."

Rhonda Philips and Ralph D'Angelo said 'no'. She was wearing a linen-cotton blend salmon short-sleeved summer dress, a black silk scarf with tan highlights, a large tan leather designer bag, and matching shoes with block heels.

Rosie Jordan said: "Let's look at the Texas situation first. It's very much of interest to us, but may not have much bearing on the case at hand. Jamie."

He began: "This's based on our data banks which are connected to all state and most local data banks; I'm paraphrasing what our Dallas field office told us. As suspected, for the person you call Adnan, there're no birth records in Texas or any other state for Edgardo Rodriguez with those parents' names and on the date given or any other date. Rodriguez is such a common name it'd be like looking for the proverbial needle in a haystack. Unless we have strong reason to do so, we won't check further.

"There were entries in law enforcement data banks for persons with that name, but none that match this person. Edgardo's a common name too. Computer-based data banks that can be easily searched don't go back all that far. There're no matches on the finger prints. Again, unless there's a strong reason, we're not going to search more.

"We found a Texas driver's license with an address in Mesquite, Texas, a Dallas suburb. When a driver's license was issued to him, requirements for proof of identity were limited in most states and used mostly for proof of age; if a person was obviously old enough to legally drive, there was no scrutiny. Here's his picture. We also located a 1995 Toyota Corolla registered in Texas in his name.

"The Dallas field office sent an agent to contact the Mesquite police. It's a working-class suburb with a relatively high Hispanic population, most of whom would be citizens, often for a few generations. There'd also be green-card holders and some illegals, but this isn't a place we'd look for significant illegal activity. They're basically law-abiding residents who work hard.

"The Mesquite police force is typical: under-funded with limited resources, reasonably well trained and professional, doing the best they can under the circumstances. We're always careful when dealing with local police if there's a possible terrorist issue because we don't want to alarm them. We implied, but didn't lie, that the person and car might be involved in illegal immigration.

"Mesquite police, at our request, contacted the rental office of the apartment complex for the address on the driver's license and automobile registration, making vague comments about a disturbance complaint, but not directly lying. The office manager was surprised because they'd received no complaints. There're too many apartments and residents for her to know them personally.

"The apartment's rented to three men, all with Hispanic names, who've all signed the lease as policy requires. Rent has been paid regularly. The police asked if all three were still living there and copied down the names which included Edgardo Rodriguez. The manager said no one informed them of any change and they're required to be notified if anyone moves out or a new person moves in. The police officer thanked her,

DISCOVERIES • CHAPTER 28

saying maybe they'd been given the wrong apartment number, but she'd check with neighbors.

"As the officer walked towards the apartment, she noticed a parked car that fit the description and matched the license plates of the one we found in the data base. When the FO was notified, we requested a stake out. The police weren't pleased to have resources used like this, but went along; the officer remained until an agent from the field office arrived. Fortunately, our agent and the local police didn't have to wait long; in early evening, a young man drove the car out of the parking lot. Once they were on a public street, the police pulled the car over.

"Our agent pretended to be a plain-clothes police officer, but didn't take an active role, just listening. The driver had a driver's license matching a name of one of tenants. The police officer said they'd received information the car might be stolen, carefully avoiding 'reported stolen'. The driver was visibly nervous, spoke good English but with an accent that didn't seem Hispanic, and didn't respond when the police officer addressed him in Spanish.

"To cut through dialogue, he said the car belonged to Eddie who must've left it for them to use. The three of them work construction, sometimes go out of town for weeks at a time, and don't always notify each other where they're going and for how long. Eddie had taken his car to work some place up north, New York he thinks. One day about three weeks ago when he came home from work, he saw Eddie's car parked outside the apartment, but Eddie wasn't around. They assumed he left the car and went immediately to another job. They have keys to each others' cars, so he drives Eddie's car from time to time to keep it running.

"He also said a package came in the mail addressed to Eddie with his wallet and a note saying it'd been found in the DFW airport. The sender took money for postage, but everything else was inside including a small amount of money. They assumed Eddie'd gotten a job that he had to fly to quickly, and somehow lost the wallet at the airport.

"The police officer asked him to park the car and get Eddie's wallet to show them. When he returned with the wallet, the police officer asked if they could take it to check things out further, and suggested the car be left parked until the police could check further.

"The young man was so nervous he almost dropped the wallet and ran back to the apartment. The police officer gave the money back saying there'd be no need for the money.

"Mesquite police are well trained in police procedure and this particular officer was very alert and quick-thinking. They have the wallet in the FO and will check it for finger prints and other forensics, but we don't expect anything useful; the FO gave it low priority.

"The driver's license looks legitimate. There's a social security card that might be fake; as a minimum it was obtained fraudulently with his name. We'll inform the Social Security Administration.

"The most unusual thing was a couple days later. The FO asked Mesquite police to patrol the apartment complex, look for unusual activity, and for the man we met. They spotted him and another young man loading belongings into a pick-up truck, seemingly moving out, leaving the Toyota behind. The police called for an unmarked unit to follow. They apparently moved into a similar apartment complex in Grand Prairie, a suburb on the other side of Dallas.

"After a few days, Mesquite police can take the car as abandoned and find a valid reason to turn it over for a forensic examination. If they come up with anything from forensic tests, you'll be informed. This has all the earmarks of a sleeper cell of al Qaeda; we'll be watching it closely."

Rhonda Philips began immediately: "We might use that photograph for identification of the obviously Arab guy at Guantanamo. His face is so badly injured, we might not get a direct comparison, but we have experts who can measure eye and nose placement, forehead dimensions, and things like that. Once bandages are off, we might get pictures to compare. The FBI and CIA may have better facilities to analyze faces; if you want to, go ahead and start."

"Does anyone else have anything to add before we go to the New York side of the case?" Rosie Jordan asked.

After a moment of silence, he said: "A short break and Debbie will begin."

Chapter 29

Thursday, May 11, 2006
Quantico, Virginia, USA

Debbie began: "We readily found birth records in New York State matching dates and parents' names for Bob and Boudi. There're driver's licenses with their names and addresses in Lackawanna, New York; here're pictures. There're no vehicles registered in their names. No criminal records.

"We found a late model BMW very recently registered to Mohammad Fadel in Lackawanna, New York; it's likely the same one because late model BMWs would be unusual in a place like Lackawanna. We made a routine check of data banks around the country. Police in Fort Lauderdale, Florida, impounded a car with that exact description. Our Miami FO checked further.

"The car'd been parked at least a week. At first it didn't cause concern because New York license plates are common in South Florida. After a while, they were suspicious because it wasn't in an area where winter snow birds stay. They suspected drug dealers, but DEA didn't have anything and no probable cause for impoundment. There were no reports of stolen vehicles matching the description. They did a routine license plate check and contacted New York State. Finally, they contacted the registered owner, Mohammad Fadel, who seemed both surprised and relieved, but nervous on the phone.

"He said two employees took off with the car over three weeks ago and he didn't hear from them since the Friday before Easter. He's really worried and trying to locate them. When Fort Lauderdale police asked why he hadn't reported missing persons or stolen cars to the police, he said the boys' parents were afraid of police; they're simple immigrants who distrust all police. They're good boys and faithful participants in the mosque, so they wouldn't do anything bad. He said he's a simple imam who runs small businesses on the side.

"Even though this sounded suspicious, it didn't involve the Fort Lauderdale police. They said he must send someone to pick up the car. He agreed, but so far hasn't contacted them. He did say it'd take a while to find someone because he's short-handed due to the two guys' disappearance.

"They did limited forensics tests in the impoundment yard which they offered to share with us. We would've liked to have a much more thorough forensics test, but we don't have a good reason for them to turn the car over to us. Fort Lauderdale police offered to inform us if anyone comes to pick it up. We're exploring possible cigarette smuggling to see if that'd give us probable cause, but Florida's not a place cigarette smugglers normally go.

"We asked the Buffalo field office to go to Lackawanna, a suburb of Buffalo. It's a grimy old steel mill town. Many groups of immigrants have come and gone; most recently, Yemenis, Central Americans, and some Asians. It's not a crime-ridden ghetto, but it's not the law-abiding suburb like Mesquite, Texas. Law enforcement activity, other than traffic, would mostly be petty crime and violence. People who live there come mostly from places where police are corrupt and abusive, so they don't trust them. The comment of the imam to Fort Lauderdale police is consistent.

"The FO contacted New York State police and local police in Lackawanna. We discovered Mohammad Fadel runs a coffee and tea shop where local Yemenis socialize and a general purpose convenience store. There's no indication of cigarette smuggling, but it'd likely be hidden. He's also imam for a store-front mosque.

"The Buffalo FO also checked with the border patrol. Lackawanna is on Lake Erie no more than 10 miles from the nearest bridge to Canada.

DISCOVERIES • CHAPTER 29

There're numerous entries of the two men re-entering the U.S. from Canada and a note in the computer that they're locals coming back from visiting friends and family in Canada. The FO talked to border patrol about suspicions over persons with Arabic names. Yes, there're suspicions, but ethnic profiling's strictly forbidden"

"Those are definitely the two I talked to at Guantanamo even if they do have facial injuries," Rhonda Philips said.

"Anyone else?" Rosie Jordan asked. "Ralph?"

"Right now we're not seeing anything of immediate interest to the CIA," Ralph D'Angelo answered. "There might be something involving Canada indirectly. We're more interested in Syria and possibly Mexico."

"The next from us is cell phones and calls," Rosie Jordan said. Allen."

"Three cell phones arrived by mail on April 27 to headquarters in DC with a note that these phones belonged to terrorists who we didn't catch," he began. "We checked for fingerprints, but they were too faint for identification. We might compare them with prints from other sources.

"Two of the phones were registered to Ibrahim al Asadi and Abdullah Zakawi, who we now know as Bob and Boudi. The third was registered to Edgardo Rodriguez, who's Adnan. We recharged them and called our land-line numbers to get a trace. Our calls alerted the NSA that was monitoring the numbers. When NSA realized the calls were going to a sensitive government office, they made transcripts of all calls and notified us and you at the CIA.

Allen reviewed the sequences of calls monitored by the NSA, then said: "So far we don't have proof all these Alis are the same; it's a very common name."

A DIA analyst quickly stated: "Our man in Iraq thinks we can get more information out of the Russian doctor if we give him information on Ali's wellbeing. Apparently he has a strong fatherly-type attachment and is worried. Incidentally, the Russian doctor we have in custody is Viktor Ilarionov, likely the Viktor on the phone conversations. The person identified as Jihad is no doubt Jihad Noussayri, the person identified as being Syrian Moukhabarat who ran the operation. Our resources in Syria weren't able to locate anything about him; he just disappeared."

Allen continued: "The one referred to as 'that guy' is almost certainly the U.S. Army officer who's been doubled. He must've been kept at another location, the place where Adnan was located. At best he was in a position that he could look at his private parts reluctantly. At worst he was dead and Adnan could look at his body and that's the reason he was reluctant. An Army officer who's murdered or missing would surely be detected by now.

"Our Cincinnati FO found the usual number of unidentified bodies, but none that fit the description of Ali or a double. Likewise, local police have no reports of missing persons fitting this description. We think he must still be alive and DIA's checking further."

A DIA analyst quickly said: "We found no reports of Army officers AWOL from anywhere in Ohio. We're also checking leave records and so far haven't found anyone close to that description who's on leave for two weeks or more. We can only assume the officer doubled is on duty and has been silenced or unaware of what went on."

The CIA analyst continued: "We had strong indications during the cold war era that Soviets made doubles of persons to infiltrate them. We suspect Israelis do also. We've heard nothing about this type of activity in several years, but a Russian doctor who claims to have made a double is consistent, and a frightening new chapter in al Qaeda's methods. Any infiltration would surely work for only a short time, but could be long enough, for example, to put a pilot on another airplane."

Rosie Jordan interrupted: "Let's see if there're any questions for Allen. If not, we can take a short break while our agents return to their duties. We can call them back if something comes up.

Chapter 30

Thursday, May 11, 2006
Quantico, Virginia, USA

After the short break, the CIA analyst continued: "Merely being identical in physical appearance isn't enough. Voice, mannerisms, and the like can quickly betray someone. It's consistent his girlfriend's away and he's sick so he can avoid close contact. This could be an experiment to see if they can get someone into the country and while they're at it get information. From their reaction, it's a failure. One of our Syria specialists has information that might be useful."

Before the Syria specialist could speak, a DIA analyst added quickly: "Wright-Patterson has lots of joint-service and DOD-level activities that would definitely be of interest to al Qaeda and many others. We're focusing attention there.

"He's apparently of Arab Christian ancestry, but there're thousands, maybe a couple million, of Arab-American Christians in this country. They've sometimes changed their names or have names so similar to American names they don't stick out: Danny Thomas the entertainer, Spencer Abraham the former senator from Michigan, John Sununu the current senator from New Hampshire, Congressman Nick Raha from West Virginia and Donna Shalala the immediate past Secretary of Education."

The CIA Syria expert then began: "Lattakia is Syria's major port. It has a population of about 500,000. Demographically it's different from inland cities. Muslims are likely a minority or at most a very small majority. Half or a little less of the population are Christian, going back some two millennia. About 10 per cent are Alawite, an ancient split off from Islam. Overall, Christians are about 10 per cent of the population of Syria and Alawites even less.

"Alawites dominate the ruling Ba'ath party, the Moukhabarat, the army, and the government. The current president, Bashar Assad and his father Hafaz Assad, the ruthless dictator, are Alawite. Hafaz Assad is a native of the Lattakia area and attended school there as a boy.

"In addition to being a major port, it also has a major university with a medical school and hospital. Lattakia's favored by the government in many ways, but also has an intense Moukhabarat presence. It doesn't attract international attention like the capital Damascus which is ten times larger and location of almost all government activity. it'd be consistent for al Qaeda to operate in Lattakia.

"A Syrian diplomat with the name Salman was assigned to the U.N. in the 1980s. The City of New York likely has records of family members who were with him, but in those days there were no computer data banks and a manual search takes time. They're working on it but we wonder how important it is to verify he was there as a child.

"Ali's father was transferred to the foreign ministry in Damascus in what appears to be a routine transfer. We checked records of the English-speaking International School in Damascus, even though they were manual, and he was a student there, a very good one at that.

"Apparently his father became out of favor and was put out to pasture. He says to Aleppo, the second largest city Syria. If it's important to go verify, we might be able to do so, but we're straining resources as it is. His father wasn't in very bad graces, or else Ali wouldn't go to medical school; university attendance in Syria is tightly controlled. The father may have merely outlived his usefulness."

"It's possible that Ali and his family could be persecuted or tortured if we repatriated him. Syrians can be ruthless with those they don't like or who fail."

DISCOVERIES • CHAPTER 30

"That's a lot to digest," Rosie Jordan stated after a short pause. "Does anyone else have anything before we go to the Mexico connection? I've asked Margarita to be here."

She began: "Apparently the persons abducted were rendered unconscious and taken to Mexico in a vehicle identified as an old dark blue jeep. 'Jeep' can refer to a specific brand, although it's unlikely they could've made a specific identification. More likely they're using 'jeep' as a generic term to refer to a large SUV. We have no information on who it may belong to, or what license plates it might have. They apparently were released on the day after Easter. We speculate that captors would return to the U.S. quickly in order not to attract attention from Mexican authorities.

"We also speculated they'd've used the closest, most direct border crossing from Ohio, which could be one of the three in or near Laredo, the one in Eagle Pass, or possibly Del Rio. There wouldn't have been time to go to other border crossings in Texas close to Coahuila. The Laredo crossings are nightmares because of long lines and intense scrutiny due to drug activity, so we focused attention on Eagle Pass.

"We asked the Border Patrol for records of entry into the U.S. from all border crossings in Texas for the week beginning April 17. We sorted them by location, by vehicle type, and by license plate. It's not quite like looking for a needle in haystack, but we have lots of possibilities. We also contacted field offices in San Antonio and El Paso to see if they had anything useful. So far, nothing."

"Thanks, Margarita," Rosie Jordan said. "Does anyone have any comments or questions before we go to the CIA?"

Ralph D'Angelo began: "Since nine-eleven, we've been curious about Mexico because terrorists might find it a useful place for sleeper cells, staging areas, or slipping into the U.S. The Mexican government shares our concern and doesn't want our war on terrorism to spill over. They have as good of control over their airports and land borders as we do except for the long border between Mexico and the U.S. They rely on us to control people coming into the U.S.

"The Mexican government has reasonably good intelligence capabilities and cooperates with us and other countries. If Mexican intelligence discovered four suspected Arab terrorists, it'd make sense to get rid of them as soon as possible, and turn them back over to us. That's where things get tricky. The last thing they'd want is publicity. Mexico's in the middle of a heated presidential race and relations between the U.S. and Mexico are tense over immigration.

"This maneuver to send them to Cuba and have the Cubans force them into Guantanamo seems like a stroke of brilliance. They can force us to take them back, but with virtually no risk of publicity or damage to bilateral relations. Actually, Mexico may have done us a big favor by making sure we got them back and become aware of the serious breach of our national security.

"The Cuban government likely owed the Mexican government favors. Cuba doesn't have many reliable friends and wouldn't likely reject such a demand. Nothing justifies rapes and beatings Cubans gave them, not even in the murkiest low levels of dirty tricks. We can speculate the Cuban government relied on low-level thugs who got out of control during drunken May Day celebrations. We could contact Mexican intelligence and internal security, but it's probably not wise to pursue that now."

"Thank you Ralph," Rosie Jordan said. "Does anyone have anything else? Rhonda?"

"Thanks, I'm taking notes furiously," she said. "I think we need to digest this before commenting further.

"Maybe we can review the next step for each of us. I'll send or take the photographs to Guantanamo for more positive identification. I'll get people there to take pictures of them without raising too much suspicion that'd cause them to clam up. Ali's photo could be especially useful to identify the person he was made to double.

"We might get voice recordings. We have to be careful because they wouldn't be legally admissible. If it turns out they're innocent and being kept only for humanitarian purposes, it'd cause political problems if it were discovered we're obtaining information surreptitiously. Anything else you can think of?"

DISCOVERIES • CHAPTER 30

"It'd be very helpful to know the Army officer's last name," a DIA analyst added. "Maybe the guys at Guantanamo or in Iraq can be persuaded to give a clue."

"We've identified quite a few other things that need to be done soon," Rosie Jordan commented. "The only thing I can add here is we need to get this resolved quickly as possible and with as minimum publicity as possible. Let's meet one week from today, same time and place. Thank you all for coming. I wish it could be a bit more pleasant."

Chapter 31

Saturday, May 13, 2006
Fredonia, New York, USA

As sun was setting, Omar Abu Deeb drove his ten-year-old battered and fading Honda Civic past the Fredonia and Dunkirk exit on the New York State Thruway, Interstate Highway 90, heading northeast. He was wearing sloppy blue jeans and a hoodie. Solid black plastic-rimmed glasses had one ear piece held on with black electrical tape. Wavy black hair, like that of many graduate students, badly needed a trim. He was five feet eight inches tall with a medium build, had intense brown eyes, and medium complexion.

He thought: *Fredonia; isn't that where a small state university wanted someone to teach religious studies? Got a teaching assistantship and didn't have to come to a place like this. Finish the PhD sooner then get a job I want. Allah knows I need money bad; get paid by both Mohammad and the FBI. Maybe Allah's way of arranging it.*

Some on committee'd have heart attacks, try to kick me out if they knew I'm working for the FBI to find out if really a terrorist cell or just smuggling. Either way, likely benefits al Qaeda, and I'd do anything, Allah willing, to stamp it out.

Mohammad's taken everything at face value. FBI created a story about a family in Yemen he knows who said I'm a poor Yemeni boy who needs a job.

DISCOVERIES • CHAPTER 31

How many friends'd abandon me if they knew? How could I support Bush who's invaded Iraq and supports Israel? He's stupid and incompetent and Rumsfeld and Cheney worse. How can Bush be compared to bin Laden and al Qaeda who desecrate Islam, the world's most beautiful religion. Bush's stupid and incompetent, but not evil.

Who's the Great Satan? Who ranks with Hitler as the most wanton destroyer of human life? Bin Laden's killed so many innocent people just because they were in his way, and in the name of Allah. My mother, father, and precious little sister and brother weren't enemies of Islam; they were the most faithful. Persons in the World Trade Center weren't enemies of Islam. People on the train in Madrid weren't enemies of Islam. Persons on bus and underground in London weren't enemies of Islam.

United States isn't anti-Islam. There's a mosque in almost every town; operate freely; easily found one in South Bend yesterday for Friday prayers.

U.S. has gone to war twice to support Muslims in Bosnia and Kosovo against Christian oppressors; Europeans twiddled their thumbs. U.S. supports Israel, but Bush's support's less than predecessors.

Israel's perceived as anti-Islam. Israel's anti-anyone it feels like bullying. Been as ruthless against Christian Palestinians as Muslim Palestinians, maybe more so. Teach that in Middle Eastern history courses like I just finished. How many people want to believe this? Not stupid evangelical Christians. Think Israel is great friend of Christians, but many wouldn't view Christians of Palestine as legitimate and they've been Christian since the days of Jesus Christ, for God's sake. Need to read their bibles.

Stupid Muslims don't read glorious Qur'an. Believe what any imam tells them. Probably like this Mohammad.

Stupid Bush, stupid evangelical Christians, stupid Islamic extremists. How much more stupidity can the world tolerate? Can't solve all the world's problems, but I can do my little bit here against al Qaeda.

How much further? Need to get out of this car. Can't believe how tired I am. Grading for the course I taught; exams in my own courses; drive 1,000 miles. Too old for this and I'm only 26. Here's the toll booth. Next exit then left.

Two hours later, Omar spoke in fluent, slightly accented English on a cell phone in a secluded place in Lackawanna: "This is Omar Abu Deeb; I was told to call."
pause
"Shouldn't talk long. They think I'm calling friends in Minneapolis to say I arrived safely," he continued.
pause
"So far he's buying everything, but I'm cautious," he added. "I'm not sure he's all that bright, but too early to tell.
pause
"I think mostly he wants me to take the place of the guys who disappeared," he continued. "He says first thing is go to Florida tomorrow or Monday to drive back the car they left there. Fort Lauderdale police are bugging him and charging high storage fees. I hope I can get out of it. I've just driven a thousand miles and don't want to drive more any time soon. Surely someone else can go and I can do that person's work; keep my eyes and ears open for you."
pause
"What!? You want me to get that car and turn it over to you?" he exclaimed. "The break you've been looking for?"
pause
"Leave it with your Jacksonville field office for a while," he repeated. "That'd give me a chance to rest."
pause
"I'm staying with a family in the same apartment building where one of the guy's family lives," he answered.
pause
"Before this Florida trip came up, I was going to SUNY Buffalo to arrange to use their library," he replied. "I really need to do research for my dissertation. Even if he has me followed, it wouldn't be easy for them to get into the library. I could call from inside there or maybe meet in person there."
pause
"I'll do my best to get to call tomorrow and let you know the Florida plans," he continued. "If you don't hear from me, that means they kept me

in their sight. Once I get on the way to Florida, I should be able to call you."
pause

"You have my cell phone number" he added. "If it's urgent, call and pretend it's inquiring about a grade."
pause

"I should go now," he said. "They might get suspicious."

Chapter 32

Tuesday, May 16, 2006
Jacksonville, Florida, USA

From his motel, Omar called on the room phone; after greetings he said: "I actually turned it over to them yesterday afternoon. Supposed to check later this morning. Am I supposed to do anything with the car after they finish?"
pause
"Oh, OK, just turn it over to Mohammad as though nothing happened," he repeated. "It's dirty from having sat so long. Maybe I should get it washed somewhere. I knew better than to wash it before the forensic tests."
pause
"Oh, they'll wash it," he said.
pause
"The first thing was make me get a haircut and put on better clothes," he answered. "Didn't want customers to see someone so sloppy. It's OK to wear nice jeans or chinos and a sport shirt, but not sloppy t-shirts or hoodies."
pause
"I haven't met customers yet," he replied. "He said he might want me to stop in North Carolina for some things, but backed off. He always has two people going, he says, and he can't get anyone free to go all the way to

DISCOVERIES • CHAPTER 32

Florida and back to North Carolina. I think he doesn't trust me alone and I'd be surprised if he did. He also said he wants the car back to use while other cars take passengers to Canada."

pause

"He has some business taking older people on day trips to Niagara Falls or visit friends and relatives in the Toronto area," he explained. "Didn't want to ask too many questions."

pause

"I was only there one full day before flying to Fort Lauderdale," he said. "Two things might be useful. Brahim's mother got a call about a week ago from someone who claimed to have contact with a chaplain at the Guantanamo Naval Base who said Brahim had been beaten, but was recovering in the hospital in American custody. The word going around is Brahim was captured, beaten, and tortured just because he's Arab. Everyone knows Brahim's a good boy, and wouldn't do anything bad. It's inflaming anti-American attitudes, but I don't know how far it's gone."

pause

"I haven't heard anything about Boudi," he continued. "They say Brahim and Boudi are always together and suspect he's there too and has been beaten."

pause

"The other thing's about the Saudi Arabian guy," he added. "Brahim's mother thinks he may have led her son into some kind of trouble that caused him to get captured. They didn't like and trust him from the beginning, just like the Saudis who try to move in and dominate them back in Yemen. I asked his name saying I had dealings with them in university back in Sana'a. They said it might be Adnan something al Wahab. In case you don't know, Wahab's a family name in Saudi Arabia associated with the Islamic fundamentalists who dominate religious activities there."

pause

"Once I get back to Lackawanna, I may not be able to phone undetected for a while," he said. "I'll call just before I get there to let you know I'm back. The very first chance, I'll go to the SUNY Buffalo library."

pause

"I still don't think Mohammad's very bright, but maybe bright enough he's a loose cannon," he added. "The sense I get is he's a petty village chief like in the villages back in Yemen. So far, I haven't seen any al Qaeda activity, but it's only been a couple of days."
pause

"OK, I'm going to get some breakfast," he concluded. "You can call me on the cell phone for at least the next two days if something comes up."
pause

"Bye."

Chapter 33

Thursday, May 18, 2006
Quantico, Virginia, USA

Rosie Jordan opened a meeting again promptly at 2 p.m. The same persons as at the previous week's meeting attended with two newcomers. Rhonda Philips wore a burgundy red linen pants suit closed at the neck, a burgundy and cream silk scarf, matching burgundy block-heeled shoes, and a large cream colored leather bag. Ruby ear studs complemented her outfit.

"Rhonda, would you like to introduce your colleagues?" Rosie Jordan asked.

"This is Colonel Sawyer of the DOD IG office and his assistant," Rhonda said. "Because of issues involving the IG, which is part of our agency, he asked to attend."

"We have lots of new information," Rosie Jordan began. "Let's start with the DIA."

A DIA analyst began: "We leaned on Viktor to get a name for the person doubled in the U.S. We offered him information about Ali if he told us. He said the family name is 'fair something' or 'far something'. He said he heard the given name once or maybe twice. It's a common-sounding name, but he didn't remember it. We kept pushing him, but it was obvious this's all we can get from him.

"Using that information, we really pressed Abed. He reluctantly gave the Arabic name فارس which you see on the screen. It's usually transliterated as 'Fares' but sometimes as 'Fahres' or 'Phares'. It's not rare in the U.S. because it's a common surname for Lebanese Christians and plenty have immigrated to the U.S. We searched military records using the three common spellings and found some, but not matching the person we're looking for.

There's a prominent pro-Syrian Lebanese politician with that name from the far north of Lebanon who very recently left the parliament because of allegations of corruption and collaboration with Syria. It's always possible the person we're looking for has connections to this politician. We must be careful because this's a common name in Lebanon, and such accusations would be like suspecting everyone in the U.S. named Cunningham just because Congressman Randy Cunningham resigned a few weeks ago after pleading guilty to accepting bribes.

Rhonda Philips began: "We sent photographs to Guantanamo and readily verified that Bob and Boudi are indeed the ones with New York driver's licenses. We took pictures of all four persons there from a distance and blew them up. The quality's not good, but you can see the match.

"Adnan's face is bandaged, but you can see similarities. Our face analysis specialists are working on it. We also gave it to the CIA. Have you gotten anything?"

"Our analysts think it's a positive match, but haven't had time for a conclusion," a CIA analyst said.

An FBI agent added: "The Buffalo FO has a resource in place who learned his family name, al Wahab. We turned it over to INS who found a record of a person with that name entering the U.S. in 2000 with a student visa, but who disappeared. We also gave the name to the CIA."

A CIA analyst immediately said: "As soon as we had a full name for Adnan, we turned it over to our agents in Riyadh. It's too soon to get anything from them."

The FBI analyst added: "Our resource said someone relayed a message to Bob's mother that he's being held at Guantanamo and was beaten. Word's going around that the government captured him, beat and tortured him, and holding him without access to anyone but a chaplain."

Rhonda Philips said: "That's what I was afraid of. Either we get this resolved quickly, or the story about beating them may be blown so big we'd never recover.

"This picture of Ali is the only one anyone seems to have. It matches physical descriptions we got from Iraq; I don't know if it'd do any good to show the picture to the two guys there; he's injured and it might upset Viktor if he has such an attachment.

"We forwarded the finger prints to all of you. We also recorded voices, although Adnan's not talkative. Our voice analysts have a positive match with Bob speaking English with Adnan on the phone, and a likely match for Adnan speaking English. We haven't recorded Bob speaking Arabic and probably can't. The CIA has the recordings and might get more. We don't have anything yet to match the voices we have for Boudi and Ali."

Rosie Jordan said: "What about the CIA?"

A CIA analyst began: "The only other thing is that telephone number in Lattakia; nothing. Our resources haven't found anything either. Jihad has just disappeared."

"We at FBI found out quite a bit," Rosie Jordan said. "If we have nothing else, let's go to Debbie."

She began: "In a major stroke of luck, our resource in Lackawanna was sent to get the car impounded by Fort Lauderdale police. He took it to the Jacksonville FO for a forensic examination. We have strong positive fingerprint matches for Ali, Bob, and Boudi, all of whom drove it fairly recently; Bob and Boudi were also back-seat passengers, so there were likely three in the car at one time.

"The most unusual matches were from data banks for Frank Reynolds, a major in the Marine Corps, and Francisco Mendoza, a practical nurse employed by the Veterans Administration nursing facility in Cincinnati. Both are finger-printed because of their jobs. We investigated Frank Reynolds and turned his name over to the DOD IG. We also began investigating Francisco Mendoza.

"We asked local police to check hotel registrations in the area where the car was found. Frank Reynolds and Francisco Mendoza were registered in the same room of a guest house on the night of April 22. Jamie has something."

He began: "Our Dallas FO checked the Toyota Corolla the police impounded and the wallet. The car has finger prints that match Adnan's; no surprise. It also has prints of Ali as a front and back seat passenger. There were also prints for Frank Reynolds and Francisco Mendoza as drivers and passengers. There were other prints that had no match; they may have been from the other men in that apartment.

"The wallet had prints from Adnan as expected, but also from Francisco Mendoza and Frank Reynolds and some others we couldn't identify. At that time, we didn't know what the Jacksonville FO had found.

"We too gave Frank Reynolds's name to DOD IG, but did some checking ourselves and started examining Francisco Mendoza. There's a Florida driver's license with a Daytona Beach address issued to Frank Reynolds who we believe is the same person; here's a photograph. Among other reasons, the name 'Frank' seems to be a given name, not a nickname for 'Francis' or 'Franklin'.

"We discovered Debbie and her group had found the same two men's finger prints in Florida, and we wondered how they traveled from Texas to Florida so soon. An agent in our Dallas FO used a special contact at American Airlines to discover a passenger named Frank Reynolds flew one way from DFW airport to Dayton by way of Nashville on the night of Saturday, April 16. We couldn't find anything about Francisco Mendoza. When it was apparent that we were looking at the same set of people, we let Debbie's group take over because they're involved more."

"Incidentally, the cell phones at our headquarters had finger prints that could match their three presumed owners, but also had prints that could be Frank Reynolds and Francisco Mendoza,"

"Now, perhaps, this is a good time for the DOD IG to tell us what it has," Rhonda Philips said almost interrupting.

"Maybe we should stand and take a short break," Rosie Jordan said.

Chapter 34

Thursday, May 18, 2006
Quantico, Virginia, USA

After a break, Rosie Jordan said: "Colonel Sawyer."

Colonel Sawyer, irritated at what he perceived as lack of deference to his position, began: "Major Reynolds is a career officer with 14 years' service currently assigned to a joint-service small weapons systems development activity at Wright-Patterson Air Force Base. He was involved in a scandal in Okinawa a few years ago," then described the circumstances. "Major Reynolds was transferred, and has been assigned to administrative posts since. Subsequent investigations by the IG and others didn't find any wrongdoing by Major Reynolds.

"He's a model officer in all respects, a third-generation Marine Corps officer from a distinguished old-line Florida family. He graduated from The Citadel, which has a long tradition of producing distinguished Marine Corps officers. Here's his official photograph.

"There's no record he signed out on leave at the time of his apparent flight from Dallas to Dayton. That's a technical violation of rules, but armed forces personnel do it all the time if they're away only for a weekend without missing duty. He did sign-out for a week's leave beginning Friday 21 April with a leave address in Daytona Beach, Florida, that's his official home of record and the address on the driver's license. We presume it's his parents' address.

"The office where he works has plenty of classified material al Qaeda and others would like to see. There've been no reports of missing classified material from that office or anywhere at Wright-Patterson. Major Reynolds has top-secret access to any material in the office and top-secret access is shared by two work colleagues, Navy Lieutenant Commander Jennifer Lewis and Army Captain Patrick Ferris. An Air Force civilian employee, Khadija Cavanaugh, has lower level access. So far we've not found anything to connect these other three to this case, but we've just begun our investigation."

"What was that name of the civilian?" a senior CIA analyst interrupted.

"Khadija Cavanaugh. Why?" Colonel Sawyer replied annoyed at the interruption.

"That sounds like the Arabic name خديجة that's given to Muslim girls," he said as he held up a sheet of paper on which he had written the name with a felt-tip marker in large Arabic script. "It is the name of a wife of the Prophet Mohammad. It's used any Islamic country."

"But she's Philippine," Colonel Sawyer stated.

"There's a Muslim minority in the Philippines on the southern islands," the CIA analyst stated. "Islamic terrorists are known to operate there. I'll turn this over to our Philippine specialists. They have good resources there and a good rapport with Philippine intelligence. What was the Army officer's name again please?"

"Patrick Ferris," Colonel Sawyer answered haughtily.

"That could very easily be فارس". The CIA agent held up another sheet on which he had written the name in large Arabic script. "Please put the Arabic script back on the screen you had earlier. As you can see, it's the same. Middle Easterners are not consistent in transliteration of Arabic names into western characters, and spelling isn't important to them, even among educated people. You can walk down the streets of Beirut and Amman where English is widely used and see signs on shops with different transliterations of the same Arabic name. When passports are issued by Middle Eastern countries, including Lebanon, names and other details are written in western characters; there's not a consistent pattern.

DISCOVERIES • CHAPTER 34

Brothers have been issued passports with different western spellings of their family name.

"If this Army officer's family is from Lebanon, it's possible they received a passport with the name spelled 'Ferris'. Maronite Christians frequently give their children French names, often saints. Patrick, while not common, isn't rare and fits the pattern. We know an Army officer with an Arab Christian background was likely duplicated. Do you have any pictures?"

"My assistant can get them quickly if I can get access to a secure internet connection," Colonel Sawyer replied.

"We can arrange that," Rosie Jordan said. "While she's away, we can continue with Debbie."

"An agent in the Cincinnati FO went to the Veterans Administration nursing facility in Cincinnati to inquire about Francisco Mendoza," she continued. "He's better known by his nickname Paco, has worked there ten years, is well liked, almost beloved by the elderly former soldiers, and he performs nursing duties in an exemplary manner. There's nothing even remotely suggesting illegal activity. He has an address in Hamilton, Ohio. He's a citizen of Mexico with a green card. The agent also noticed he'd taken comp time before and after Easter.

"The director asked if the agent wanted to talk to him. The agent declined, emphasizing the information was based only on a name and that there must be hundreds of men in the U.S. with the name Francisco Mendoza.

"We then asked INS to check immigration records. Francisco Mendoza has been a legal resident with a green card for over 30 years. He obviously immigrated to the U.S. legally with his parents when he was an infant. There are no suspected violations or a failure to register.

"We found an Ohio driver's license with the same address. Here's the photograph. We found a few criminal records for that name, but none matched the finger prints, photograph, and description we have. Tomorrow or Monday, the Cincinnati FO will send someone to Hamilton."

Colonel Sawyer's assistant returned and said: "Here's the official photograph for Patrick Nabil Ferris, home of record Russellville, Alabama, and place of birth Russellville, Alabama; graduate of Auburn University and the University of Alabama. Distinguished service record."

"That's Ali!" Rhonda Philips exclaimed. "Our photo isn't very good, but I've seen Ali with my eyes and talked to him for an hour or more. If Patrick Ferris is the one being duplicated, it's a very good job."

"Nabil is a common Lebanese Christian man's name," the CIA analyst offered. "It's almost certain this person is of Lebanese Christian origin. I presume you can get names of parents from birth records. If they're immigrants, we have good resources in Lebanon who can get information."

"I can send someone to search birth records right now," Rosie Jordan interjected. "It'll take a few days for INS to search its records. Their immigration would've been around 30 years ago and records were manual then. We can check driver's license and other data banks."

"Would it be possible to check the, er, private parts which was seemingly the reason this project went wrong?" a CIA agent asked.

"It's not unheard of to require someone to bare himself," Colonel Sawyer's assistant replied, "but it'd be done only in unusual circumstances. Right off hand, I can't think of a way for us to do this for Captain Ferris without causing problems we don't want to deal with."

"I wonder how well he speaks Arabic," a DIA analyst said. "From time to time we recruit active duty officers for the DIA, like Major Armstrong. Maybe we can recruit Capt. Ferris or pretend to recruit him. A preliminary step could be a physical exam. We'd need cooperation of the examining doctor or use one of our own doctors. Let's think about that one. Rhonda, can we examine Ali in Guantanamo?"

"I can't think of any way we can re-examine him without causing extreme suspicion on his part, and maybe his refusal to cooperate," Rhonda Philips replied. "Remember, he's a medical doctor and would be right on top of anything we'd do. Also, we're not detaining him; we're offering humanitarian medical assistance. I'll get back in touch with Guantanamo and see if the doctor who did the original examination can remember anything."

An FBI agent gave documents to Rosie Jordan who glanced at them and said; "Here's an Alabama birth certificate for Patrick Nabil Ferris, parents Nadine and Raymond Ferris. An Alabama driver's license was cancelled about a year ago and replaced by an Ohio driver's license. Here're driver's license photographs that obviously match the Army photograph. No records of criminal activity.

"We've had a very significant breakthrough, here. We have a person who we didn't know about before who's obviously connected and is also a Mexican citizen. Does anyone have anything else right now?"

A DIA analyst commented: "Last time we reported, Viktor thought the double was going to Daytona, which didn't make sense at the time because there's no Army activity in that part of Florida and attention shifted to Dayton. We thought Viktor had confused the names. Now we know there's a connection to Daytona Beach. Maybe Ali was going to meet Frank Reynolds at his home in Daytona Beach. Or maybe Frank Reynolds's recent visit to Daytona Beach was to meet someone about the classified material."

The rest of the group sat silently for a moment when Rosie Jordan said: "Thanks to all of you. We have quite a bit to reflect on. We need a short recap of who's going to do what before the next meeting. I suggest we meet again here next Tuesday, but be ready to meet earlier if necessary."

He gave the recap and closed the meeting.

CHAPTER 35

Friday, May 19, 2006
Hamilton, Ohio, USA

In mid-morning, FBI agent Thomas Gruenwald parked the standard-issue late model dark green Ford Taurus near the Hamilton police station. He stood 6 feet tall with medium brown closely trimmed hair. He had a trim body reflecting workouts for the FBI academy and now daily gym visits. Bright blue eyes revealed confidence and hid underlying nervousness of his first task alone. He wore the FBI 'uniform', a solid light gray suit with a white shirt that had very thin navy blue stripes, and a conservative navy blue tie.

ENTERING HAMILTON, OHIO.

DISCOVERIES • CHAPTER 35

He met police lieutenant Lech Glenkowski whose duties included liaison with other law enforcement agencies. He wore a slightly crumpled uniform barely covering his developing paunch.

"What can we do for the big G today?" he asked

"We're following through on a report a resident might be involved in illegal immigration," Agent Gruenwald said. "All we have is a name, Francisco Mendoza; we give local police the courtesy of asking first if you know of anything."

Lieutenant Glenkowski chuckled: "You mean Paco Mendoza; he works at the Veteran's home in Cincinnati."

"Yes, that's a nickname we have for him," Agent Gruenwald replied, surprised, "and that's where he works."

"We know him pretty well but not for any official reason," the lieutenant continued, smiling. "His cousin Luie, or Luis Mendoza, has the best bakery in town, in fact the best within miles and miles. It has all sorts of Mexican specialties, and good Polish ones too. We police go there all the time for pastries and coffee, and just to hang out. Paco's in there a lot when he's not on duty, so we know him too. Illegal immigration you say?"

"Yes, just a report based only on names," Agent Gruenwald repeated.

"You're barking up the wrong tree there," the lieutenant continued. "Paco, Luie, and their families are model residents. Don't make 'em any better, even if they are Mexican immigrants. They're here legally, or so it seems; we haven't actually verified their green cards or naturalization. I couldn't imagine any circumstances they'd be involved in illegal immigration, especially right under our noses since we're in an out of the bakery so much. Don't mean to imply we're watching them official like, but just about everyone on the force goes there including the plain-clothes officers. I bet they've figured out all of our plain-clothes officers by now."

"That's a testimonial if I ever heard one," Agent Gruenwald said. "I should go see how great it is. Can I safely say there's nothing in your files about him?"

"You can safely say that," Lieutenant Glenkowski replied, "and for sure go to the bakery. It's close to the station here. Get one of the apple fritters; they're to die for. Luie says he got the recipe from a bakery in New Mexico where they grow good apples."

"Thanks, you've been very helpful," Agent Gruenwald said, stood to shake hands, and left.

He easily found the bakery and parked on a side street.

Hey, he realized, *that jeep behind the bakery matches the description of the one in the file. Let me see if I can get the license plate number without being obvious.*

He called on his cell phone to report the license plate number, and agreed to call back later. He then walked around the block in order to approach the entrance from the opposite direction just in case someone noticed his interest in the four-by-four. Once inside, an attractive young Hispanic woman in a white dress asked with a cheerful smile if she could help.

"An apple fritter and coffee; cream no sugar," he said.

"For here or to go?" she asked.

"To go," Agent Gruenwald replied. *Hey, all this looks good,* he said to himself. *I could buy bread to take home.*

When she brought the coffee and pastry, he asked for a loaf of bread. He paid and asked on the spur of the moment: "Has your boss returned from Mexico yet?"

"Yes, he returned a couple of weeks ago," she answered. "Would you like to speak with him?"

"No thanks; I see he's busy," he hastily replied. "Just tell him Tom from Cincinnati stopped by." He said to himself: *that must be him in the back; Hispanic-looking, all white clothes, a white apron dusty with flour, and a hairnet.*

Back at his car, he called to relate what he discovered and find out about the license plate.

pause

"Oh, you want me to keep him under surveillance?" he spoke in the phone.

pause

"What about, Francisco, or Paco they call him here, the one you sent me to check on?" he asked. "From the address you got tracing this Jeep, they live next door."

DISCOVERIES • CHAPTER 35

pause

"OK, I'll hang around the bakery," Agent Gruenwald said. "You'll send someone else when Paco comes home."

pause

"Bye now," he said and disconnected,

Meanwhile Luie brought a big tray of *bolillos* to put in the display case.

"Hey, boss," the young woman said: "A guy was just in and said to tell you Tom from Cincinnati stopped by."

"Oh, why didn't you come get me?" Luie asked.

"He didn't give me a chance," she replied. "He said he could see you're busy, took his change, and left. He asked if you'd returned from Mexico yet."

Huh? Who could that be? Luie asked himself. *Someone from the Serpent? I don't recall anyone named Tom there. How'd someone from there know I'd been to Mexico?* "What'd he look like?" He asked.

"I can't remember exactly," she replied. "Like all the lawyers who come in here. Young, maybe 25. I think his suit was gray. The rest of the clothes were nothing special or I'd've noticed. Guess he's a bit taller than you are, maybe six feet. Average build; been working out. Brown hair, cut close like a lawyer. Maybe blue eyes, but I can't remember for sure. He was nice looking, but had a wedding ring."

Like hell she didn't notice closely, Luie thought smiling. *If he's from the Serpent, he'd be wearing leather so that description's not much to go on. All types go to the Serpent and plenty could be that size and description. Maybe I'll see him tonight. Maybe that's why he asked if I'm back from Mexico because he's going tonight. Married too. Some married guys go there when they can get away.*

About three hours later, Agent Gruenwald parked in sight of Luie's house, took off his coat and tie, and called on his cell phone saying: "He left the bakery about noon and ran errands. Went to a bank, a laundry and dry cleaners, and a supermarket; then he drove here, parked, went in the back door, and hasn't left."

pause

"It's a clean, decent, and safe-looking neighborhood. It's a little old with small houses," he replied.

pause

HOUSES WHERE LUIE AND PACO LIVE, HAMILTON, OHIO.

"If you send someone to tail Paco, he should dress like one of the locals and use one of the old cars," he added. "When he gets here, maybe bring me something to eat."
pause
"Catch you later. Bye."
After several hours, about 9 p.m., Agent Gruenwald's phone rang which he answered: "Hey, Andy."
pause
"Yes, I see him getting into a Camaro, about five years old," he said. "I saw it drive up a couple of hours ago. It looks like the two of them are going somewhere together."
pause
He said: "I'll follow you," and disconnected.

DISCOVERIES • CHAPTER 35

Cincinnati, Ohio, USA

The agents parked watching Luie and Paco walk to a dimly-lit bar named Eagle @ Serpent.

EAGLE @ SERPENT GAY BAR, CINCINNATI, OHIO

"What now?" Agent Gruenwald asked on his phone.
pause
"I've heard of leather gay bars, but never went into one. Are we supposed to follow them in?" he asked.
pause
"Yeah, that's what I thought," he said. "I can imagine how I'd stick out with my suit pants and dress shirt."
pause
"Oh, they wouldn't even let me in," he said. "Sounds like you've been involved in this type of stakeout before. So what now? Can I just go home?"
pause
"OK. I'll find a better place to park and wait until you get back to me after you call the duty officer. I sure hope he says I can go," he said.

About 45 minutes later, he collapsed in bed next to his wife after having a sandwich made with the bread he bought, and a beer.

Chapter 36

Monday, May 22, 2006
Buffalo, New York, USA

In early afternoon, Omar called from the restroom in the stacks of the SUNY Buffalo library, one of the few places where cell phones can be used. A few minutes later an average-sized man in his early 40s came into a private study carrel wearing a grey suit with white shirt and royal blue tie.

"Hi, you must be Omar; Gabe Andreotti," agent Gabriel Andreotti of the Buffalo field office of the FBI said as he shook hands and sat.

Omar said: "Nice to meet you in person."

"I wish we could meet over a cup of coffee or something," Gabe Andreotti said. "It looks like you have a safe-enough place here. It took us some effort to get me a pass from campus security. We should get right to business. What've you found?"

"Mohammad's sending me to North Carolina tomorrow with another young guy to get supplies and distribute things to customers," he began. "I don't know a lot, but he has a legitimate-seeming business importing Middle Eastern goods like Arabic sweets, bottled rose water, canned hummus, and the like; he distributes them to Arab and other Middle Eastern-run shops along the way. Most of it comes from Lebanon. He complained he can't get things from Syria any more. He's also annoyed I can't help with the Canadian business because my student visa won't allow me to go in and out of Canada."

DISCOVERIES • CHAPTER 36

Gabe Andreotti made notes and asked: "Have you done any work for him before this?"

Omar replied: "I went with him to collect money from service stations and shops around western New York. It could easily be done by one person, but he wants someone to drive him. It likely gives an intimidating appearance if he has a driver and assistant with him. He claims it's money the shops owe for the goods they've bought. It's strange they pay in cash and not always at the time goods are delivered. Why don't they write a check? Middle Easterners use cash back in their home countries, but these places accept credit cards so they use banks; I know Mohammad uses a bank."

"Sounds like an extortion racket or money laundering," Gabe Andreotti said. "What else?"

"He's not quite as stupid as I originally thought," Omar said. "Not all that bright, but careful about what he says and devious. I've heard only one Friday sermon and it seemed he was choosing words carefully. He went on and on about anti-Islam activities of infidel countries and how Arabs and Muslims are so badly treated. He avoided inflammatory words that could incite persons to violence.

"He repeated how unfair it is that decent hard working young Arab men can't get jobs in this country because of discrimination against Muslims. I get the sense he's trying to convince them so he has a supply of cheap labor. Yes, the economy's bad in an old run-down place like Lackawanna, but it doesn't seem any worse for Arabs than others. They could probably find jobs if they tried, and better jobs than Mohammad gives them.

"He has small group meetings with young guys at the mosque. So far, I've not been invited and haven't asked to attend. I might not be welcome if he realizes I'm smart enough to have figured out some things.

"Brahim's mother's been saying her son couldn't get into a university even though he was a very good student and such a good boy. She said he was told Arabs didn't deserve financial aid and Allah knows they didn't have enough money to pay tuition, not even at a community college. Actually, she has a point, but it's been distorted. I can't speak for universities in New York, but Arab-Americans get financial aid at the University of Minnesota."

"Have you heard anything more about Brahim and Guantanamo?" Gabe Andreotti asked.

"Mohammad hasn't said anything, at least not where I could hear," Omar replied. "I think he's smart enough to realize an unsupported public allegation could attract attention he wouldn't want. There's still plenty of talk going on in the community, especially among parents of young men. Brahim and Boudi's parents are saying it's like back in Yemen where young men just disappear. They seem to be resigned to the idea their sons aren't coming back."

"Have you heard anything about al Qaeda?" Gabe Andreotti asked.

"Hardly anything," Omar answered. "Mohammad hasn't said anything. Some people occasionally mention al Qaeda, and not always favorably. They may have had experiences like I did with al Qaeda killing or injuring their families in Yemen. They seem to be afraid to say too much."

"What've you learned about Mohammad personally?" Gabe Andreotti asked?

"He's married and has two daughters elementary school age," Omar replied. "He's old for children that age, mid to late 40s, but in Yemen some men wait until that age to get married and have a family. I get the sense he's not that close with his wife. She seems much younger, at least 10 years, but hard to tell with the veil she wears. It may be an arranged marriage like back in Yemen. They seem to get along, but little sign of affection. He has elderly parents in Yemen he keeps in touch with."

"Is there anything we can do for you now?" Gabe Andreotti asked. "Here's $100 advance on your pay. I suspect you're too shy to ask, but you must be a little short."

"Thank you!" Omar said. "More than just a little short. I can't think of anything else right now. I can call you in an emergency, but I doubt I'll be alone long enough to report to you on the way to North Carolina and back. I'll let you know when I'm back and maybe arrange another meeting here."

Gabe Andreotti stood to shake hands, leaving Omar to bury himself in his research.

Chapter 37

Tuesday, May 23, 2006
Quantico, Virginia, USA

At 10:00 a.m. Rosie Jordan opened the meeting with the same persons at the previous Thursday's meeting. Rhonda Philips wore an evergreen short sleeve linen-cotton dress with beige block-heel leather shoes and a large beige leather handbag, a complementary evergreen, black, and beige silk scarf, and small jade ear studs set in gold.

He began: "Lots has been happening and we all have information that'll take a while, so we agreed to meet early. Maybe this time the CIA should open, Ralph."

Ralph D'Angelo began: "INS located immigration and naturalization records for Khadija Cavanaugh, including maiden name and home village. We found her sister and mother who did most of the talking saying Khadija was a bad daughter. They sent her to Manila to make money to send back to them, but instead she married an infidel and went to America. They didn't hear from her for ten years. She must've done something bad and gotten in trouble in America because men who work for a local chief forced the mother and sister to call her to say they were being hurt, and she must do what they say. Maybe Khadija's dead and Allah punished her for being such a bad daughter.

"When we asked if the mother tried to call Khadija to find out what may have happened, she became indignant saying Khadija's such a bad daughter. Allah punished her, the mother, for having a bad daughter; she hopes Khadija's dead, and of course she wouldn't call her."

A DOD IG agent said: "If I may, this might be a good time to report we put Khadija Cavanaugh under surveillance. She lives with two mixed-race children in an ordinary house in an ordinary middle-class neighborhood; apparently no one else's in the household. She drives an ordinary car. Military records show she and her deceased husband Kevin Cavanaugh have two children who match the two we saw.

"There was nothing remarkable over the weekend. On Sunday they went to the local Roman Catholic church. There they met Army Captain Patrick Ferris who was with his apparent significant-other. There was short social interaction among the five of them, especially the children and Captain Ferris. We'll report on him shortly. We can't see a reason to continue observing her."

Ralph D'Angelo continued: "We have a report from our specialist on Arab countries who discovered quite a bit."

The specialist began: "Our agents in Riyadh discovered Adnan's full complete name, Adnan Mohammad Abdullah al Wahab. He's from the big extended family, tribe might be a better word, the Wahabis, which includes religious extremists, often called religious police, who're given license to control religious activities of Saudis Arabians and punish them on the spot. We've all surely heard of their antics, like carrying large sticks to beat people if they're out of line. His immediate family doesn't seem to be involved, but it seems they do share extremist religious beliefs.

"He was allowed to study molecular biology at a university, but after graduation he worked in a hospital as a laboratory technician. Apparently he went to Afghanistan as a humanitarian worker. We and the Saudi government know now he almost certainly was with al Qaeda. In 1999 he returned to Saudi Arabia, obtained a student visa for the U.S., entered the U.S., and shortly disappeared.

"He's not well liked by anyone in Saudi Arabia and the government wouldn't want him back. If we prove he's a citizen, they'll have little choice. We can't rule out the possibility he'd be tortured by others while the government looks the other way. Anything before I go on to Lebanon?

DISCOVERIES • CHAPTER 37

pause

"We found passport records in Lebanon readily. Many records were destroyed in the civil war, but it was in the interest of all of parties to be able to get passports issued readily so those records weren't damaged. They were kept manually, of course, but we found passports issued in 1976 to Raymond Ferris and Nadine Ferris with names transliterated as 'F-e-r-r-i-s'. Their actual names in Arabic were indeed فارس like you see here and you saw before.

ANALYST DISCOVERS MAJOR CLUE WITH ARABIC NAMES.

"In Lebanon, people identify themselves with their families' original home village, and Raymond Ferris identified himself as being from Beino, the same village that's the home of the prominent politician named فارس, transliterated F-a-r-e-s. We went there to inquire. There's no apparent connection between Raymond Ferris and the politician. These are large extended families and at most they'd've been distant cousins. Raymond actually grew up in Beirut and had little contact with people in the village.

"We showed photographs of Patrick Ferris to people there. Some remembered seeing him about a month ago walking around with a slightly older man who was pointing out landmarks. They thought it strange they didn't stop and visit because the same young man was there in 2001, and he was so nice. They remembered the date they saw him a month ago because it was the Sunday before Latin Easter when everyone goes to church in new clothes and children walk around with palm leaves. This young man didn't attend church, but in 2001, he went to church like a good Maronite.

"We located an elderly lady with whom Patrick and a cousin stayed in 2001. She recognized the photographs and remembered him as a pleasant young man just like she'd expect a son of Abou Patrick to be. No, they haven't kept in touch. She hears from Raymond and Nadine occasionally.

"With this information, we checked official immigration entry and exit records which're now computerized. In 2001 Patrick Nabil Ferris, or someone with a U.S. passport in that name, entered through the Beirut airport in April and departed about a month later in May. Both entry and exit were by way of Amsterdam on KLM flights. In May 2001 there was also a departure and return a day later at the land border in Masnaa, a very busy border crossing on the main road between Beirut and Damascus. Day trips or overnight trips from Beirut to Damascus are very common, especially for tourists.

"There was another entry through the Beirut airport on April 5, 2006, by someone with a U.S. passport in the name of Patrick Nabil Ferris and a departure on April 10, both on Czech Air from and to Prague. We learned Czech Air is now a popular airline for flights from Lebanon to Europe and the U.S. Fares are lower than other European airlines; it offers reasonable service and connections, and the Prague airport is more convenient for transfers than major European airports. It's especially popular with young tourists. It's consistent the person posing as Patrick would use Czech Air because it'd look like a tourist visit.

"When our agent in Beirut discovered this information yesterday, he immediately notified us. Because of the time difference, we got the information in the morning and immediately notified you. Maybe you have information."

An FBI agent said: "INS records show Patrick Ferris entered the U.S. at Kennedy Airport in New York on a Czech Air flight from Prague on April 10, 2006. It was a routine entry in the data base."

DISCOVERIES • CHAPTER 37

A DOD IG representative said: "When we got the information yesterday, we immediately asked the IG office at Wright-Patterson to perform an unannounced check of the deployment readiness kits, classified document security, and similar things. Unannounced checks are the norm, and it'd been a while since we checked this office so a check now wouldn't cause alarm.

"We located Captain Ferris's passport and verified entry and exit stamps for Lebanon on April 5 and April 10 this year. There were also stamps for entries and exits in 2001. Everything about classified documents was in order.

"We checked leave records. Captain Ferris didn't sign out any time in April. Sometimes people don't sign out if they're gone only a day or two. It'd be totally unheard of for him to be gone for a week, especially to a sensitive foreign country, without permission and signing out.

"The only conclusion that makes sense is someone took his passport out of the file and let someone else use it. We've heard Khadija Cavanaugh was forced to do things and she had access to the passports. By the way, she uses the name Felicia, not Khadija, even though it's her legal name"

The CIA analyst began again: "We concur someone using Captain Ferris's passport to enter and leave Lebanon is the only explanation that makes sense. I suspect it's two someones: one from the U.S. into Lebanon getting all the proper entry stamps, and Ali leaving again. Airlines make only a cursory check of pictures in passports when someone leaves the U.S. and passport control in Beirut is not all that thorough to verify the person entering actually matches the passport. All that'd be needed is a young man about the same age and with physical features that aren't out of line.

"Lebanese resources also found Jihad Noussayri, who's Syrian, recently imprisoned in the infamous Lebanese Roumieh prison. He was convicted of theft of household items in seemingly an open and shut case with a relatively fair trial under Lebanese law. It's well known Moukhabarat stole televisions and the like from shops and houses in Lebanon and sold them in Syria. During the Syrian occupation of Lebanon, Moukhabarat were untouchable. Now when Lebanese have evidence, they're convicting them and putting them in prison. Any questions or comments?"

Rosie Jordan said: "We checked INS records and discovered Raymond and Nadine Ferris became naturalized citizens in the early 1980s. An agent from our Birmingham field office went to Russellville. The Ferrises are well liked and respected. They own a local supermarket that apparently has plenty of business.

"It's time for a short coffee break. I could use a cup."

Chapter 38

Tuesday, May 23, 2006
Quantico, Virginia, USA

After the coffee break, Rosie Jordan called on the DIA; an analyst began: "We sent Patrick Ferris's photographs to Iraq. Abed didn't recognize him. Maybe he didn't bother to look at Ali after surgery. Viktor immediately said 'that's Ali'. When we said it was Captain Ferris, he realized how much we've uncovered. He was terror-stricken we might turn him over to Russia or Tajikistan. For now, there's no problem keeping him in the prison. A much greater problem's the four at Guantanamo. Rhonda can speak to that."

Rhonda Philips began: "I went to Guantanamo with photographs of Luis and Francisco Mendoza and Frank Reynolds. The best interrogators were assigned; I was present with Ali, Bob, and Boudi. It was 'good cop, bad cop'. Interrogations were taped.

"Ali was first and vague with answers, saying he didn't remember and couldn't identify them. The interrogator caught a reaction in his eyes he knows all three. We tried to trip him up about Daytona and Dayton because of a possible connection between him and Frank Reynolds. We asked who of the persons in the pictures was from Daytona, not using the full name Daytona Beach. He said he recalled reading or hearing about a Daytona automobile race, but that's all. The interrogator thought it was the truth.

"I had a sudden inspiration to play a geography game, asking if he'd been in cities along the routes he'd have taken from New York to Dayton, and then to Mexico. The interrogator caught on and looked for differences in eyes and body language. When we said Daytona again, he didn't know which state; the interrogator said he didn't know.

He readily answered correctly to Harrisburg, Columbus, Louisville, and Memphis. He must've suspected what I was after, though, and tried to be clever. I mentioned Wheeling; he didn't know which state and said he hadn't been there. If he drove, he'd have surely noticed Wheeling, even if he didn't remember it's in West Virginia. The interrogator said he indeed recognized Wheeling. For Little Rock, he said it's the home of Bill Clinton. He claimed not to know Texarkana, although he could've guessed. The interrogator again verified he recognized it. The last one he tried to deny, but the interrogator said he recognized, is Mesquite. I won't go over each place, but he's familiar with U.S. geography and was conscious for a good part of the long road trips he made.

"In summary: he is alert and bright enough to know what's going on, but frightened. He's trying to protect the three persons in the photographs. He continued to ask what'll become of him and implied he won't implicate anyone if he's going to be punished anyway.

"We need to get him away from there soon. We're not going to get more information until we tell him what'll happen to him next. There're too many investigating what we're doing in Guantanamo and the hospital's coming under increasing scrutiny. Our own personnel may get suspicious and tell people back home. We concocted a story, implying without lying, that he's an Arabic-speaking medical student on rotation. We didn't say he's American, but with perfect American English the conclusion can readily be drawn.

"I asked the doctor who examined Ali about intimate details. He doesn't remember, but they're trained to notice anomalies. He's sure he'd've made a note or notified someone if Ali were uncircumcised.

"Boudi was next. The interrogator warmed him up talking about sports. He said Boudi's well versed on American sports, further confirming he's a long-time resident if not native. He was glad to get exercise. He'd like to go swimming now that his wounds are healed, but doesn't have a swim suit.

DISCOVERIES • CHAPTER 38

"When we showed the photographs, he recognized them and reacted really negatively to Frank Reynolds. I'll not go through all of the dialogue. We promised him a swim suit if he'd tell us more, and I made a point to get it for him. The major points are Frank Reynolds and another man abducted him at gun point. Frank Reynolds wore what looked like a military uniform, but had his shirt off. The Mendozas put them in a jeep and drove them to Mexico. I had a photograph of a dark colored Jeep. He said it looked like this, but couldn't be sure. Paco injected them to knock them out. They thought Luis and Paco were Arab terrorists.

"Boudi said their boss told them to get Ali in New York City in the BMW and turn him over to Adnan in Dayton. They thought Adnan might've been part of this other group, but Paco and Luis roughed him up worst of all. Adnan was always giving orders and telling them what bad Muslims they were. When they were in the same cell in Mexico, Adnan started beating on him and Bob because they weren't being proper Muslims. Boudi and Bob fought back to protect themselves, and Ali tried to break up the fight.

"Ali was supposed to take the place of an army officer, but Adnan didn't trust them enough to give details. They were just supposed to take Ali to Canada the next day. They had done only what they were told, and didn't hurt anyone.

"He didn't say much about their work driving to North Carolina and Canada. He may have realized he'd said too much. He asked what was going to happen to him, that he just wanted to go home and see his mother and family. We told him if he wanted to see his mother again, he'd need to continue to cooperate.

"Next was Bob. He asked why we were questioning him again, didn't he have rights, etc. The interrogator said he's free to leave any time he wants to return to Cuba.

"I softened him up by asking what he thought of the books I left behind with discussion back and forth about the authors and how they developed their plots. He liked going to the library, but it'd be better if he could borrow books or buy some of his own. He also said he only had hospital scrubs to wear, which limited where he could go. At the end I went to the base thrift shop and bought used clothes. If we get them out of there, they'll need something to wear.

"He immediately recognized Paco and Luis as Arab terrorists who took them to Mexico. I'll not go through the dialogue. He confirmed Boudi's story and had the same reaction to the Jeep picture. He, too, didn't like Adnan and confirmed Adnan's beating them up in jail in Mexico.

"He seemed to detect that we hadn't yet talked to Adnan and suggested the interrogator call him 'spaghetti'; that would really make him mad. When the interrogator asked why, he said Paco and Luis had called him that because of his penis.

"We asked about working for Mohammad Fadel. He was surprised we knew his name, suspected we knew about smuggling, and described briefly what they did. He told the same story about picking up Ali in New York City and Ali's driving the BMW to Dayton. Like Boudi, he said they just did what their boss told them and had done nothing wrong.

"I asked why were they afraid to go back to the U.S. if they'd done nothing wrong, reminding him of his comment about Moussaoui. He said the Arab terrorists, referring to Paco and Luis, told them they'd be prosecuted like Moussaoui. He assumed these two could frame them, Arabs have no rights, and after nine-eleven the government finds excuses to prosecute Arabs.

"I asked what he'd like to do with his life. He said he really wanted to go to a university to study history and government, and become a teacher. He'd even thought about being a lawyer. I encouraged him to keep his dreams. I admitted it'd been difficult for him, but dreams do come true. I emphasized if he wants any hope of achieving his dreams, he needs to be honest with us, and tell us what he's been hiding. I left money to be given to him to buy books. We'll see how cooperative he'll be next time.

"Our highest priority is to get Boudi and Bob out of there. We're sitting on a time bomb. The longer we keep U.S. citizens there, the greater the chance for serious political fall-out. It makes no difference how guilty or innocent they may be; we can't keep them in Guantanamo one day longer than the absolute minimum time necessary. I hope we can devote time to this issue.

"Next was Adnan and very disturbing. He was in a room where I could hear. The interrogator identified him as Adnan Mohammad Abdullah al Wahab, a Saudi Arabian citizen. When he protested, the interrogator shut him up saying that certain people, naming two in Saudi Arabia would like to see him again, and also gave the names of the men in Texas he shared an apartment with, saying he'd never see them again. He was stunned and silent.

"The interrogator showed him the photos. There was a terror-stricken reaction to all three. The interrogator said 'These are the other Arab terrorists who abducted you, aren't they? Other terrorists just like you.' His body language indicated a positive response, but he didn't answer. The interrogator said: 'What do you want, Spaghetti? You want us to turn you back over to the Cubans? You'd like that; they're not spaghetti like you.'

"He physically attacked the interrogator. They can defend themselves if necessary, but're trained to use restraint, which this one did. Until help came, Adnan hit the interrogator saying: 'You show respect for Arabs and Muslims. Those guys aren't proper Arabs; they're infidels who don't respect Allah and true believers. We're not terrorists, they are. We're the true sons of Allah who're fighting to regain respect we're due. When al Qaeda defeats infidels, then the world'll know Allah and the true servants.'

"Big muscular security guards pulled Adnan off, and applied handcuffs and leg restraints. He was taken to a cell-type hospital room. Remembering he urinated in the bed, the staff was told to apply an adult diaper. He went berserk, screaming, shouting, and trying to attack anyone who came close. Eventually he was subdued and physically restrained with a straightjacket and the diaper attached.

"It's not as urgent to get him out of Guantanamo as it is Bob and Boudi, or Ali for that matter. "He's not likely to attract attention. Even if there's unwanted publicity, we have tapes that prove he said he's with al Qaeda. We don't want it to come to that point, but the political fallout would be less.

Rosie Jordan said: "If there's else for Rhonda let's break for lunch.

Chapter 39

Tuesday, May 23, 2006
Quantico, Virginia, USA

After lunch, a DOD IG agent began: "We also put Captain Ferris and everyone in their office under surveillance. For Navy Lieutenant Commander Jennifer Lewis, there was nothing remarkable; I can give details if you like.

"For Captain Ferris, little was remarkable. He lives in an ordinary rented house. He does drive an up-market car, a BMW about a year old. He apparently lives with a young woman who he picked up at the Dayton airport Friday night; she was wearing what appears to be a USAirways flight attendant uniform. We could follow up on that, but it doesn't seem to lead us anywhere. There were two cars in the garage indicating she lives there also. Military records don't indicate he's married, but living with a significant other is hardly remarkable these days.

"On Saturday they went shopping in her car, an older Toyota Celica; she was driving. On Saturday night they stayed home. On Sunday, as we heard, they went to the local nearby Roman Catholic church, driving the BMW, where they met Khadija Cavanaugh and her children. Afterwards, they worked in the yard. On Monday, Captain Ferris went to work. Every indication's a normal domestic life."

"We found a 2005 model silver BMW registered to Patrick Ferris at the address on file in several places," an FBI agent added. "We have the license plate number and VIN if you like. We'd like to do a forensic check for finger prints to see if Ali drove it, but we can't think of a way to get a court order without unwanted publicity."

The CIA Arab specialist interrupted: "Now we get the significance of the late-model BMW Mohammad Fadel recently bought and why it was important for Ali to drive it from New York City to Dayton. When he took Captain Ferris's place, he must've driven his car to get onto the base. Ali spent his teen-age and adult life in Syria and likely had little opportunity to drive a car, and certainly not a BMW. Taking it to Fort Lauderdale was likely to throw us off course. This's well beyond my responsibility as a Middle East specialist. I can tell you that a young Syrian, doctor or not, would need experience driving it if he were to drive as though it were his own and not draw attention to himself."

A senior DIA analyst added: "Captain Ferris has an appointment tomorrow in DC for a physical exam. We contacted him Friday saying he's being considered for a DIA assignment because of his Arab ancestry and our serious need for uniformed personnel who have Arab backgrounds.

"He was surprised saying he doesn't speak Arabic, and wondered how we came upon him. We concocted a story that we're always keeping eyes and ears open for possible recruits and heard mention of his Lebanese background. We said we need an interview with him and he needs a physical exam by one of our doctors. He protested he'll get married soon and doesn't want an overseas DIA assignment with its risks. We implied that he has no choice in the matter."

The DOD IG representative resumed: "Major Reynolds lives in a middle-class neighborhood in a house typical of his income range that he owns. He apparently lives alone. He drives a late model Mercury Mountaineer SUV that's trendy with persons of his income level and social class. On Friday night, he drove it to Cincinnati to a bar that caters to gay men with a leather and sado-masochism fetish. Our agent didn't go inside, but kept surveillance of the door.

"He entered about 10 p.m. and left shortly after 2 a.m. in the company of three other men. We showed pictures of Luis and Francisco Mendoza to the agent who said two of the men could be the two Mendozas, but it was dark so he couldn't make a positive identification. They parted company with rather public displays of affection, the two Mendozas leaving together, and the other two going separately. Major Reynolds drove straight to his house. The lights in the house went off shortly.

"The rest of the weekend was unremarkable. Saturday he ran errands and went to the base gym to work out. On Sunday he worked in his yard and drank beer with his neighbors. On Monday he went to work as usual."

Debbie interrupted: "That's consistent with what our Miami field office discovered in Fort Lauderdale. The guest house where Major Reynolds and Francisco Mendoza were registered caters to gay men with a leather fetish. I didn't mention it because it seemed incidental."

Colonel Sawyer interrupted forcefully: "Now we know he's going to criminal hang-outs like that homo place so we can discharge him before he steals more classified. In the old days we could've just discharged him. Now with 'don't ask don't tell' it's more difficult. This must be where al Qaeda got hold of him."

"Colonel, I think you're a bit hasty and not entirely correct in your characterization of that establishment in Cincinnati," Rosie Jordan said gently. "Perhaps you'd better wait until you hear the report from our agents."

"What do you mean, too hasty?" Colonel Sawyer replied forcefully. "Everyone knows homosexuals are easily corrupted by intelligence agents, and have been for years."

Rosie Jordan cleared his throat loudly and said: "Debbie, please go ahead."

She resumed: "It may be useful to fill you in how Luis Mendoza, Paco Mendoza's cousin, was identified." She then described agent Gruenwald's visit adding Luie's jeep was on the list of those crossing the border into the U.S. at Eagle Pass, Texas, on April 17, about 11 p.m.

"I'll return to Hamilton in a moment," she continued. "We asked the San Antonio FO to go to Eagle Pass with Luis's and Paco's photographs. After a few inquiries, the agent located an older, family-run motel where the owner thought he remembered Paco Mendoza arriving late one night recently; he didn't see another person. The owner is likely Indian and was visibly nervous; he may have told the agent something to make him go away. It's well known Indian immigrants have been buying older independent motels all over the U.S. for several years, especially in the southern states, and bringing extended families and friends to work in them, not always legally.

"The agent noticed a bakery across the street, bought coffee and a roll, and asked if anyone recognized the persons in the pictures. They immediately recognized Luis Mendoza because he'd talked to the owner and, even gave a recipe for apple fritters he'd gotten in New Mexico.

She then described Agent Gruenwald's visit to Hamilton and concluded: "Both agents followed Paco and Luis to the same Serpent Bar in Cincinnati and weren't dressed suitably to go inside. Luis and Paco Mendoza came out about 2 a.m. with two other men. Our agent's reasonably sure one is Frank Reynolds, but as mentioned it was dark. The four parted company, as we heard, with public displays of affection, and Luis and Paco returned to Hamilton."

Colonel Sawyer interrupted: "Now we have this terrorist gang operating out of gay S&M bars. At least they have a ready-made training ground for torture techniques. Someone should shut them down. The local police must be taking pay-offs instead of doing their jobs."

"Colonel Sawyer," Rosie Jordan said with increasing anger, "you are obviously jumping to conclusions without hearing all of the report. Debbie, please continue."

"Yesterday morning," she continued, "the Cincinnati FO contacted Cincinnati police to inquire about the Serpent Bar. We have good rapport with the Cincinnati police force, which is professional and well trained. They said the bar goes to extreme lengths to operate within the law and makes sure its customers do also. It will not allow drugs or other illegal substances to be used; it has called in police to arrest customers who're apparently using or handling drugs. It will not sell liquor to clients who appear to be intoxicated and will do what it can to make clients take taxis if they appear unable to drive safely. It has called police to remove customers who are disorderly.

"Prostitution is of course illegal in Ohio, but Cincinnati police like most big-city police, don't actively enforce prostitution statutes unless some other illegal activity's involved. Nonetheless, this bar refuses to allow prostitutes to operate and will evict suspected ones.

"Cincinnati police send undercover officers to observe from time to time and the owners welcome such visits, although they don't know when they are. The Serpent operates within the law in every respect. The clientele come from a broad cross-section of society who're from all indications decent, respectful, law-abiding citizens, and appreciate a safe place in which to engage in their special interests. Because of the type of activities that occur there, customers wouldn't want attention drawn to themselves if illegal activity occurred and police raids were common. The activities in this bar would likely be viewed as, er, unsavory to many members of society, but aren't illegal."

"They run terrorist cells," Colonel Sawyer blurted out.

"Colonel, if you please, it's been a long day and we have more to go," Rosie Jordan said tersely. "You have a serious misunderstanding of modern law enforcement and its relationship to persons with homosexual orientation, which frankly I find surprising for a person in your position.

"I can speak only for the FBI, but we do know how professional police forces operate. Whether we approve of homosexuality or not, we must deal with people who have this orientation. The vast majority are ordinary, decent, law-abiding citizens; in fact, they're more law-abiding than society as a whole. Most crime involving homosexuals, by far, is crime against them not crime by them. Almost all larger, professional police forces have homosexual officers, male and female, many recruited specifically because they're homosexual to deal with some of the horrible crimes that're committed against homosexuals. Debbie, please."

"The last item," she continued, "is from the Buffalo FO. Our resource has discovered quite a bit." She then gave a summary of what Omar had reported to Gabe Andreotti.

Rosie Jordan said: "Thank you Debbie. Anyone else? Questions or comments? Rhonda's eager for us to discuss what to do with the men at Guantanamo, and we need to think about what if anything we'll do with the other persons. Let's take a short break and go to that topic.

Chapter 40

Tuesday, May 23, 2006
Quantico, Virginia, USA

When the meeting resumed, Rosie Jordan called on Rhonda Philips, but Colonel Sawyer interrupted: "First thing I'm doing when I return to the office is begin the process of discharging Major Reynolds."

"If I may," Ralph D'Angelo stated, "the CIA has had to deal with homosexuals in many capacities, some of which you'd surely not like to hear about. Homosexuals have been forced with fear of exposure to do many things that were treasonous and worse, but that was in the past. Attitudes have changed; it's not an issue any more.

"I don't see any indication whatsoever that it's an issue here. There's nothing so far that even remotely indicates that Major Reynolds is involved in delivering classified material to enemies of the U.S. The phone calls clearly indicate the classified material was in the hands of the persons who are now at Guantanamo.

"It's almost certain that Ali posing as Captain Ferris took the classified. It would make no sense for Major Reynolds to have assisted him. If Major Reynolds were passing classified secrets to the enemy, it'd make no sense whatsoever for al Qaeda to go to the extremely elaborate scheme of putting a double in the office to get the classified material; Major Reynolds could pass it along himself.

"Although I've not thought this through, I'm getting the strong idea that Major Reynolds unintentionally discovered Ali was the double and, along with his buddies, took matters into their own hands. I can think of a few ways he made this discovery and reasons he'd take things into his own hands, all related to his supposed homosexuality.

"We need more time to reflect on these issues and get more information. In the meantime, Colonel, from a CIA perspective, we would be very much opposed to action against Major Reynolds at this time. Among many other reasons, it could lead to public exposure of a serious breach of the country's security and that'd be disastrous."

"Colonel," Rhonda Philips began, barely containing anger and pointedly looking at her rose gold watch: "If you pursue that, not only will I not support you, I will do everything I can to stop you. You do not have the faintest shred of evidence that Major Reynolds jeopardized the security of the U.S., nor do you have any indication he's derelict in his duties. You, yourself, said he's a model officer in every respect.

"It's apparent your opinion of him changed only when it became known he's likely homosexual. You, yourself, said the U.S. armed forces has a 'don't ask; don't tell' policy, and Major Reynolds has not told us he's homosexual. All we know is agents placed him in two locations that are frequented by homosexuals. That's far from proof. If you pursue a discharge of Major Reynolds, you'll expose the breach of U.S. security by al Qaeda, seriously endangering international relations with several countries. You'll bring even more unfavorable publicity onto the Guantanamo Naval Base, further damaging international relations.

"As for domestic political relationships, you'll do irreparable harm. Don't be misguided by the current proposal by the so-called religious right to amend the constitution to prevent gay marriage. It won't get out of the Senate; public sentiment in the U.S. is just not that strong.

"From the other side, attempting to discharge a distinguished Marine Corps officer for homosexuality would open Pandora's box of U.S. politics. Gay activists and advocates would have a field day in the run up to the November elections. Policy makers like Mary Cheney, the Vice-President's daughter, are actively involved in gay rights issues. The Log Cabin

DISCOVERIES • CHAPTER 40

Republicans, a gay group, have supported the current administration on most issues. I cannot imagine the damage that would occur.

"If you want to discuss this further with me, we'll do so back at the Pentagon, not here. Now can we go to crucial issues of what to do with the guys at Guantanamo?"

Colonel Sawyer, stunned, chose to sit silently.

Rosie Jordan began: "Rhonda, if this were an FBI issue, we'd think of getting them to agree to prosecution for a lesser charge than national security, and agree that they must never disclose what happened or face much more serious charges. It's ultimately a DOD decision, but if it has any appeal we could discuss it further."

"That's an approach I wouldn't've thought of," she replied. "If it'd eliminate, or at least postpone, the chance word would get out, I'm in favor. Of course, I'd need to clear it with my bosses."

Rosie Jordan replied: "For this to work, all of our ducks must be in order. Any arrest'd have to be in the U.S. and the moment they set foot here, they're entitled to rights of U.S. citizens. They need to be immediately arrested or set free, and they'd have to have access to legal representation."

"Mohammad Fadel would need to be neutralized. If they contact him immediately, not only could he provide them with legal services that could upset plans, but he'd have a chance to bolt and save himself. Even if we have something we can arrest him for, there could be problems if they have access to the same lawyers."

Ralph D'Angelo began: "With publicity over extraordinary rendition, we can't snatch him on the streets of the U.S. and send him somewhere. The trick'd be to get him to leave the U.S. voluntarily, hopefully going to a country where we have good resources and cooperation with the government, and confine him there, at least temporarily. Can the FBI get more information about him from INS?"

"Debbie, can you start on that now?" Rosie Jordan said. "We can ask our resource in Lackawanna also.

"Rhonda, if you want to pursue this, we'll contact the section of the Attorney General we usually work with and start things going. You and

I can work on this together over the next few days without involving the whole group. Maybe someone else has some ideas."

"Thanks, Rosie," Rhonda Philips stated. "I'll stay after this meeting. In the meantime, we need to get the other two out too. Adnan is so belligerent, I think we should turn him over to Saudi Arabia as soon as we can. I can't see much damage to U.S.-Saudi Arabia relations knowing what we know now. There wouldn't be political fallout in the U.S., so long as we can keep his transfer quiet and not allow any publicity related to his role in getting Ali into the U.S. I'm hoping the CIA might give guidance. Sitting here, the thought occurred that maybe the prison in Baghdad could be a place we can keep him until we can transfer him."

The CIA Middle East specialist said: "If he's medically fit to travel, moving him to the prison in Baghdad just might not be a bad idea. The only question is when and how. With the Council of Europe watching every move we make in these so-called renditions, and with a big exposé report due any day, we might need to move him immediately while we can. We're returning detainees from Guantanamo to Iraq now. Maybe put him on one of the flights so he wouldn't stick out. Rhonda, I think this is one we can solve quickly."

"Thanks, Scott," Rhonda said. "That only leaves Ali."

Another senior DIA analyst said: "Rhonda, why can't we send Ali to that same prison in Baghdad? He may not like it, but it can't be any worse than the alternatives, and likely better. You've said he won't tell any more until he knows what'll happen to him. Maybe if he's presented with the alternatives, that'll be enough."

"Why didn't I think of that?" Rhonda asked. "Scott, can we do this one also?"

"I don't see why not," he replied. "You might dangle a carrot in front of him that we might eventually relocate him to another Arab country in the area, perhaps one of the friendly Gulf states. Surely he's bright enough to realize that staying in North America can never be an option.

"You said you concocted a story he's a medical student on a special rotation for this type of medical practice. Put him on a flight as a medical assistant then he conveniently stays behind in Baghdad.

DISCOVERIES • CHAPTER 40

"You have your own expert interrogators, but if we can lend any assistance, let me know. Most of the remaining information we want from him relates to the capers in the U.S. and Mexico. Much of that's an FBI issue, so maybe they'd like to be in on the interrogation also."

"Yes, Rhonda, we'd be interested in being involved," Rosie Jordan added."

"That's a relief," Rhonda Philips exclaimed. "Thanks."

"Thanks again to all of you for coming," Rosie Jordan said. "This might be the last meeting all of us need to attend, except perhaps for a final wrap-up session. Given the nature of the topic, we can't say it's been a pleasure. Still the degree of collegiality and cooperation has been remarkable."

He pointedly avoided looking at Colonel Sawyer.

Chapter 41

Tuesday, May 23, 2006
Winston-Salem, North Carolina, USA

About 7:30 p.m., Omar called from a room in a Day's Inn: "Hi, this is Omar. I'm in Winston-Salem, North Carolina, at a motel where Kamal stays when he's here. I should make this quick because I don't know how soon he'll return."
pause
"We drove all day," he continued, "stopping a few times. He says we'll stop more on the way back."
pause
"Kamal Ashfoor," Omar answered, then spelled the name. "Seems he's Mohammad's favorite, number one assistant; he's a little older and worked with him the longest."
pause
Omar replied: "Not a common name in Yemen, but not unusual. The girl he's with calls him her big camel jockey."
pause
"Late 20s, I'd guess," Omar added. "He has girlfriends up and down the road. He offered to line me up with one of her friends, but I declined saying I needed to read for my thesis; I did bring books to read so it's legitimate."
pause
"I'll see if I can get names of the girls," Omar said. "I hope you don't want me to go with them. You know I'm not fundamentalist, but I do

DISCOVERIES • CHAPTER 41

accept the Islamic belief that a man should not be with a woman until they're married."
pause

"OK, good." Omar said relieved. "I picked up a little about their operations, but maybe I should tell you something first in case I have to leave suddenly.

"He recently went to Yemen," Omar began. "He used another person's passport to go and his own to come back. Went to Beirut first, entering on the other guy's passport and met a guy, a real asshole using his words, who took him into Syria. Kamal gave him the other person's passport and documents like driver's license. Then he got a flight to Sana'a using his own passport. Jihad arranged for him to leave Syria without first having entry documents, apparently paying baksheesh, and he entered Yemen paying a small amount of baksheesh, 'a smile from Abraham Lincoln' he said."
pause

"No, and I didn't ask the guy's name because I didn't want to appear to be too curious," Omar continued. "He said they picked him because he resembled the guy, they lightened his hair and cut it really short, had him gain weight to fill out the cheeks, and had him wear photo-sensitive glasses to cover his eyes. He wasn't supposed to look directly at anyone so long as he wasn't obvious about it and start coughing covering his mouth, turning away from the person examining passports. He shaved in the Prague airport so his darker facial hair wouldn't be obvious."
pause

"You mean Kamal?" Omar asked then continued. "About five-ten, dark brown hair, medium brown eyes, average build, maybe a little on the thin side, and light skin for a Middle Eastern person, but about average for Americans. Doesn't look like a stereotypical Arab, but there're plenty who'd look like him. He wouldn't attract attention in Sana'a except young women'd find him attractive. American girls must find him attractive too. Maybe that's another reason why Mohammad likes to use him because he blends in well."
pause

"No, apparently hasn't traveled much except down here and to Canada," Omar continued. "Mohammad had him get his first passport just

for that trip. He was talking about the excitement of being in an airplane the first time."
pause
"He said it was interesting to see places his parents and their friends talked about," Omar added. "He met his grandparents for the first time, which according to him, was a strange experience. They were all over him with affection, but to him they were strangers with some strange habits, especially men chewing foul tasting leaves getting high."
pause
"I didn't have to ask him about Mohammad's family; he talked about it on his own," Omar replied. "He took things for Mohammad's parents and met the extended family. He said Mohammad isn't well thought of. Only his parents showed much interest and they kept saying over and over to tell Mohammad to please come visit them before they die because they're getting old and're in bad health."
pause
"Who? Kamal?" Omar asked again and continued: "He mostly goes to and from Canada. He's doing this trip because Brahim and Boudi disappeared. Feigning idle curiosity, I asked what he thought had become of them. He said it's probably an American group who thought Mohammad's encroaching on their territory, so they abducted two of his men to teach him a lesson. I asked: 'Isn't Mohammad's an American group also?' He said Mohammad's part of Canadian operations, and only worked the area around Buffalo and a few places up and down the road to North Carolina. It sounds more and more like rival tribes back in Yemen that have their territories staked out, but fight each other along the edges because they don't have clear borders for whose territory is whose."
pause
"He says they'll likely'll be released soon with a message to Mohammad that he's pushing limits too far. This is the U.S., not the Middle East. If Brahim and Boudi were killed, police'd be all over them investigating and might find out too many things. I stopped asking questions because I didn't want to push limits."

DISCOVERIES • CHAPTER 41

pause

"So far, we've stopped at gas stations and shops that're run by Middle Easterners, not all Arabs," Omar replied. "We gave them Middle Eastern products and collected money in cash. They don't seem happy getting the merchandise. I looked around some shops and it looked like they had plenty gathering dust. They grumbled about so much money.

"So far we haven't paid for gasoline, either. This car must use a lot of gasoline because we've put in a lot more than I'd have thought necessary. He says we're headed back north tomorrow and he's already looking forward to seeing some girl in West Virginia."

pause

"Maybe I can call you tomorrow night, especially if he's with a girl again," Omar said.

pause

"Ok, bye for now," Omar said and returned to reading.

Chapter 42

Wednesday, May 24, 2006
Summersville, West Virginia, USA

In the restroom of Applebee's where a public phone was located, Omar said: "Hello, Gabe; Omar. I'm in Summersville, West Virginia, in a restaurant restroom. If someone comes in, I may need to be quiet for a while."
pause

"In the motel room with a woman," Omar replied, Super 8 next door. They wanted me to be with them because she had a friend. I pretended I was embarrassed, and it didn't take much pretending, saying I'm shy and never did anything with other people around. I hope he doesn't keep putting me in these situations. If I keep refusing, they'll get suspicious."

SUPER 8 MOTEL, SUMMERSVILLE, WEST VIRGINIA

DISCOVERIES • CHAPTER 42

"Oh, wouldn't have thought of that," Omar said. "Pretend I met someone when I drove up from Florida then you arrange someone I can meet and go to a movie or something. Where do I say I'll meet her?"

pause

"OK, you'll set it up and let me know," Omar said.

pause

"He seemed to accept my excuse although the girl was disappointed," Omar said. "She was hoping it'd be like with Bob and Bud. Said Katie'd be really disappointed. She was especially interested in Bud. I think she's talking about Brahim and Boudi. Sometimes people named Ibrahim or Brahim are called Bob."

pause

"Oh, you already know about Bob but haven't heard of Bud," Omar commented. "That's not a name we'd use in Arabic, but maybe they use it so they don't sound like Arabs. Bud is close enough to Boudi."

pause

"Her name is Sheryl Summers," he replied. "S-h-e-r-y-l and Summers. Sheryl Summers from Summersville she said giggling. She's a ditzy blonde like in movies although the blonde doesn't look natural. Her friend is Katie but don't ask me how to spell it. They spell names funny here."

pause

"I said I'd come to Applebee's and read so they could be in the room as long as they like," Omar answered. "He'll call after he takes her home. She must still live with family."

pause

"The big thing is buying guns today," Omar said.

pause

"Yes; pistols," Omar repeated. "I don't know much about guns. Know the difference between a pistol and a rifle, but that's about it."

pause

"A place called Appalachian Outdoors just outside of Beckley," Omar continued. "Right after we left the turnpike to go onto Highway 19."

pause

"Wanted me to buy a couple of pistols," Omar added. "Said all I had to do was show my driver's license as ID. I said I wasn't sure, that I'm on a student visa, and didn't want to get kicked out of the country in case someone got suspicious over an Arab-looking guy with an Arab name and a Minnesota driver's license. I hastily added I'd consider it next time after I had a chance to find out more.

"He was a bit angry saying I wasn't doing them much good not being able to go to Canada and not buying guns. I pretended to be angry, too. saying if someone'd told me what I'd be doing, maybe I could've checked things out and made arrangements. He calmed down saying Mohammad sometimes does things without thinking them through."

pause

"One was smaller and one larger, but not so small you can hide it in your hand like in the movies," Omar replied. "He also bought ammunition; I think he said 22 and something else. I can pay more attention next time."

pause

"Yes, that'd be good to fill me in on this type of thing," Omar said. "I can't let them see me studying guns."

pause

"In the car, I asked him more about the guns and what we did with them," Omar continued. "He seemed surprised, saying didn't I know that we take them to Canada? I asked him what goes on in Canada that I wasn't useful for, wondering if I could be useful in some other way."

pause

"He acted surprised and suspicious asking 'didn't Mohammad fill you in?'" Omar said. "I started to say 'no', but suddenly realized that'd not be a good answer. Words came to me to say Mohammad told me a few things when I arrived, but I was too tired and didn't remember. When I mentioned Canada again, he was busy but said he'd tell me more when I got back from Florida. I showed fake annoyance asking Kamal if he didn't remember I'd immediately been sent to Florida and Mohammad has me

running around all over the place. I guess he bought that. I'm not sure how bright he is, but he gets suspicious quickly."
pause

"Actually he did," Omar replied. "They take older people across the border, let some off in Niagara Falls if they want to go sightseeing and pick them up at a specific point later. The rest go to Missisy-something, a suburb of Toronto. They let them off there and tell them that they have to be back at a certain time at a store-front mosque there.

"Someone takes the car and empties the gas and takes out the other things and then loads it up with the drugs. When I asked why they take out the gas, he got annoyed and suspicious again saying didn't I know anything? Gas is more expensive in Canada so that's why they buy gas in the U.S.; they have to stop at a gas station in Niagara Falls, New York, on the way back. Now it makes sense why the car takes so much gas; must be two tanks.

"They drop off the drugs in Virginia, Wittsville or something like that. I remember stopping there, but I didn't pay attention. I just thought it was one of the places we dropped off merchandise and got gas. I didn't ask more because it'd raise even more suspicion. I sure don't want to be involved in drug dealing."
pause

"Oh, prescription drugs," Omar said.
pause

"Cigarettes are much more expensive in Canada, also?" Omar asked. "Maybe that's what's in the boxes we loaded this morning. I don't know what's in them, Kamal didn't say, and I didn't ask. I saw lots of signs for places to get cheap cigarettes and tobacco products just before the state line."
pause

"That's a clever one," Omar said. "Smuggle cigarettes hoping authorities focus on that if they get caught and not look for other things that'd be a more serious offense."

pause

"Yes, it'd help if you filled me in especially things like gas prices in Canada so I don't get caught again," Omar said a bit forcefully. "I know it's as much for my safety as it is for your security you don't tell me much. I really don't want to know much, but some things would help."

pause

"I'm sure I can get away to go to the library after I get back," Omar said. "I really do need to do my research. Friday's out because of Friday prayers. Maybe Saturday or Sunday. Maybe Sunday so I can nose around on Saturday and learn more things while the others are gone to Canada."

pause

"OK, bye for now," Omar said.

Chapter 43

Sunday, May 28, 2006
Buffalo, New York, USA

Omar, disturbed by Gabe Andreotti in a study carrel of the SUNY Buffalo library, said after pleasantries: "Sorry you have to come out on Sunday and on a holiday weekend too. Things are happening quickly and I need to go with Kamal to North Carolina tomorrow early. He's not happy about going on a holiday weekend either."

"Comes with the territory for me," Gabe Andreotti replied. "I have things for you but tell me what's going on."

"Mohammad got a phone call from Yemen," Omar began. "His parents are in bad shape and need him to go see them right away."

"We thought that might happen," Gabe Andreotti said.

"You arranged this?" Omar asked.

"Not exactly," he answered. "This is one thing it's best you not know too much about. When's he going?"

"Late this week or over the weekend depending on flights," Omar answered. "He asked me to help book flights because I know how to use the internet."

"That's a big help for us," Gabe Andreotti stated. "Book him on a Middle Eastern airline so he can change in Jordan, Dubai, Qatar, or someplace similar. Amman would be ideal."

"OK," Omar said. "He wants me to drive him to New York City. I mentioned taking a local flight or bus but he said he needs to do business along the way and collect money. I don't want to drive anymore and he smokes heavily so I'll lean on him to let someone else drive him."

"Oh, please drive him yourself," Gabe Andreotti said. "You can be sure he got the flight and notify us immediately. We'll make it up to you. Take time to relax and have fun in New York City. We'll pay for it."

"Omar grumbled and said: "Everyone's in a dither. Mohammad's on the phone to Canada all the time. They want more and more of something from him. He complains he's giving them all he can now."

"We're beginning to learn more what's going on in Canada," Gabe Andreotti said. "Again, best you don't know too much. What's this trip tomorrow?"

"Because he's leaving for Yemen, Mohammad wants us to go now instead of later in the week," Omar replied. "He wants Kamal to take care of business while he's gone except his wife'll run the shop like she does anyway. He actually asked me to give Friday sermons and lead prayers."

"This's helping us more and more," Gabe said almost gleefully. "Maybe you can find out more about the boxes of medicine you drop off. We strongly suspect it's in Wytheville, Virginia, at the junction of two major interstate highways. It'd fit that a drug distribution business would be there a way away from the border."

"What do you want me to do?" Omar asked.

"Just keep your eyes and ears open to find out as much as you can about the packages of drugs," Gabe Andreotti said. "I checked and we agree it's not a good idea for you to buy firearms. It'd not be a good to find your name on a record. We're not in a good place to clear the record without revealing you're working with us."

"That's a relief," Omar replied.

"We talked about setting you up with a woman," Gabe Andreotti continued. "When you're in Winston-Salem a young female agent from our Charlotte field office will pretend to keep you company."

DISCOVERIES • CHAPTER 43

"Oh!" Omar exclaimed, "That's good, I guess. On the way back from Summersville, he made snide remarks about gays, not directly accusing me of being gay, but pointed. I won't be expected to do anything, will I?"

"No. Even if you were interested and willing, our agents wouldn't do that," Gabe Andreotti said, "but she'll put on a good act I'm sure and you'll need to go along. Follow her lead. We'll tell her you're inexperienced."

"OK. How do I contact her?" Omar asked.

"Sometime tomorrow, maybe when you're in Wytheville, call me," Gabe Andreotti replied. "I'll have details and a phone number for you to call her."

"What if Kamal sees me on the phone?" Omar asked.

"It wouldn't hurt and may help if he sees you on the phone for one phone call, maybe not two," Gabe Andreotti said. "Now that I think of it, it might help if you make a point of his seeing you on the phone. Then you can say you're calling a girl you know and you're setting it up for the night. You're bright; you can think of something."

"OK," Omar replied. "Anything else?"

Gabe Andreotti answered: "Look at these photographs."

"That's Mohammad," Omar said, "and that's Kamal."

"That's what we thought," Gabe Andreotti said. "These're from public data bases like drivers' license, but it's good to have confirmation. And the other two?"

"They're not familiar. Wait. Is that Brahim or Boudi? I think I've seen a picture on one of their mother's shelves."

"Which one?" Gabe Andreotti asked.

"Maybe that one," Omar answered pointing to Brahim, "but I think he had glasses on."

"OK," Gabe Andreotti said. "There's a meeting Tuesday to work out details how to get them away from Guantanamo. Mohammad's trip fits right into that. I'm sure we will be using you. You said Kamal's taking over business. Does that mean someone else'll drive to Canada in cars loaded with gasoline, cigarettes, and firearms?"

"I don't know yet," Omar replied. "I doubt it. With Brahim and Boudi gone, the only others are a couple of young kids just out of high school who work in the garage with the cars and move boxes around. Kamal's complaining about how much driving he's having to do now so I suspect it'll be him."

"Please let us know as soon as possible," Gabe Andreotti requested. "We'd especially like to know exactly when he'll go to Canada."

"OK," Omar said. "Anything else?"

"You said cars. How many are there?" Gabe asked.

"Two full sized Chevrolets I know of," Omar replied. "They need big cars to carry more passengers to Canada and big trunk space helps when they have boxes of cigarettes, or I suppose they're cigarettes; they won't let the passengers take much. They'd need big cars for extra gas tanks, too."

"That fits the pattern," Gabe Andreotti commented.

Omar continued: "They have one car to drive to Canada while one is being driven down to North Carolina. And, oh, there's the new BMW. I think Mohammad wants me to use that to go to New York City. He keeps complaining people in Canada are putting pressure on him to sell it and get the money back, but he says they're just going to have to wait until he gets back from Yemen."

"Interesting," Gabe Andreotti said. "Call me tomorrow from Wytheville. We'll work out things with the girl."

"OK," Omar said as he stood up to shake hands.

Gabe Andreotti also stood, shook hands, and walked quickly out of the room.

Chapter 44

Monday, May 29, 2006
Wytheville, Virginia, USA

Kamal told Omar to fill the tank while he went to find the owner of the gas station. They soon returned and removed a cardboard box from the trunk. When he could dawdle no longer without drawing attention, Omar slowly replaced the gasoline nozzle and walked towards the restroom.

Outside the restroom in sight of the car, he called Gabe Andreotti: "This is Omar. We're in Wytheville where a cardboard box was unloaded."
pause

"Sleepy and tired," he replied. "We left early. Traffic's heavy because of the holiday. We only stopped a couple of times to drop off things and pick up money. We'll do more on the way back since we take two days to return."
pause

"Wilco, W-i-l-c-o," he said. "It must be local. I've seen stations here and North Carolina, but nowhere else."
pause

"Just off the interstate on the road going into town on the east side," he continued. "In a long commercial strip."
pause

"There's a Texaco station across the road and Exxon across the local street on the same side," he said. "There's a McDonalds next to the Exxon

and a Hardee's just down from the Texaco station. I'm sure someone can find it."
pause

SAM'S WILCO, WYTHEVILLE, VIRGINIA

"Sam's Wilco," he continued. "I suspect the owner's named Sami, Samer, Issam, or something like that. He looks Arab. He and Kamal speak English."
pause
"Yes," he replied. "Leaving Saturday night and is going to buy the ticket from a travel agent tomorrow. I made the reservation last night. Royal Jordanian from JFK at 11 p.m. We'll leave Lackawanna early Saturday morning."
pause
"OK. I should be able to call you from Summersville tomorrow night like last time," he said.
pause
"I should take her phone number and call her now," Omar said. "I don't think he's seen me make this call yet. I'll do my best to let him see me make the next call."

DISCOVERIES • CHAPTER 44

pause

"I'll enter it in my cell phone," he said. "What name should I put?" he asked.

pause

"Missy for Melissa," he repeated.

pause

"I'll call you tomorrow. Bye," he said, dialed again saying: "This is Omar. I'm supposed to call, er, Missy."

pause

"A little nervous and shy," he said, "but I'll try to be better tonight."

pause

"Oh, OK, you can play into that," he said.

pause

"We're in Wytheville, Virginia," he replied. "It should be a little more than an hour before we get there. We stay at the Days Inn on Germanton Road. I'll find out more details and tell you later. I've only been there once before."

pause

"OK. I'll call you when we get close to town and you'll be waiting for me in the parking lot," he said.

pause

"It's a big Chevrolet, a few years old, dark green with New York plates," he said. "How'll I recognize you?"

pause

Oh, you'll look for me," he replied. "How do you know what I am like?"

pause

"Gee, you people think of everything," he said.

pause

"See you in about an hour," he said and disconnected.

Kamal walked up and asked: "Oh, you were on the phone. Ready to go?"

Omar replied: "I was just calling a girl I'm meeting tonight. You remember a couple of weeks ago when I drove back from Florida? I met her then. I was going to ask you if you're going out with your girl like last time."

"You're meeting a girl tonight?" Kamal asked as he got into the driver's side. As they drove away: "Here I thought you're maybe gay or one of those strict Muslims who don't do anything before getting married. I was afraid you might tell Mohammad about me, but I think he fucks on the side too. I doubt his wife gives him much."

"Well, I'm shy and like to do things in private," Omar said, "but I was being cautious at first because I didn't know you and how you felt about things. If I'd known ahead of time, I probably would've called her last time, but I really did have work to do. That thesis is really hanging over my head and I need to do lots of reading. After I found out different, it was too late; she was already busy."

Kamal chuckled asking: "Where're you two going?"

"I'm hoping you'd go out like before so I can use the room, alone," Omar answered. "If not, we'll have to go somewhere else. She lives too far away to go to her place."

"Yeah, I'm going to Charlene's," Kamal said. "Don't make too much noise. That motel has paper thin walls."

Chapter 45

Monday, May 29, 2006
Winston-Salem, North Carolina, USA

Kamal parked near the reception of Day's Inn where a young woman in her mid-20s walked up to Omar saying loudly: "Ohh-marr **huhh**-nee," in a pronounced Carolina Piedmont accent giving him a big hug and kiss on the cheek.

DAY'S INN WINSTON-SALEM, NORTH, WINSTON-SALEM, NORTH CAROLINA.

She stood 5 feet seven inches, had short-ish streaked blondish hair teased into ringlets, and amply applied eye shadow, eye liner, and lipstick. She wore a blue-jean skirt that barely came half-way down her thighs, a pink polyester tank top that revealed her skimpy endowment, red imitation leather thong sandals, and a small matching purse. Omar was startled and backed away.

"Oh, arn chuh glaad to seee me, huhh-nee?" she asked moving closer. "Yew naw-thun bo-uzz arr sooo ruh-zervd."

Omar put his arm around her shoulder taking a few seconds to understand her heavy accent.

"Whooz your free-yund, Oh-mar huh-nee?" she asked.

He thought a moment to understand then said: "Oh, sorry. This is Kamal; we work together."

"Pleeez'd t' mee chah, Kamal," Missy said holding out a hand to shake. "Kamal, like a cam-muhl driver. Ah bet th' gurrlz just luv hav'n' a cam-muhl jockey if yourr as sweet as mah Omar hee-ur."

Kamal blushed as he thought: *She sure is forward, but seems nice. Where'd Omar find a girl like her?* He then replied: "Thanks, nice to meet you too."

"Ohh, yew naw-thun guys. So for-mull. Guess that's what makes yew sooo nah-iss," she said.

Kamal said awkwardly: "I should go check in."

When he entered reception, Melissa quickly reached into her purse and pushed three twenty-dollar bills into Omar's pocket saying in a cultured, educated, but detectably southern accent: "This's for dinner tonight. You're treating if Kamal can bring his girlfriend."

Omar, startled, said: "OK. Sorry if I'm messing up."

"You're doing just fine," Melissa said. "Maybe relax more and touch me a little bit more affectionately."

"OK," Omar said as he put his arm around her and pulled her close. "I have problems understanding your accent, the first accent, so I have to stop and think what you're saying. I don't want to ask you to repeat yourself."

"OK, I'll see what I can do, but I have to act the part," Melissa answered. "I want to meet his girlfriend; that's why you're taking us all out to dinner if they'll go."

DISCOVERIES • CHAPTER 45

Kamal returned handing a key to Omar saying: "Room 208, upstairs at the back. I'll leave the car here."

While they walked to the room, Omar and Kamal with backpacks, Missy said: "Yew have uh date t'night too? Why don' cha bring her along and we-ull all have din-uhr. Omar's takin' me out, arn cha huhh-nee. Yew two come along."

Kamal remained silent while Omar thought: *I should take more initiative* and said with a forced smile: "Yes, please. It'd be nice for us all to have dinner together. I just got paid so I'll treat. Where should we go, sweetie?"

"Welll, therzz Golden Corral just down the road at Haines Mall," Missy said. "It's mah fave-rite place. Yew c'n git all ya want uv sooo many thangs."

Kamal thought: *Damn, I just wanted to see Charlene fast as I could then maybe eat something after. How can I say I'm not interested without making them upset? Can't say she lives too far away because she lives close; that's why I stay here. Don't know Omar that well yet. He gets pissed off, might notice some things and tell Mohammad.* He said with a distinct lack of enthusiasm: "I could call her and see."

Missy sat on a bed and started bouncing up and down while Kamal called on the room phone saying: "Hi, Charlene baby. It's Kamal."
pause

"Yeah, me too," he said
pause

"Listen, the new guy who travels with me is here with his girlfriend," he said, "They want us to go with them to dinner at Golden Corral,"
pause

"Oh, you like it," he said. "Pick you up in five minutes."
pause

"See you," he said as he hung up the phone. "She lives close so I can go there quickly."

"Weee'uhl just go in mah carr 'nd meecha they-uhr," Missy said. "Weee-ll just wait inside the door where it's coo-ull if yer not goin' to be long."

Once downstairs, Melissa guided Omar to an old Mustang, at least eight years old, a fading red color with small dents and scratches.

Once inside, she said in her regular accent smiling: "Some car isn't it? The bureau knows how to pick 'em. Probably impounded in some bust. You wouldn't want to see the car they usually assign. It'd scream cop car."

Omar chuckled: "You really pulled that one off. I hope we don't have to wait long; I'm starved. What's this place like? We don't have Golden Corral in Minneapolis."

Melissa answered: "You pay when you go in, get a tray, tableware and drink, then serve yourself to lots of different things. They have everything. You should be first in line so you can pay for all four of us. Someone'll bring drink refills and you should leave a little tip at the end. If Kamal's polite, he'll offer to leave a tip."

"Oh, there're places like that in the twin cities, just different names," Omar commented. "Students like me go there a lot because there's lots of food for a low price."

"It must really be cold there," Melissa said while they stood inside the restaurant waiting. "Don't know if I could live there or not. Minneapolis's where the agent worked who blew the whistle on the bureau's failures after nine-eleven."

"Not so bad once you get used to it," Omar said. "Buildings're designed with walkways connecting them so you don't have to go outside hardly at all in the winter. I sure suffered when I first got there. Most of Yemen's hot and humid year 'round, I guess you know."

"I don't know much about Yemen except where it is and something of its involvement in terrorism," Melissa commented. "Maybe that's not a good topic for you."

"I don't mind," Omar said. "Do you know my family was killed just because they were in the way? It was very painful to talk about at first. Sometimes it helps to talk."

He stopped abruptly when he saw Kamal and a young woman walking towards the door. She was wearing pink shorts, straw sandals and a matching straw clutch purse, and a white shirt that was fastened by one

DISCOVERIES • CHAPTER 45

button just below her breasts with the opening revealing she was not wearing a bra and the bottom tied in a knot to reveal her naval.

Kamal opened the door for Charlene who smiled at Omar and Missy as he said: "This is Charlene and this is Omar and Missy."

All said a perfunctory: "Pleased to meet you", which came out: "Pleeez'd tuh meee cha" from the two women.

Kamal made a pretense at being willing to pay for him and Charlene, but Omar waved him off, gave the three bills, and pocketed the change without counting it.

While they were eating exchanging small talk, Missy looked at Charlene and asked: "Yew must lee-uv close t'hee-yur if yew all got hee-yur so fast."

"Yay-uh, just a few blocks," Charlene replied. "What about chew? What part uv town yew live in?"

Omar strained to listen thinking: *Better pay attention so I don't get tripped up.*

"Ohhhh, I yum from Charrr-lutt," Missy answered. "Mah fokes live there. Now ah live norrrth uv there with other fam-lee at Lake No-ur-man. Better jobs they-ur in summer in all the rest-raunts and lounges. What 'bout chew? Yew work 'round here?

"I use ta wurk at a diner clooose. That's where I met camel boy hee-yer," Charlene said as she looked at Kamal squeezing his arm. "Now I work at the Shan-gree-laww Lounge as a cocktail wait-russ. Not too bizz-ee on Mun-day nights 'spesially t'night bein' th' last night uv th' holiday weekend. I just say-ed I-ud be late t'night when my bee-ug camel jock-eee called and said heez commin'. B'sides I worked my ass off last three nights bein' it's uh hol-uh day."

After helping themselves to desert, they sat quietly until Missy said to Charlene: "Ah need to pow-duhr mah nose. Yew want t' come with me?"

"Yeay-uss," Charlene replied.

Both went to the women's restroom while Kamal said: "You got lucky it seems. Wasn't sure you had it in you."

Omar gave a big grin without saying anything.

"You seem nervous; this isn't your first time, is it?" Kamal asked.

Omar replied: "Oh, I'm still shy. These Carolina girls are so forward; Minnesota girls aren't like that." His mind drifted: *I'm sure Minnesota women're no more or less virginal. Could've gone to bed with some of 'em, 'specially students and female grad students who've come on to me subtly. 'Subtle'; that's the word. Girls there're subtle and here so forward it's scary.*

Kamal asked: "How long you think you'll be at it? You heard Charlene say she needs to go to work tonight. Otherwise I might've stayed over at her place like I do sometimes. I'm tired, too. I'm sure I'll want to go to sleep soon as I can, but don't want to disturb you, lover boy."

"Missy has to go early back to Lake Norman," Omar said, thinking: *Gee, glad I remembered that one.* "I'm pretty tired too. Wish there were some way I could let you know we are through and you can come back."

"Gee, you really aren't experienced are you?" Kamal said. "Call me and cancel the call after one good ring. I'll hear it, see the missed call, and know I can come when I want to."

Omar shyly said: "No, I've never been out with another guy and his girl before."

When the women returned giggling, Kamal jumped up obviously eager to go and guided Charlene to the door.

Missy nuzzled Omar's cheek and whispered: "tip".

Not wanting to fumble for small change, he put a five-dollar bill on the table, took Missy's hand, and walked out.

Chapter 46

Monday, May 29, 2006
Winston-Salem, North Carolina, USA

As they drove to the motel, Melissa asked: "Bob and Bud are the guys we're trying to get out of Cuba, aren't they?"

"Yes, how'd you know?" Omar answered

"Charlene told me," she replied, "except she didn't say Cuba. They're popular with girls here. She goes with Bud, a girl named Tammi with Bob."

"She's not, er, a, er, prostitute is she?" Omar asked.

"I wouldn't call her exactly that," Melissa replied. "I'm sure she gets something out of it, maybe just a nice meal and some pocket money or a very nice tip if they go to a place she's working. You really caught on quick back there."

Omar blushed and mumbled: "Thanks."

"Did you notice I didn't tell any lies?" Melissa commented. "I really did grow up in Charlotte and my folks still live there and I do live near Lake Norman now with other family. I guess they briefed you about not lying but not always telling the full truth either."

"No, not really," he said, "but some things are easy enough to figure out."

"Good," she said. "Did you notice I didn't actually say I work at Lake Norman? I just said jobs are better there than in Charlotte because of the restaurants and cocktail lounges, which is true. They can draw their own conclusions."

"No, guess I didn't so your subtlety worked on me," Omar said thinking: *This southern lady is every bit as subtle as any I've known in Minnesota.*

Once inside the motel room, Melissa broke the tension by opening her purse, pulling out a wrapped condom saying: "Go into the bathroom, put this on, and masturbate, then tie it in a knot and put it into the trash can. Maybe leave it hanging on the edge like you weren't careful when you threw it away. Unwrap it here and leave the wrapper on the night stand so Kamal can see it."

Once inside the bathroom, Omar's thoughts raced: *Never done anything like this before. Well, here goes.*

When he returned, Melissa lay on the bed fully clothed except for shoes, under the sheet, with the bedspread where it had been carelessly kicked.

"We have to make this look good," she said. "Take your shoes off and get under the sheet also."

He removed his shoes and nervously climbed under the sheet as she immediately began: "There's a big meeting tomorrow afternoon. How much've you been told?"

"Not much," he answered. "Gabe mentioned it yesterday. Something about bringing Brahim and Boudi back from Guantanamo. He wants me to call him tomorrow night. Maybe he'll give me more details then."

"That's Gabe Andreotti, isn't it?" she asked. "I don't know him nor talked directly to him, but I've been briefed."

"Yes, that's him," he replied.

"I've been instructed to tell you some details," she continued. "The two guys at Guantanamo will be returned to the U.S. soon, maybe Monday a week from today as soon as Mohammad Fadel and Kamal are out of the country."

"What? Kamal's leaving the country too?" He exclaimed. "Haven't heard about that."

"Gabe'll surely fill you in tomorrow," she replied. "You'll have a role and you may have to travel more."

Omar gulped: "Guess it comes with my job too. Gabe mentioned something when I called him from Wytheville."

She said: "I'll need to know what you observed in Wytheville because I'll be involved in uncovering the prescription drug business that's apparently run from there."

"OK," he said his mind whirling.

"The other thing I was instructed to tell you is that you must pay close attention when you stop to get the cigarettes tomorrow," she continued. "We need to know exactly how the procedure works, especially how payment's made."

"OK. Who do I tell? You or Gabe?" he asked.

"Tell Gabe when you call him tomorrow," she replied. "It's not a good idea for you to have contact with me for the next few days unless it's extremely urgent. The fewer contacts you have with agents the better, but you know that."

"Yes, Gabe told me," Omar replied.

"I'll give you my card just in case," she said. "You can always use that cell phone number you have. If you're some place where you need to make urgent contact with the bureau and can't talk freely, just call the cell phone and say: 'Hello Missy'. I'll know what to do."

She rummaged in her purse to extract a business card saying: "Here, keep this as well hidden as you can in case someone gets curious and searches."

"Maybe in my money belt?" he suggested. "One of the few things I brought from Yemen."

While putting the card in his belt, he noticed her full name: Melissa Andrews.

"You must have about as much as your mind can absorb," she said. "Tell Gabe tomorrow what you found in Wytheville. What time is it? I need to go, but we need to make this look good. When'll Kamal come back?"

"He said call him when we're finished but hang up before he answers," Omar replied.

"He knows all the tricks" Melissa chuckled. "We've been here about 30 minutes. Let's watch news on television and I'll go."

When the next half-hour break in the news came, Melissa put on her shoes and said: "It's really nice meeting you, Omar. You're a nice guy. The things you're doing are VERY much appreciated."

He got out of the bed facing her saying: "I can't say it's my pleasure because this is ugly business. Working with people like you, though, makes it more tolerable. Today's a holiday. Hope it didn't mess up your plans."

"Part of the job," she said as she gave him a quick friendly peck on the cheek and left.

Omar, his head still spinning, called Kamal, undressed to his briefs, got into bed leaving the sheets rumpled on the other side, turned out the lights making sure not to disturb the condom wrapper, and quickly went to sleep.

Soon Kamal opened the door, turning on the light causing Omar to stir and said: "She really must've worn you out," grinning as he saw the condom wrapper.

Omar mumbled sleepily: "Yeah, I'm exhausted."

Kamal returned from the bathroom a few moments later giggling and saying: "I see you did have a good time."

Both quickly went to sleep.

Book 3
CONSEQUENCES

CHAPTER 1

Tuesday, May 30, 2006
Baghdad International Airport, Iraq

With a bright new shoeshine from one of the many men working in Baghdad to earn a few dinar, Major Armstrong knocked on Colonel Jones's office door in mid-morning.

"Joshua. Or should I say Josh?" Colonel Jones said. "It's been a while. Coffee?"

"No thanks, not now;" he replied, "maybe later and, yes, Josh is fine. We have interesting ones for you today."

"You called ahead; what's up?" Colonel Jones asked.

Major Armstrong replied: "Guess who's coming to join Abed and Viktor today?"

"You got the Syrian guy?" Colonel Jones asked.

"More bizarre than that," Major Armstrong said. "We have Ali, the guy who was made into a double, and a Saudi guy who was running the operation in the U.S."

"You don't say!" Colonel Jones exclaimed.

"It's a long story, the most bizarre and convoluted you'd want to hear," Major Armstrong began. "I'll have to tell you the full story, or as much as I know, over beer."

He then gave a brief description of the events leading up to departure from Cuba and continued: "They've committed enough crimes to get themselves locked up for years, but the knowledge that'd come out would cause a political uproar you wouldn't believe; they're here until we work out what to do with them. There's a plane due soon with detainees from Guantanamo who're being released. These guys are on it."

"How long do we keep them?" Colonel Jones asked.

Major Armstrong replied: "Might not be too long for the Saudi guy. We'll turn him over to the Saudis as soon as we can work out the transfer. There's one potential problem I'll get to in a moment.

"We promised Ali we'd try to get some Arab country to take him in exchange for information about al Qaeda. We can't send him back to Syria because he might be tortured. There's a problem with him too."

"Oh, what're the problems?" Colonel Jones asked.

"For that we need the doctor," Major Armstrong said.

"You said you needed to see him when you called," Colonel Jones said and asked an assistant to get the doctor.

"Briefly," Major Armstrong began, "these two and two others who were with them were raped by Cubans immediately before being chased onto the base. I'll leave the physical details for the doctor, but they could possibly be infected with HIV, especially the Saudi guy. We can't send them anywhere else until we know what their status is."

"Where should we keep them so they won't infect others?" Colonel Jones asked. "From what I know about HIV, and we have to know a fair amount in the funeral business, it's transmitted mostly by sex and shared needles, but also blood to blood contact. I suppose we need to keep them in separate cells, but our space is kind of limited."

"Your concern is valid, Colonel, but that may not be necessary," Major Armstrong replied. "For sure, you can't put them in the same cell. The Saudi guy's violent and might attack Ali. He has a pattern of attacking people.

"The thought came to mind we put the Saudi guy in the same cell as Abed. They're both religious zealots. I can't imagine they'd do anything that'd transmit HIV. Abed is mild mannered and a little stupid, but he could probably defend himself. The report says the Saudi guy attacks persons who he thinks are not showing proper respect to Muslims or Muslims who are not behaving properly. Probably wouldn't have a reason to attack Abed."

"What about Ali?" Colonel Jones asked.

"Remember Viktor's very attached to him," Major Armstrong said. "We could put them in the same cell. I can't imagine two doctors knowingly transmitting HIV even if they were inclined and of course we'd have to tell Viktor. You're in charge of where to put prisoners. I thought of these possibilities since you asked."

"Sounds good to me," Colonel Jones said.

Dr. Sensenberg arrived and Major Armstrong said: "I've been telling Colonel Jones we have two prisoners coming from Guantanamo soon. I need to give you these medical files. You'll find out soon enough one of them, Ali, is the one who Viktor made into the double. Maybe I'll have something to drink now, but something cold if possible."

Colonel Jones asked: "What about you, Bob?"

"No thanks. I just had something," he replied.

Colonel Jones asked Carrie to bring cold drinks and for her and Jimmy. All sat in silence while the doctor read the files. She returned with the drinks while he was reading.

He laid the folders aside and said: "I'll read these in more detail later, but I get the idea. Nasty business. Fortunately, we don't deal with it much in pediatrics. We don't have HIV testing capabilities; we'll have to send blood to Germany. What do we do with them if they're positive?"

Colonel Jones replied: "There must be policies and procedures for HIV positive detainees. I'll look them up, but let's not cross that bridge until the time comes."

"I'll look you up when the plane lands and we get the prisoners sorted out," Major Armstrong said.

All stood and shook hands. Major Armstrong and Dr. Sensenberg left together but went separate ways.

Chapter 2

Tuesday, May 30, 2006
Quantico, Virginia, USA

Rhonda Philips walked sprightly into Rosie Jordan's office for a 10 o'clock meeting wearing a hot pink cotton and linen summer dress with pearl white block heeled leather shoes, large matching leather bag, pearl necklace, and pearl ear studs set in gold.

Rosie Jordan greeted her saying: "Roger Chen from the Attorney General's office will be here shortly. We can catch up in the meantime. You've solved two of your problems at Guantanamo it seems."

"Ali and Adnan arrive in Baghdad any minute if not already," Rhonda Phillips replied. "I heard Ali opened and gave your interrogators a lot of information."

"Yes," Rosie Jordan said. "We got an indication of the fourth person involved in the abduction. It must've been a gay police officer in Middletown, Ohio, where they went before they left for Mexico. Those last cell phone calls show Middletown, Ohio, also. His physical description matches the fourth man outside the bar in Cincinnati. The question's whether we want to pursue the issue. It could open up lots of things we don't want open now."

"For sure," Rhonda Philips agreed.

"Our undercover person in Lackawanna has been traveling to and from North Carolina with the guy who traveled to Lebanon using Patrick

Ferris's passport," Rosie Jordan added and continued to describe circumstances. "There're some amusing things about girls along the way, but that'll wait for another day.

"The big thing we found out is there's much more to the Canadian part than we thought. We're eager to know more from the two guys still in Guantanamo.

"With the cooperation of the CIA, we enticed Mohammad Fadel to leave the U. S. for what he thinks is a temporary visit with his parents who're in poor health. When he leaves, we can bring your guys back from Guantanamo.

"We also want to get the guy out of the way who's supposed to take over while Mohammad's away so your guys won't have support from anyone in Lackawanna and'll be more likely to go along with what we offer them. They're really small potatoes. We want to park them out of the way and not punish them much. You feel the same."

"Essentially, yes," Rhonda agreed. "They're not bad guys; just got caught by circumstances."

Roger Chen arrived with a confident professional air. He was in his late 30s, average build and height, and dressed in a typical lawyer's navy blue pin stripe suit along with a white shirt and a yellow tie that complimented his square-ish face, nicely trimmed slightly wavy black hair, and dark brown eyes typical of his Chinese ancestry.

After introductions and exchanging pleasantries, he summarized information he had and concluded: "You want them out of there, but you don't want to prosecute them publicly. Instead you want to convict them on lesser charges so they can be kept quiet, at least for a while. Is that right?"

"Conviction on lesser charges was my idea based on what the bureau often does," Rosie Jordan said.

"That's a good summary," Rhonda Philips said.

Roger Chen continued: "Their crimes include smuggling prescription medicine from Canada into the U.S., smuggling firearms, cigarettes, and gasoline into Canada, and maybe extorting cash from shopkeepers in the U.S., maybe for the benefit of al Qaeda. Is that right?"

"That's our conclusion," Rosie Jordan added.

Roger Chen continued: "There're pitfalls, but we might pull it off if they cooperate and we have a little luck.

"When they set foot in the U.S. they have rights of U.S. citizens. I presume you'll land at a military facility. They don't have the right to be on a military facility without an invitation so you can immediately make them leave. At that point they're free to go. You could get warrants and immediately arrest them on some charges. It wouldn't be easy to convince a judge to issue an arrest warrant or establish probable cause based on the evidence you have so far. If they have good lawyers, they could get off; you risk a backlash that you're targeting Arab-Americans, not to mention exposure of details you don't want exposed."

"They don't have any money," Rhonda Philips interrupted. "Literally they do not have one cent. If we take them to the gate and just drop them, what'll they do? How do they contact a lawyer, much less pay for one?"

"They're in an al Qaeda cell," Roger Chen answered. "Maybe it can provide them with a lawyer."

"Don't be so sure," Rhonda Philips said. "DIA's knowledge of al Qaeda in the U.S. is limited. They operate outside the U.S. based on religious zeal and fervor so they don't think of having lawyers on retainer just in case one is needed. Maybe Rosie can tell us what it's like in the U.S."

"Al Qaeda's not a crime organization that has lawyers ready on a moment's notice," Rosie Jordan began. "Our resource hasn't mentioned lawyers. From all indications, it's a one-man operation led by Mohammad Fadel and it looks like he's taking orders from Canada.

"When they arrive in the U.S. from Guantanamo there'll be no one to contact for help. Their parents are poor and poorly educated immigrants, not likely able to provide them with lawyers nor money to pay for one. So what does that leave them? The public defender?"

"Don't underestimate public defenders," Roger Chen said. "Many if not most of them are good at what they do and can be very aggressive. We can't control how they'd defend them and wouldn't want to if we could. Still the situation you describe makes it more likely we can get them to bargain and plead guilty to a lesser charge. The issue is to which lesser charge. Smuggling cigarettes and gasoline out of the U.S. is not a U.S. federal crime so long as tax has been paid. There might be an issue of not having export licenses, but that's not important enough for a judge to incarcerate them; at most, it'd probably be a fine.

"The firearms issue is a possibility. Just like cigarettes and gasoline, it's likely not a U.S. federal crime to smuggle firearms into Canada, but there're laws about interstate transportation of firearms that aren't for personal use. It'd take some warrants, but we could get access to records of that dealer in West Virginia and find their names as purchasers of a large number of firearms. We can start working on this, but it'll take a while to put together a case a judge might buy.

"We could pursue the extortion issue. If we can get enough shop owners to testify, we might have a good case. It'd likely come out that they're extorting money for Mohammad Fadel and al Qaeda. You may or may not want that. We can start working on this, but again, it'll take time.

"After consulting with some colleagues, we think the best thing you can use fairly soon is prescription drugs. If they can be caught with prescription drugs manufactured in Canada in their possession, we can probably build a case just on that alone and not bring in al Qaeda unless the defense brings it up. If we get more evidence from the drop off place in Virginia, it can help even more. That means you have to arrange for them to have the medicine in their possession and ideally stopped by local police who search and find the drugs. Could you do that?"

"We might," Rosie Jordan replied. "Our undercover person in Lackawanna is pretty good at arranging things."

Roger Chen continued: "there're risks. It's possible a defense attorney could claim entrapment by placing the medicine in their car without their knowledge. We have to make sure they agree ahead of time."

"This is intriguing," Rosie Jordan said. "I told Rhonda you guys're the best. How soon can we get together and work out the details."

"I might get some things pulled together by tomorrow or maybe Thursday," Roger Chen said.

"Works for me," Rhonda Philips said. "I'll drop everything and come to another meeting whenever."

"I'll get our operations persons working on possible arrest scenarios," Rosie Jordan stated. "Let's go to lunch. We'll use my private dining room and we can talk more."

Chapter 3

Tuesday, May 30, 2006
Baghdad International Airport, Iraq

Dr. Sensenberg and Viktor waited in the clinic with other medical staff for an influx of new detainees. Medical staff rolled Adnan in on a cot restrained by a straight jacket and leg clamps. Ali followed wearing shabby clothes rumpled from long hours inside an airplane.

"Ali!" Viktor almost screamed with a huge surprised smile rushing with his arms open to give him a big hug.

"Viktor!" Ali opened his arms also with a big smile.

Ali gave Viktor three Arab kisses on the cheeks, left, right, left then they locked in a tight embrace.

That's a bit intense for fatherly affection, Dr. Sensenberg thought and said: "I'm Dr. Sensenberg, the medical officer. You're Ali Salman and a medical doctor."

"Yes, I'm Doctor Ali; pleased to meet you," he said distracted watching Adnan wheeled in. "Be careful how you deal with him. He can be violent if a woman touches him. Let me help you. I tended to him on the plane. He speaks good English, but is calmer when I speak with him in Arabic. He was badly injured."

Dr. Sensenberg went quickly into an examining room saying: "Alex, he'll only let men touch him and is violent."

Moments later, a young female nurse came away leaving only Alex and a male orderly inside.

Ali continued: "He needs cosmetic surgery too. He's not a nice person, but no one deserves to go through life with a badly disfigured face."

You're a cosmetic surgeon? Dr. Sensenberg asked.

"Yes, I trained under Dr. Viktor," Ali replied.

The young female nurse returned saying: "Rich'll be here in a minute. Do you still need me or shall I go and come back when the other detainees arrive?"

She was a stereotypical Nebraska 'farm girl type', about 5 feet 5 inches with medium brown hair cut short and swept to the back in a 'duck tail' haircut, sparkling blue-green eyes, and dressed in a white nurse's uniform with pants and a top. She always had a cheerful smile.

"Please stay for now, Angie, if you will," Dr. Sensenberg said. To Ali: "We can talk about your background later. Now we need to examine you. Do you object to female nurses drawing blood and other things?"

"Oh, no," Ali replied.

Dr. Sensenberg said: "Wait here and come into the examining room when we call you. Angie can take blood, history, and other things. You surely know what I mean."

"Yes, I know the procedure," he replied. "Don't you want me to help you with Adnan though?"

Dr. Sensenberg answered: "Let's examine you first. It won't take long. It won't hurt him to wait. Angie, please come with me; I'll tell you what to do."

She followed miffed, wondering what he needed to tell her because she knew her job very well.

Dr. Sensenberg made a fuss about looking at the supplies on the table motioning for her to come closer then said softly: "There's a small chance he's been infected with HIV involuntarily. Be extra careful although you know your job very well and always follow procedure. Draw enough blood for another HIV test. I'll tell you more later if need be. I'll ask him to come in."

Ali went in, did not shut the door, and Angie began the examination. A young man came into the reception area wearing a rumpled white medical orderly uniform looking like he had just been disturbed, which he had.

"In there, Rich, please, and thanks for coming on such short notice," Dr. Sensenberg said motioning towards the other examining room. "Maybe you and I should go see what's going on. To Viktor: "It might be a good idea to take the bandages off his face while he's still restrained. I'd like your opinion about his facial injuries."

Alex was holding Adnan's legs while Brandon, an average sized 'boy-next-door type' orderly was washing Adnan's mid-section after having removed a soiled diaper. Rich immediately put on rubber gloves and began picking up the soiled diaper to dispose of it and other used supplies, making a point not to look at Adnan's mid-section. Alex pointedly looked away from the exposed genitals as did the doctors, having been trained to respect Islamic sensitivities.

"How's it going, guys?" Dr. Sensenberg asked?

"He's uncooperative, trying to kick us even if he's restrained," Alex answered. "He doesn't respond to anything we say, but maybe he doesn't understand English. Do we need to put another diaper on him?"

"He speaks English well enough we're told," Dr. Sensenberg said. "Let's wait 'til the Syrian doctor comes in; he tended to him in the airplane. Cover him with a sheet and hope he doesn't do anything before he gets here."

"Oh, he's a doctor?" Alex asked. "I thought he was another detainee."

"He's both," Dr. Sensenberg said. "We can talk about that later. Now, we want to examine his facial injuries."

The two doctors moved to the head of the examining table. Adnan started moving his head as much as he could from the neck screaming: "Don't touch me!"

"We know you speak English, Adnan Mohamad Abdullah al Wahab," Dr. Sensenberg said. "We also know you're a strict Muslim and we'll respect your sensitivities. We must examine you and you must understand that. We're going to remove the bandages and examine your injuries. The other doctor here is a specialist in this type of injuries. If you cooperate, it'll make it easier. Your record says you were a battlefield medic so you must obviously know why we're looking at your wounds and changing dressings."

Meanwhile, Viktor had washed and sterilized his hands and started removing bandages. Adnan, surprised the doctor knew his full name in Saudi Arabian tradition, lay still moving only when adhesive tape was removed.

"Now I see what Ali meant," Viktor said. "He does need surgery urgently to make it possible for full repair."

Hearing a knock at the door, Dr. Sensenberg said: "That must be Angie. Alex, please come here a moment."

Outside, he told Alex about Adnan's possible HIV infection and asked him to draw additional blood. He then went to the other examining room where Ali was sitting on the examining table with his shirt off.

"You're ready for me," he said. "Let's look in your eyes. Now your ears. I see very faint scars. Are they from the surgery Viktor did on you?"

"Yes," Ali replied while Dr. Sensenberg continued: "Viktor's been telling me quite a bit about this type of surgery. Maybe we can talk about it later. Heart's good. Deep breath. Another deep breath. Cough. Cough again. And again. You don't have a hernia do you? You'd know so maybe I don't need to examine there.

"No, no hernia," Ali replied.

"That's enough for now except penile swab and urine sample and you can surely do that yourself," Dr. Sensenberg said. "You can put your shirt back on too. I hate to bring up another topic, but did the medical staff at Guantanamo say anything to you about HIV?"

"Yes, there's a slight chance I might be infected," Ali replied. "They seemed to assume I'd know being a doctor. I know how HIV's transmitted and how I may have been infected. I asked questions about ease of transmission, incubation periods, and the like. We concluded the likelihood of infection is low, but I must be cautious until I've been tested negative a few times."

"You may have detected we took enough blood for an additional test," Dr. Sensenberg added. "We don't have lab facilities so we'll send it to Germany. You know how HIV's transmitted so obviously you're expected not to engage in any activity that could transmit the virus. In addition to no sex, that means no surgery, although you wouldn't be likely to perform surgery anyway."

"Yes, I understand," Ali replied.

"My major concern is the Saudi Arabian guy," Dr. Sensenberg continued. "We're taking blood from him also. Is there anything you can add to what's in his record?"

"I haven't read his record," Ali replied. "I'm well aware he may've been infected; I watched it happen."

Dr. Sensenberg added: "I suppose you wouldn't know he had rectal damage and bleeding, ideal conditions for transmission. Apparently you had no damage."

"They told me I had no damage," Ali replied, "and I didn't have any discomfort."

"I'm not sure how much they told Adnan," Dr. Sensenberg continued. "It seems he was uncommunicative after he regained consciousness and became belligerent at the slightest thing. You seem to be the only one who has any rapport with him. Somehow he must be informed and told not to engage in activities that'd transmit HIV. His record says he was an al Qaeda battlefield medic, but I can't imagine they'd've briefed their people on HIV."

"He told me he'd been an al Qaeda medic," Ali said, "and I told interrogators. He was also a laboratory technician in a hospital. I can't imagine there'd be any problem with his spreading HIV by his own activities. He's an extreme Islamic fundamentalist and wouldn't consider sex outside of marriage or drug use and neither will occur in this prison I'm sure."

"Thanks for your offer to help," Dr. Sensenberg said. "I know you're tired from a long flight, but anything you can do would be appreciated."

"I'm pleased to help," Ali replied. "I can't say how much I calmed him down. At least he wasn't kicking and screaming like before. He's like a caged animal. I'm no psychologist and had only minimal psychiatric training, like you I suppose. Still he's angry, frightened, confused, and both emotionally and physically stressed all at the same time. He suffered a terrible trauma, both emotionally and physically when he was raped. It was bad enough for me, but think of a Muslim fundamentalist who might believe he's unclean before Allah the rest of his life.

Chapter 4

Tuesday, May 30, 2006
Baghdad International Airport, Iraq

When Dr. Sensenberg and Ali entered the other examining room, Brandon and Rich were attempting to hold down Adnan's legs while Alex was trying to draw blood. Viktor was examining his face the best he could.

"He's really uncooperative," Alex said. "He keeps screaming 'No! Leave me alone!'"

"Let me try," Ali offered and spoke to Adnan in Arabic who responded with a torrent of angry invective in Arabic.

"He thinks you're injecting poison or knocking him out like the guys who abducted us," Ali explained.

"Doesn't he realize we're just making a routine examination?" Dr. Sensenberg asked. "They must've done the same thing at Guantanamo."

"He was unconscious. He's not rational now, but he hears and understands everything we say."

Ali spoke Arabic to him again and slightly less belligerent-sounding Arabic responses came from Adnan.

Ali said: "I told him you're not injecting him with anything, just taking blood samples for lab analysis like when he worked in a hospital. I added you don't inject substances for torture or truth serums like he did in Afghanistan. I reminded him Americans treat detainees humanely; his response was something about Abou Ghraib, you have him restrained and put on diapers."

"His file said he urinated in the bed to punish people in the hospital," Dr. Sensenberg replied.

Adnan immediately started speaking angrily in Arabic.

"He said he urinated in the bed because women were trying to help him urinate and under the law of Allah he can't let a woman touch his body," Ali paraphrased. "Finally he couldn't hold it any longer. The indecent Americans made him stay in the urine-soaked bed to torture him."

"Here we have male medical staff because we know Muslim men won't allow women to see them or touch them," Dr. Sensenberg said. "They're overworked because there're not enough medically-trained men in the reserve units. We said we'll respect his religion. He'll have a male attendant to help urinate with as much privacy as possible."

Again, Adnan spoke in Arabic only slightly less angry and Ali said: "He says he's capable of urinating and also defecating on his own in privacy, but you have him restrained like the infidel monsters did at Abou Ghraib."

"His record says he attacked an interrogator there," Dr. Sensenberg commented forcefully.

More angry Arabic came from Adnan; Ali's said: "He says he's doing the will of Allah to protect Islam and Islamic people from disrespectful acts. The infidel in Guantanamo insulted him and threatened him with heathen acts."

Dr. Sensenberg spoke directly: "You obviously understand me Adnan Mohamad Abdullah al Wahab. When you're in this medical unit you do not have the right to impose your interpretation of what you think is the will of Allah on other people. We have the obligation to do the will of God, the same God as your Allah, to protect our people from violent attack. All religions including your Islam clearly say one person will not cause harm to another. Until you can accept that fact, you'll be kept under restraint. You can discuss this with your chaplain any time you like after we finish this medical exam.

"We have the obligation from Allah to protect other detainees, all presumably loyal followers of Islam, from infectious disease and we have an obligation from Allah to protect you from the effects of any disease or injury that may not've been detected. You worked in a hospital and as a medic so you must understand what I'm talking about. You must also understand we're going to examine you, one way or another, and we'll do it as humanely as possible with Allah watching everything we do. I'm more than willing to incur Allah's judgment on me for anything I do and I suspect these other fine gentlemen are too."

Everyone in the room was stunned. Ali spoke to Adnan in Arabic who answered in Arabic.

"He'll allow the examination to proceed if I'm watching every step," Ali stated. "I assured him he won't be harmed and he says he'll trust me. He knows there're enough people with the physical strength to restrain him."

When Dr. Sensenberg finished examining the upper torso, he said to Ali: "In view of his attitude, maybe we don't need to examine for hernia."

"I can't imagine anything that'd cause a hernia," Ali said. "You can safely forget about it for now."

"The last thing is a penile culture and a urine sample," Dr. Sensenberg added. "It'd be a violation of procedure if we omitted them. Any suggestions?"

Ali and Adnan conversed in Arabic then Ali said: "He definitely will not allow anyone to touch him. He agreed to allow me to watch just enough to see that he's doing it properly. He doesn't need anyone watching to give the urine sample. You should hold up the sheet and turn your backs."

After Adnan finished, Dr. Sensenberg said: "We need clothes for him so he can be taken to his cell. He can use scrubs until he can be issued clothes. We don't have underwear so he will just have to do without."

"My roommate's skinny like him," Brandon offered. "Maybe he can spare a pair."

Dr. Sensenberg was at the point of saying 'no' when Ali quickly said: "Oh, good idea."

Dr. Sensenberg said: "Please tell security we're ready for them to escort him to a cell. We can go outside while he dresses but leave the door open so we can watch him and go inside quickly if he moves."

CONSEQUENCES • CHAPTER 4

"Sorry if I overruled you on the underwear, Doctor," Ali said once outside seated. "Perhaps you don't understand how important it is to Arabs to have underwear to cover their mid-sections. If we meet his needs on a small issue, it might be easier to deal with him when there're bigger issues."

"It's OK. I didn't think about that," Dr. Sensenberg replied. "What'd you say to him to get him to cooperate?"

Ali replied: "I said if he wants to do what he thinks is the will of Allah, he'd better cooperate because otherwise he'll never be out of constraints. I also told him that if Allah trusted me enough to send me on that mission then Allah surely trusts me not to violate his principles."

Dr. Sensenberg continued: "How'd you know al Qaeda uses needles to inject things to torture or control people?"

"Just a guess," Ali replied. "His reactions to the needles were extreme. The thought just came to me."

"I should've thought about that," Dr. Sensenberg commented. "Young children are terribly afraid of needles if they've been forced to have IVs or something."

"When can we do surgery on his face?" Viktor asked.

"We need to talk about that," Dr. Sensenberg replied. "There're potential complications. Ali knows about them."

"Oh, what facilities do you have for cosmetic surgery?" Ali asked.

"We don't," Dr. Sensenberg replied. "We did it once the best we could in a near emergency situation."

"A bit like out on the battlefield," Viktor explained and recounted the experience briefly.

"I'll bet you'll be glad to finish this tour and get back to school," Dr. Sensenberg said to Alex? "Have you had any surgical rotations yet?"

"Oh, what kind of school?" Viktor asked. "You didn't tell me you're attending medical school."

"Not medical school," Alex replied. "I'm studying to be a nurse practitioner. I'll be very happy to get back and so'll my wife."

"What's a nurse practitioner?" Ali asked.

"In most states there's now a profession called nurse practitioner that's between a doctor and a nurse," Dr. Sensenberg began. "They're allowed to be in private practice, do some types of examinations, do some routine procedures, and prescribe certain types of medicines. It's a real benefit in rural areas and small towns where there's not enough work to justify a doctor. People can get medical attention they wouldn't seek if they had to drive to a big city. It's really great for pediatrics. Lots of baby checkups are routine and don't need a doctor; nurse practitioners can find potential problems and get care sooner."

"Lots of people, especially older ones, want to be seen by a man even if it's a nurse practitioner," Alex added. "It should be a good living and serve the community."

Brandon entered with underwear and hospital scrubs asking: "Shall I give them to him now?"

"Should we shut the door and let him get dressed alone?" Dr. Sensenberg asked Ali.

"Probably," Ali answered. "Let me talk to him."

He spoke sternly in Arabic, took the clothes from Brandon, gave them to Adnan, shut the door, then said: "I told him we're making an exception, but he'd better hurry and get dressed because the door's going to be opened in five minutes and we'd check pockets and the inside of his underwear if anything's missing."

Major Armstrong came in, shook hands with Dr. Sensenberg, greeted Viktor, looked at Ali and said: "I need to talk to this detainee. It won't take long."

Inside an examining room the major began: "I've been designated to tell you formally you are here as a detainee. This is not like Guantanamo where you were allowed on the base for humanitarian reasons. You have committed crimes against the United States. We do not view you as an immediate security threat nor dangerous. It doesn't serve our purposes to bring you to trial at this time so we're not formally charging you at this time.

"We won't return persons to a country where they'd be tortured or persecuted. So far you haven't made a case that you'll be tortured or persecuted in Syria, but we've decided we won't pursue returning you there for now. Instead, with your consent, we brought you here until we can make arrangements to send you to a suitable location.

"You'll be treated humanely while you're here. Unlike Guantanamo, though, you don't have freedom of movement. I'm sure you understand, but I'm still obligated to notify you formally. Do you understand what I've been telling you?"

Ali gulped, and said: "Yes, I understand."

"Good," Major Armstrong added. "You must be tired from your long trip. We can talk later if necessary."

Meanwhile, guards took Adnan to the cell where Abdulrahman was sitting silently. After tense uncomfortable moments, Abdulrahman spoke in Arabic: "I'm Abdulrahman al Baladi. Why're you here?"

Adnan replied in Arabic: "I'm Adnan," and gave a vague answer about why he was there.

Abed gave a vague response. From then on, the two of them talked very little praying together five times daily.

Chapter 5

Tuesday, May 30, 2006
Summersville, West Virginia, USA

About 7 p.m. Omar called from Applebee's saying after greetings: "He's with Sheryl again,"
pause
"Very well," he chuckled. "She really knows how to handle things. Do you give your agents training in acting?"
pause
"He seems to," he continued. "He made crude remarks about, er, my keeping a winning streak going."
pause
"I said I really needed to work tonight because of having fun last night," Omar said. "He made crude remarks about not having my priorities straight choosing school work over sex. Also made snide remarks about my being a college guy who thinks he's so important. He feels threatened."
pause
"I observed what I could," Omar replied. "He paid cash, taking it from what he collected on the way down."
pause
"Yes, we got guns too," he continued. "He was annoyed again I wouldn't buy any; said Canadians complain because we're not getting them enough. I said I'm still checking."

pause

"Yes, M, er, Agent Andrews said there's a meeting today," he replied.

pause

"What? I have to drive there again?!" Omar exclaimed.

pause

"How'n hell am I supposed to do that?" Omar said forcefully. "I take Mohammad to New York City on Saturday like you want me to. Then I have to drive back to Lackawanna and then to North Carolina by noon Monday? No way. There're only 24 hours in a day and I need to sleep. You know I want to help, but some things I just can't do."

pause

"If it's Tuesday, it might be possible, but it's a heck of a lot of driving!" he continued annoyed. "Why not stay over in New York City and drive to North Carolina from there?"

pause

"OK," Omar groaned. "You need a car there with drugs in it? How'n hell am I supposed to get drugs in the car? I don't have anything to do with that end of the operations."

pause

"He's already feeling threatened, maybe thinking I want to shove him aside and take over," he said. "That's what a Yemeni'd do. If I start nosing around, he'll really get upset.

pause

What? You want me to do that too?" he almost shouted. "What do you think I am? Some magician or miracle worker. How the hell am I supposed to make sure he has guns and cigarettes in the car he takes to Canada?"

pause

"OK, OK, I'm bright, but there're limits," he replied.

pause

"Let me go over this again," Omar said. "Kamal must go to Canada on Saturday and have guns and cigarettes in the car. I'm supposed to notify you which car he's driving."

pause

"But how'm I supposed to do that? I'll leave early Saturday before he'd take off." Omar asked.

pause

"Ok, I'll get you the license plates for both cars just in case," Omar repeated.

pause

"Then when I get back from New York City, I'm supposed to take off again to drive one of the Chevrolets to North Carolina," Omar continued.

pause

"What reason do I give for taking off for North Carolina so people won't get suspicious?" he asked.

pause

"Why'd the phone call come to me that they got away from captors? I don't get those kinds of calls."

pause

"Oh, now I'm supposed to have Mohammad's cell phone," he stated sarcastically.

pause

"Phone call's going to come from one of you, but sound like it's from the captors. Damn, this is getting complicated," he exclaimed. "And I'm supposed to make sure that there's a load of prescription drugs in the car I take to North Carolina. How'm I supposed to do that?"

pause

"This's too much to get my head around. If there're not drugs there for me to take to North Carolina, then Kamal has to bring some back on Saturday then he goes to Canada again on Sunday and doesn't come back."

pause

"For sure we need to meet," he said. "I'm getting the idea, but need to think it over. You're expecting too much."

pause

"I'll make some excuse to go to the library on Friday, maybe late-ish, after prayers," he said.

CONSEQUENCES • CHAPTER 5

pause

"OK, I'll call or text," he said.

Omar hung up frustrated and annoyed thinking: *Damn, what've I gotten myself into? Didn't bargain for this; Can't do everything? How can I get out of this gracefully and just go back to Minnesota!?*

Chapter 6

Wednesday, May 30, 2006
Quantico, Virginia, USA

Rhonda Philips, wearing an off-white linen and cotton summer dress with bold chocolate brown zig-zag patterns on the skirt, chocolate brown leather block heel shoes and large matching leather bag, chocolate brown scarf, and plain gold ear studs, met Roger Chen again in Rosie Jordan's office.

After pleasantries, Roger Chen reviewed issues they discussed the previous day and continued: "I've been checking with colleagues. A major issue is probable cause for police to stop their car and search it. One possibility is for them to buy large quantities of cigarettes in North Carolina, someone notify police in another state, say Virginia. Police stop them, find cigarettes, and arrest them on state charges of bringing in cigarettes without Virginia tax paid for commercial purposes. Then when searching the car, the prescription drugs are found."

"We have a good working relationship with Virginia State Police," Rosie Jordan offered. "Our operations people have already begun working on different scenarios. We'd be justified having FBI agents watching large tobacco sellers in North Carolina who'd notify Virginia police of suspicious activity. I'm not a lawyer, but wouldn't that help the probable cause issue?"

"Yes," Roger Chen replied. "It'd be better to have the arrest in the western part of Virginia near the drop-off point for the medicine. Among other things, federal judges in the Western District of Virginia are no-nonsense. What kind of punishment do we bargain for?"

Rhonda Philips replied: "They're basically good persons who came under the spell of Mohammad Fadel. I've read about minimum security prisons where people are locked up, but otherwise have an easy existence; places disgraced CEOs are sent. Maybe send these two to some place like that, hopefully a long way away from Lackawanna. Is there a place like that in Montana or North Dakota?"

Rosie Jordan interjected: "I've been thinking along the same lines: a short prison sentence to keep them out of circulation a few months and then supervised work-release for a few years until this blows over."

Rhonda Philips said: "Both these guys just want to live normal lives and earn a decent living. Brahim especially wants to go to a university. Can we make going to school and being steadily employed part of a work-release?"

"We've been thinking alike," Roger Chen said. "I gathered you wanted them far away so I did some checking. There's a minimum security federal prison in Duluth, Minnesota, on an old Air Force base that has capacity. We can build a case a judge'd accept for sending them there.

"Doing community service and re-integration into society is often part of a minimum security prison stay although most prisoners are much older men like CEOs you mentioned. It's not out of reason for a work-release to require employment and attendance at school. From what I picked up, Duluth's an open and tolerant community and the economy is good so we might be able to require they stay in Duluth until their work-release is up. There're a couple of universities there too. I can work on this more."

"Sounds good to me," Rosie Jordan commented.

"Sounds good to me, too," Rhonda Philips said. "Let me clarify some things: "I presume you expect me to arrange transportation through the DOD to get them out of there. Yes, Roger, it'd have to be to a military installation. Landing at a non-military airport would raise questions we wouldn't want to deal with. You want them to pick up cigarettes along the way and that could be around Winston-Salem.

THREE KISSES

"I did some homework and found Fort Bragg and Pope Air Force Base, joint installations, not far from Winston-Salem. It's a major logistics and staging area so there's a lot of military traffic from all over. We could surely get a flight there from Guantanamo without drawing attention. If you think this's a good place, I'll do some more checking."

Rosie Jordan said. "Our operations people are working on a North Carolina arrival as one likely scenario. An agent from Charlotte's already involved so it could work."

Roger Chen added: "Makes sense to have them close to the cigarettes and Virginia where they'd be arrested."

Rhonda Philips continued: "Roger, you mentioned their rights as U.S. citizens. Remember Brahim's very well informed about individual rights, the Constitution, Bill of Rights, government, history, and the like, especially for someone with just a high school education. He also says Arabs have no rights in the U.S. What do we do if he talks to a public defender or the judge along these lines?"

"You've got a point," Roger replied. "Wait. I have a possible solution or way to get guidance. A new guy's just joined our office. He's Arab-American from near Detroit, Yusef Shaito but goes by Joe. Many people think he's Japanese until they see him because of his name. We went to a lot of effort to recruit him from the University of Michigan law school. He's Muslim, although we couldn't use that as a criterion. Ideally I'd like to have him talking to these guys face-to-face. He's sharp as a tack and has good people skills. Don't think he has enough experience to be sent to Guantanamo alone. We have to be careful about too many people knowing underlying details, but surely Joe wouldn't be a problem. I can work on that."

Rosie Jordan added: "Our operations have worked on one possibility. We can have one of Mohammad's cars waiting with the prescription drugs inside, maybe just outside the base or maybe we'll drive them in an FBI car to some place nearer Winston-Salem where the car's waiting."

Roger Chen interjected: "You need to be careful about taking them too far in an FBI car without first arresting them or else they might have another good defense point. Just be sure you coordinate with us first on the legal implications."

Rosie Jordan continued: "If plans go the way they're supposed to, we'll have Mohammad and Kamal out of the way this coming weekend and we could fly these two guys out on Monday. That means we need to get them to agree to this plea bargain by the end of the week if possible. For that we need to have someone at Guantanamo. You'll need to be there I'm sure, Rhonda. Who else? You said your young Arab-American attorney shouldn't be there alone, Roger. You going also?"

Roger Chen said: "We're used to dealing with accused persons' attorneys not with them directly. We'll need someone there, probably me along with Joe, but need to be careful not to overwhelm them."

"It could be helpful to have an FBI agent there too," Rosie Jordan added. "Maybe the agent from Buffalo. You're right; we don't want to have too many to intimidate them."

"The base commander'll likely insist on having someone present, probably from security," Rhonda Philips said. "When'll we have this meeting?"

"It seems I'm the only one here who won't be there," Rosie Jordan said, "which is fine with me! We don't want to give them too much time to think about this. I hate to tell everyone to work on a weekend, especially when we had two of our field agents working over the holiday weekend, but maybe Sunday's the best day. It seems everyone except our agent from Buffalo will be traveling from DC. Maybe we can bring him down from Buffalo on Friday so he's here to tell us that Mohammad left the country."

Rhonda Philips added: "This project's occupied most of my weekends so far so another won't hurt. The sooner we get this over the better."

Roger Chen gulped and said: "We don't usually work weekends, but sometimes it has to happen. I don't know how Joe'll feel about it."

They reviewed details and exchanged goodbyes.

Chapter 7

Friday, June 2, 2006
Buffalo, New York, USA

At night, Gabe Andreotti was waiting in a study carrel in the SUNY Buffalo library and said to Omar who walked in: "What's up? You don't look so good today and you were upset on the phone on Tuesday."

"You're asking too much of me," Omar blurted out. "I want to help because I hate al Qaeda and I badly need the money you're paying me, also the money Mohammad's paying me, but damn it, there's a limit to what I can do. I just want to be an Islamic scholar and an imam someday, not a professional spook."

Gabe said: "I'll see what I can do about money. We don't want a matter of money to interfere, especially at this delicate and crucial point. You know we treat people fairly."

Omar gave a faint nod but made no comment.

"At the same time," Gabe Andreotti continued, "we don't buy loyalty. We know you're not here just for money."

Omar gave a faint grunt of confirmation.

"I also told them that it has to be Tuesday, not Monday, when you'll have the car in North Carolina. They agreed," he said. "Better for me too. I have to go to Washington and then fly to Guantanamo."

"OK," Omar grunted.

Gabe Andreotti thought: *Gee, thought he'd be pleased*, then continued: "I can tell you a little more now. What we thought was a small-time operation in Lackawanna and an attempt to smuggle an al Qaeda operative into the U.S. has taken on MUCH greater significance and you've played a big role in helping us discover that. The Canadian part is BIG. You'll likely find out more over the next few weeks."

He paused as Omar showed surprise and continued: "Things in Guantanamo are tense and we need to get those guys out of there NOW or we could have major problems. These Guantanamo problems are not directly related to al Qaeda, but certainly play right into their hand."

Again, he paused and said: "Please hang on just a little while longer. It'll be over in a month's time. MAX."

Omar's facial expression softened slightly then Gabe asked: "Are you set to go tomorrow?"

"Yes, leaving early; about seven," he answered tersely.

"You said his flight leaves at 11 p.m.? Please stay with him until he checks in and goes through security and then call us," Gabe Andreotti continued.

"Well, you want me to drive back to Lackawanna and then to North Carolina," Omar said tersely. "It's an eight-hour drive back to Lackawanna and then about 12 hours to Winston-Salem. Don't you think I should sleep sometime? You want me to make sure the cars are loaded with some things going to Canada and some things going with me to North Carolina. When will I have time to do that?"

Gabe Andreotti thought: *Gee, I had no idea he's so upset.* Then he said very gently: "I'm sorry you're so upset. I had no idea until now. What can we do about it?"

"Start treating me like a human being who gets tired and not like a machine," Omar replied, "and don't expect me to be a miracle worker. If it weren't for al Qaeda's involvement and Mohammad such a disgrace to Islam, I'd be in my car back to Minnesota right now."

How's that for a slap on the face? Gabe Andreotti said to himself. *We haven't had a resource talk to us like that, but most of them are not from very high levels of society. Some'd just do what they pleased and not tell us their objections.* He said: "I'm sorry. I don't know what to say. Maybe we got carried away. So much has been going on all at once; I've been working day and night too."

"Let's get on with it," Omar said. "I'm tired; really tired and stressed. I can overreact, but let's not go there now. So I baby sit Mohammad until he goes through security."

"Yes, we need to be as certain as we can he'll actually get on the plane to Amman," Gabe Andreotti said gently. "Maybe convince him to check in early and go through security. Once he gets past that point, it's unlikely he'll come back out again. If it helps, get a hotel room in New York City, even one at JFK airport, and get a good rest."

"OK. I'll see," Omar said.

"About the telephone," Gabe Andreotti continued: "We'd like to check calls he's made and is getting. Someone'll call that number to say come to North Carolina get the two guys. You're the one who needs to take the call and it needs to come to Mohammad's phone."

"Makes sense," Omar said.

"Maybe convince him he can't use it in Yemen so just have you give to Kamal," Gabe Andreotti suggested.

"OK", Omar replied. "He doesn't like to use cell phones anyway. Don't you need to fill me in on how Kamal's going to be gotten out of the way and what I'm supposed to do?"

"I should tell you a little," Gabe Andreotti said. "Again, it's for your protection we didn't."

"I know and I appreciate that to a point," Omar said, "but when you're expecting me to coordinate things like a stage director for a play, I need to know a few things."

"Kamal's going to make a one-way trip to Canada, we expect," Gabe Andreotti continued. "We hope tomorrow but depends on whether there's at least one box of prescription drugs for you to take to North Carolina. There needs to be a box of drugs in the car when Brahim and Boudi're arrested."

"Oh, they're going to be arrested?" Omar asked. "I thought I'm supposed to bring them back."

"No, they're going to drive themselves and be arrested by local police," Gabe Andreotti explained.

"So how'm I supposed to get back?" Omar asked.

"We haven't had a chance to tell you," Gabe Andreotti said. "You're going to fly back. You're going to take over and be in charge. You need to be back quickly so you let them drive back and you fly. We'll make the flight arrangements."

"Oh, I'm in charge, am I?" Omar asked.

"Yes, who else?" Gabe Andreotti retorted. "You said there're only two young kids who work in the garage. Someone's got to wind things up; can't leave them hanging. We'll give you guidance behind the scenes. We may need to gather lots of things for evidence, but we don't need to go into that today. Back to the main point: are there drugs you can put in the car you'll drive to North Carolina?"

"Don't think so," Omar replied. "I looked like you asked even though I was ticked off. I didn't ask the young guys because they might tell Kamal and Mohammad."

"Oh, damn," Gabe Andreotti said. "Kamal has to make a trip on Saturday to pick them up and then make his one-way trip on Sunday. He'll bring some back on Saturday, won't he? And he'll make another trip on Sunday, won't he?"

"I guess he'll bring some back," Omar replied. "I don't know that end of the operations and he goes both days."

"Will he have guns in the car both days?" Gabe Andreotti asked. "Does he take the same car both days?"

"Hey, I don't know things like that," Omar answered. "I'd guess he delivers guns on Saturdays; haven't noticed. I think he takes different cars on Saturday and Sunday. That way they can deliver more gasoline. I think the guys service the car that went on Saturday so it can be ready to go to North Carolina again Monday or Tuesday."

"We've got to get some guns inside both cars," Gabe Andreotti said emphatically. "Otherwise, this'll fall apart."

"What do you mean, 'we'?" Omar asked. "I need to get some guns in both cars. Again, a miracle worker."

"Yes, you," Gabe Andreotti said softly. After a few moments, his face brightened. "Maybe you need to put Mohammad's luggage in the BMW tonight or check something out on the BMW. You've discovered you may have lost something on your trip a couple of days ago. Ask the young guys for the keys to both Chevrolets so you can check. Look in the trunks of both of them and make sure at least one gun is in the trunk of each car."

"OK, OK." Omar grumbled.

"The best solution is to put a box of drugs in the car you'll take to North Carolina," Gabe Andreotti emphasized.

"Look, I've got to go," Omar stated tersely. "Can't we talk more when I get back from New York City on Sunday? Supposedly by then I will be in charge of everything"

"Yes, we can be in contact on Sunday," Gabe Andreotti replied being as eager as Omar to bring the session to an end. "Remember I won't be here. I'll be in Washington getting ready to go to Guantanamo."

Omar left giving a half-hearted hand shake.

Late that night he called saying to Gabe Andreotti who had obviously been wakened: "I found a box of drugs that I put in the car for North Carolina. Go ahead with plans."

He pushed the button to disconnect cutting Gabe Andreotti off in mid-sentence.

CHAPTER 8

Saturday, June 3, 2006
Fort Erie, Ontario, Canada

About 8:30 a.m. Kamal drove the green Chevrolet across the Peace Bridge that crosses the Niagara River at the point Lake Erie flows into the river and spans the border. Passengers sat two in the front seat and three in back. He glided to a stop at the Canadian border control as he had done dozens of times.

He routinely handed over his and the passengers' passports; the official asked looking at the license plate number displayed on a monitor: "Where are you from?"

"Lackawanna," Kamal answered.

"Why are you going to Canada?" the officer asked.

"Taking these people to visit friends and relatives in Toronto and in the Falls," Kamal answered like every time.

"May I see the automobile registration," the officer said.

Kamal, surprised, gave automobile documents.

The officer said: "Drive over there and park."

Kamal protested: "I never had to do that before.

"Park over there. You're holding up traffic," The officer commanded.

A Canadian customs officer and an officer of the Royal Canadian Mounted Police said: "Get out."

Kamal, nervously got out.

"Open the trunk," the customs officer commanded. "Take those bags out."

"I never had to do this before." Kamal protested.

"Take them out now!" The officer commanded.

Kamal began lifting out passengers' bags. Upon seeing their bags being removed, some of the bewildered passengers got out of the car to retrieve them.

The RCMP officer pointed to a place next to the building and said gently: "Go stand over there. You'll get your bags back with everything in them if there're no illegal items. The rest of you get out and go stand over there."

When passengers' bags were removed, the customs officer said: "Now remove the other items."

Kamal removed two large cardboard boxes.

"These smell like cigarettes; smuggling them I see," the customs official said. "Now remove the carpet, open the compartments on the side, and open the spare tire well."

Two small bundles were obvious.

"Hand them to me," the officer commanded. "Well, look what we have here. Firearms; illegal fire arms," he said.

"I, uh, didn't know they were there," Kamal stammered. "Someone planted them."

"Someone planted firearms that you're on record for buying in West Virginia?" the RCMP officer said mockingly.

Kamal gulped realizing what was going on and broke out in a cold sweat while the RCMP officer radioed: "Please come get them."

A young uniformed female RCMP officer came, spoke to the passengers in Arabic, directing them to a police van asking them to surrender their cell phones.

"Whhhhat's going to happen to them? They haven't done anything," Kamal asked nervously.

"They'll be released and their property returned if there's nothing illegal," The RCMP officer replied. "They'll be returned to the U.S.

You come with me. You'll be taken to the offices of the Royal Canadian Mounted Police where you'll be formally charged."

"What? What about my rights? You can't just take me away without reading me my rights," Kamal exclaimed.

"Let me remind you that you're in Canada not the United States," The RCMP officer said tersely. "Your rights as an accused are protected under Canadian law. You have at least as many rights in Canada as an accused person has in the United States. That doesn't mean we're obligated to follow the same procedure. Now come with me!"

Kamal dejectedly got into the back seat of a police cruiser. The RCMP officer and the police van with the older passengers drove to the police station. A police auto transport truck took the green Chevrolet for further search.

Several hours later, the passengers were sitting in a holding room in the police station, very nervous, upset, even crying. They had been given two meals but left alone.

A young U.S. consular official approached the officer at the desk yet again and asked: "When'll they be released? They've been here over ten hours and haven't been charged," she continued. "You confiscated their belongings and examined them in their presence. Nothing was found. They have rights under international law that we'll enforce if necessary. Either arrest them or let them go."

Damn, why's it me who had to be on duty today, she said to herself. *Bet they're green card holders, not citizens, not that I bothered to check. The Canadians said they're from the U.S. so here I am.*

The police officer looked directly at her and said: "I told you we'll release them as soon as we get authorization. That hasn't come yet. If you want to call your embassy in Ottawa and complain, go right ahead. You can use that telephone over there; I can locate the telephone number if you don't have it."

She grumbled and sat down.

The police officer thought: *Another damned arrogant American thinking they're so damned important and can throw their weight around here in*

Canada telling us what to do. Wonder why they're being held so long. Must be some reason the higher-ups want to hold them here so long.

Shortly after 9 p.m. the telephone rang and the police officer said: "OK, I'll release them."

Speaking loudly enough to wake the consular officer: "I just received authorization to release them and their belongings. We'll return their telephones and other belongings to them. They need to sign a release. Do you have vehicles to transport them? We'll help you to load their belongings."

Chapter 9

Sunday, June 4, 2006
Amman, Jordan

A Royal Jordanian Airlines plane taxied to the terminal of Queen Alia International Airport after a long flight from New York. Mohammad Fadel and other travel-weary passengers collected belongings and left the aircraft barely acknowledging smiling faces of flight attendants who said 'thank you' in English and 'shouqran' in Arabic. His face and eyes were especially tired-looking as he looked for signs to the international transit lounge saying to himself in Arabic: *I can't stand these long flights. I have to have a cigarette now!*

A uniformed officer of Jordanian security forces was watching passengers carefully, looking at a photograph, then said as he approached: "Mohammad Fadel."

"Yes, I'm Mohammad Fadel," he replied in English.

"Come with me," the security officer said in Arabic.

"Uh, what? What's this?" Mohammad asked in Arabic.

"Just come with me. Now!" the officer commanded in Arabic moving behind Mohammad to guide him.

Mohammad, startled demanded in Arabic: "What's going on? I need to smoke a cigarette."

The officer responded forcefully: "Go inside."

Using a push-button code, he opened a door and almost pushed Mohammad inside to the uniformed chief of airport security seated at his desk; two men were sitting with slacks and short-sleeved dress shirts and non-descript ties.

"Mohammad Fadel," the chief said in English with a slight British accent: "This is Charles DuPuy of the Canadian Embassy," pointing to his left, "and this is Benjamin Davis of the United States Embassy," pointing to his right. "They want to speak with you. Give the officer your ticket with your baggage claim check."

Mohammad stammered in Arabic: "What? I need to go to my elderly parents who're sick."

"Your parents are taken care of," the chief of security said in Arabic. In English: "You'll be taken to a security facility where these two gentlemen will ask you questions."

"We want to know about your activities with the so-called imam at that supposed mosque in Mississauga," the Canadian official said. "If you cooperate, you may be able to go on to Yemen."

Mohammad stammered but was interrupted by the U.S. official: "We're very interested in activities of you and your employees; things they've been buying in North Carolina and West Virginia are very much of interest to us as well as our Canadian friends. If you cooperate, you may be allowed to go on to Yemen."

"What?" Mohammad stammered again, stunned they knew about his operation: "What about my rights? I live in the United States; I have a green card. I have a family there."

"A green card does not give you the right to commit crimes," the U.S. official stated. "It does not give you the automatic right to go back. You'll likely not be allowed to enter the U.S. again except possibly to be tried on criminal charges. You're a citizen of Yemen. It's up to Jordanian authorities to inform the Yemeni government you are here and for the government of Yemen to determine what rights it wants to pursue on your behalf."

The Canadian official said: "You'll not be allowed to enter Canada except possibly to face criminal charges."

"What about my family, my wife and children? My children are U.S. citizens," Mohammad asked pleadingly.

The U.S. official replied: "Your two daughters are U.S. citizens; it has been well established in law that having children who are citizens of the U.S. does not automatically give non-citizen parents right of residence in the U.S."

Mohammad gulped in stunned silence.

The chief of security said in Arabic: "An officer will take you to a holding cell here in the airport until we get your luggage. Then you'll be transferred to a jail."

A security officer took Mohammad by the elbow and guided him out of the room.

Chapter 10

Sunday, June 4, 2006
Lackawanna, New York, USA

In late afternoon, Omar, sound asleep, was jarred awake by ringing of a cell phone. Reaching for his telephone, he discovered it was Mohammad's and mumbled 'hello'.
pause
Startled, he replied in Arabic: "We're supposed to send someone to pick them up? When and where?"
pause
"Let me get a pencil and paper to write that down," he continued in Arabic.
pause
"OK! I'll write it down later," Omar said in Arabic annoyed. "That's Sanford, North Carolina, the Food Lion Shopping Center, Highway 87 going to Fayetteville."
pause
"When?" he asked in Arabic.
pause
"OK. Tuesday, 12 noon," Omar repeated in Arabic but the connection had been cut.
Still groggy, he thought as he found a pen and paper: *Gabe said a call'd come to Mohammad's phone, but in Arabic? Is that really the FBI?*

Must be concerned phone's being monitored. Need to call Gabe anyway so I'll verify this.

A short while later, he unlocked the door of the storefront mosque. He took off his shoes and socks, placing them on the shoe rack, walked down the corridor that had been created with plywood to lead from the front entrance directly to the restroom in which a large basin had been installed for foot washing, crowding other fixtures.

He closed the door, turned on the light, and called saying: "This is Omar," omitting the usual 'hello'.
pause

"I tried to call you a few times, but your phone wasn't turned on," Omar stated.
pause

"Oh, hadn't stopped to think you'd be flying today and would have your phone turned off," Omar said less tersely. "Sorry, I'm exhausted even though I did have a nap."
pause

"You got my message that we got to the airport early," Omar continued. "He was so desperate for a cigarette he wanted to find a smoking area. He knew I wouldn't go there and insisted I leave. Couldn't think of a good way to verify he did go through security. I decided not to stay at the airport hotel because it was still early and there was daylight. Found a motel along the Thruway and slept, but not very well.

"I needed to take a nap when I got here, but lots of people are upset over Kamal's arrest. His passengers were really upset over being detained for so many hours and wanted to talk to me. Finally told them I just had to go and got a few more hours sleep."
pause

"Oh, it was you who was responsible for having them detained so long," He said.
pause

"But you don't realize they were hysterical, terrified, traumatized. Some of them may never fully recover. They come from societies where

police can be ruthless. They didn't do anything wrong and on top of that, it was a hassle for them to get back to Lackawanna."
pause

"Well, I don't agree with you that it would've been worse if they had contacted people in Lackawanna who would notify Mohammad and people in Canada," Omar said forcefully. "What's done is done and we're not going to resolve anything over the phone. Let's get on with it."
pause

"That's why I am calling," he continued. "Speaking Arabic no less. I hope his rudeness was just for show."
pause

"It's written down," he said. "What do I do there?"
pause

"Oh, she'll be there," Omar said. "Give her the keys."
pause

"How do I get back here?" he asked.
pause

"She'll drive me to the Raleigh airport?" Omar asked. "Isn't that close to the University of North Carolina in Chapel Hill? I really need to go to a library that has more material than SUNY Buffalo. How about she takes me to Chapel Hill instead? You promised me a couple of days in New York City. I'll take them in Chapel Hill."
pause

"Get me a ticket to come back on Thursday night," he said. "I need to be here Friday to give the sermon."
pause

"Bye," Omar said perfunctorily.

He washed his feet, turned off the light, and walked into the mosque performing the ritual of his prayers with genuine feeling, sharing his thoughts only with Allah.

Upon finishing, he surveyed the area thinking: *What a pitiful mosque, but better than nothing. There're oriental rugs on the floor even if they are threadbare. Wouldn't it be good if they had a proper mosque like in South Bend?*

There's where I give the sermon on Friday. What'll I say? Something will come to me, maybe while doing research in Chapel Hill. For sure, something Mohammad never gave them: a message of love and tolerance, the true Islam, not the bitter invective he was using to control them.

He slowly put on his shoes and returned to his room and slept peacefully for the first time in a long time, not thinking of his long drive the next day.

Chapter 11

Monday, June 5, 2006
Guantanamo Bay, Cuba

Rhonda Philips sipped coffee in Colonel Walker's office wearing an indigo linen-cotton modified shift with uneven bold white spiral patterns complimenting the weave of the fabric cut on the bias. White block heel shoes and matching large white leather bag and sodalite beads strung on silver with silver sodalite bead ear studs completed her outfit. Brahim and Boudi were shown in, startled to see her with the chief of security. They wore clean worn jeans and shirts from the base thrift shop, the only clothes they had.

She immediately began: "You surely remember we said we need to move you, but we can't release you in the U.S. because you've committed major crimes."

Brahim grunted: "Er, yes."

Boudi merely nodded his head.

"We've arranged for you to plead guilty to lesser crimes," she continued. "You'll serve a short time in prison and then have a supervised work-release during which you'll go to a college or university, work, and do other things for your future. You remember I said I'd see what I could do to help you get an education."

"Er, yes," Brahim stuttered.

"Er, OK," Boudi replied.

She continued: "We'll go to the next room where U.S. Attorneys will explain legal issues and an FBI agent has more details. For now, there's one important thing that you must agree to: you must never under any circumstances tell anyone, ever, you were at Guantanamo. Not even your attorneys. It may not be a good idea to say you were in Mexico, but that's your choice. You must never let anyone know you were at Guantanamo. Do you understand that?"

"Er, yes, I guess so," Boudi answered.

"Why's that?" Brahim asked testily. "Don't we have a right to free speech?"

"The right to free speech can be waived in exchange for something else," Rhonda Philips replied. "The lawyers next door are experts. All I can say is you must agree or else the rest of this deal won't be valid and you'll be subject to conviction on the crimes."

Brahim gulped saying: "OK."

Rhonda Philips persisted: "You both agree that you will never tell **anyone** you were at Guantanamo."

Both nodded their heads and grunted a faint 'yes'.

"Ok, let's go next door," she said.

Joe Shaito, Roger Chen, and Gabe Andreotti stood in deference to Rhonda Philips. Joe Shaito stood about 5 feet 9 inches with average build, slightly dark complexion, and closely trimmed slightly curly black hair; he had rectangular frameless glasses and used a small moustache and goatee to give age to his boyish handsome face. Rhonda Philips sat next to Joe Shaito who was alongside Roger Chen; Gabe Andreotti sat across the table. Colonel Walker pointedly sat between Brahim and Boudi.

Rhonda Philips introduced Joe Shaito who said: "*Marhaba.*"

Boudi thought: *Oh, does he speak Arabic?*

She continued introducing Roger Chen and Gabe Andreotti then said: "Mr. Shaito will present the U.S. Government's conditions for your transfer from this base."

He began: "Dr. Philips has outlined conditions under which you will be convicted of lesser crimes. Is that right?"

"Yeah, you'll lock us up and forget about us," Brahim, having become visibly agitated, stated testily.

Rhonda Philips was startled at his attitude change as Joe Shaito continued: "After a short sentence, you'll have supervised work-release to prepare for re-entry into society."

"Yeah, as ex-cons, Arab ex-cons, which is even worse in this country," Brahim again interrupted rudely with others noting he said 'this country' even though they were in Cuba.

Joe Shaito continued calmly: "Perhaps we should review the situation. You have committed serious crimes against the government of the United States. You were in possession of classified documents that you intended to give to a known enemy of the United States. In addition, you assisted in the infiltration of a known enemy agent into the United States. These are treasonous, capital crimes."

"So what're you going to do? Fry our asses? Or I guess it's a lethal injection these days," Brahim almost shouted.

Even Boudi was startled at the forcefulness of his cousin's comments.

Joe Shaito, unfazed, continued: "It's not in the interest of the United States government to pursue prosecution of these crimes **at this point in time**. You've can also be charged with other crimes including acquiring large quantities of firearms with the intention of taking them out of the country illegally, bringing prescription drugs into the country illegally, and extorting cash from supposed sales of merchandise in violation of federal racketeering statutes."

Boudi was startled to learn how much they knew.

Brahim spouted out: "Is that all you have against us? Ha! You can't lock us up without having a trial; even Arabs have to have a trial. The guy we work for can get us off or keep us somewhere you can't touch us."

Gabe Andreotti interrupted: "If you're talking about Mohammad Fadel, he fled the U.S. and is in foreign custody. His assistant Kamal Ashfoor is in foreign custody also. They're not going to help you with anything."

Boudi was startled again, but Joe Shaito calmly continued: "I should inform you there's no statute of limitations on treason; we have the right to try you for these crimes the rest of your life if you fail to cooperate."

CONSEQUENCES • CHAPTER 11

He continued describing in general terms arrangements to have local police arrest them.

"Oh, you're going to break the law and plant evidence. We'll use that to get off," Brahim continued testily.

Joe Shaito, finally becoming annoyed, replied: "No, not planted. When you agree to this arrangement you agree you know the drugs are there. You'll be shown the evidence so you can agree they're the same drugs you usually transport. Now let's continue. When you're arrested, you'll have the right to legal representation. We won't interfere in any way with your using any attorney to represent you."

"Big fucking deal!" Brahim blurted out. "We have no money and you say guys in charge back home can't help."

Rhonda Philips winced at the obscenity; until now he had pointedly avoided such language around her.

Joe Shaito continued unfazed: "Then you'll have access to the public defender. All accused persons have the right to defense in the United States."

"Oh, yeah," Brahim exclaimed: "Another government lawyer to railroad Arabs."

"Be assured you'll receive competent legal counsel from public defenders in federal courts," Joe Shaito stated emphatically. "I was a public defender in my internships."

"Gee, some lousy defense they got," Brahim retorted.

Rhonda Philips, visibly agitated, immediately stated: "Just a minute, Ibrahim al Asadi. What's gotten into you? Until this point, you've been polite and respectful. We've gone to great lengths to find a way for you and your cousin to not only receive minimal prison time, but also achieve your personal goals. I've put my reputation on the line to work out a way for you to get into a university like you want to. I don't like what I am hearing out of you!"

She paused a few seconds and continued: "What would your mother think if she heard you talking like this?"

At the reference to his mother, Brahim became suddenly quiet and Boudi spoke: "Sorry, Ms. Rhonda. We just don't know who to trust now.

Mohammad always said he'd take care of us, but now he's run away you say. You want to put us in prison. We haven't done anything wrong. We just did what he told us to and didn't hurt anyone."

Rhonda Philips bristled at what she perceived as insulting first-name familiarity, her face becoming visibly angry and her eyes like blue-hot gas flames.

Joe Shaito quickly leaned to speak softly into her ear: "When an Arab addresses someone with a title followed by a first name, it's a sign of respect." To all: "Please let me be alone with these two men for a few minutes."

Colonel Walker started to protest: "I don't know …"

Roger Chen stood and said: "Let's go," and walked towards the door.

Rhonda Philips and Gabe Andreotti followed him.

Colonel Walker stood and reluctantly walked away saying: "OK. We can go into my office."

Chapter 12

**Monday, June 5, 2006
Guantanamo Bay, Cuba**

Inside Colonel Walker's office they heard a forceful voice through the door, but not distinct enough to be understood.

Colonel Walker said: "I still don't like the idea of leaving them in there alone."

"I understand your concern, Colonel," Roger Chen said deferentially. "You're in charge of base security. What about Joe? He's great, isn't he? One of the best rookies I've worked with and we have lots of good people. I had a good feeling about him. Let's see what he comes up with."

Rhonda Philips nodded her head 'yes'.

Colonel Walker said: "Would anyone like coffee or something? I could sure use a cup."

"A cup of coffee would be great," Rhonda Philips said, "cream and sugar please."

The others gave coffee orders which Colonel Walker gave over the phone to an assistant.

"That was a brilliant comment," Roger Chen said to Rhonda Philips, "asking what his mother would think."

"Thanks; it was a sudden inspiration," she replied. "When I talked to him before, he was obviously polite and respectful to older women. He learned it somewhere; must've been from his mother. What got into him today?"

"Maybe we'll find out soon," Roger Chen answered.

An assistant brought coffee which they sipped in silence a while until they heard a knock on the door.

Joe Shaito said: "You can come back now."

As Rhonda Philips entered, Joe Shaito looked directly at Brahim and Boudi and lifted his eyes. In response, Brahim and Boudi stood up. Joe Shaito looked directly at Brahim.

Brahim said: "Sorry, Ms. Rhonda. I got carried away."

"Let's begin again," Joe Shaito said. "You have agreed to this plea-bargain arrangement. Is that right?"

They each meekly said "Yes."

"Tomorrow morning, you'll be flown to an air force base in North Carolina," Joe Shaito continued. "The moment you arrive in the U.S. you have all the rights of U.S. citizens. Those rights do not include remaining on a U.S. military installation except by invitation and you have not been invited. Do you understand?"

Brahim and Boudi nodded 'yes'.

"If you **choose not** to cooperate," Joe Shaito continued, "you will be immediately escorted to one of the gates where you will be released to find your own way to wherever you want to go next. All criminal charges against you remain and you'll be subject to arrest as soon as we can locate you. Mr. Andreotti will explain what happens if you cooperate."

"When you leave the base, you'll be driven to a car you'll recognize," Gabe Andreotti explained details.

"How do you know it's a box like we've supposedly brought from Canada?" Brahim asked.

Gabe Andreotti replied: "We know quite a bit about your operations: The garage and warehouse where you keep the cars and drugs until you take them to Virginia and where you keep the cigarettes until you take them to Canada. Just off Ridge Road, close to the botanical garden, Holy Cross Cemetery, and Our Lady of Victory Basilica."

CONSEQUENCES • CHAPTER 12

Brahim and Boudi were stunned then Boudi said: "Gee, you know a lot about the area. Have you been there?

"I work in Buffalo," Gabe Andreotti said.

Brahim thought: *Andreotti. An Italian name. There're lots of Italians there. Should've guessed. He's a local.*

Gabe Andreotti continued stating: "You'll be subject to immediate arrest. Do you understand?"

They nodded their heads again in agreement.

Gabe Andreotti continued concluding: Mr. Shaito will continue discussing legal aspects."

"A U.S. attorney will represent the U.S. government and will be familiar with this plea-bargain arrangement," Joe Shaito said. "You have the right to have your own attorney represent you. Do you understand that? All accused persons in the U.S. have the right to the attorney of their choice."

Brahim and Boudi again nodded their heads and Boudi said meekly: "We have no money to hire a lawyer."

"We've been over that," Joe Shaito said. "It's important you understand you have the right to have the attorney of your choice. As mentioned, if you have no money, you'll be assigned an attorney through the public defender. Do you understand that?"

Brahim and Boudi grunted: "yes."

"The U.S. Attorney will formally present the agreement," Joe Shaito continued. "If you, with the advice and counsel of your attorney, agree to accept, it'll be presented to a U.S. federal judge. We cannot guarantee the judge will concur. As you surely know, the judiciary in the U.S. is an independent branch of the government and cannot be controlled by another branch."

"Yes, I know that," Brahim said. "What would happen if the judge doesn't agree?"

"That's impossible to predict," Joe Shaito replied. "Each judge is independent, but his or her decisions are subject to review by higher courts on appeal so we can say with some confidence there'll be no significant deviation from the agreement. In the vast majority of cases, the agreement is accepted; the U.S. attorney won't allow it to be presented unless he or she's confident the judge'll concur. In rare cases, a judge has not accepted a guilty plea and required an actual trial or sometimes imposed a lesser penalty than was agreed. I've not known of any circumstances where a more severe penalty was imposed."

Roger Chen commented: "Likewise, I haven't known a judge to impose a harsher penalty."

"But what'll the penalty be?" Boudi asked

"The penalty we're recommending is six months imprisonment in a minimum security prison where you'll have substantial freedom of movement," Joe Shaito replied. "After serving your sentence, you'll have supervised work-release for five years during which time you'll be required to study in a university or vocational school and be gainfully employed. You'll be given assistance to enroll in school and find employment."

"Oh, gee, really?" Boudi asked.

Brahim showed visible relief, but did not comment.

"Let me emphasize," Joe Shaito said, "we cannot guarantee this outcome. Judges are independent. Your attorney may not concur and convince you that you should negotiate some other type of arrangement."

Boudi asked: "Will we be able to see our families?"

"You'll be allowed telephone contact under specified conditions while you're in confinement," Joe Shaito replied. "During the work-release phase, there's no limit. It'll be the decision of the judge which prison you'll be assigned to. It can be anywhere in the U.S. and there's no guarantee it'll be close enough for your family to visit. Likewise, with the location of your work-release. These are issues to be discussed between your attorney and the U.S. attorney. Mr. Chen is the U.S. Attorney in charge of this operation. I'll turn the rest of the discussion over to him."

"Mr. Shaito has done an excellent job of presenting the government's position," Roger Chen said. "Dr. Philips has emphasized that you must never disclose to anyone you've been at Guantanamo. If your presence at Guantanamo becomes public, the U.S. government has the right to charge you for your medical care and other costs incurred in keeping you here during your recuperation. Any time a civilian non-dependent is treated at a U.S. military facility, whether emergency or humanitarian basis or not, the government has the right to collect if it chooses. For the foreseeable future, we do not intend to charge you for your medical care. We are also aware you do not have financial means to pay. Still, the U.S. government maintains the right to charge you and would consider exercising that right if it becomes known you were here at Guantanamo. Do you understand that?"

Brahim and Boudi gulped muttering: "Yes".

"Good," Roger Chen continued. "You'll be given the rest of the day to consider what has been presented to you. Colonel Walker can explain further what arrangements have been made for your departure."

Colonel Walker said: "No matter what you decide, you will be required to leave this base tomorrow. There is no longer any medical or humanitarian reason for you to be here and, as you have just heard, non-military persons are allowed to be on military installations by invitation only and that invitation expires tomorrow morning. We cannot force you to get on the airplane, but your only other alternative will be to be escorted to the gate where you entered the base voluntarily so you can return the same way you entered.

"The plane will depart at zero nine hundred hours. You must be ready at zero eight hundred. You'll be escorted to the flight line where you will meet the other people here. Now you'll be escorted back to the hospital."

CHAPTER 13

Monday, June 5, 2006
Guantanamo Bay, Cuba

After Brahim and Boudi left, Colonel Walker asked: "Can we get you anything? More coffee? It's early for lunch."

"A cup of coffee would be wonderful," Joe Shaito answered, "and maybe water."

"That was amazing," Roger Chen said to Joe Shaito.

"Thanks," he replied modestly.

"Could you tell us what you said while we were gone?" Rhonda Philips asked. "It certainly must've been effective."

"First I spoke in Arabic, rather forcefully," Joe Shaito began. "They wanted me to speak English, but I wanted to impress on them that I was speaking as one Arab to another and they'd better get the point. I had the idea from the outset they were a little like me, a fish out of water, an Arab in the American culture. Maybe a better description would be 'neither fish nor fowl'. Raised Arab, but not completely Arab, not completely American either."

An attractive young female enlisted Marine set coffee in front of Joe Shaito with a big smile noticing his handsome good looks. She gave bottles of water to the others.

He continued: "My parents came to the U.S. from Lebanon as young adults and settled in a community of other Lebanese Shia Muslims in

CONSEQUENCES • CHAPTER 13

Dearborn, Michigan. I was born there and raised as a good Arab, Muslim boy. I went to American schools where there were plenty of Arabs, but plenty of others too, and we became Americans during school hours. We watched American television, went to American movies, listened to American music, and the like.

"I went to the University of Michigan for undergrad and law school where I became more American, but at home I'm still an Arab boy. If I hadn't moved to DC to take this job, I'd still be expected to live at home no matter what my job and income level. I'm very pleased to be an employee of the U.S. government and represent its interests. I don't feel any conflict between being an Arab and an American. Still a big part of me is Arab."

"My parents say the same thing," Roger Chen said. "They were born in the U.S. and are now close to 70."

"It was my grandparents," Gabe Andreotti commented. "My grandmother's in her 80s."

Rhonda Philips reflected on her mid-America heartland upbringing in Missouri, pleased she had escaped to DC at a young age to obtain a PhD at Georgetown and remained in Washington working her way up to her current position.

Joe Shaito continued: "When you said what would his mother think, I observed he got quiet. I realized he must be a lot like me: Arab inside worrying about staying on the good side of his mother, not disrespecting her upbringing of me."

"I also suspected, almost from the beginning, he deeply resented another Arab kid just like him, his age and family status, becoming what he wanted; it's pretty easy for one Arab to detect whether another Arab is from a prominent family, especially among first generation immigrants. He may also have resented another young Arab selling out to the 'enemy' since he's indirectly involved with al Qaeda.

"I told both of them, but really directing comments to Brahim using language one young Arab'd use to another, that I was tired of taking their er nonsense, they'd better stop, or they'd really er have problems. The Arabic words don't translate readily.

"I also lambasted Brahim for his disrespect of you, Dr. Philips, re-emphasizing what would his mother think when she finds out, emphasizing **when**. Again, the Arabic words don't translate well, but you get the idea. I'm not even sure they understood fully because Yemenis speak a different dialect, but they got the message.

"I switched to English and told Brahim I'm tired of his whining that Arabs have it so bad in the U.S. I even told him directly that he's likely jealous and envious of me, but I come from a poor hard-working family too. They put aside just a little to get me in the door of a university, but I had to use student loans, which I'm still paying off, and will be for years, and I worked my er tail end off in er undesirable jobs just to get by. I made it. I told him there're plenty other Arab kids from Dearborn, men and women, doing the same thing.

"Brahim began saying: 'But Mohammad told us….' I shut him up in mid-sentence, saying er forget Mohammad; they should know now what kind of a er bad person he is."

"I then challenged Brahim, taunting him a little about being so good at history, to tell me the major immigrant groups that've come to the U.S. He fumbled and mentioned Irish, Italian, Polish, Chinese, and Mexicans. I then asked which of these groups had an easy time and found doors open to them. He fumbled trying to avoid the question by saying something about affirmative action for blacks.

"I cut him off and said er forget affirmative action; we're not going there. Every one of these groups has had to work their er tail ends off to get somewhere and that he, Ibrahim al Asadi, is no different, and the same for Abdullah Zakawi, just like it for Yusef Shaito, and I still don't have it made now.

"Then I softened them up because I didn't want them in such a down mood when you returned. I asked what they really wanted for their lives. No need to repeat their answers. I finished pointing out the plan **you** are largely responsible for is just that. When I felt their mood was better and cooperative, I called you back."

"Wow, very well done!" Roger Chen exclaimed.

"Amazing!" Gabe Andreotti stated.

"Good job," Colonel Walker said.

"I definitely want to add my congratulations and appreciation also," Rhonda Philips offered emphatically. "If I may, I have a question for you."

"Yes, of course," Joe Shaito said.

"When we've been here together, you call me Dr. Philips," she began. "Yet, you whispered to me that Boudi's calling me Ms. Rhonda was a sign of esteem and respect; I suppose it's the same when Brahim called me Ms. Rhonda. Is Dr. Philips not so respectful or esteemed? I'm not one who's hung up on doctor in front of my name, but I do expect a certain amount of politeness and respect."

Joe smiled and replied: "Arabs, especially younger ones or those clearly in a serving capacity like maybe a shop attendant, use a title like 'Mr.', 'Mrs.', or these days 'Ms.' in front of a person's first name to show esteem, respect, and a bit of intimacy, but intimacy with an appropriate distance. I think American blacks in the old days did something similar.

"Arabs would use 'doctor' followed by a first name if they knew the person is a doctor. I can only guess they weren't aware or had forgotten you're a doctor and likely didn't pay attention when I called you Dr. Philips so they just called you Ms. Rhonda. I'm sure they would've called you Dr. Rhonda if they'd known. I can't imagine there're many female doctors in their society; there weren't where I grew up so it may not have occurred to them.

"It was obvious to me that Boudi was genuinely trying to show respect and esteem and didn't like his cousin's behavior. Later when Brahim said the same thing, it was respect, esteem, intimacy, and an apology. It was more genuine than it would've been if he hadn't used Ms. Rhonda.

"As for me, I'm Americanized with my years in university and law school. Calling someone 'Dr. so-and-so' using last name comes automatic Now if we were back in Dearborn among family and friends, you'd be Dr. Rhonda."

She smiled warmly and said: "Thanks, Joe. That's my way of expressing esteem, respect and a little intimacy calling you by your nickname. I can't imagine I'd call you Mr. Shaito or Yusef unless we were in a group where that's the only appropriate way to address you."

After a few moments silence, Colonel Walker said: "Shall we go to lunch now? It's a bit early, but the officer's club'll be open by now. Try some of their Cuban specialties if you haven't already."

Chapter 14

Tuesday, June 6, 2006
Sanford, North Carolina, USA

Omar parked and soon heard: "Omar, over here."

A young woman approached wearing a light gray worsted woman's business-style pants suit with a pale blue blouse and a loose navy blue scarf at the neck, black flat heeled shoes, tasteful small gold earrings, lightly applied makeup to complement her medium brown hair with blond highlights that falls over her ears in a gentle wave.

She held out her hand for a professional handshake saying in a cultured Sothern accent: "Hello, Omar, it's nice to see you again."

"It's nice to see you, too, M er Ms. Andrews. I must admit I wouldn't have recognized you," he replied.

"I noticed," she smiled; "please call me Melissa. Actually, it's Mrs. Andrews. One reason you were safe with me is my husband wouldn't tolerate any activity, even in the line of business. I wouldn't either. Remember I said I live with other family at Lake Norman? I live there with my husband and little girl. Listen, are you hungry? There's Wendy's just down the road. There's also Golden Coral if you want another big meal. I need to look at your car; then we can eat and go to Chapel Hill."

"I had a big breakfast," Omar replied. "I could go for something lighter like Wendy's.

CONSEQUENCES • CHAPTER 14

She opened the trunk of the car Omar had driven and said: "This must be the box of prescription drugs. I won't touch it and get finger prints on it. Anything else in here?"

He replied; "There're firearms I didn't touch."

"Please show me where they are," she said. "How was the trip down?" she asked while looking.

"I told them I had to come here to clean up some business," he replied. "To make it look good, I took some merchandise and stopped at one place along the way. A guy in Western Pennsylvania isn't doing a good business selling Middle Eastern goods in a remote place on the interstate where people stop only to buy gasoline. He's always been nice. I left a small amount of merchandise saying pay me later. He was surprised but filled my tanks. It wasn't too far from Lackawanna, so it didn't take much. It didn't feel right taking free gasoline from someone who's in the business of selling it. I don't intend to go back to collect. If anything, I'll buy back the merchandise.

"Stayed overnight in Wytheville to get a better look around. I didn't go to Sam's Wilco because he'd probably automatically open the trunk and take the drugs."

She locked the car and said: "That's mine over there."

"You're right," he chuckled, "It does scream 'cop car'"

While eating, she asked: "What more can you tell me about the place in Wytheville?

"Not much," Omar answered. "I watched the station from across the street. Seems to do a good business."

"That's typical all over the South," she added. "Middle Eastern people buy small local business. You can be sure there's an extended family there somewhere."

"I tried to get an idea where they store the drugs and if someone comes and picks them up," Omar continued. "There're storage rooms at the back, but any gas station'd have them. There're a couple of delivery trucks too."

"I'd guess someone picks them up once a week or so," she said. "It'd be just chance you saw someone. The prescription drug business is probably a sideline, especially you say gas business is good. I'd bet he has a cousin, or cousin of a cousin, somewhere who runs the drug business. These things're sold mostly over the internet. Thanks for the information. Please tell me more about your studies. What'll you do with a PhD in Islamic theology?"

"My dream's to be imam at the biggest mosque in Washington, DC," Omar replied. "Being more realistic, it'll likely be an academic job, professor of comparative religion or Middle Eastern studies, and maybe imam on the side."

She asked: "How'd you come to study this and have those aspirations? You said al Qaeda killed your family. Or would you rather not talk about it."

Omar, surprised she remembered a brief comment a week ago said: "It helps to talk at times. Al Qaeda destroyed the apartment building where my family lived taking them in the process because an anti-al Qaeda government official lived in the same building. I was away visiting friends; I was 18 and old enough to go out on my own at night.

"They were wonderful loving parents. They moved to the capital city, Sana'a, when I entered high school so we children could get a better education and have a better future. They left their family and whole life back in the village just for us. They worked hard to save money for us to go to the university. My little brother and sister were so sweet and innocent. They were at least as bright and deserving to live as I was. I wished they'd killed me instead. I might've killed myself to join them in heaven, but Islam forbids suicide despite what suicide bombers are doing.

"I wanted to hurt al Qaeda in the worst possible way; I wanted to kill them like they'd killed my family. It was tearing me up inside. A friend's family took me in so I could finish high school, but no one wanted to be around me because of my anger. Friends avoided me. I was lucky the family didn't kick me out. Teachers didn't want to have me in class. I started failing my subjects. I finally got physically ill and was forced to stay in bed.

"Somehow an imam and professor of Islamic theology at the university found out about me. I still don't know how he found out and what motivated him to come to see me. The ways of Allah cannot be known to us mere humans. Illness forced me to surrender so the will of Allah could take over, although I didn't realize it at the time. Allah sent him to me when the time was right and I was ready.

"This wonderful man was like my substitute father. He convinced me Islam is a religion of tolerance, justice, acceptance, spirituality, love, peace, and hope. Yes, it's right and good to be angry and demand justice to a point, but Allah gives justice in His way and at His time, not like we humans think it should be. It took a while for this to sink in, but because of him, I was able to finish high school and enter the university to study Islamic theology myself."

"Amazing," Melissa Andrews said in awe. "How'd you get from there to Minnesota?

"I was a good student," he continued. "I felt inside Islamic theology was what Allah wanted me to study. I wanted to stay in Sana'a because they have some of the best Islamic scholars in the world. My mentor convinced me studies there'd be only in the context of the Muslim world; if I really wanted to understand Islamic theology, I should do it in the context of other religions.

"Because of my anti-al Qaeda anger, I didn't have strong negative feelings against the U.S. I disapprove of a lot of this country's policies and actions, but let's not go there. Nothing kept me in Yemen. My grandparents were old and senile. Aunts and uncles had large families of their own.

"The university in Sana'a has exchange programs with the University of Minnesota, but I was stubborn and didn't go there automatically. I applied to other programs and almost came to the University of North Carolina at Chapel Hill. In the end, I surrendered to Allah and was soon in Minneapolis.

"I have lots of anger inside still. I'm furious your agency left those people in the police station in Canada for so many hours terrified, traumatized; some may never recover. Gabe tells me to wait and I'll see the alternative might've been worse. I'm learning to control my anger and not let it destroy me, but I'm still damned angry inside."

"What can I say?" Melissa Andrews replied. "I don't know specifics, but we sometimes have to make difficult decisions, balance the lesser of two evils. We're human too. Sometimes with hindsight we realize we didn't make the best decision, but we're not evil out to hurt people."

Omar grunted "OK. I'm really getting anxious about my dissertation. I feel it's the will of Allah for me to finish as quickly as I can so I can get onto other things. I'm grateful you're taking me to Chapel Hill."

"Where do you want to go in Chapel Hill?" she asked. "I went to school there myself and know my way around."

"Somewhere near the library, I suppose," he answered. "Maybe find a cheap hotel."

"There're hotels right next to the campus," she said. "That's where my family stayed when they came to visit. Don't worry about how much they cost. Gabe promised you a couple of nights in New York City at our expense. Chapel Hill's a whole lot less expensive. I'll tell him when I see him later today that he needs to pay."

"Oh, thanks," Omar said.

As they were finishing eating, Melissa Andrews asked: "What's your dissertation about?"

He replied: "It's how Islam has neglected its spiritual roots. Islam works from inside individuals, not externally imposed force. Christians have a similar belief that's often overlooked that the Kingdom of God is within. Also, I'm exploring the notion that the words of the glorious Q'ran, you usually say Koran in English, must be read in the context of the times when it was written and the culture and beliefs of that day, and not be taken literally today. This is a controversial subject. My thoughts are not well developed; that's why I need to get busy reading more."

"This's fascinating," she said, "but we need to get on the road. Your discussion about spiritual issues is interesting; I want to hear more. My family are Episcopalian and I grew up with some of the same views of God's spirit working inside not being imposed from outside. I also grew up in a big ocean of Southern Baptists and other churches whose views are different, as I'm sure you know. Let's talk more in the car. It's about a 45 minute drive to Chapel Hill."

Chapter 15

Tuesday, June 6, 2006
Pope Air Force Base, North Carolina, USA

Before refueling and service, Rhonda Philips descended from a military transport airplane followed by Brahim, Boudi, Roger Chen, Joe Shaito, and Gabe Andreotti. Inside the operations building before reboarding she said to Boudi and Brahim: "Most of us will leave you now. Agent Andreotti will stay until another agent takes you to the next location."

"An agent from the Charlotte field office will meet us soon," Gabe Andreotti said. "I'll call her right now."

"All the best wishes to both of you," Rhonda Philips said. "You'll both do well when you apply yourselves; I have confidence in you."

Boudi and Brahim fumbled with words; Boudi saying: "Thanks Ms. Rhonda."

Brahim said: "Thanks Ms. Rhonda. We really caused you a bad time. Sorry."

Roger Chen said: "Best wishes to you also."

Joe Shaito said: "Good luck; yalla bye."

Gabe Andreotti said: "She's on her way; it'll be 20 minutes at least. Would you like something to drink? It looks like a snack bar over there. I'll treat."

Both expressed thanks and while sitting Boudi asked Gabe Andreotti timidly: "You know a lot about Lackawanna. Are you from there too?"

"I grew up on the south side of Buffalo," he answered; "spent time around Lackawanna."

Brahim asked: "Would it be possible for us to call our folks, Agent Andreotti? We can call collect."

Gabe Andreotti thought a moment and replied: "You're free to do what you like, but think a moment. Maybe this isn't the best time. You might get their hopes up that they'll see you soon, but you'll be arrested, put in jail, and later in prison. You can't very well tell them you **will** be arrested. You'll be given a chance to make at least one phone call after you're arrested. Maybe it'd be better to wait until then, but you're free to do what you like."

Brahim pondered while Gabe said to himself: *Quick. Gotta find something to distract 'em.* He asked: "Say, did you guys get briefed you must never lie when you do call?"

"What?" Brahim asked while Boudi looked confused.

"Don't tell lies about the things you've been through," Gabe Andreotti continued. "If you tell lies you can betray yourself if you don't remember exactly which lie you told. If you always tell the truth, that's less likely to happen. That doesn't mean you have to tell the whole truth."

"But Ms. Rhonda made us promise never to tell anyone we were at Guantanamo," Boudi said.

Gabe Andreotti said: "Shhh. Don't ever use that name. Just say 'that place we were' or something like that."

"I still don't get it," Brahim stated argumentatively.

"It could be something like this," he began. "You can say you were abducted by guys a little older than you who you thought're from a rival Arab gang. Note that you said you **thought**. That's a true statement, isn't it?"

Both nodded their heads and mumbled: "Yeah".

"You did **not** say you were abducted in Ohio," Gabe Andreotti continued. "Do any of your family and friends know exactly where you went?"

Boudi, still confused said: "No."

Brahim answered: "No, only Mohammad, I guess, and maybe Kamal, but we don't know who they told."

Gabe Andreotti continued: "You were knocked out; you can even say it was from an injection of the drugs you brought with you, if you want. That way it clearly fits into being arrested on prescription drug possession. OK?"

Both nodded their heads again.

"You can say when you woke up, you were in a place you didn't recognize," he added. "That's true. You didn't recognize you were in Mexico until later."

Both nodded their heads again.

"There's nothing wrong with saying you were in Mexico from our perspective," Gabe Andreotti continued, "but it wouldn't fit the rest of the story so it might not be a good idea for you to say anything about Mexico."

"That's what Ms. Rhonda said," Brahim commented.

Gabe Andreotti continued: "You can say your car was taken to Florida, but you were brought back to North Carolina where Mohammad was told to come get you. Notice you haven't said you were in Florida, but if the listener draws that conclusion, that's OK. You could even talk about heat and humidity, palm trees, or whatever in the place you were. The place has lots of similarities to Florida."

"Oh, it does?" Boudi said. "I've never been to Florida.

Brahim quickly retorted: "But no one told us the car was in Florida. How're we supposed to say that without lying? And what's this about telling Mohammad to come get us. We don't know that either."

"Well, I just told you now, haven't I?" Gabe Andreotti said smiling. "Yes a call was made to Mohammad's telephone to tell him that you need to be picked up in North Carolina. He didn't take the call, of course, but someone else did bring the car down here."

Boudi had a slight gleam in his eye finally catching on and asked: "Who's coming to get us?"

"You'll find out soon," Gabe Andreotti replied. "For now, I'll just say the person who drove the car down here had to leave on urgent business.

Also notice you didn't say you were abducted in North Carolina. When you say 'back to North Carolina' that doesn't mean necessarily that you'd been here recently. It's still a true statement you've been brought back to North Carolina and listeners can draw whatever conclusions they like."

Both nodded in acknowledgement and Brahim asked: "What about these injuries and scars? How do we explain them? Or is that another thing we can't talk about because it happened down there?"

Gabe Andreotti pondered and said: "As we've said, you have rights of free speech and can talk about anything that you want except 'you know what'. Maybe you can say something like when you were transported from one place to the next, they might think it is from North Carolina to Florida, the persons transporting decided to beat you up on their own without being told to do so. When you were dropped off, you were in such bad shape the persons who received you took pity and got you emergency treatment. I don't think I need to go into details now about how this's not a lie, but you're not disclosing everything either. You could even say that the reason you were held so long was to allow your wounds to heal enough that you can travel safely."

I wish she'd hurry and get here, Gabe thought. *I'm running out of things to stall them.*

Brahim and Boudi nodded and mumbled: "OK."

Gabe Andreotti's phone rang; he answered and after a few seconds he said: "OK" and disconnected. "She's on her way," he said. "We need to go out front."

When they were on the way, Gabe Andreotti said to Melissa Andrews: "Say, how about your opinion. I just told these guys it might be a good idea to wait until after they're arrested to call their families so the folks at home don't get the idea they'll be home soon. Of course, they're free to do what they like and I told them that."

She replied: "Sounds good to me. Also, time's pretty tight. Wait 'til there's not so much time pressure so you can have a nice long talk. If it were my family, I wouldn't like to hear: 'I'm free and OK. Gotta go. Bye.'"

CONSEQUENCES • CHAPTER 15

Brahim thought: *Do they think I'm falling for that? He's not asking her opinion. They're probably right. Boudi might want to bolt and run if his mom pressured him. I'm not about to let him do that. We'd both be screwed. Get it over as quick as we can, but, don't treat us like we're stupid.*

He drifted off to sleep. Boudi was already sound asleep.

Chapter 16

Tuesday, June 6, 2006
Sanford, North Carolina, USA

About half an hour later, Boudi and Brahim woke up and Boudi exclaimed groggily: "Hey, that's one of our cars."

FULL SIZE 2001 CHEVROLET IMPALA USED IN MOHAMMAD'S BUSINESSES

Gabe Andreotti told Brahim and Boudi: "Please stand by our car." To Melissa Andrews: "I'll get the front."

He looked underneath the front seat, running his hand in the crack between the seat and seatback, and opened the glove compartment.

CONSEQUENCES • CHAPTER 16

Melissa Andrews kept one eye on the two young men while she examined the back seat.

"You can come here now," Gabe Andreotti said.

Melissa Andrews held out keys saying: "Here's a set for you. Agent Andreotti has another set."

"I get driving duty," Boudi said taking the keys.

"Examine the car thoroughly including all the hidden compartments," Gabe Andreotti said. "Save the trunk for last. Open the glove compartment. Under the seats. Under the car."

"We don't have hidden compartments," Brahim stated.

"What about extra gas tanks?" Gabe Andreotti asked.

Brahim replied: "That's not a compartment."

"Check it anyway," Gabe Andreotti said.

Brahim crawled underneath the car and two distinctly different sounds were heard.

Back upright, he said: "One's almost empty, but the other one sounds like it has gas in it. I swear we don't have hidden compartments. We only use the trunk and the glove compartment to carry anything."

"Please check them," Gabe Andreotti requested.

Boudi, opened the trunk raised the lid and looked inside while Brahim opened the glove compartment.

"Only maps and car papers inside," Brahim said.

"Yes, I know," Gabe Andreotti said. "I checked myself. Now you've verified there's nothing hidden for someone to find when the car is impounded."

Boudi saw a cardboard box and said: "That's just like the ones we bring with us."

Gabe Andreotti said to Brahim: "Come verify that."

Brahim said: "Yes, that's like the boxes we bring."

"Please open it," Gabe Andreotti requested.

Boudi began breaking the seal as Brahim protested: "We don't know what's inside; we never opened them."

"What about the medication used to knock you out and the other guy?" Gabe Andreotti asked.

"Oh, that," Brahim said. *Gee, they know everything*, he said to himself. "I forgot about that."

"Look inside the box," Melissa Andrews said. "Does that look like the medicine you carried before?"

"I never opened a box and looked; honest," Boudi said.

"I guess that looks like the one we opened," Brahim answered. "I didn't open it and didn't pay much attention."

"Pick up some of the little boxes inside, both of you," Gabe Andreotti said. "Read what's on them."

"There's a name I can't pronounce," Boudi said, "and a name of a laboratory and address in Toronto, Canada."

"Same here," Brahim said. "Print's small but seems to be from a laboratory in Montreal, Canada."

"Both of you verify this is prescription medicine made in Canada," Gabe Andreotti stated. "You actually saw it here in front of Agent Andrews and me as witnesses."

"Yes," Boudi answered in resignation.

"I can't verify it's prescription medicine," Brahim said testily. "I don't know enough about pharmacies to recognize prescription medicine from something else. I know what you're getting at. I verify I saw it."

"Now remove the carpet and spare tire cover," Gabe Andreotti again requested.

Brahim said to himself: *They know about the guns.*

Boudi exposed two bundles wrapped in newspaper.

"Now pick up the things in the newspaper and unwrap them but do not touch what's inside," Gabe Andreotti said.

Boudi and Brahim each picked up a bundle and started to remove the newspaper as Melissa Andrews said: "Be sure you don't touch them. Make sure you're not putting on your finger prints as a result of anything we asked you to do."

Brahim thought as he unwrapped and exposed a pistol: *gee, they really have this figured out.*

Boudi unwrapped a different type of pistol.

Gabe Andreotti said: "Please verify these are the types of pistols you buy in West Virginia. They might be ones that you actually purchased."

Brahim asked testily: "How would you know these might be pistols we actually bought?"

"We can check serial numbers against purchase records that you've signed," Gabe Andreotti answered. "Now verify these are the same types of pistols you've purchased before, you're aware they are here in the trunk, and you did not touch them and leave fingerprints."

Both replied with resignation: "Yes, I verify that."

"Wrap them up again, be careful not to touch them, and put them back where you found them," Gabe Andreotti said.

They complied while Melissa Andrews brought two bags with the name of the store T.J. Maxx prominently in red saying: "This is yours, Boudi, so this must be yours, Brahim,"

Each removed one pair of new chino-type pants, one new polo-type pullover shirt, one pair of briefs, a belt, a new black leather wallet, a toothbrush, tube of toothpaste, disposable razor, and a small tube of shaving cream.

Both were startled; Boudi said: "Gee, thanks and you got me the right size."

Brahim mumbled: "Thanks," opened the wallet, and exclaimed: "You have my driver's license, social security card and five dollars."

"Where'd you find our driver's licenses?" Boudi asked.

"They're new," Gabe Andreotti replied. "You need them to drive and the social security card for ID, especially if you don't have your numbers memorized."

Melissa Andrews interjected: "You'll find a map in the car. Turn left out of the parking lot. Follow Highway 87 to 421 all the way through Sanford and then into Greensboro where you'll get on I 40 west to Winston-Salem. Take the business route I 40 through Winston-Salem to Highway 52 North that goes to Mount Airy. I'm sure you know that road. Tobaccoland is right on Highway 52. It's about an hour and a half drive from here."

"Yeah, we know," Brahim grumbled.

"Just at the exit ramp you take to go to Tobaccoland, there's a McDonald's," she continued. "Drive in there and park as far away from the other parked cars as you can. We'll drive up and park next to you."

"Yeah, we know that McDonalds," Brahim said.

"OK, let's go," she said. "You first; we'll follow."

Chapter 17

Tuesday, June 6, 2006
Winston-Salem, North Carolina, USA

A little less than two hours later, Boudi parked in the far corner of McDonald's parking lot. The drive had been mostly in strained silence, listening to the radio, with the occasional comment that it was nice to listen to *good* music.

Boudi said: "Hope they get here soon. Don't know how much more I can take. I just want to run away and see Mom."

"Run away with what?" Brahim asked. "We've got $10 and not enough gas to get home. They'd just get us again."

"I know," Boudi said with a dejected sigh. "If it's got to happen, I'm glad you're here with me, Bob. Don't think I could take this by myself."

"Yeah," Brahim said also with a dejected sigh. *I'm glad Boudi's with me too*, he thought.

Melissa Andrews soon arrived and parked alongside where Gabe Andreotti handed Brahim an envelope saying: "Here's money to pay for the cigarettes. Please count it."

Brahim counted then said tersely: "Exactly enough."

Gabe Andreotti then said: "Drive over there and park where you usually do. We'll park a good distance away, out of sight of others, but able to see you. When you're done, drive back over here and park; we'll be right behind you."

"Can we get something to eat here when we come back?" Boudi asked. "I'm hungry and I bet Bob is too."

Melissa Andrews replied: "We can all go back up the road to Golden Corral. You know where it is I'm sure. It's close to where Charlene lives."

Both were notably startled; Boudi asked: "Whaaat? You know Charlene?"

"I've met her," Melissa Andrews answered. "She and Tammi like you two a lot."

"You know Tammi, too?" Brahim asked.

"I just met Charlene, but she told me about you and Tammi," Melissa Andrews said. "We're taking up time. Go get the cigarettes and drive straight to Golden Corral. We'll follow you. Agent Andreotti'll pick up the tab, won't you?"

Before he could answer, she said: "Sorry if I put you on the spot; I could see Brahim getting angry so thought it best to say something. Those two're under a lot of stress. I wouldn't want to be in their shoes. I'll put this on my expense account if you like. Besides, I'm starved too."

"No, problem," he said. "I'll pay but we have to be careful that they don't sit next to each other and have a chance to bolt. What kind of restaurant is this?"

"It's self-service, all-you-can-eat," she answered. "I guess you don't have Golden Corral in New York. Omar hadn't heard of it either."

"I think I know the kind of place you're talking about," he said. "Let's see if we can get a booth and make sure the two guys are on the inside.

She said: "Let one of them go first, I go next, then you be at the end to pay," as she parked where they had a good view of the Chevrolet.

When they saw boxes of cigarettes being loaded, Gabe Andreotti called: "They have the cigarettes. Give us time to eat, then we'll head north. I'll call when we're on the way."

At the restaurant, Boudi opened the door for Melissa Andrews who said chuckling: "Thanks, but why don't you go first, Brahim. You're skinny; you look like you need to eat first." Brahim was startled but she continued teasing: "Oh, go ahead. We don't need to stand on ceremony. I do appreciate your good manners."

CONSEQUENCES • CHAPTER 17

She got in line behind Brahim, motioned for Boudi to follow with Gabe Andreotti at the end who paid.

She pointed to a large booth then got behind Brahim indicating he should go in first and she sat beside him. Boudi went in the other side and Gabe Andreotti quickly followed.

They ate with little conversation. Once next to the cars, Gabe Andreotti said: "This's the last time we'll likely see each other. You know the way. We'll follow you until you get stopped. All the best. Ciao."

On the highway, he called again: "We're on our way."

Chapter 18

Tuesday, June 6, 2006
Poplar Camp, Virginia, USA

Melissa Andrews and Gabe Andreotti drove wearily along Interstate Highway 77 northbound following Boudi and Brahim. June days were long providing daylight for at least another hour. Soon, they saw a sign saying 'Enter Wythe County leave Carroll County'. They noticed a Virginia State Police patrol car entering the highway just ahead.

"Finally" Gabe Andreotti sighed: "Can't wait for this to be over."

"That's two of us," Melissa exclaimed. "I bet they waited until they got to Wythe County; did you see the sign? That way they can keep them in Wytheville overnight, not in some small town county seat a way off the interstate."

"Wytheville?" Gabe asked. "Where the drugs are unloaded?"

"You've got it," Melissa replied. "Not only is it a little bigger than other county seat towns around, it's right on two of the busiest interstates in the U.S. Easier to take them to Roanoke tomorrow, or whenever. Roanoke's the nearest U.S. federal court."

The police cruiser drove up behind the Chevrolet, followed a few moments, and turned on its flashing lights.

"There's no place to pull over and watch what happens without calling attention to ourselves," Gabe Andreotti said.

CONSEQUENCES • CHAPTER 18

"Maybe we can find a place to cross over, come back the other way, and stop on the other side," Melissa Andrews said. "We can justify crossing the median with our credentials. We need to go back the other direction anyway."

Soon the two sets of lanes of the divided highway came close together and there was a crossover, which she took, made a U-turn, and drove southbound, stopping to observe.

"They finally got us," Boudi said wearily as he stopped on the shoulder and rolled down the window.

A male uniformed police officer came to the window and said in a Virginia mountain accent typical of the region: "Get out of the car and place your hands on top of the car."

Boudi complied and the officer patted down his body.

The officer then said: "Turn around and hold out your hands then with one hand take out your driver's license."

Boudi complied and the officer read: "Abdullah Zakawi, Lackawanna, New York. Mr. Zakawi, may I see your automobile registration?"

Brahim gave him the car papers which he handed to the officer who said: "Registered owner is Mohammad Fadel of Lackawanna, New York. Who's Mohammad Fadel?"

"Man we work for," Boudi answered.

The officer signaled his partner and said to her: "Please check the passenger." To Boudi: "Get in the back seat of the police car while I check these."

"Mr. Zakawi," he began after entering data in the computer, "we stopped you because you were clocked driving 70 miles per hour in a 65 mile per hour zone."

My speedometer showed exactly 65," Boudi protested.

The officer continued: "We've been requested to have you open your trunk and examine the rest of the car."

In the meantime, the other police officer repeated the process with Brahim and guided him to the rear of the car where Boudi had opened the trunk.

The first officer asked. "What's in those two boxes?"

"Er," Boudi fumbled for words.

The officer continued: "You were observed having large quantities of tobacco products loaded into your car. Take out the two boxes."

"It smells like tobacco," the other officer confirmed.

"Open the boxes," the first officer ordered.

Each broke the seals on the cardboard boxes. Cartons of Winston cigarettes were obvious in one box and cartons of Salem cigarettes were obvious in the other.

"These are obviously too many for your personal use," the first officer said. "May we see your license to transport tobacco products commercially across state lines?"

"We, er, don't have one," Boudi said.

"Look, there's another box in there that's already open," the other police officer said.

"Take that one out also," the first police officer said. "Open the flaps so we can see what's inside." Seeing smaller boxes inside, he continued: "Take out some of the smaller boxes and give them to us."

"Looks like prescription drugs. 'Made in Canada' it says on the box," the other officer said.

The first officer commented: "The state pharmacy board'd be interested in these and federal authorities, too. May I see your license to transport prescription medicine?"

"We don't have one of them either," Brahim said.

The other officer said: "We should look further and see what's in the spare-tire well and any hidden compartments. Unload the other items and let us see the spare tire."

When bundles wrapped in newspaper were visible, Brahim said: "I suppose you want us to unwrap these."

"Yes," she said.

Each unwrapped a package being careful not to touch them and held them out to be seen.

The first police officer asked: "What're these?"

"Er, we bought them in West Virginia and're carrying them back with us," Brahim replied.

"You entered Virginia from North Carolina," the first officer said. "You must've transported them across Virginia into North Carolina and back into Virginia. Let me see your permit to own and transport them."

"Er, we don't have any," Brahim replied.

"It's illegal to transport commercial quantities of tobacco products in Virginia without having paid Virginia tax or without having a license to transport them to another state," the first officer stated. "It's also illegal to possess commercial quantities of prescription medications in Virginia without a pharmacy license. Federal officials will be interested in the prescription medications because they appear to be illegally imported from Canada. Federal officials may also be interested in the firearms."

He looked at the driver's licenses again and said: "Abdullah Zakawi and Ibrahim al Asadi, you are under arrest. You have the right to remain silent. ..." he continued to recite the remainder of the 'Miranda' statement. "You will both go sit in the back seat of the police car; my partner will take the car keys from you. For the moment, we don't think you need restraints if you cooperate. You will be kept in custody overnight at the Wythe County jail and formally charged tomorrow morning."

"What about the car?" Boudi asked. "What about our personal things?

"I'll call a truck to transport the car and impound it while it's being investigated," the first officer continued. "Your personal belongings will be delivered to you in jail."

Gabe Andreotti let out a big sigh, saying: "Finally. Nothing more we can do here. What's the nearest airport?"

Melissa Andrews replied: "Closest airports are in Roanoke and Greensboro, but the Charlotte airport's only a few miles further away and it's a major hub. You might get a direct flight to Buffalo from there. You'd likely need to change in Charlotte anyway if you left from the other two airports. Also Charlotte's where I need to go."

"Oh, OK," he said. "How far to Charlotte then?"

"Hour forty five," she replied. "Maybe two hours to the airport itself; it's on the other side of the city. Say, why don't you stay overnight with us. We have a big house on Lake Norman with an extra bedroom. You can meet my husband Dan and my little girl tomorrow morning. You can even come to the office. Are you in a big hurry to get back?"

Too tired to object and really not wanting to, he said: "Sounds good to me. Thanks a lot. Sure sounds better than an airport hotel. Yeah, I'm in a hurry to see my wife and kids too, but I'm sure I couldn't get a flight this late."

She called on her cell phone: "Hello, honeybun.
pause

"On the way home; about an hour and a half," she said.
pause

"Say, I've got another agent with me. We've been working this case together. I invited him to stay overnight with us. He can't get a flight tonight anyway. He's nice. You'll like him. He's from Buffalo," she continued.
pause

"Could you look at the guest room and see if it needs freshening up," she said. "Last time I looked, it was OK."
pause

"Is Susie still awake?' she asked.
pause

"Hello, little sweetie pie," she said with another big smile on her face and in her voice.
pause

"Mommy luvs ya. Big kiss and I'll see you in the morning. Please give the phone back to Daddy," she said.
pause

"See you in a bit," she said.
pause

"Luv ya," she said, disconnected the call and drove southward towards Charlotte and Lake Norman.

CHAPTER 19

Tuesday, June 6, 2006
Wytheville, Virginia, USA

About half an hour after their arrest, Brahim and Boudi were led into the Wythe County sheriff's office where a deputy with a rumpled uniform that barely fit over his paunch was sitting in a swivel chair near a door leading into the jail.

WYTHE COUNTY SHERIFF'S OFFICE, WYTHEVILLE, VIRGINIA

He leaned up saying: "Hey, Phyllis."

She replied: "Hey Bubbah, two guests for you tonight."

"Noo Yoh-urk," he said in a Virginia Appalachian mountain accent looking at their documents. Er, Ihh-bruhh-himm awlll Uhsss-ahh-dee. Wich one'r' you?"

Brahim responded tersely: "I am."

"Ab-dul-ah Zah-kah-wee must be yew," he said. "Ain't that th' name uv that A-rab terrr-ust in Eye-rak? he asked.

"No! That's Zarkawi!" Boudi stated very tersely wincing at hearing 'A-rab'.

The deputy handed them two large envelopes saying: "Puh cher pers-null bee-long-ins in these on-vlopes."

"Here're their driver's licenses," The officer said.

The deputy gave them forms saying: "Sign hee-yur on these forms that yurr dee-poz-tun yurr pers-null thangs thee-un see-ull th' flaps, and sign yurrr names on th' seal."

When he put the envelopes and forms away, he lifted his bulk out of the chair and said: "Stay-up this way."

"Bye, Bubbah," the police officer said

"Bye, Phyllis," he replied.

The deputy waddled to open the door saying: "Hope y' had yurrr supp-ur. Ain't got no more food t'night."

As they passed an open room with a telephone, Brahim asked: "Don't we get to make a telephone call?"

"Yupp. That's yurrr right," the deputy said. "'Structions on th' wall. Y' gotta call collect."

Boudi, who was closest to the phone, placed a collect call then said in Arabic: "Mom it's Boudi."

pause

"Mom, I'm OK," he continued in Arabic.

pause

"No, Mom, they didn't kill us," he said in Arabic. "We got caught by guys who said they're Arabs. We were held a while and they took us back to North Carolina."

CONSEQUENCES • CHAPTER 19

pause

"Who told her that?" he asked in Arabic.

pause

"Yes, the car was left in Florida. But they didn't **confine** us at that place," he continued in Arabic.

Brahim, amazed at his cousin's ability to avoid lying, started agitating to be able to talk.

pause

"No, Mom, the government didn't beat us up," he said in Arabic. "Some other guys taking us from one place to another roughed us up a little."

pause

"No, Mom, he's OK too." he said in Arabic. "He's right here; talk to him yourself."

"Hello, Auntie Dima," Brahim said in Arabic.

pause

"Yes, I'm sure she's been worried, but I'm OK," he continued in Arabic.

pause

"You can tell her, but I'll call her myself as soon as Boudi finishes," he said in Arabic. "Here he is again."

"Mom. We're in Virginia. We've been arrested," Boudi said in Arabic.

pause

"Calm down, Mom," he said in Arabic. "They're not going to beat us up again. They don't do that here."

pause

"Someone brought a car down to North Carolina for us to drive back," he explained in Arabic. "Police stopped us for driving too fast and found things in the trunk they said are illegal. Mohammad always told us it was OK."

pause

"Mohammad's gone?" he said in Arabic. "Where?"

pause

"No one's heard from him?" he asked in Arabic. "They're calling from Yemen to ask where he is?"

Both said to themselves: *He really did flee the country.*

pause

"Who brought the car to us?" he asked in Arabic. "Was it Kamal? Whoever it was had to go back quick."

pause

"What?" he exclaimed in Arabic. "He got arrested in Canada?" *Oh, that's what he meant when he said Kamal's out of the country,* he said to himself.

long pause

"I'm sure it was terrible for them," he said in Arabic.

pause

"Who's Omar?" he asked in Arabic interrupting.

pause

"What? He came after we left and now he's running things?" he continued in Arabic, "and he's the imam too?"

Brahim, increasingly impatient made gestures for Boudi to hang up the phone.

pause

"Mom, I've got to go," Boudi said in Arabic. "Bob needs to call his mother too."

pause

"Yes, Mom, I'll call you when I can," he said in Arabic. "Bye, Mom. Tell everyone hello."

Brahim tried to call then said: "Damn, no answer."

"OK, boyzz," the sheriff said. "Time tuh go. Not many others tuh'night. Yuh each gits uh cell uv yurr own."

Once the deputy left, Boudi said: "Mom said a guy named Omar runs things now. He brought the car down."

Brahim replied: "Maybe he's the one who set us up."

"Yeah," Boudi continued. "Maybe he's part of that gang who captured us and took us to Mexico."

CONSEQUENCES • CHAPTER 19

"Those guys weren't from a rival gang," Brahim replied. "Didn't you figure that out? They weren't Arabs. Didn't you notice one guy was wearing a uniform?"

"Yeah, but why'd they take us to Mexico and dump us?" Boudi asked.

"Man, you're asking too many questions," Brahim replied. "Maybe we'll never find out, but for sure they want us out of the way. They seem afraid someone else'll want to ask us questions also."

"This is too much right now," Boudi said. "Maybe we just try to sleep and see what happens tomorrow."

"Yeah," is all that Brahim could say.

Chapter 20

Thursday, June 8, 2006
Roanoke, Virginia, USA

About 8:30 a.m., Richard Harris parked his ten-year-old Toyota Corolla on Mountain Avenue several blocks from the Poff Federal Building, location of the U.S. District Court for Western Virginia, where he could park free and save his meager income. He was wearing a solid light gray suit, white shirt, navy blue tie with a non-descript pattern, and black shoes with black socks for his first free-lance assignment with the U.S. federal public defender's office.

He is a stereotypical middle class WASP who predominate the Appalachian mountain region of the eastern US: 23 years old, 5 feet 10 inches tall, with medium brown hair trimmed professionally short. He recently bought plastic faux-tortoise shell glasses to replace the gold ones he had worn for years, thinking it makes him look more lawyerly.

Sure not going to get rich from this job, he thought as he walked up First Street SW. *Not enough to pay for clothes and glasses. Gotta start somewhere. Beats defending red-necks for drunk and disorderly. Hey, who's that over there? Looks like James Edward. Must be going to the same place I am. He got the job I wanted with the U.S. Attorney. Maybe he's prosecuting this case; his first, too. He looks the lawyer part too: Charcoal gray suit and a white shirt and navy tie. At least he has a regular pay check to pay for them.*

"Hey, James Edward," he called loudly to his former classmate at Washington and Lee Law School.

James Edward Goodwin, startled, deep in thought over the upcoming bar exam said to himself: *I heard Rich moved back to Roanoke. Looks like he's going to the federal building and parked here to save parking fees too.* He crossed the street and said enthusiastically shaking hands: "Hey, Rich, how goes? I heard you joined a local firm in Roanoke. You going to the federal building too?"

"Not exactly joined," Richard said. "A local firm allows me to use office space, the law library, phone, and have them take calls. They refer some criminal clients to me, usually the dregs, but gets me started. Doing free-lance public defense work for state, local, and federal courts. Could've had jobs in general law, but wanted to specialize in criminal law like you. Moved back in with my folks. Going to the federal building. We're probably on opposite sides of the same case."

"Most likely," James Edward replied. "Young guys from New York."

"That's the case," Richard confirmed.

James Edward thought: *Hey, maybe he can help me meet people here; it's been damned lonely so far. He always had nice friends.* "Where do your folks live?" he asked. "I remember here in the valley somewhere."

"In Salem," he replied. "Where do you live?"

"Got a place in a big complex on 419 close to Tanglewood Mall," he answered. "Not the greatest, but it's OK to start. That's close to Salem, isn't it?"

"Not far at all," Richard said. "My parents' house is in the south side of Salem not far off Electric Road."

"Say, maybe we can get together sometime," James Edward said.

"Sure," Richard responded eagerly, "but what about Amy, the girl you were dating so seriously?"

"That's over," James Edward replied. "I broke it off."

"Sorry to hear," Richard commented.

"Don't be," James Edward replied; "I'm sure not. Took a while to see, but if I continued, I'd have lost any and all independence."

"How's that?" Richard asked.

"We didn't talk marriage directly," James Edward explained, "but there were indirect references as graduation was coming near. She made it clear the only place she'd live is Richmond and anyone she married would have to move there. She's from an old-line family, one of the Fine Families of Virginia who believe Richmond's the center of the universe and certainly no decent, self-respecting Virginian would ever consider living anywhere else. Her family had connections so getting a job'd be no problem, but career advancement would depend on how well I fit in.

"The proverbial last straw was one night she was having her period and we couldn't do anything. She was really disappointed, not because we couldn't have sex, but because she had a period. We'd decided she'd take care of birth control although I was willing to wear condoms. It all fit into place; she was trying to get pregnant so I wouldn't have any choice but to marry her and she could pull me into her spider web and suck the life out of me."

"Man, that sucks," Richard said. "Oops, sorry for the bad choice of words. Your family's pretty blue-blooded too; Goodwins are pretty well known in this state."

"I don't know how blue our blood is," James Edward said, "but, yes, Goodwins've been prominent in Madison County since colonial days. Never been fabulously wealthy, but we have every bit as much right to be one of the Fine Families of Virginia as Amy's family and the FFV distinction never had much to do with money. May've been why she wanted me in her clutches because my family was as good as hers or even better.

"Goodwins feel comfortable about ourselves, who we are, what we've accomplished by our own efforts, and don't hold ourselves up to be prominent. Each person finds their own way. My family's happy I got a good job in Roanoke, even if it is on the other side of the Blue Ridge."

"I wish I had a more independent life," Richard said. "My parents are happy enough to have me back home and I'm happy enough for now to be back We get along fine. I've been away for six years and living with them requires adjustment on my part and theirs."

"You dating anyone?" James Edward asked.

CONSEQUENCES • CHAPTER 20

"Not at the moment," Richard answered. "Back in school you must've noticed I dated around, but none turned out to be serious. Still have friends here, but no potential girlfriends yet. Kind of like starting over again, but not completely from scratch."

They entered the federal building and learned the case would be heard before Judge Martha Bishop.

Judge Bishop, Richard said to himself. *Ashley Sue said she c'd be a tough one when she briefed me. Must've had run-ins herself, but wouldn't give me details.*

POFF FEDERAL BUILDING, ROANOKE, VIRGINIA

Oh, Judge Bishop, James Edward thought. *Back in the office they said if the case were before her I had to be really careful. She's extremely fair to a fault, but strict.*

"See you inside the court room," Richard said to James Edward. "I've got to find my clients and talk to them."

Chapter 21

Thursday, June 8, 2006
Roanoke, Virginia, USA

Just before 9 a.m., Brahim and Boudi entered the courtroom wearing their new clothes and sat at the defendants' table with Richard Harris between them. James Edward sat at the prosecutor's table. No one else was in the courtroom other than court officials.

A moderately heavy-set woman about 5 feet 6 inches, well into her 50s with gray hair over her ears styled neatly with the slightest natural wave entered. Her black robe covered a simple cotton summer dress. Dark brown plastic rimmed glasses hung on a chain on top of her breasts. The bailiff announced the cases of U.S. vs. al Asadi and Zakawi.

Judge Bishop said: "You are charged with illegal possession and interstate transportation of controlled substances, and interstate transportation of firearms without a permit. How do you plead?"

Brahim stood and said: "Guilty, Your Honor."

Boudi also stood and said: "Guilty Your Honor."

Judge Bishop, surprised, looked directly at them saying: "Let me be sure I heard you. How do you plead?"

"Guilty Your Honor," they both said.

She looked at the two lawyers saying: "Would counsel for both sides approach the bench."

She turned on a noise-neutralizer, looked directly at both lawyers, and said: "This case has a distinct odor and I don't mean sweet perfume. Mr. Harris, how is it your clients plead guilty when there are very obvious lines of defense? Are you not aware of cases overturned because a public defender did not offer adequate defense?"

Richard, momentarily stunned, thought: *Ashley Sue's right; she's a tough one, but what've I got to lose?* He began: "Your Honor, there was a fairly recent case in the third circuit, or was it the sixth circuit; I'd need to do more research to find the exact detail. A conviction was overturned because of inadequate defense by the public defender. The case here has substantial differences. In that case, the public defender had only minimal education and experience in criminal law."

He paused a moment then continued: "In that case, the defendants wanted to plead not guilty, but were advised against it by the public defender. In this case, I've explored several avenues of defense with my clients, but they insist they want to get this situation behind them as soon as possible so they can get on with their lives.

"Mr. al Asadi, is well versed on civil rights, public trials open to the press, and the like. I've talked to them individually and together. They've given me nothing I can use to develop a defense and insist on pleading guilty."

Judge Bishop, startled momentarily, thought: *This young man's no dummy and seems to know his law. He was clever enough to imply, but not say directly that he's better educated in criminal law than the PD I was referring to. Still, I bet this's his first case because he seems a bit nervous, but he's got some spunk about him.*

She then turned to James Edward and said: "Mr. Goodwin, this case positively reeks with the potential for official misconduct. A car is stopped on the ridiculous pretext of driving 70 miles an hour in a 65 mile per hour zone. Then police observe the driver and occupant are Arabs from New York; guess what? They're asked to open the trunk. In case you haven't noticed, the press's having a field day with ethnic profiling; civil rights groups and Arab-American politicians are getting involved too.

"Guess what again? Police find not only cigarettes, but prescription medicine and firearms. Are you not aware of cases overturned in federal courts because police had no probable cause to look for evidence?"

James Edward's knees felt like they wanted to buckle as he thought: *My first case and the judge's trying to rake me over the coals. The office was sure right about her; she's hell on wheels. Rich spoke up for himself and she didn't seem to mind.*

"Your Honor," he began, "the facts of this case show the defendants were observed by undercover agents in North Carolina loading commercial quantities of tobacco products in their car. It's well known in judicial circles that various states place observers in North Carolina from time to time to observe potential law-breakers importing untaxed cigarettes into their state, notifying various state police forces to look out for cars with the license plates and descriptions that match those observed. The federal courts have upheld this procedure, although I'd have to do more research to provide citations and details."

He paused, thinking: *Whew, good thing I attended that seminar on legal issues of the tobacco industry and remember at least some of what I heard.*

He continued: "When the Virginia State Police stopped the defendants' vehicle, they routinely reported the license plates and vehicle identification number along with driver's license details. Headquarters relayed instructions they should examine for commercial quantities of tobacco products.

"This is far from ethnic profiling; it can be demonstrated that this procedure has been followed in several similar circumstances, not only in Virginia but in other states. Virginia State Police are well trained in proper procedure, especially in the area of ethnic profiling, because of the proximity to Washington, DC. This training is state-wide and not limited to northern Virginia because Virginia State Police officers can be transferred temporarily or permanently from one part of the state to another. Therefore, there is no *a priori* reason to suspect ethnic profiling."

He paused to catch his breath and calm his nervousness saying to himself: *It's a good thing I went to law school in Virginia and had plenty of exposure to Virginia law and police procedure. She hasn't stopped me so here goes again.*

"Your Honor, to continue with the issue of probable cause: there've been cases in the federal courts, again I'd have to look up details, that've established probable cause exists when police have reason to examine an automobile for other reasons, especially on state charges like possession of commercial quantities of tobacco, and then discover illegal drugs. Although there've been no cases to my knowledge that involve prescription medications as in this case, the same legal reasoning should apply. Likewise, for possession of firearms. Therefore, Your Honor, I respectfully submit there was no official misconduct in this case."

Judge Bishop thought: *This young man also knows his law. He must've gone to law school here in Virginia as well versed as he is on state issues. He has quite a bit of spunk too. Still he's awfully nervous; must be his first case also.* She said: "If you and your offices think I'll rubber stamp this case and find them guilty, you've got another thing coming. None of my cases has been overturned on appeal and I'm not about to let that happen.

"This case'll be scheduled for further hearing at the earliest possible time, hopefully early next week. In the meantime, you need to go do your homework and look up details of those cases you mentioned, among other things. You can go back to your seats."

Looking at the defendants, she announced: "Ibrahim al Asadi and Abdullah Zakawi, the court does not accept your pleas of guilty; I'm entering pleas of not guilty on your behalf. The case is recessed until further hearing."

She banged the gavel, rose, and exited.

Brahim and Boudi were startled, with Brahim asking: "What's going on?"

In a low voice, Richard said: "I need to consult with my office. I'll get back to you just as soon as I can."

The bailiff escorted Brahim and Boudi to the holding room to await transport back to the jail.

Chapter 22

Thursday, June 8, 2006
Roanoke, Virginia, USA

Richard walked out of the federal building; saw James Edward in earshot, and shouted: "James Edward, wait."

He waited for Richard to catch up and said: "I figured you'd need to talk to your clients."

"I need to consult with the head public defender and tell her what happened," Richard said. "I told 'em I'd get back to them soon as possible."

"I need to inform my office, too," James Edward said.

Richard then said: "When can we get together and do something? You free this weekend?" He remembered: *We learned in law school not to let professionalism get in the way of a social life, and vice versa. Opposing attorneys, no matter how bitter and intense the court room battle, can be friends in private lives.*

"Uh, no," James Edward answered, "You're not busy?"

"Like I said, I'm sort of starting over again," Richard replied. "I could find something to do, but to be honest, lot of my friends have gone their own way and I have too. I think I have something with family tonight, but the rest of the weekend's free. You don't go home on weekends? Or back to Lexington?"

"I'd thought about going to Lexington for lack of anything better; it's only an hour," James Edward replied, "but almost everyone I know's away for summer break. I was just with my folks and no desire to go back so soon. Madison's much smaller than Lexington, I guess you know, so people like me move away when they finish school. I'd be happy to do something with you. What do you have in mind?"

"I know where clubs and bars are here and I could take you on a tour. Also, my folks have a place at Smith Mountain Lake and summer season's just getting going. We could go swimming, boating, or water skiing over there. There'll be other young people hanging out there too."

"Sounds good to me," James Edward said.

"Let me get your phone number," Richard said, "and you can have mine."

They exchanged cell phone numbers then James Edward said: "Here's where I need to turn."

"We'll definitely see each other this weekend," Richard said and exchanged a warm handshake.

Meanwhile, in the locked holding room, the television was broadcasting a news program.

Boudi said: "Wonder if I can get ESPN."

"Wait!" Brahim exclaimed. "That's Abou Hassan!"

The bottom of the screen read: "BREAKING NEWS: TERROR PLOT FOILED IN CANADA".

They sat stunned watching a person they recognized, the imam at the mosque in Mississauga where they picked up passengers, being led away in handcuffs by police.

Brahim immediately turned up the volume to hear: "… Royal Canadian Mounted Police have arrested several persons in connection with a terrorist plot to destroy landmarks in Toronto, Niagara Falls, and Ottawa. Details are sketchy, but sources state the RCMP had been investigating this imam and members of this mosque suspecting an al Qaeda cell. Recent information from the FBI and intelligence sources in the U.S. prompted the RCMP to act now, apparently just days before blasts were to occur. More information on this breaking story as we learn more. …."

"Wow," Boudi exclaimed. "Mom said Kamal was arrested entering Canada. Maybe that's how they found out."

"Maybe," Brahim said, thoughts racing.

"Folks at home must be scared shitless," Boudi added, "worried sick police'll come arrest them next because they've been to Abou Hassan's mosque. They're not going to let us get off easy like they said, not with this."

With that, he almost broke down crying.

"Wait a minute," Brahim said. "Maybe they knew this's going to happen. Maybe they want us out of the way before the shit hits the fan." He was a frightened as Boudi but didn't want to admit it.

Within a few minutes, the U.S. marshal came to take them back to their cell at the jail.

Chapter 23

Thursday, June 8, 2006
Raleigh, North Carolina, USA

Omar waited for a flight in the Raleigh-Durham airport thinking: *Can't read another thing, not even a newspaper or novel;* **really** *need new glasses when I go back to Minneapolis.*

Got sermon written. Took a while to come up with the topic. Tempting to speak on spirituality and strength of Allah within, like discussing with Agent Andrews. Wonder if I'll see her again. She's nice, very bright, interesting to talk to. Her husband's sure lucky. Wonder if I'll be so lucky.

His mind drifted to the sermon he had written in his mind: *Allah wants us to lead a modest life. Even if we're a minority in a land that follows another religion we don't have to give up on our own beautiful Islam; can be proud, good Muslims in non-Muslim society. The Prophet himself said that in early days of Islam when they lived among non-Muslims.*

Careful to not condemn Christians and call them infidels. Jesus was the last great prophet before Mohammad, peace be upon Him. Christianity is beautiful religion too, for Christians. We're Muslims, can be proud, follow our own ways, live a respectful modest life, respect others, not give into the ways of the world.

His thoughts stopped as he glanced at the overhead television, startled seeing a banner at the bottom of the screen: 'BREAKING NEWS: POLICE ARREST SUSPECTS IN CANADA TERROR PLOT'. Pictures showed men in handcuffs being led away from a store-front mosque much like the one in Lackawanna.

He forced his rebellious eyes to focus on smaller moving lines of print at the bottom of the screen: '... Targets included CN Tower, Parliament, and Niagara Falls....'

He sat up startled, thoughts popping into his mind: *Niagara Falls! That's close; I've been there. Never heard of those other places; well Houses of Parliament. Other places must be in Toronto. Destroying Niagara Falls? How many killed? How many without electricity?*

'Canadian police had been monitoring suspected al Qaeda cell', the moving lines continued. 'FBI tip-off led to arrest today because attacks imminent. Reports of firearms smuggled from the U. S. to support attack'.

He thought: *Must've been the mosque Kamal was talking about where they met for the ride home. Older ones must be scared to death police coming after them like back in Yemen. They need someone, but is it me they need? What am I supposed to do, Allah? Can't make planes fly any faster. Was going to take bus from the airport, but would take couple of hours. Wonder if Fadi or Fouad could pick me up.*

"Fadi, it's Omar," he said into his cell phone calling.

pause

"Yes, watching television right now," he replied.

pause

"Waiting for flights to Buffalo. Can you or Fouad drive the BMW to the airport to pick me up?" he asked.

pause

"Great," Omar continued. "United flight 1876 from Washington, arriving 7:45 pm."

pause

"That's right," Omar confirmed. "Park in short-term parking as close as you can to the baggage claim exit. You know where things are at the airport, don't you?"

pause

"Oh, you don't?" Omar asked. "Ask someone. Or go to the airport early so you can find your way around. Don't try to go into the terminal;

just park where you can see people coming out of the baggage claim exit. If you can't park close enough to watch from the car, then walk up to the baggage claim exit and wait on the sidewalk."
pause

"You can't call me. Have to keep my phone turned off on airplanes. I'll turn it back on when I get to Buffalo."
pause

"I'll call you from Washington if there's a delay."
pause

"I never saw them," Omar said. "Just left the car."
pause

"They're arrested?" Omar exclaimed.
pause

"Tell me more when I get there," he said. "It's time to get on the plane. See you at baggage claim."
pause

"Bye," Omar said and turned off the telephone. *For sure I can't preach that sermon I had planned*, Omar said to himself. *Maybe I can think of something else on the way.*

Chapter 24

Sunday, June 11, 2006
Baghdad International Airport, Iraq

Ali woke up just past dawn after a restless night, thinking: *Can't sleep? How much longer in limbo? At least they don't lock the door so Viktor and I can go to the clinic on short notice. Don't flaunt it in front of other prisoners. Need to pee. Go to the restroom by the clinic, not disturb Viktor. Never liked peeing in a bucket.*

He put on hospital scrubs and sandals and walked to the restroom. While relieving himself, he heard a loud noise that shook the whole complex followed by shouting.

What's that? he asked himself. *A bomb? What do I do now? Maybe just stay here.*

He went to the clinic where two medical corpsmen on standby night duty asked: "What're you doing here?"

"Couldn't sleep so came here to pee," Ali replied. "Any idea what's happened?"

Almost immediately, night shift guards escorted two prisoners saying: "These two're injured from flying debris, not seriously. Bad cases'll be here soon."

Dr. Sensenberg arrived groggy from deep sleep. Alex and Angie, the two head nurses, arrived shortly afterwards.

CONSEQUENCES • CHAPTER 24

What's he doing here so soon? Dr. Sensenberg asked himself, but was preoccupied by the commotion.

"Direct hits on a couple of the cells," one of the guards said. "These two caught shrapnel and debris. Not badly injured. A couple who took direct hits're on the way."

Ali sensing Dr. Sensenberg's question said: "I had to urinate and came to the restroom next door. I was there when it happened."

Alex and Angie quickly went to the two having their wounds dressed by corpsmen. Guards pushed in two hospital cots with bodies; Ali recognized them immediately as Abdulrahman and Adnan.

"These two took direct hits," a guard said. "Ceiling and beds crushed them."

Angie and Ali rushed to Abdulrahman who was nearest; Dr. Sensenberg and Alex rushed to Adnan.

"He has shrapnel wounds and maybe internal injuries," Dr. Sensenberg said.

"This one has internal injuries; only superficial skin cuts," Ali stated. "Breathing is very labored."

"He's trying to say something," Angie said.

Ali moved his ear close to Abdulrahman's mouth then said: "He said something like: 'They were supposed to free us, not kill us.'"

He reached for a stethoscope to listen to his chest.

"It's too late, doctor," Angie said with her fingers on the arteries in his neck.

"Better let me confirm that," Dr. Sensenberg said. "I'm the one who has to sign death certificates."

Ali went to Adnan's cot where Alex said: "It looks like he has shrapnel lodged in his throat blocking his breathing."

Bending for a closer look, Ali said: "He needs immediate surgery."

Dr. Sensenberg pulled the sheet over Abdulrahman's head and said: "I haven't performed surgery in years, but this's an emergency."

"I'm a surgeon," Ali said. "I haven't worked in emergency rooms for a while, but I know what to do."

"OK, but be careful," Dr. Sensenberg said to Ali. In a very low voice he added: "Be *very* careful. His test results came back inconclusive yesterday. Yours are negative."

"Should I help like I helped Dr. Viktor?" Alex asked.

"I don't know, Alex," Dr. Sensenberg said softly: "He might be positive; do you want to take the risk with so much at stake in your life now? I'll assist Dr. Ali."

"But doctor," Alex replied, "you have a wife and family and a medical practice. You can't take the risk."

"We need to start immediately," Ali pleaded as he was scrubbing his hands and arms. "He doesn't have much time."

"OK." Dr. Sensenberg said, "We'll both assist at least until someone comes in who needs the attention of one of us. Angie, would you please look after the others."

"We can't anesthetize him," Ali stated as he put on gloves. "He's not strong enough."

Two guards came in with another body on a cot saying: "This one didn't make it; died on the way."

"Viktor!" Ali screamed running to his cot.

Angie put her fingers to Viktor's throat to verify the lack of a pulse and gently pulled a sheet over his head.

Realizing his sense of duty, Ali returned to the table to begin surgery on Adnan.

"Unfortunately he didn't make it," Dr. Sensenberg said removing his fingers from Adnan's neck and pulling the sheet over his head.

Ali slumped into a chair, sobbing, trying unsuccessfully to stop the flow of tears.

Dr. Sensenberg, thought: *Why's he having such a reaction? Death's tragic, of course, any death, but doctors must be able to deal with it without emotional breakdown. He's a good doctor. He has to get past this or he'll be limited in what he can do. Maybe I should talk to him and give him some support.*

He removed the gloves, walked to Ali, placed a hand on his shoulder, stood silently a moment and asked: "Is this your first exposure to death as a doctor? It can be emotionally stressful. Just sit for a minute. Can we get you something? Water? Coffee?"

"It's Viktor," he said. "He's the only person I ever cared for. He's the only one who ever really cared for me."

Dr. Sensenberg pointed and used lip movements to tell Alex and Angie to leave and take the others with them.

"My parents," Ali continued, "I left them for good when I went to America, but they'd left me emotionally when they were forced to move to Aleppo. The government, the regime, took their life away from them; they just survived day to day and it was because of me. Viktor was my life, first as his student, then as he worked on me. It hurt when we had to say goodbye, but he knew I was going away to a new life. Preparing me for my new life was what he'd dedicated himself to. Then we found ourselves back together, dreaming about helping with our skills, repairing faces and bodies of innocent people ravaged by war. Being with Viktor kept the dream going. Now it's over."

Dr. Sensenberg stood silently, his hand still on Ali's shoulder remembering the scene when Viktor and Ali exchanged a very warm, tender embrace. He thought: *Was Viktor more than just a friend or a father figure? That'd account for this type of reaction. This's the 21st century and we recognize homosexuals have intense emotional attachments also. Should I say something? Maybe later.*

Dr. Sensenberg saw Alex, Angie and others standing at the door and said: "You may come in now. Maybe one of you'd get him some water and a cup of coffee."

Ali, his composure returned, said: "Yes, coffee please."

"Cream? Sugar?" a corpsman asked.

"Just sugar, please," Ali said faintly.

Two guards escorted two more prisoners with superficial injuries. The remaining corpsman and Alex examined them and started dressing their wounds.

"That's all," a guard said. "Hits were specifically on two cells. Very little collateral damage, but the cells next to them can't be used for a while. We need to find a place for these two prisoners and the other two also."

Ali winced, realizing his cell had been directly hit.

Chapter 25

Sunday, June 11, 2006
Baghdad International Airport, Iraq

While Ali was drinking coffee, Dr. Sensenberg asked the guards: "Is there a place you can keep these prisoners until cells can be found? As soon as word gets around, this place'll be full of prisoners feigning injuries."

"There're a couple of holding cells," a guard replied.

"Please use them," Dr. Sensenberg said. To the medical corpsmen: "The day shift should come soon. When they get here, you can freshen up and maybe take a nap. It's hard to say just how busy we will get. ..."

Before he could finish, two prisoners resisted moving, protesting loudly in Arabic, using fingers and other gestures to suggest they were badly injured and should not go.

Ali became more alert, went and spoke to them in Arabic, and then said: "Let me examine them."

Without waiting for Dr. Sensenberg's consent, he began. When he tapped on their knees, they cried in pain. He spoke to them forcefully in Arabic.

He said to the guards: "They'll go with you now."

As they left, Dr. Sensenberg asked: "What was that?"

Ali replied: "They were looking for excuses not to go back. It's damned unpleasant and they know they can't go back to their cells. If they're really seriously injured, I suggested we might transfer them to an Iraqi hospital under guard. Then I examined them. You saw what happened."

Dr. Sensenberg, amazed at Ali's skills with troublesome patients, said to himself: *He'll make a damn good doctor. If he and Victor did have a homosexual attachment, he needs to deal with it. There's nothing wrong with being gay. I knew gay doctors in medical school, internship, and residency. They were as good as any of us; some damned good. I'd gladly go to them for treatment and send my family.* To the corpsmen: "Before you go, though, please take these three who've expired to the storage room until we know how to deal with them with appropriate dignity." To Alex and Angie: "Sorry to say, we might need you both. I suspect it'll be a while before word gets around and people start showing up. Maybe take turns going to freshen up. If we don't get too busy, you can take turns going back for a nap or whatever."

Alex helped move the cots with the three expired bodies. As Viktor's cot was taken out of the room, Ali stood in obvious pain walking slowly to the cot as it left the room. He then sat down again slumping and sobbing.

Dr. Sensenberg put his hand on Ali's shoulder again and commented gently: "Maybe you should go too. You need to rest. You've had quite a bit to deal with today."

"But don't you need me?" Ali protested. "If you get a lot more people today, I can help like I just did."

"OK, if you're up to it," Dr. Sensenberg replied thinking: *dealing with prisoners took him out of emotional distress momentarily. He really does throw himself into work and can separate feelings from duty. He can't always avoid his feelings by throwing himself into work; best for him to confront them, but not right now.*

Angie heard Dr. Sensenberg say to Ali: "We wouldn't need you right away. Go freshen up; maybe take a nap."

Ali replied: "Where'll I go? My cell was destroyed."

Angie said: "There's an empty bed in Mike's room. His roommate was Lindsay who air-evaked for surgery." She put her hand on his other shoulder, saying: "I can take you when I go soon as Alex returns."

When Alex returned, she added: "Wait. Maybe Mike's still asleep. Maybe it'd be best if you took him, Alex. You can go first to take a shower, if you like, and take Doctor Ali with you. I can wait 'til you get back."

Dr. Sensenberg said: "that seems a good idea." To Ali: "You've had quite an emotional upset. Let me examine you quickly before you go."

Inside the examining room with the door shut, Dr. Sensenberg took Ali's blood pressure and temperature and spoke in a low voice: We need to talk more soon if you're going to spend time with medical personnel and others. It'd be a good idea if you weren't seen publicly. Ask them to bring meals to you so you don't have to go to the dining room." With the exam complete: "Everything normal. Again, I'm sorry about Viktor."

Back in the reception area, Angie gave Ali a small hug and said: "I'll come later to see if you need anything".

Dr. Sensenberg thought: *Angie's been paying lots of attention to him lately, not just today, and now she's getting more affectionate. Need to keep my eyes on this too. Ali's possibly being gay is only a small part of the issue.* Then to Alex: "Would you see if you can get a towel, soap, and things like that. Also, maybe borrow underwear."

"Got ya," Alex replied then guided Ali out of the room.

Just as they were leaving, Colonel Jones entered, surprised seeing Ali being led out.

Dr. Sensenberg said: "I was going to come see you as soon as I could. We've been busy here."

Colonel Jones replied: "That's why I came here. What's happening with Ali? I heard his cell was destroyed."

Dr. Sensenberg answered: "Apparently he got up in the middle of the night to relieve himself and came to the restroom next door. You remember we agreed we wouldn't lock their cell so they could come to the clinic when they can help so long as they didn't abuse the privilege and flaunt it."

Colonel Jones nodded and said: "Yes, I know."

"He was here when the injured arrived." Dr. Sensenberg said. "He heard Abed say: 'They were supposed to get us out, not kill us,' just before he died."

CONSEQUENCES • CHAPTER 25

"Oh," Colonel Jones said. "The DIA'll be here soon; they'll want to know that. What're the consequences here?"

"Three dead," Dr. Sensenberg continued. "Abed, Adnan, and Viktor. Apparently they took direct hits. Four others in the cells next to them had superficial injuries."

Colonel Jones muttered: "Viktor too?"

"Yes," Dr. Sensenberg answered lowering his voice significantly and walking to the far side of the room so others couldn't hear. Ali was really emotionally distraught. I need to talk to you more about that. He pulled himself together and calmed down the prisoners who didn't want to return to the cell block."

"Where's he going now?" Colonel Jones asked.

"I told him to relax and freshen up; that we'd call him when we need him. I expect we'll be getting plenty of business when word gets around to other prisoners who claim to be hurt or emotionally injured. I suspect plenty of 'em'll be just plain scared. He doesn't have a cell to go back to so Angie said there's an empty bed now that Corporal Myers has gone. I'm not sure it's a good idea for him to stay with the troops and I really don't think we should send him to another cell. There're extra rooms in the officers' wing."

"I see your point," Colonel Jones said. "We need to think it through, but yes we might keep our eyes on him better there. I'll bring it up with DIA. He's their prisoner. We'll talk later. You could use freshening up yourself. I'll stay here a while. I can't do doctor things, but I can make command decisions if necessary so Angie there doesn't have all the burden. My staff knows where to find me."

"Yes, Doctor, go ahead," Angie said. "When Alex returns, I'll stay here until you get back. I know two nurses don't equal a doctor, but we can keep a lid on things."

"I'll be back as soon as I can," Dr. Sensenberg said.

Chapter 26

Sunday, June 11, 2006
Baghdad International Airport, Iraq

In late morning, Colonel Jones was sitting in his office musing: *I didn't become a successful funeral director and unit commander allowing disasters to set me back. I've had plenty of experience dealing with distraught people...*

Major Armstrong's knock took him from his thoughts as he said: "Hello Josh. I was hoping you'd show up soon. Please take a seat. Coffee? Cream and sugar, isn't it?"

"Yes, thank you," Major Armstrong answered.

Colonel Jones called to Jimmy, who responded somberly, asking him to bring two coffees and something for him and Carrie.

"They're scared and upset, understandably," Colonel Jones said. "They never expected to be called to active duty much less attacked."

"I'm sure," Major Armstrong commented. "What're the specifics here?"

"Three persons dead: Abed, Adnan, and Viktor."

"Oh, Viktor, too," Major Armstrong said sighing.

"Yes, direct hit on their cells," Colonel Jones replied.

Major Armstrong asked: "Any others injured?"

Jimmy returned with coffees, handed Colonel Jones the change, and left without comment, his face showing stress.

CONSEQUENCES • CHAPTER 26

Colonel Jones replied: "Superficial injuries to four others from shrapnel and debris." He explained Ali's help in calming them and putting them in holding cells. "Others are scared, some panicking. The clinic's busy with prisoners feigning injuries."

Major Armstrong added: "The website of the Majahideen Shura, that's the al Qaeda-linked organization that took over when Zarkawi was killed, had an item that translates: 'the loyal servants of Allah fulfilled the divine command to destroy the false servants who failed in their duties and sought refuge among the infidels'. Then it referred to this successful attack on the prison."

Colonel Jones said: "Something else now makes sense: Ali heard Abed say something in Arabic just before he died like 'they were supposed to free us, not kill us.'"

Major Armstrong said: "Pieces of the puzzle are fitting together. We couldn't figure out why they'd want to bomb this prison. They don't have enough firepower to destroy the walls and we have back-up guards all around the perimeter to immediately close any gaps. They do have weapons to make pin-point hits if they know specifically where."

"Makes sense, sadly," Colonel Jones said.

"We've known from the beginning that chaplains, our translators, and other local help are not all reliable," Major Armstrong continued. "At least they've tipped their hand so we can narrow down unreliables.

"It stretches our imagination to believe they view themselves as servants of Allah to kill those who screwed up. We're sure they wanted to limit information that might fall into our hands. A big part is probably al Masri, the new guy in charge, wants to prove to us and others that he and the group are as powerful as Zarkawai and his network."

"Would they know Ali survived?" Colonel Jones asked. "That's another point I need to bring to you today, what do we do with him now?"

"What've you done so far?" Major Armstrong asked.

Colonel Jones explained where Ali was taken and continued: "He's really emotionally upset over Viktor's death, Bob tells me; much more than a close working relationship would indicate, if you get the idea. He may be back in the clinic now; he goes out of his way to help."

"I think I get the drift," Major Armstrong replied, "but that's not today's issue. How many'd've seen him and know he survived other than your medical personnel?"

"The four prisoners who were treated," Colonel Jones answered, "and any others he may have seen in the clinic later. Bob told him he should have his meals brought to him so he's not seen wandering around."

"I doubt spies would risk being around today," Major Armstrong continued. "Unless a prisoner knows who Ali is and tells a spy, then no one'd know. Besides, I doubt anyone in Majahideen Shura knows what Ali looks like. If he's dressed like an American doctor and people hear him speaking flawless American English, they likely wouldn't suspect anything even if he does speak Arabic. It's well known we recruit Arabic speakers when we can. Bob's right; best to keep him out of sight except in the clinic."

"Bob suggested we put him in an extra room in the officer's quarters," Colonel Jones continued. "It could raise questions if someone found out we're keeping a prisoner among our officers, but otherwise it seems a good idea to me. He's your prisoner, though."

Major Armstrong said. "Go ahead and move him there like he's an American doctor under Bob's supervision."

"One problem solved," Colonel Jones said. "Next and most pressing is what to do with the bodies? We can't keep them in the storage room. We don't have a morgue and the weather's hot. The remains have to be treated with proper Islamic respect, at least the two Muslims. If something isn't decided by late today, we'll probably have to air evak them to Germany where there's a morgue. Any ideas?"

"Gee, you sure come up with tough ones," Major Armstrong chuckled. "As you surely know, Islamic tradition doesn't allow embalming and requires burial within 24 hours if at all possible. Cremation's not allowed."

"Yes, we've had Muslims in our funeral home," Colonel Jones commented.

"We should notify the Iraqi guy's uncle, the parliamentarian, immediately," Major Armstrong continued. "The family'll immediately jump to the conclusion we killed him. Fortunately, we have that web site item. With luck he can be gone by tonight."

"OK, that's one," Colonel Jones said. "Two more."

"The Saudi Arabian's a challenge," Major Armstrong continued. "We've been avoiding dealing with Saudi Arabia until we knew his HIV status. I can't imagine they'd blame us for killing him, especially with this web site thing. He's one of the extremist religious tribe the Wahabis who'd be upset if he's not shown proper religious respect."

"His test results came back inconclusive," Colonel Jones added. "Ali's still negative, by the way."

"It's just as well we waited. They're surely not going to do a blood test on a dead body so we can avoid any issue of HIV. There's still the 24 hour tradition. I don't see how he could be returned to Saudi Arabia in 24 hours from this morning. We have our channels of communication with the them. Let's wait and see and be hopeful. Maybe we can air evak his body to Bahrain or Qatar instead of Germany. I'll definitely be back to you on that one as soon as I can."

"Good," Colonel Jones said, "and for Viktor."

Major Armstrong replied: "At least we don't have the 24 hour tradition. He's likely not religious, but we have our own sense of dignity and respect for the deceased."

"Yes, I'd thought about a memorial service," Colonel Jones commented, "but I'll get to that in a moment."

"He has no known family," Major Armstrong said. "We kept up inquires, but stopped when it was obvious we were using resources and getting nowhere. For sure, the Russian government wouldn't want to be associated with him. His Tajik passport is fake. It's up to us to decide. Maybe send him to Germany for cremation?"

"As I mentioned," Colonel Jones said, "Bob detects a very close attachment between him and Ali. Maybe we could ask Ali what he'd like us to do with Viktor's remains."

Major Armstrong replied. "Maybe ask but lean on him to agree to cremation. It'd certainly be the most cost-effective as well as dignified way.

Let's think about this one for a moment, but if you or Bob could ask him later today, it's worth pursuing."

Colonel Jones said: "I'll take care of that so long as we understand we have to do something by tomorrow. The thought occurred to have a memorial service. I was going to speak to the chaplain today, maybe involve a Muslim chaplain. Everyone deserves some type of last rites; funerals and memorial services are for the living, not the deceased. Some of our people are really upset at their first encounter with death. I'm a funeral director and think in different terms. What do you think, Josh?"

"Sounds good to me," Major Armstrong replied. "Maybe I should check with protocol before giving a final answer, but go ahead and pursue it with your chaplain. After all the bad publicity we got from Abou Ghraib, to have an U.S. Army Reserve unit actually arrange a memorial service for prisoners who were killed may be a nice touch."

"This isn't for publicity," Colonel Jones replied tersely. "I'm not going to be a part of any publicity stunt."

"Yes, understood," Major Armstrong replied meekly. "Sorry, it's been a stressful day."

"No problem," Colonel Jones said. "It has for all of us. You might as well stay for lunch. No one here feels much like eating but we need nourishment."

"Yes, thanks. I think I will," Major Armstrong replied.

Chapter 27

Sunday, June 11, 2006
Baghdad International Airport, Iraq

Ali lay in bed in the officers' quarters, tossing and turning, agonizing: *Viktor's gone. What do I do now? He was my life. Without him, life's not worth living. Why do I feel this way? Never felt like this about someone before.*

It was sad when I left him before; not like this. Big hole inside me. When we met again and he hugged me, something happened. Am I gay if I feel like this towards another man? I can't be gay. Doctors can't be gay.

Why's Angie paying so much attention to me? Always nice to know someone likes me; what's she want? Is she like that Swedish girl who just wanted sex with an Arab? Angie's nice, attractive, and pleasant, but do I have sexual feelings? Did that Swedish girl damage me from sexual feelings towards women? If I were with Angie would it change me?

Why's it so nice around men? Is that sexual attraction? What's sexual attraction? What's it feel like? Exciting watching guys in Mexico. I came without touching myself. Is that what being gay's about? Forced and violent sex.

Felt good, nice, sleeping in the bed with that nice old man. Would I've have wanted sex with him? What'd we have done? It couldn't've been violent.

What's it like other ways? Violent sex is all I've known. When I was raped it was horrible and exciting at the same time. Humiliated, brutalized, victimized, but felt, felt, can't find words for what it felt like. Came automatically then too.

Guy in Mexico said there're other ways. What other ways? Said I must get used to being gay; much easier for me. How? A doctor can't be gay and I can't be anything but a doctor. I know that.

What're my feelings towards Viktor? The thought, the very idea of being close. Can't describe. Kinda like with old man in Mexico. But different. Viktor and I couldn't be close. Wanted to be close; felt he wanted to be close too, but in cell everything out in the open.

Do I love Viktor? Or did I love Viktor? What's love? Never felt love before. Not like in all those movies and TV shows they made me watch. What I felt for Viktor wasn't that.

I can't be gay. I'm a doctor. Viktor was a doctor. Doctors can't be gay. No one'd let me touch them if I'm gay.

What'm I going to do? Can't deal with this. At least I'm in a private room. Bathroom's shared but not out in the open.

If I had to go back to a cell, I'd just kill myself. Easy to do at night in the clinic. Plenty of knives.

What're they going to do with me? Don't have anything that's my own. Yes, gave me a toothbrush and razor. I don't even have clothes. Nothing.

Over there I felt like a caged animal let out sometimes. Now feel like a trained animal. Comfortable but must perform. I want to perform. I'm a doctor. My destiny. Can't keep on like this. What'm I going to do, Viktor? Why'd you leave me? What'm I going to do now?

Eventually he fell into a listless sleep being waked when there was a rush in the clinic the next morning.

Chapter 28

Monday, June 12, 2006
Buffalo, New York, USA

A little after noon, Omar walked wearily into Gino's Diner, asked to be seated at a booth in the far corner, saying he would be joined by someone else.

Oh, man am I tired, he said to himself resting his head in his hands. *Good to get away, but in no mood to talk with Gabe. If I'm a good imam, I'll face worse than this, but the very first time and not even a proper imam yet....*

A middle-aged waitress, slightly overweight, in a white dress arrived with a glass of water and a menu, asking with a pleasant smile: "Are you OK?"

"Just really tired," Omar replied. "Thanks for asking. There'll another person. We'll order when he gets here."

"OK, I'll bring another menu," The waitress said. "Let me know if you need anything in the meantime."

"Wait, a cup of tea. Please bring a cup of tea," he said.

He looked over the menu saying to himself: *Specials for the day: grilled chicken breast, mashed potatoes, vegetable of the day, salad, rice pudding. Haven't had a decent meal like that in a long time.*

Gabe Andreotti arrived, shook hands, sat opposite, and said: "You don't look good. What's going on?"

"Just tired as hell," Omar replied. "They're really upset over the bust in Canada; it was at the mosque where they went to be picked up. They recognized the people led away in handcuffs. Brings back images of police in Yemen, what they thought they got away from. I'm their imam now; they look to me for answers and I can't give them."

"I can imagine," Gabe Andreotti replied. "But are you sure you're OK? We can arrange for you to see a doctor. We didn't talk about health care. We normally don't when we have a contractor like you. We just assume you have something for yourself."

"I have student health insurance," Omar said. "I'll be OK with some rest. I haven't had any real sleep since Wednesday night. Had to stay up all night Thursday re-writing the sermon for Friday. People've been coming to me with every kind of issue imaginable. A few are basically in sympathy with al Qaeda, but when it comes to blowing up Niagara Falls and Blue Jays stadium they don't know.

"Kamal's mother and family are really worried and upset that he's in custody in Canada. Brahim and Boudi's mothers and families are worried because they're in custody far away, Virginia they said."

"I can imagine," Gabe Andreotti continued. "Actually I can't imagine. We see lots of messy things in this job and this's no worse or no better. Unless one's right in the middle of it, it's hard to imagine. How was your sermon?"

The waitress arrived to take their orders, Omar ordering chicken and Gabe Andreotti meatloaf.

"The sermon," Omar continued. "Thanks for asking. I think it was OK considering it was my first ever and under the circumstances. I couldn't give the one I wrote in Chapel Hill. I asked 'what are these people feeling?' I couldn't condemn the planned bomb attacks directly; there's too much divided opinion. Finally, I came up with the message Muslims get our strength from Allah, strength inside. It's not necessary to use external means although I didn't specify which external means I was talking about.

"I made a point of saying religious terrorism has been around for many centuries with the worst examples so far in history at the hands of the Christians during their crusades. I didn't dwell on this topic, but I let them know that religious terrorism is not unique to any religion.

CONSEQUENCES • CHAPTER 28

"Finally I said that Islam can exist in any country and in any place. We can be good Muslims and live in any country. It's not necessary to have our own country. What's important is we remain true to ourselves and the words of the great Prophet, not demanding things of other people."

"Wow," Gabe Andreotti exclaimed. "You must've really impressed them. You certainly impressed me."

"I don't know about that," Omar replied. "I think I did all right. Remember these're simple people and not easily impressed by things that'd impress you and me."

The waitress brought the food with a big smile saying: "Enjoy your meal."

Both ate in silence, especially Omar who ate eagerly, finishing his food first.

While waiting for Gabe Andreotti to finish, he said: "I don't know how much longer you'll have me here working for you. We need to talk about that today. These people need an imam to follow me. I do want to be an imam one day and I do care for these people, but now I need to go back to finish my PhD. I need to find someone to take my place."

Gabe Andreotti stopped eating to say: "Why not contact mosques here in the Buffalo area and see if they can help?"

"I don't know where they are," Omar replied.

Gabe Andreotti said: "I can ask in the office to see who remembers where mosques are located."

"What?" Omar replied surprised. "You have a directory of mosques in your office?"

"No," Gabe answered. "After nine-eleven we located mosques to see if any illegal activity might be going on."

Omar exclaimed: "You're spying on mosques?"

Gabe Andreotti replied: "No! Not spying, but, yes we did observe their activities. If there was no indication of illegal activity, we stopped. We don't have a list. Not only would it be inappropriate to keep such a list, the media, civil rights organizations, and even some members of Congress would be up in arms in ways you might not even imagine. All I meant was some people in the office might remember where some mosques are located."

Omar thought: *Calm down. I'm tired and not thinking clearly. But damn it, investigating mosques?*

Gabe Andreotti continued: "Just for the record, we have done and continue to do the same thing for churches, or groups that call themselves churches. Almost since the beginning of the United States, some have sought to cover up illegal activity under the guise of freedom of religion using so-called churches, sometimes legitimate churches. For what it's worth, I assure you there've been many times more churches under investigation than mosques."

The waitress asked if they were ready for dessert and cleared away the dishes. Conversation stopped while they ate. Later she asked if they wanted anything else.

"Coffee for me," Gabe Andreotti replied.

"Another cup of tea, please," Omar said.

They sipped in silence until Omar said: "The bust near Toronto was the big event you told me about wasn't it? The something that was going to happen when I talked about the old people who were held in custody for so many hours."

Gabe had a faint smile gave a slight nod of his head.

"So the suffering of those old people was worth it to avoid the possibility that the bombs might be set off early and thousands of innocent people killed," Omar continued.

"You know I can't answer that," Gabe Andreotti said.

"It would've been terrible if they killed so many thousands, compared to five elderly persons," Omar persisted. "But did you have to keep them so long? Did the 11 or 12 hours you kept them make that much difference?"

Gabe Andreotti, visibly trying to control increasing annoyance, said: "Be careful how you say 'you'. It was the Canadians, not us who held them. If you want me to say they made a mistake holding these old people when it wasn't necessary, I can't do that. Or if you want me to say by holding them they kept thousands of people from being killed, I can't say that either.

"I can't speak for the Canadians, but I suspect they operate much like we do. Sometimes there're difficult decisions to be made. We make the best decision we can based on what we know or suspect at the moment. Sometimes it's a good decision. Sometimes with hindsight it's a bad decision. Sometimes we just don't know if it is a good decision or a bad decision and we'll never know."

"Agent Andrews said something similar," Omar said more calmly. "But you don't know what it's like for guys like me who have to deal with them."

Gabe Andreotti replied: "Omar, you don't know what it's like for law enforcement agents who have to make decisions like that, either. You're not the only clergyman to face a difficult situation. If this's the worst you have to deal with, you'll indeed be fortunate. Maybe you should look at the civil rights movement in the U.S. in the 1960s when clergy had to deal with horrendous human rights abuse, some of it because of decisions made by law enforcement officers and some at the hands of law enforcement officers themselves. Clergy had to deal with abusers who were their parishioners and thought they were doing God's will.

"Just a couple of years ago, a man in his 80s was tried and convicted for murder in a notorious civil rights case from the 1960s in Philadelphia, Mississippi. I don't know his church-going habits, but many like him were prominent active Christian church members. Think about the clergyman today who must deal with parishioners for events going back forty years. It's easy to say things should have been left alone after 40 years and not traumatize the frail old man, his family, and friends, rather than dumping them on the clergy to deal with. I could go on and on, but you get the point. It was not a pretty scene, but one we must live with."

They sat in silence for a moment then Gabe Andreotti continued: "Shall we get to the business for today. And, oh, if you want me to say that you uncovered and reported information that led to these arrests and saved thousands of lives, I can't exactly do that either because I can't speak for the Canadians. I can say there's a very high likelihood. So if you want to take the credit for having saved thousands of lives, then go ahead.

You deserve the credit. It was your intelligence, foresight, perception, and intuition that did it. I wouldn't always be so strong in my praise because some resources get too much of a big head and become arrogant and difficult to deal with. You're much too humble for that."

Omar blushed and said: "Gee, I don't know what to say. Thanks, I guess …."

The waitress, noticing the pause in conversation, came with a coffee pot in one hand and a pot of hot water in the other with a new tea bag to offer refills. Both accepted.

Chapter 29

Monday, June 12, 2006
Buffalo, New York, USA

Gabe Andreotti and Omar sipped coffee and tea a few moments until Omar asked: "How long do you want me here? I was expecting to be here all summer because I need money so bad. With Mohammad gone and the big arrests in Canada, what's there for me to do?"

"Don't worry about the money," Gabe Andreotti said. "We committed to pay you for the summer and we'll do that. There's still plenty to be done. We need you to wind up the operation and give us access to more information."

"You told me on the phone I'd be winding things up," Omar replied. "I don't know how to do that and now you want me to do more spying and get you more information?"

"Don't worry. It's a small operation," Gabe Andreotti said. "You can ask us for guidance. Mostly we need financial records so we can trace money movements. We'll have court orders requiring you to surrender records to us. We want to serve the order on you, not on someone who might be confused, afraid, angry, or just uncooperative, like maybe Mohammad's wife."

"Can I legally do that?" Omar asked.

"You can now," Gabe Andreotti answered as he gave a document to Omar. "Here's your power of attorney."

"How'd you get this?" Omar asked. "Notarized by the U.S. Embassy in Amman, Jordan. Mohammad's signature. You got him to agree?"

"Actually, it was his idea," Gabe Andreotti replied. "When Mohammad suggested you, they contacted us."

"He suggested?" Omar asked incredulously.

"Apparently it came to that after he was informed that Kamal and Brahim are in custody," Gabe Andreotti continued. "He didn't want the two young guys; I can't remember their names."

"Fadi and Fouad," Omar interrupted.

Gabe Andreotti continued: "He apparently thought they're too young and afraid they'd tell what they found out."

"That's a pretty good guess," Omar confirmed. "They're good kids but still close to their parents. I don't know his relationship with them, but I'm sure Mohammad wouldn't want too many knowing about the business."

"He definitely didn't want his wife involved," Gabe Andreotti added. "I'd guess he doesn't trust her."

"That's a good assessment," Omar said. "I haven't seen her so cheerful. I'd guess he's been abusing her; abusing in what way I don't know and don't even want to think about. She's pleasant to me, but let me know in no uncertain terms that the tea and grocery shop is hers and I'm not to touch it. She doesn't seem to have money problems either."

"I see," Gabe Andreotti commented.

"She's worried," Omar continued, "not like a woman would about a husband she cared for, but the uncertainty of not knowing where he is and what'll happen now."

Gabe Andreotti said: "Maybe people in Amman can get word to her that he's never coming back and she's free to do what she wants, like get a divorce. I'll even give you name of divorce lawyers."

"But she's Muslim," Omar interjected. "Muslim women don't just decide to divorce their husbands. Even though it's possible here in the U.S., she'd be in disgrace in the community if she tried to divorce him. For men, it's much easier. Wait. If you're in contact with the embassy in Amman, they can convince him to divorce her under Islamic law. All he has to do is say three times on three separate occasions 'I divorce you'. It's not quite that simple, but simple enough. If they're in Jordan, they can figure out details of Islamic law."

"Hmmm. Good idea," Gabe Andreotti replied. "I'll get on it right away when I get back to the office."

"So now he and everyone in Jordan know I'm an undercover spy for the, er, for your agency," Omar asserted.

"Oh, no, not at all," Gabe stated. "They don't even know who you are other than a name. Mohammad doesn't know or he'd never have suggested you. Apparently he still thinks you're the friend of the friend back in Yemen who can be trusted because of old ties. Even though he doesn't know you well, you're more trustworthy than the others.

"As for our officials in Amman, they know we have a resource in place, but they have no idea who or what kind. The mere fact your name's on this power-of-attorney document doesn't reveal anything to anyone."

"Oh, OK." Omar said relieved. "Now what?"

Gabe Andreotti took other documents from his briefcase saying: "Here's a request he signed giving you signature authority over his bank account at HSBC. If you discover other bank accounts, let us know so we can get court orders and hopefully signature cards for them.

"What you need to do now is start going through files and finding out what's there. Find out how much money there is. Pay any bills. If there's not enough money to pay the bills, let us know and we'll do something. We don't want the risk that electricity is cut off for nonpayment or someone sues to collect a past-due bill.

"Get Fadi and Fouad to help you. You don't want them looking at financial details, but they can move boxes, open file cabinets and the like. From what you say, he's the old fashioned type who wouldn't keep records on a computer. Even if he does, these young guys can probably hack into it; most guys that age can. If his relationship with his wife is so bad, he'd surely have records in an office, not at home."

"Good idea," Omar said. "Fadi and Fouad don't have much to do now that the two big cars are gone and there's only the BMW to take care of. I don't want them suddenly unemployed. Speaking of the BMW, what do I do with it? I'm driving it now. My old clunker will do good to get back to Minnesota, so I'm giving it a rest."

"You have a power-of-attorney. Sell it to yourself," Gabe Andreotti answered. "You'd have to pay market price or else there could be some questions raised."

"Nice idea, but no," Omar replied. "If I arrived in the Twin Cities with a flashy nearly new BMW, it'd raise more questions than I'd want to answer. Besides, I need the money to live on. I don't want my electricity cut off either."

"Give it to the wife, then," Gabe suggested.

"Baria doesn't know how to drive," Omar said. "Most Yemeni women her age don't."

"She's never too old to learn," Gabe Andreotti continued. "Maybe now's the time to take driving lessons."

Gabe Andreotti gave him another envelope and said: "Here's some money. You must be short with Mohammad not paying you."

"Thanks," Omar said.

Gabe Andreotti added. "We're hiring you as an independent contractor and consultant; you were told that when we first contacted you."

Omar nodded and said: "Yes."

"Despite being undercover, we still have to operate within the law, the tax law," Gabe Andreotti continued. "You're subject to income tax. We don't withhold it. Instead, at the end of the year we'll give you a form 1099 showing the amount. The form won't have the name of our agency, but instead something like Special Services U.S. Department of Justice. It's no secret you're consulting with the government based on your research."

Omar nodded his head.

"The next advice is unofficial," Gabe Andreotti continued. "You'll need to file a tax return and you'll probably need help. It can be complicated because you're self-employed, have to fill out special forms, and can deduct travel costs and similar things. Also, the money you get from Mohammad is subject to tax even though he paid you under the table. You might claim some is for services as a clergyman and special tax rules apply to the clergy. You'll be subject to New York State income tax too.

CONSEQUENCES • CHAPTER 29

If you can't find someone in Minnesota to do your taxes for you, get in touch with me. I can find someone reliable. You're in a pretty sensitive position now. You don't want you get tripped up on something like messing up your taxes."

Omar, confused, said: "Thanks. I have so many things in my head, I can't think about all them at once."

"You obviously need to rest," Gabe Andreotti said. "Do you have a place you can be undisturbed for a while?"

"I guess I could go to the mosque," Omar replied. "Not too many people go there during the day."

"Good. We'll obviously be in touch," Gabe Andreotti said. "Get a GOOD rest before you do much else."

The waitress noting the break in the conversation brought the bill saying: "Thanks for coming. Hope you enjoyed your meal."

"Yes, very much," Omar said enthusiastically.

"Yes, and thank YOU," Gabe Andreotti said took out a credit card, put three one-dollar bills on the table, then walked to the cash register to pay.

When Gabe Andreotti had his back to the table, Omar added a dollar bill to the tip, smiled at no one in particular, and walked to the door.

They shook hands outside without comment and walked to their respective cars.

Chapter 30

Monday, June 12, 2006
Wright-Patterson AFB, Ohio, USA

Patrick sat at his desk before 8 a.m. reading a newspaper and drinking coffee. Felicia, came in wearing a cream-colored summer dress with a multi-colored floral pattern that complimented her petite figure.

"Good morning, Sugarlump," Patrick greeted her. "You look chipper this morning."

"Oh, yes," Felicia said as she made a cup of tea. "Last week of school. Children are happy and easy to get off in the morning."

"They told me at church yesterday you're going on a trip," Patrick continued.

"Yes, we're going to the DC area for a few days," Felicia replied.

Frank walked in with his normal military bearing, helped himself to coffee, and sat saying: "Good morning."

"Good morning, Frank," Felicia said cheerfully. "How was your weekend?"

"Hey, Frank," Patrick said.

"Nothing special," Frank replied. "Met friends. Worked around the house a little. You know what it's like to keep a house and yard." *Can't tell 'em Paco came up and we're trying to patch things up slowly*, Frank said to himself. *Can't even say we went out with Jen and her girlfriend.*

Jen walked in, stopped for coffee nodding and smiling.

CONSEQUENCES • CHAPTER 30

"Oh, yes," Frank added, "Jen and I went to that new restaurant in Beavercreek. Wasn't all that great."

"No, nothing special," Jen commented and drank coffee thinking: *Wonder why Frank brought that up.*

"Anything in the paper about the al Qaeda bust in Canada?" Frank asked. "I haven't heard anything today."

"It's now coming out how much the U.S. is involved," Patrick replied as he folded the newspaper. "Firearms had been smuggled in from the U.S. and the FBI tipped them off they'd picked up intelligence that pointed to the cell there."

"Getting pretty close to home," Frank commented. "Time to get to work. I have that appointment with Marine Corps personnel at ten. Wonder if I'm being reassigned."

Two hours later, he arrived at the Marine Corps personnel office where the administrative assistant said: "They're waiting for you in the conference room there."

Frank was surprised to see three 'bird' colonels, one each from the Marine Corps, Army, and Air Force.

The Marine Corps colonel said: "Come in and have a seat, major. I'm Colonel Ramsey from Marine Corps Personnel. This is Colonel Granger with the DoDIG; and Colonel Ross, deputy associate director of the National Security Agency.

"Let's get right to the point. We're here to tell you you're being reassigned as commander of the Marine Corps security guard detail at the National Security Agency headquarters at Fort Meade, Maryland. You'll begin your new duties one August. That should be time to sell your house. You don't have a family to move and settle."

Frank thought: *It's time for a new assignment, but why tell me like this? Even brought the NSA deputy director. How do they know I own a house? Personnel records show I have no family and give an address, but not who owns the house.*

"Let's be blunt," Colonel Ramsey continued. "We're bringing you to the DC area so we can keep our eyes on you. We know about your adventure with the infiltrator and the men helping him. The end result may have been beneficial, but ends do not justify means."

Colonel Granger of the DoDIG said: "Your actions stopped an attempt to obtain military secrets and infiltration of terrorists into the U.S. Your actions may have stopped them sooner than if you'd turned the situation over to us. The consequences gave us valuable information we may not've gotten otherwise. At the same time, you committed major crimes, notably a federal crime of abduction and transporting persons across state lines, not to mention state crimes. We understand why you may have been motivated to take things into your own hands, but that does not excuse committing criminal acts and that we cannot condone."

Colonel Ramsey said: "This's the second time in your career you've come to the attention of the highest levels of the Marine Corps in negative ways. In the Okinawa situation you weren't culpable. Still, as you're surely aware, you've been receiving assignments that will not allow you to be in a similar position again. You did nothing to put yourself in this situation. You did nothing to put yourself in the situation in Okinawa. Still there's something that causes you to be involved in such activities; accident prone some people say. Now you **have** committed illegal acts and you've put the Marine Corps in a delicate position.

"You've had a satisfactory career and you come from a family with three generations of distinguished Marine Corps officers. So long as you keep your nose clean, you'll be allowed to serve out your twenty years and retire, but we're going to keep our eye on you."

Colonel Granger spoke: "It's not in our interests to prosecute you. You might be aware there's no statute of limitations for this type of crime. The FBI said to tell you to suggest your companions take U.S. citizenship to avoid automatic deportation if something comes up in the future."

Frank gulped, astonished they were aware of Paco and Luie not being citizens.

"There's another role we have for you, major," Colonel Granger added. "The DIA, of which the IG is a part, has realized it needs to know more about homosexuality and how to deal with it. Other intelligence services are ahead of us realizing society's attitudes have changed.

CONSEQUENCES • CHAPTER 30

"Until now, the DIA, being an agency of the DoD, had the attitude that homosexuality has no place in the armed forces and has seen no need to deal with it. Now we're realizing, somewhat reluctantly on the part of many people, we must as a minimum learn more about homosexuality and how it affects our intelligence activities. By this we mean not only the members of our own agency, but those we deal with, the resources we use, the targets, the whole spectrum."

Frank's stoicism turned suddenly to a cold sweat.

Colonel Granger continued: "As you probably know, all U.S. intelligence services have avoided using homosexual agents and resources and have eliminated persons when it was discovered they're homosexual. That was based on the notion homosexual agents would be unreliable; if enemy intelligence discovered the homosexuality, the threat of public exposure would cause the agent to be turned; at best become a double agent and at worst, you can imagine.

"According to other intelligence services, society's attitudes have changed. Many homosexual persons are not afraid of being exposed and aren't readily turned. We've been losing too many good people with crucial skills by automatically discharging them. The DIA's the only intelligence service that routinely does this any more and it's costing us a fortune. Maybe more important, the enemy's aware of this policy and may be using homosexual gathering places to conduct clandestine activities knowing we likely wouldn't be in these places."

What the hell?! Frank thought. *Do they suspect me because I go to the Serpent? Did they follow me?*

Colonel Ross added: "This aspect of your duties does not involve the NSA even though it's your work place."

Colonel Granger continued: "Your duties will involve DoD personnel, military and civilian, and finding out more about homosexual activity from their perspective. ..."

"What?!" Frank blurted out forcefully. "You want me to spy on members of the Armed Forces and report them to you?! I'll resign my commission before I do that!"

The colonels were surprised at Frank's reaction.

He said to himself: *The words just came out of my mouth. Would I really out myself?*

Colonel Ramsey stated: "Absolutely not! This is a point I was going to bring up next. The DoD has a strict don't ask; don't tell policy. Enforcement's left to each service. The Marine Corps comes under the Navy and the Navy's enforcement of the policy is the strictest or some would say the most liberal because strict enforcement of the policy results in tolerance of homosexual members who don't flaunt themselves. If you were to discover individual members who you suspect of being homosexual, you must NEVER disclose that fact officially or unofficially. That would indeed result in termination of your career."

Frank asked: "What do you want me to do? Why me?"

Colonel Granger replied: "We want you to observe homosexual people in general. Get to know them so you can understand more about their mind-set, in particular how much of a threat are they to us from a military intelligence perspective. Where do they go? Where do they congregate? Is there clandestine activity going on at these places?"

Frank thought: *You stupid ass. Gay people are just like others, come in all types, the only thing they have in common is sexual attraction to the same sex. Until you can get that through your fucking head, you'll never understand. ...*

His attention was brought back as Colonel Granger continued: "Why you? It's obvious you've been exposed to a broad range of people and have shown sensitivity to individual differences, er ..."

Sensitivity? Frank thought cynically. *Paco should be hearing this.*

Colonel Granger continued: "Maybe lack of prejudice would be a better expression. In Okinawa you saw the Asian girls as human beings to be respected and treated with dignity, not objects for enjoyment with no concern for their human-ness. In your latest activity, even though you abducted the individuals, you didn't show prejudice against them because they're Arabs. We think you might be able to interact with homosexuals with the same lack of prejudice."

Colonel Ramsey said: "Also there's a matter of your availability. Your job at NSA does not require full time attention. Being at the NSA provides good cover because you'll not be directly associated with a DoD activity. We must remind you that you must exercise caution in the places you might go. You cannot discredit yourself and the Marine Corps by going to establishments that are, shall we say, disreputable or where illegal activity might occur."

Colonel Granger interrupted: "Our interaction with the FBI Indicates most homosexual establishments are no more disreputable than others and may be even more law-abiding. There's no indication you'd be inclined to go to such places. Still we must state for the record this task is not intended to encourage you to visit certain types of establishments."

Colonel Ramsey stood to end the session and said: "Major, you'll receive your orders soon. When you arrive at Fort Meade, you'll receive more details about your duties."

Frank, startled at the abruptness of Colonel Ramsey's dismissal, stood, pausing for a moment wondering whether to come to attention and salute.

"At ease," Colonel Ramsey said. "That's all."

Chapter 31

Monday, June 12, 2006
Wright-Patterson AFB, Ohio, USA

On the way back to the office, Frank thought: *I sure was naïve thinking no one'd trace this to me. Gotta tell the guys. Paco's working day shift. Can't remember when Fred's working. Luie'd probably know. Call him at the bakery and ask. Really have to get in touch with Fred and tell him he may've been outed. Suspects the police force knows and're happy to have him, but needs to hear it from me.*

Wonder what would've happened if I'd told the IG? Likely worse than this. 'Don't ask; don't tell' they emphasized. I sure would've told. Besides, they'd have dithered so long, damage would've been done and they know that. Colonel said as much.

Moving to DC isn't bad. Not much attraction for Ohio. Only Paco's here and we're patching it up maybe. Wonder if he'd want to come to DC? Would I want him to? Could I share my life with anyone? How the hell should I know?

Maybe just resign commission here and now. Only reason I'm in the Marine Corps is to please my father; get him to accept me. Be proud of me. Finally figured out nothing would please him. Even if I walked on water, he'd criticize something. Should've walked faster or not gotten clothes wet.

Weird a religious metaphor popped into my mind. He's so agnostic wouldn't even know what walking on water is. Guess he taught me to be just as agnostic.

CONSEQUENCES • CHAPTER 31

Can't resign commission now. No marketable skills and need an income. Going to DC gives me time and places to learn something new. For sure, not much in Dayton.

In the office, he said: "You want to buy a house, Patrick, now that you're settling down with Elsie?"

"Well, er maybe," Patrick replied. "You get a new assignment like you thought?"

"Yeah, to Maryland near DC, commander of the marine guards at the NSA," Frank answered.

Jen looked up and asked: "When're you going?"

"One August," Frank replied.

"We'll miss you, Frank," Felicia added.

"Catch you at lunch time for the gym?" Frank asked.

"Yeah, sure," Patrick answered.

As they drove to the gym, Frank asked: "Did you ever hear anything more from the DIA about your reassignment?"

"No, not a word," Patrick replied. "I told them I wasn't interested. They insisted on flying me to DC anyway and giving me a physical exam. Maybe there was something wrong, but why wouldn't they say something so I can go to the doctor here. Come to think of it, it was a weird exam. They seemed to be more interested in the hernia test than anything else. Just went through the motions. I still don't see why they couldn't've had a local doctor do it."

When dressed in gym clothes, Patrick said: "Catch you in the showers maybe.

If he only knew what catching him in the shower used to do to me, Frank thought. *It hasn't done anything to me since then. Maybe it's like seeing my brother in the shower only I don't have a brother. Other gay guys say seeing their brothers doesn't do anything for them.*

Frank began running along the track seeing Patrick in the distance allowing his thoughts to drift.

Suddenly he said out loud even though no one was close: "What the fuck!" To himself: *Hernia test with his shorts down. Sent him all the way to*

DC to be examined by a doctor from DIA headquarters. They were checking him out; must've known how I found out.

His mind continued to drift as he ran lap after lap then suddenly he startled himself so much he almost stopped running: *They don't want me as part of a project to find out about gays and how to deal with them. Telling me it's OK to keep going to gay bars and'll even cover for me. I have 'em over a barrel. That's why he was so abrupt in dismissing me. They try to get rid of me or take sanctions, I disclose the whole thing. Accident prone. Maybe I am, but sure as hell know how to cover my ass and make 'em kiss it.*

Probably realized I'd out myself if I had to. Said I'm from distinguished Marine Corps family. Maybe they've figured out that my father and mother didn't give a shit about me and never have. Sure they'd be embarrassed to have a gay son. So-called friends'd feel sorry for them, feel sorry for themselves. Disown me and I'd not get any money. Who the fuck wants their kind of money.

Who needs this fucking Marine Corps any more anyway? Can't just walk away now. Why should I? Let 'em pay me to have fun in DC. Only got little over five years left.

In DC figure out what to do next. Maybe get an MBA like Patrick. What about foreign affairs? Didn't that colonel say I'm sensitive to different nationalities? Maybe master's in foreign affairs. What the hell, I'll get a PhD.

He finished his run with his thoughts winding down and drifting back to the weekend with Paco. Upon entering the locker room, he noticed Patrick was already in the shower. He leisurely undressed and joined him.

CHAPTER 32

Tuesday, June 13, 2006
Roanoke, Virginia, USA

Richard Harris walked towards the federal building thinking: *Doesn't look like James Edward's here, but I'm early to meet Ashley Sue. Sure was fun with him over the weekend.*

Approaching the federal building, he saw Ashley Sue Hunter dressed in a cream colored summer suit with a blue blouse open at the neck, the best J.C. Penney offered. The outfit along with plain flat-heeled shoes and eye glass frames from the Wal-Mart vision center was carefully chosen to give a suitable business-like appearance her public defender clients would expect, but not overwhelm them.

He thought: *She was dressed more upscale yesterday when she had lunch with the guys from DC. She'll take over today. It's sensitive now.*

Some minutes later, Brahim and Boudi entered the courtroom, Ashley Sue Hunter between them and Richard Harris following. Roger Chen, Joe Shaito, and James Edward Goodwin were accompanied by Randolph 'Randy' Walker, U.S. Attorney for the Western district of Virginia.

All rose when Judge Bishop entered; she thought: *Ashley Sue's here today; she asked to join as defense counsel. Obviously she's taking this case more seriously rather than leaving it with a contract lawyer.* She said: "Will counsel please approach the bench."

As the six attorneys approached, she thought: *Nice to see Ashley Sue looking so good. Almost as proud of that girl as my own Becky. How many years ago did they became best playmates? At least 25. Best friends though school and Virginia Tech. Becky stayed for masters in computer engineering. Ashley Sue wanted law and I was her mentor. Went to UVA Law, and now's chief public defender for Western Virginia. Hope they get quick resolution; otherwise have to recuse myself. Couldn't preside over her case.*

She activated noise neutralizing and said: "Ms. Hunter, you've appeared before this court before and we have a good relationship with your office. You're petitioning to be added as counsel for the defense."

"Your Honor," Ashley Sue Hunter replied. "Mr. Harris said you raised issues about the adequacy of the defense by the public defender's office. To meet your concerns, I decided to join the case myself, with your approval."

"I'm inclined to grant that request," Judge Bishop stated. "Let me emphasize I did not question Mr. Harris's competence; he presented the situation quite well. Still there were obvious issues I felt obligated to raise.

"Mr. Walker, you too have appeared in this court many times and we have a good relationship with your office. You other two are from the U.S. Attorney General's office in Washington. I have a petition for all three of you to be added to the case. And you are?"

"Roger Chen, Your Honor," he replied.

"Then you must be …" she said.

"Joe Shaito, Your Honor," he interrupted.

"It says here Yusef Shaito," Judge Bishop stated saying to herself: *he doesn't look Japanese. Yusef sounds like an Arabic name. That'd fit this case.*

"Joe's the name everyone calls me, Your Honor," he replied. "Yusef Shaito is my actual name."

"I'll get to this petition later," Judge Bishop said. "I said last time this case has an odor to it. Today it has an even more distinctive odor, but a very different one. It's obvious the defendants are involved with the arrest of alleged terrorists in Canada and don't try to pretend otherwise."

"Yes, Your Honor," Roger Chen responded. "Or rather no, Your Honor."

CONSEQUENCES • CHAPTER 32

"But all the government's doing is charging them with petty little crimes," she continued.

"Your Honor," Roger Chen stated, "It's not in the best interests of the United States Government to pursue other charges against these defendants ..."

"That's a no-brainer," Judge Bishop interrupted. "You'd have to present evidence that might upset the case in Canada, you might have to extradite witnesses from Canada, and heaven forbid you might expose weaknesses in the so-called war on terrorism."

Roger Chen replied: "These two young men are at the lowest level of the organization, errand boys so to speak; they're naïve and didn't fully understand the consequences."

"So why didn't this come out in court at the last hearing?" Judge Bishop asked. "Why're we waiting until today for big guns from Washington to come down here to our backwater mountains and valleys to push this case through the system as quickly and quietly as possible?"

"Your Honor," Roger Chen continued, "another agency deals with Canada on this matter and for obvious reasons did not inform us ahead of time that such action was planned. The United States government did not want even the faintest risk something would come out in open court that could have even the remotest slight chance of affecting the operation in Canada. We didn't have information we could have brought out in court before.

"Hrrmph, I see," Judge Bishop said."

"We've since been in contact with defense counsel," Roger Chen continued. "We'd like the defendants to have an opportunity to rehabilitate themselves with a minimal legacy from the consequences of their actions. In exchange for their guilty plea, we'll recommend a minimal sentence of six months in a minimum security facility followed by a five-year period of supervised work and study."

"And what do you think of that, counselor?" Judge Bishop asked saying to herself: *if Ashley Sue goes along, I'll agree; she's no pushover for the big guns from DC and she knows her law almost as well as I do. I still think this's a big set-up, but no way to prove it from the bench.*

"Your Honor," Ashley Sue Hunter began, "I've discussed the issues at length with my clients. Just as with my colleague Mr. Harris, the defendants'll give absolutely nothing with which to pursue a defense. They're aware of possible lines of defense and refuse to follow any of them. Now that additional events have occurred, I discussed issues with them in even more detail. They're aware additional charges could be brought against them. I presented the offer from the prosecution and they accepted."

"Well, I see," Judge Bishop stated. "If you have things so neatly arranged, I see no reason to approve adding additional prosecution counsel from headquarters. Mr. Walker, this court has a long-standing professional relationship with you and your office. If you feel strongly you should be added, I'll grant that request. Nonetheless, it seems to me Mr. Goodwin is very capable of proceeding on his own so you can be free to continue giving your two visitors from Washington the orientation tour."

The four U.S. attorneys looked at each other with perplexed looks and mumbled: "Orientation tour?"

"In case you haven't noticed," she continued, "a judicial reporter from the *Roanoke Times* is in the courtroom. Someone at the paper must've gotten wind there might be something interesting and sent a rookie reporter.

"As Ms. Hunter and Mr. Walker know, this court'll go to whatever lengths are necessary to respect the right of defendants to have an open public trial, including open to the news media. This court'll also uphold to the maximum extent the constitutional guarantee of freedom of the press. What I will not do is have this courtroom become one ring in a three-ring circus full of national media. The last time that happened was in 1984 when a Virginia Tech student was denied the right to register to vote merely because she was a student. The national media flocked in here like bees go for nectar. That's not going to happen in this case.

"What I will do is entertain a request from you that as a professional courtesy the visitors be allowed to accompany local counsel to this conference before the bench while Mr. Shaito's taken on an orientation tour of federal courtroom procedures in field settings. Do I hear such a request?"

CONSEQUENCES • CHAPTER 32

Randy Walker said to himself: *With rumors flying that the Attorney General's getting rid of U.S. attorneys to make places for political appointees, I'd better not make waves.*

He responded: "Your Honor, I so request."

"Your request is granted," she replied.

"When you return to your tables, I'll ask the defendants to plead again. If it's still guilty, as you say it'll be, I'll schedule a sentencing session as soon as I can."

"Your Honor," Roger Chen began, 'we've already…"

"Just a moment, counselor," Judge Bishop interrupted angrily. "Did you not just now hear me that I denied your request to join this case? Mr. Goodwin is attorney of record. If he were alone and were to ask for a brief recess in order to consult with the U.S. Attorney's office by phone, I'd grant the request. I don't think a telephone call's necessary.

James Edward Goodwin stepped forward and said: "Your honor, I request a recess of a few minutes to consult with representatives of the U.S. Attorney's office."

"Request granted; you have five minutes," she replied.

James Edward Goodwin, Randy Walker, Roger Chen, and Joe Shaito conferred a few moments then James Edward Goodwin stepped forward saying: "Your Honor, the prosecution anticipated the issue of where to incarcerate the defendants. We've determined there's space in a minimum security facility in Duluth, Minnesota. This possibility has been discussed with defense counsel."

"Hrmph," Judge Bishop mumbled. "Ms. Hunter?"

She replied: "Defense counsel presented this possibility to the defendants and they concur."

"Thank you for visiting our courtroom Mr. Chen and Mr. Shaito," Judge Bishop said. "I'm sure the visit will be instructional under Mr. Walker's capable guidance. The bailiff can show you to the side door."

Chapter 33

Tuesday, June 13, 2006
Roanoke, Virginia, USA

Randy Walker, Joe Shaito, and Roger Chen slipped quietly into seats on the back row while Judge Bishop called the court to order saying: "For the record, Ms. Ashley Sue Hunter, Esquire, has been added to the case as counsel for the defense. Two representatives of the U.S. Attorney General's office are on a tour to give a new employee an orientation to court procedure in the field. The head of the local U.S. Attorney's office is guiding them. As a professional courtesy, they were allowed to observe proceedings at the bench. Now, I will re-entertain pleas from the defendants. How do you plead?"

Brahim and Boudi repeated their guilty pleas to which the judge responded: "Abdullah Zakawi and Ibrahim al Asadi, based on your pleas, this court finds you guilty as charged. The court will reconvene at the earliest possible time to pass sentence. Court dismissed."

When James Edward didn't see his colleagues outside, he thought: *they must've gone to the office. I'd better beat it before that reporter gets hold of me.*

As Ashley Sue Hunter and Richard Harris were leaving she said: "We'll talk in my office. I'll call you when to come."

They started walking in separate directions when a young man rushed to them dressed in blue jeans, Nikes, a non-descript short-sleeve

CONSEQUENCES • CHAPTER 33

sport shirt, black metal-framed glasses, and with longish medium brown hair over his ears saying: "Marcus Porter from the *Roanoke Times*. I'd like to ask you some questions."

Ashley Sue Hunter said: "The Public Defender's Office is always pleased to cooperate with the media," thinking: *If I stall him, that'll give prosecutors time to get away.*

Richard Harris stepped back and stood quietly.

"Could you comment on your successful plea bargain for the defendants?" Marcus Porter said holding a miniature tape recorder close enough to get her voice. "They're involved with the terrorist arrest in Canada, aren't they?"

"Plea bargain?" She replied. "Sorry, I think you're confusing me with someone else."

"No," he stated emphatically, "the case you just joined and defendants pled guilty. You obviously joined as part of a plea bargain presented to the judge at the bench."

This guy's on the ball, she said to herself and replied: "I think you must be jumping to conclusions, Mr. er …"

"Porter, Marcus Porter," he replied. "Why else would you have petitioned to join the case?"

"I can answer that," Richard Harris interrupted thinking: *maybe I can relieve some pressure from Ashley Sue.* "She joined the case because the judge questioned my competence to defend the defendants at the hearing last week when you weren't present. When I notified Ms. Hunter, she appeared in the court today to inform the judge she has confidence in me, but not wanting to create further concern for the judge, she asked to join the case."

"I most certainly did," she confirmed thinking: *Gee, Rich's quick on the uptake.*

"Then why were attorneys from the Attorney General's office in the court today?" Marcus Porter persisted.

"Didn't you hear the judge's comments?" she said. "They're visiting federal courts to orient a new employee to practice in the field."

439

"Yeah, sure," Marcus Porter said. "Why'd you have lunch with them yesterday if not to discuss a plea bargain?"

She said to herself: *so that's how they got onto this. Someone from the paper obviously saw me at lunch at the Hotel Roanoke yesterday, smelled something, and sent this young rookie to check it out.* "As a professional courtesy to me," she stated pointedly. "In case you're not aware, I too am an attorney employed by the Department of Justice even if I'm the public defender on the opposite side of cases. Don't you think I deserve to be included in meetings with visitors from the national office? Moreover, as the head of the public defender's office in Western Virginia, they asked if they could observe this case as a courtesy to me. I told them the only time I had was over lunch. I'm quite busy being the only full time attorney in the public defender's office. If you'd done your homework, you would have known that. Just in case it makes any difference to you, I took the opportunity to talk shop. I don't get much of an opportunity to know first hand what's going on at the top of the federal judicial system."

"So why'd they pick Roanoke and this particular case for an orientation visit?" Marcus Porter asked skeptically.

Damn, she said to herself. *This guy doesn't give up. He knows damned well I won't go too far to antagonize him because of the relationship we cultivate with the media.*

"You'll just have to ask them that," she replied.

Richard Harris interrupted: "Perhaps it'd be useful if you consulted a map first. Roanoke's in a somewhat isolated location but only 200 miles from Washington and it's easy to travel here. The judicial experience here is substantially different from highly urbanized places like Philadelphia that're the same distance in the other direction."

"Are you trying to tell me, then," Marcus Porter asked, "there was no plea bargain for these two guys right after that big arrest of terrorists in Canada? They're Arabs from New York close to where it happened."

"Mr. Porter!" she began angrily. "Maybe you should talk to your editor and maybe I'll talk to him myself. The media are all over the law enforcement community for ethnic profiling and all over public defenders saying we don't give adequate defense to people who're poor, black,

Arab, or whatever. Now who's doing ethnic profiling? You're jumping to conclusions just because they have Arabic names that they're terrorists and involved in a big operation in Canada."

"Well, those are the facts," Marcus Porter said. "Arabs from New York and Arabs were arrested in Canada. You want to keep it quiet don't you?"

"Mr. Porter," she asked angrily. "Where're you from?" thinking: *Quick; he's speaking with a mountain accent, maybe I can get him.*

"Bluefield," he replied startled.

"Virginia or West Virginia?" she continued. "Must be West Virginia with that accent of yours. Down in the coal fields. Bet y'r old man has all sorts of stills set up in the old abandoned coal mines. That's all you rednecks do over there. Bet you and your brothers and cousins bootlegged the moonshine. I s'pose you grow weed out on the mountainside up the hollow these days. You peddled it to other students to finance your way through college too, didn't you? How much you got with you to sell today? Right here on the steps of the federal building too."

Marcus Porter turned red, livid with anger saying: "How dare you! If you were a man I'd clobber you."

Richard Harris immediately jumped in: "Yeah, that's the only way you rednecks know to solve your problems. Then you'd have a public defender like me to defend you because you attacked an officer of the court on federal property. You rednecks spend your money as fast as you get it so you wouldn't be able to pay for your own defense."

Marcus Porter dropped his tape recorder, paper, and pencil and lunged towards Richard Harris.

Ashley Sue Hunter deftly stepped in front of him and said: "Cool it, Marcus. We're riling you up on purpose to show you what ethnic profiling's really like. These two defendants are first generation Americans; their parents are poor immigrants. They grew up in a rundown town in New York. They come from decent but poor, uneducated families. Most of the other people in town are other immigrants. All their lives they've been taunted like I just taunted you.

"Along comes a petty smuggler. He offers these guys a job. All they have to do is drive the car and drop off things and pick up others. Don't bother to look to see what's inside. See some more of the world. Make a little money. Get away from people making fun of you. It happens all the time in this country and has been happening for years.

"Next time when you do your homework you'll find this type of petty smuggling is commonplace. The vast majority don't get caught. My clients had the misfortune of getting caught. Their boss tells them 'don't worry, you're not doing anything really wrong. We'll take care of you.' Now where's their boss?"

Marcus Porter muttered: "Oh."

"So when you write your story," she continued, "write about how these guys had the good fortune to fall into the hands of public defenders who do their damnedest to make sure their rights were defended to the utmost by very well qualified and bright attorneys like Mr. Harris here, about the same age as you are. You're working hard to make a name for yourself and do good for society. Well, so is he. Put that in your story."

"Well, er" Marcus Porter fumbled for words.

"We do appreciate the cooperation of the media and especially the *Roanoke Times* in making sure all members of society know they have access to fair and competent legal representation," she said in dismissal. "Tell your editor hello for me. We dated at one time."

Marcus Porter said: "Thanks," and left in a daze.

Richard began to say: "Tha...."

"See you in the office," she interrupted. "I'll call you."

Chapter 34

Thursday, June 15, 2006
Quantico, Virginia, USA

Rhonda Philips arrived early for a 2 p.m. wrap-up meeting wearing a sleeveless olive green linen-cotton summer dress, a slightly off-white large silk scarf draped around her shoulders because of the well air-conditioned room, patent leather block-heeled shoes in the same off-white color and matching large leather bag, all complemented with a silver necklace with large pearls and large pearl ear studs.

After initial pleasantries, Rosie Jordan said: "I just spoke with Roger Chen. He said your boys are on their way to Minnesota so that one's tied up for you."

"Not completely," Rhonda Philips said. "There's one point I want to get to during the meeting."

"He says the judge was a real pistol," he continued and described events in the courtroom.

"Oh, that must have been Joe, the young Arab-American lawyer we met in Guantanamo," Rhonda Philips said. "He's good. Sounds like we need a few more judges like her, too."

He continued: "Roger also said she jumped on the big guns, her words, from Washington coming down to a rural backwater, her words again, thinking they didn't know how to do things properly in the sticks of Appalachia."

"Well, sounds like maybe she was right on that one too," Rhonda Philips said.

"Yeah, she was," Rosie Jordan agreed. "Too many here get caught up in the Washington mind set, inside the beltway thinking, and forget there're capable bright people everywhere. We get that in the bureau often enough, but we have a big field network that keeps us on our toes."

"Some of our people think they're dealing with Neanderthals at our installations," Rhonda Philips added thinking: *It's easy for me to slip into the inside the beltway mindset for sure. Missouri's a distant memory.*

Ralph D'Angelo from the CIA entered along with an Army colonel; Rhonda Philips said: "Please let me introduce Colonel Otis Granger of the DoDIG."

After pleasantries, Rosie Jordan said: "We agreed to one last meeting to wrap things up. There's one small item under the FBI's purview." He explained briefly about discovering a Middletown police officer saying they would not pursue the issue concluding: "The fewer people who know the better. Ralph, the CIA's been in contact with our Buffalo field office. What can you tell us?"

"Mohammad Fadel's in custody in Jordan," he began. "He's been cooperating with us and the Canadians, although not that willingly.

"The biggest issue's what to do with him now. As you know, the President's taking a lot of heat for keeping people in foreign custody with no charges against them and using alleged torture techniques to get information. While the Canadians are doing most of the interrogating, we certainly don't want his presence there to be known. He's a citizen of Yemen. We're trying to work out their putting him under house arrest there. If he tries to continue contacts with al Qaeda, the Yemeni government has enough on him to deal with him under Yemeni law."

"Thanks, Ralph," Rosie Jordan said. "Rhonda?"

"Maybe we should let Colonel Granger speak," Rhonda Philips replied. "What I have's best left to the end."

"I'm coming late to the process," Colonel Granger began. "I've read files and Rhonda's filled me in. I can report I was at a meeting on Monday with Major Reynolds ..." and continued with a brief description of the meeting concluding: "Some wanted to discharge him now because he's seemingly homosexual. Finally, the agreement was to let him serve his 20 years and retire; he has a little over five years to go.

"The biggest risk's someone'll push him too hard and he'll blow the whistle in order to avoid more harassment; there's no longer a great stigma about being homosexual. We concocted a DIA task force to study and observe homosexuality and how it might affect intelligence activity. We told Major Reynolds he's on it so he could go to gay bars and the like. The Marine Corps reluctantly went along. In effect he has permission to keep on going to gay places so long as he doesn't get himself in trouble.

"The only real hold we have over him is financial, allowing him to retire at 20 years. He doesn't seem to be hurting financially, so that may not be much of a hold. Any questions or comments?
pause

"The only other issue from our perspective is we don't think it's wise to keep Captain Ferris at Wright-Patterson much longer. We can't transfer him immediately, right on the heels of Major Reynolds, and he's done nothing wrong. We have to make a transfer look routine. We have a few things in the works I'm not at liberty to talk about now, but I can take comments or questions."

Rosie Jordan said: "Thank you. It seems the two who weren't citizens were taken to our prison in Baghdad and are safely out of the way."

"Not exactly," Rhonda Philips interrupted. "I'll get to that in a minute. We got them out in the nick of time just before those detainees at Guantanamo committed suicide and the commander made his asinine comment about the suicides' being an asymmetric act of aggression" She described briefly events of earlier in the week in Baghdad concluding: "There's little doubt al Qaeda's targeting people associated with this operation to silence them. Our concern at the moment is for the survivors. Ali's now housed in the officers' quarters, working in the clinic because he's doing a valuable service, but otherwise kept out of sight; his survival's not common knowledge. Over the long run, we need to make other arrangements. We'd welcome any thoughts you have."

"Let me check with our people in the field and I'll get back to you," Ralph D'Angelo said.

"The other two who are citizens," Rhonda Philips continued, "were transported to an Air Force Base in North Carolina ..." and described briefly the events leading to their conviction and imprisonment in Minnesota. "My biggest concern," she continued, "is them. Is al Qaeda going to track them down and attack them while they're in a minimum security facility? Maybe I'm too emotionally involved."

Rosie Jordan replied: "I see your point Rhonda. Right now hardly anyone knows they're in the U.S. much less in Minnesota. They've contacted their families, but we think we've severed the link between Lackawanna and al Qaeda. If someone in the U.S. were dedicated to silence them, they could have done so in Roanoke and we couldn't have stopped it. The question is how well coordinated is this al Qaeda group in Iraq with activities in the U.S."

"From what we've gathered," Rhonda Philips said, "the group in Iraq under al Masri is a maverick group and not well coordinated with any other al Qaeda group."

"That's what our intelligence tells us," Ralph D'Angelo added. "It sees Zarkawi setting himself up as a rival to bin Laden and trying to take over the whole network. With him dead, we can't imagine the group in Iraq can tap into the network to do its dirty work in the U.S.

"Our reaction's the attack on the prison in Baghdad was a local operation for the new guy, al Masri, to demonstrate he's in charge and can pull off an attack. I'd suspect silencing persons involved with the failed operation was secondary. I'll run it through our Middle East section and get a more comprehensive assessment. For the moment, I don't think we have too much to worry about."

"We could also put them into a maximum security facility," Rosie Jordan offered, "but that has consequences you wouldn't be pleased with, Rhonda. You know what other inmates in the maximum security prisons are like."

Rhonda Philips nodded her head and said: "Yes."

"We have a witness protection program where we change identities and physical appearance with cosmetic surgery," Rosie Jordan continued. "I'm not sure they'd fit this program and whether they'd want their identities changed."

"Remember their faces were badly disfigured in Cuba," Rhonda Philips added. "They need cosmetic surgery and they aren't going to get it on their own. As for their identity, these're pretty proud people so would they really want to change it? From what Joe Shaito told us about Arab customs, their fathers are probably called Abou Abdullah and Abou Ibrahim so they're not going to give that up easily. How many in al Qaeda would actually know their names?

"Likely not many," Rosie Jordan said. "From what we know of al Qaeda in the U.S., once they go to work on a mission, they don't communicate back and forth with other al Qaeda members for obvious security reasons."

"Maybe they don't need to change identities," Rhonda Philips said, "but maybe we could use the witness protection program for cosmetic surgery to repair their damaged faces."

Ralph D'Angelo said: "Our agency's about to give a research grant to a well-known medical facility to explore uses of cosmetic surgery for our purposes. I'm not at liberty to say much now, but, no, we're not going to make doubles. If this comes off, and we're sure it will, the facility'd like to have Middle Eastern people, especially Arabs, to study and work on. Let me get back to you."

"Anyone have anything else? We didn't actually wrap this up completely but close enough. Unless something comes up, we'll not meet again."

All exchanged pleasantries and goodbyes.

Chapter 35

Monday, July 17, 2006
Roumieh, Lebanon

Jihad Noussayri sat in a dark cell with no ventilation in Lebanon's infamous Roumieh prison on the mountainside above Beirut. He was wearing only underwear in the stifling hot humid summer weather.

ROUMIEH PRISON IN THE HILLS ABOVE BEIRUT, LEBANON

A PRISONER LIKE JIHAD IN HIS CELL IN ROUMIEH PRISON.

A jailer wearing badly wilted gray camouflage fatigues and black leather boots, the uniform of the Lebanese National Guard, said in Arabic: "You have a visitor."

A man entered who was about 40 years old, average height and weight, with black hair. He wore thin, badly worn prison slippers along with non-descript dark pants and a loose fitting inexpensive cotton shirt

CONSEQUENCES • CHAPTER 35

with the tail out of the pants; everything had been emptied out of his pockets and he had undergone a thorough body search.

Jihad rushed to give him three Arab kisses, saying in Arabic: "Eiad, you've finally come to get me out."

Eiad responded in Arabic as he roughly pushed Jihad away: "No, you stupid ass, I've come to tell you to quit sending those damned messages asking us to get you out. You're putting us too much at risk in case someone gets hold of them and asks too many questions."

"But..." Jihad began in Arabic.

"In case you haven't heard, you ignoramus, there's war going on outside," Eiad continued in Arabic. "Hizbollah and Israel both played into our hands and are fighting each other. No matter which side prevails, we take over Lebanon again."

"Yes, I know," Jihad stammered in Arabic. "That's why I need to be out, working and helping."

"Yeah, some help," Eiad almost shouted with disgust in Arabic. "We don't need help from a fuck-up like you."

"What? How can you say that, Eiad?" Jihad blurted out in disbelief in Arabic. "I was always loyal. I was the best you had. I always delivered."

"Yeah, like you delivered yourself to the Lebanese National Guard," Eiad smirked in Arabic. "Driving across the border in broad open daylight and leaving documents in your car. That's beyond stupid. You might as well've been waving a banner saying I'm Moukhabarat, come arrest me."

Jihad pulled back not believing what he was hearing.

Eiad continued in Arabic: "Why were you running away from Syria to Lebanon right then? Running away from the job you fucked up. We trusted you, but you let the doctor get away and that stupid Iraqi guy too."

"It wasn't my fault ..." Jihad stammered in Arabic.

Eiad slapped him on the face saying in Arabic: "Shut up you stupid ninny. I'm sick of hearing your whining voice. It's never your fault. If you weren't in prison, you'd be dead. It's not worth our effort to infiltrate this prison again just to take out a low life stupid piece of vermin like you. You can't imagine what I had to go through today. Just be damned thankful that you're in prison and hope you stay here a long time. The moment you step out of here, you're gone and don't even dream of going back to Syria, EVER!"

"My wife, my children," Jihad almost cried in Arabic.

"You ought to hear yourself now," Eiad spat out the words in Arabic. "You're worse than pathetic. You never gave a shit about your wife and kids when you were in Syria. You were too damned busy fucking all the other women and fucking up your jobs. Maybe she'll find a decent man."

Hearing these last words, Jihad, enraged, attempted to hit Eiad with his fist.

Eiad grabbed his wrist, bent it behind his back, forced him to bend over, then said in Arabic: "Did you hear me? Do you understand? One more message out of this prison from you and maybe it will be worth our while to get in and take you out. Maybe we'll tie you to one of Hizbollah's rocket launchers immediately before it fires at an Israeli target. The Israelis can do the job when they take the rocket launcher out in retaliation. Then you can become a hero. Too bad you're not Muslim. You could become a martyr and have all those virgins waiting for you on the way to heaven. Maybe they can give you what your wife doesn't any more."

With that, Eiad let go of his arm, and walked out the door that the jailer had conveniently left unlocked.

Book 4
NEW BEGINNINGS

Chapter 1

Thursday, July 20, 2006
Hamilton, Ohio, USA

FBI agent Tom Gruenwald left the police station after a routine visit asking himself: *Should I go to that bakery again? They wouldn't remember me after two months.* Inside: *that's the same girl who waited on me before.*

She smiled and asked: "May I help you?"

"Coffee, cream only, and four apple fritters," he replied.

"You must like them," she said smiling. "We call them *frituras de manzana* in Spanish. Coffee here or to go?"

"Here, please," he answered, "but I'll take the freetora things with me. And some bread too; one of those whole grain loaves down there."

"You bought that last time; did you like it?" she asked.

Damn, he said to himself. *She remembers me.*

"Please have a seat and I'll put the other things in a bag and bring them to you," she said. "Luie's here and not too busy," she said. "I'll tell him you're here."

"That's not …" he began to say as she walked away.

He sat in a corner hoping he'd not be too obvious drinking coffee and nibbling on an apple fritter.

THREE KISSES

Luie walked up with a paper bag saying: "Hi, I'm Luis Mendoza."

Tom Gruenwald awkwardly stood, shook Luie's offered hand, saying: "Tom; pleased to meet you."

Luie said: "Please sit. Consuelo said you wanted to see me." To himself: *I'm going to get to the bottom of this.*

"Not really," Tom Gruenwald replied. "Just wanted to say guys at the police department are right. This is the best bakery around."

Luie persisted: "Consuelo said last time you asked if I was back from Mexico, like you wanted to talk to me."

Damn, Tom Gruenwald thought. *Maybe get the conversation onto some trivial topic.* "Oh, it was nothing," He said. "The guys at the police station said you bring recipes from Mexico. I just thought maybe you'd been there recently. They said apple fritters are from Mexico."

"Oh, no," Luie said. "They're from **New** Mexico. "Swapped recipes with a bakery in Lovington, farm and oil town near the Texas border. My mom has family there we visit. Theirs are the best in the whole world. They use local apples; New Mexico apples are the best."

BAKERY LOVINGTON, NEW MEXICO, HOME OF APPLE FRITTERS

APPLE ORCHARD NEAR MAYHILL, NEW MEXICO, WHERE THE BEST APPLES ARE GROWN.

"Well you do a good job here in Ohio," Tom Gruenwald said with a strained chuckle. "My wife loves 'em too, but she won't eat too many. Too fattening."

Oh, he has a wife, Luie thought. *That probably eliminates the Serpent, but some married guys go there. When I asked around the Serpent, no one knew anyone with his description.* He said: "Glad you like them, both of you. Ohio apples are good, but not like there."

"We don't have bakeries like this in Cincinnati," Tom Gruenwald added. "Wish we did."

"Mostly German bakeries down there," Luie said. "I tried to make some of those big German pretzels and moon-kuchen, or something like that; the things with poppy seeds. They didn't go over up here."

"Oh, really?" Tom Gruenwald asked. "Why not?"

"Not enough Germans," Luie replied. "Mostly Poles and Mexicans. Mami said they wouldn't go over here, but I didn't listen to her. Now I sure do; learned my lesson. They're foreign to the Mexicans and some older Poles have bad memories about German occupation.

"Mami convinced me to learn how to make Polish things from the ladies who make them for the bake sales at the Catholic church," he said chuckling and grinning, "They can't talk directly to each other much; Mami doesn't speak Polish and they don't speak Spanish. I guess Catholic mothers have a way of communicating even if they don't speak the same language. Now we make those paczi pastries for Easter and the angel wing cookies for wedding parties. You should come try them some time. Say, let me bring my mom over to introduce you; looks like you need a refill."

He thought: *maybe Mami can occupy him while I think of something or he says something to give himself away.*

"Thanks, but ..." Tom Gruenwald tried to say with his mouth full.

Luie said to his mother: "*Mamita, ¿puedes traer la cafetera, por favor? El señor quiere más café.*" To Tom Gruenwald: "She doesn't speak English very well, but tries."

"Oh, I know what that's like," Tom Gruenwald commented. "A few of my grandparents' cousins were like that: barely spoke English, speaking German most of the time. I was never around them much; they died when I was a little boy. Funny, I never had any desire to learn German. My ancestors were among the very earliest immigrants into the U.S.; early founders of Cincinnati. My family always spoke English as far back as anyone can remember. But wait; I studied Spanish a couple of years at the university. Maybe I can remember enough to talk to her." He thought: *Maybe he'll wear down with my bad Spanish.*

A sprightly, diminutive older woman with bright, sparkling brown eyes and short silver gray hair, wearing a white dress, came with a coffee pot in her hands.

Luie stepped aside saying: "Tom, this is my mother, Mrs. Mendoza. *Mami, te presento al Señor Tom de Cincinnati. Él piensa que las frituras de manzana son magníficas; la receta fue de Lovington donde Tío Jorge.*"

Tom stood smiling saying in bad Spanish: "*Mucha gusto conocerte, Señora Mendoza.*"

Her face lit up as she filled his mug saying. "*Encantada. El placer es mío. Habla español.*"

"*Poquito,*" he replied. "*Estudio en colegio. Recordo muy poco. Muy malo.*"

"*O, no. Es bueno,*" she said still beaming. "*Luisito dice que le gustan las frituras. Son sabrosas, ¿No?*"

"*Si. Mucha bueno,*" he replied hesitatingly.

"*Usted es abogado, parece,*" she continued. "*Hemos recibido a muchos abogados aquí.*"

'Abagado'? 'Abagado'? Damn, I know that word, he said to himself. *Oh, yes, 'lawyer'. Now how do I answer?* "*Si, estudio abagado,*" he finally said.

Maybe if I say I studied law that'll do, he said to himself.

Mrs. Mendoza glanced over her shoulder then said: "*Perdón, señor. Esa viejita no habla inglés y a ella le gusta comprar solamente de mí. ¡Vuelva pronto!*"

Luie thought: *Says he's studying law. A law student working as an intern? Seems a bit too old, but he doesn't speak Spanish all that well. Maybe he meant he studied law, but why wouldn't he just say he's a lawyer. Who'd study law, but not be a lawyer? Wait! Of course! Frank said the FBI said to tell us to get citizenship. Someone from the FBI obviously found out about us and probably in person. Got it.*

"Thanks," Luie said. "That was nice of you to speak Spanish to my Mom."

"Glad to do it," Tom replied thinking: *Can't think of any way to prolong this and so far he isn't showing signs of stopping. I'll just have to get up and go and hope for the best.*

He put the uneaten half apple fritter into the bag and gathered it and his briefcase to go saying: "Thank you for your personal attention. How much do I owe you?"

"Nothing. This time it's on the house," Luie said with a big smile.

"No, I can't let you do that," Tom said.

"Oh, I insist," Luie replied effusively. "You really made my mom happy speaking Spanish like that to her."

Damn, Tom Gruenwald thought. *Can't let him do that. My ass'd be reamed good if anyone found out I'm accepting favors from someone under investigation no matter how small the favor. Even if I didn't get caught, it's not ethical.*

"Seriously," he said, "I can't let you do that; I'll pay."

Luie sat directly across from him, leaned, and said softly: "I know you can't and I'm pretty sure I know why. I'll ask Consuelo in a minute how much you owe. Your money's good here. You're welcome as a customer any time or in any other capacity. Please promise me, I mean it, you'll come back next time you're in town. You're always welcome here."

"I will," Tom Gruenwald said meekly wondering: *How'd he figure me out. What'd I say to give myself away? Maybe he asked that police lieutenant.*

Luie returned with a cash register receipt and said: "That's eight-twenty-five. If you have the change, I'll take it or if not see Consuelo, she'll give you change."

Tom Gruenwald took a five-dollar bill and three ones from his wallet and reached in his pocket for a quarter.

"Thank you for your business," Luie said. "Seriously please **do** come back. You know you'll not get better apple fritters than ours anywhere else but New Mexico."

Tom Gruenwald said: "OK, next time I'm in town."

Luie gave Consuelo the money saying: "Please let me know next time Lieutenant Glenkowski comes in," saying to himself: *I'll ask him to confirm. Won't tell me directly, but I can get it out of him.*

Tom Gruenwald walked to his car thinking: *Should I say something to the lieutenant? An ethical police officer wouldn't tell him he's under investigation. If I do say something and I'm wrong, then he'll be pissed off and tell the bureau I'm making false accusations. I'll keep my mouth shut and hope for the best. Maybe I can get someone else to buy apple fritters for me.*

Chapter 2

Monday, July 24, 2006
Buffalo, New York, USA

Shortly after noon, Omar slid into a booth in Gino's diner opposite Gabe Andreotti who said: "You look much better today. Getting more rest now?"

"Better than last time you saw me, for sure," Omar replied, "between winding things up for you, being the de facto imam, and working on my thesis, I'm still not getting as much sleep as I need."

"The thesis going well?" Gabe Andreotti asked.

"Yes, very well, thank you," Omar replied, "and that brings up something I need to talk about."

The same waitress as before came with the order pad and a big smile; Gabe Andreotti said: "Meatloaf special."

"Oh, that's what you had last time," she said. "It's as good as ever today."

"I'll have the roast beef," Omar said.

"Oh, you'll like that," she said. "That's what I had today. Can't eat meatloaf every day."

"Thanks for asking about my thesis," Omar continued. "My supervisor really likes my proposal. He thinks it'll be readily approved and well received. He found me a part-time teaching job at The University of

Minnesota-Duluth for comparative religion courses; they're enthusiastic to have an Islamic person teaching it."

"Sounds good," Gabe Andreotti replied.

Omar continued excited: "Also there's a thriving Islamic community in Duluth and they want an imam. It's only part time. Based on my supervisor's recommendation, they gave me the position sight unseen. The work in the mosque can give me data for the thesis."

"Sounds great," Gabe Andreotti said.

"They need me there as soon as possible," Omar continued. "The university wants me there about August 15 and the Islamic community wants me there before that if possible. That gives me two weeks at the most to wind things up here and I have lots of questions for you."

Gabe Andreotti replied: "I don't see a problem from our perspective winding things up by then. We can talk about that after we eat. Did you get a new imam here?"

Yes, Omar replied: "I contacted a couple of the mosques you referred me to. They were pleased I asked. We think we've found someone."

The waitress brought food with her usual cheerfulness saying: "Enjoy your meal."

While eating Gabe Andreotti asked: "What'd you do with the BMW? Does Mohammad's wife want it?"

"Yes," Omar answered. "She's taking driving lessons; she'll get her license soon. She quit wearing her veil, too, but still wears a headscarf."

"I've seen Muslim women wearing headscarves but not veils," Gabe Andreotti said.

"There may be more women from Yemen who wear veils than from other countries," Omar continued. "It's mostly the older conservative ones; I'm sure their husbands make them. I'm pretty sure Mohammad made Baria wear one. Since he left, she stopped and some others have also."

"Not headscarves," Gabe Andreotti added. "Doesn't the Koran say that women have to wear headscarves?"

"Interesting you should ask that," Omar replied. "Some teen-aged girls and especially their fathers have been asking me that. Actually, the

Q'ran doesn't say that. The word that the Prophet copied to 'cover your *something*' does not have a clear meaning. Some scholars think it'd best be expressed cover your precious, whatever 'precious' means. The thing that makes most sense is cover your breasts; there was and still is a good Arabic word for breasts, but it may not have been used because of modesty. There's a good Arabic word for hair that could've been used but wasn't. The idea's pretty clear: women must be modest; men too but that's not the issue. They don't want to hear a scholarly argument, especially the fathers. They just want me to say 'no, you can't do that' to their daughters.

"I tell them wearing headscarves is part of Islamic tradition and culture and in the Q'ran culture and tradition are important. What's modest is a cultural thing so if a woman feels not wearing a headscarf would be immodest, she should wear one, but if having exposed hair does not make her feel immodest then she's not required to do so. They don't like to hear that. Well, the teenagers do because they don't feel immodest at school when other girls aren't wearing headscarves. Fathers feel their daughters are immodest and try to force them. I finally say they have to work it out between father and daughter, but don't expect me to say it's something required by the Q'ran when it isn't."

Gabe Andreotti commented: "Interesting. I guess fathers and daughters are alike in all cultures."

The waitress asked: "Ready for dessert?" clearing dishes. She returned with chilled lemon custard saying: "Just right for a hot day. Coffee or tea?"

"Coffee, please," Gabe Andreotti said.

"I'll have coffee also," Omar said then continued: "I hope I haven't messed things up too bad for the next imam. Oh, thanks for the referral to the woman divorce lawyer for Baria. When Mohammad delivered the final statement divorcing her, she was relieved. At first, she thought she could continue living her life and running her shop as she always did. She knew I was winding up Mohammad's other businesses and made it clear that she was to be let alone.

"I told her that I was more than willing to let her alone, but legally all those things are Mohammad's. I made it clear I didn't want them, but she needed to take steps to make them hers, like getting a legal divorce.

At first she was indignant. I pointed out that even under Islamic law Mohammad'd have a right to the property. That's when I offered to refer her to a lawyer to get a legal divorce."

"Oh, good for you," Gabe Andreotti said.

"She was nervous about seeing the lawyer just in case a man might be involved," Omar continued. "Not only are Muslim women not supposed to be in the company of a man to whom she's not related, she was worried she'd be mistreated because she was wearing a headscarf. In the end, she went with one of the younger women who's a bit more worldly shall we say."

"Oh, the headscarf thing again," he commented.

"Yeah," Omar continued. "Some're putting out word the U.S. government's trying to keep Muslim women from wearing headscarves like they do in Europe. When I tell them it's not true, they don't want to believe me.

"I ask them to tell me one instance where any woman was told to take off a headscarf for any reason. No one can give me an answer. Then I tell them there was a court case a couple of years ago in Oklahoma in which the U.S. government actually went to court to support the right of a high school girl to wear a head scarf in school and the court agreed that she could."

"I think I remember that case in Oklahoma," Gabe Andreotti added. "It came across our desks in case we had to deal with something like that, but we don't get involved too much in civil rights cases unless there's some more serious crime involved. What do they say to that?"

"They don't want to believe me," Omar answered. "They stammer and say well Hani says, or Sami says. Finally, I tell them they have to choose who they want to believe. I offer to find a copy of the newspaper article proving it, but emphasize that I don't care if they believe me or not because I know what the truth is."

"And then what?" Gabe Andreotti asked.

"They get quiet and sullen," Omar responded. "Many of them have a martyr complex and go out of their way to find reasons to become martyrs; there are plenty, including the al Qaeda types, who'll exploit them because of that. Sure there's some discrimination and distrust of women who wear headscarves, but that's not the government's trying to forbid it when the government's doing just the opposite.

The waitress refilled coffee, asked if they wanted anything else and brought the check saying: "Thank you for coming. I hope you liked it. Please keep coming back."

"Yes, it was very good," Omar answered with enthusiasm.

"Very good as usual," Gabe Andreotti said.

Chapter 3

Monday, July 24, 2006
Buffalo, New York, USA

When the waitress left, Omar began: "Thanks for referring me to the lawyer and accountant. They got us an employer ID and sent money to the federal and state governments for back taxes that were supposed to have been withheld from all of us. And thanks for locating social security numbers for Brahim, Boudi, and Kamal."

"No problem," Gabe Andreotti said.

Omar continued: "We decided not to make Fadi and Fouad pay the money that was supposed to have been withheld. Mohammad didn't pay them much; the lawyer thinks it's above the minimum wage, barely, if we pay back taxes. We can't collect from the others and Mohammad has plenty of money to pay their taxes."

"How much?" Gabe asked.

"Between his bank account and cash stashed away, well over $100,000," Omar stated."

"Jeez," Gabe exclaimed softly. "That's a lot!"

Omar added: "If it's Baria's as part of the divorce and I gave that much money to her, she'd risk disgrace if it became known her husband had been extorting it and now she gets it. I've used some to buy back Middle Eastern products he forced people to buy. Baria's glad to have them; with the war in Lebanon she's not getting her usual supply"

NEW BEGINNINGS • CHAPTER 3

"Sounds good," Gabe said.

"There was another $20,000 that Kamal had apparently skimmed off the top," Omar continued. "There're problems with that too. In effect he stole it from Mohammad but Mohammad got it by questionable means."

Gabe Andreotti interrupted: "I'm not a lawyer, but I suspect if someone tried to sort out legal claims for this money it'd be tied up for months if not years."

"Kamal wants his friends to take the money to him," Omar continued, "but he doesn't ask directly. A couple of friends visited him in jail. He told them to go to a certain location, get personal things, and give them to his lawyer. I can't stall them much longer or else the whole community will think I'm denying Kamal his personal things or maybe trying to steal them myself."

Hmmm, Gabe Andreotti thought then said: "Do you owe Kamal back pay?"

"He apparently got paid for the last trip he took to North Carolina," Omar replied. "Mohammad pays in cash so there aren't records."

"What'd you say about barely the minimum wage?" Gabe Andreotti asked. "Kamal could be entitled to more than minimum wage for the type of work he did. Talk to the accountant and lawyer and work out what might be a fair wage, err on the generous side, then prepare a paycheck with all the proper deductions. Have your lawyer send it to Kamal's lawyer in Canada and get a receipt. That way Kamal gets money for his defense and it shuts him up, hopefully. Arrange for some of his personal things to be there so his friends can find something."

"But would that be the full $20,000?" Omar asked. "I'd like to give his mother some money. I know she relied on him for money, but I can't give her the full amount."

"Why not?" Gabe Andreotti asked.

"It'd be obvious Kamal was stealing from Mohammad. It'd be a disgrace to her in the community to get a big sum of money from her son and the only way he could've gotten it is stealing. Maybe I can say he'd been saving for Ramadan and the Eid in October and she can have it now."

"What's that?" Gabe Andreotti asked.

"You know what Ramadan is, I suppose," Omar said. "The period of about 28 days when Muslims fast during the day and eat at night after sundown. It's called iftar. People take turns hosting dinners, which of course costs money. The first three days after Ramadan is the Eid; eid means holiday in Arabic. It is the biggest holiday of the year. People spend money for gifts and parties and the like. Saying Kamal had been saving money for Ramadan and Eid, his mother could take some of it and not lose face."

"Ah, I see," Gabe Andreotti said.

"I have an idea for the rest of his money," Omar said, "but we need to talk about Mohammad's money first. Now that you say Kamal gets back pay, what about Boudi and Brahim? Wouldn't they be like Kamal?"

"Yes, I guess they would," Gabe Andreotti said.

"Do I send money to them?" Omar asked. "How?"

"They'll get a work-study release out of prison in a few months," Gabe Andreotti replied. "They could probably use money then. Let me find out how to send it. But do their parents need money too?"

"These are all poor people and can use money," Omar replied, "but their parents didn't rely on them for financial support. I'm not inclined to give money to them if Brahim and Boudi themselves can use it.

Gabe Andreotti suggested: "If it'd not cause potential disgrace for you, pay yourself a generous amount. You deserve to be paid a fair amount for what you've done.

"OK, I will," Omar said, "but that leaves quite a bit and I have some ideas. First for Fadi and Fouad: When I shut this operation down, they'll be without work and an income; it's not easy for two young guys like them to get jobs. As luck would have it, there's an older gas station for sale. It doesn't sell much gas, but it does service work and has the potential to do a whole lot more. The owner's old and not up to keeping the business going; wants to sell."

"So you want to buy it for Fadi and Fouad?" Gabe Andreotti asked. "Wouldn't that cost a lot?"

"Yes and it could cause problems if suddenly they came into money to buy it," Omar said, "but if I can get them enough money to make a fairly big down payment, they might get a loan for the rest. I talked to the accountant about it. He thinks it could be done. Working on cars is all they know and they're good at it."

"Lackawanna's not a prosperous place, but people do need to have their cars serviced," Gabe Andreotti added. "They may keep their cars longer and need more service. Talk to the lawyer and accountant and see if you can work out how to give them money and of course make sure the business gets set up legally. Use Mohammad's money to pay for legal fees and the like and no one would be wiser."

"It'd be good if they could buy an old car like one of the big old Chevrolets they used to take people to Canada," Omar continued. "Lot of the old people're asking to be taken there like before and pay for the service. I let them take the BMW on weekends while I work on my thesis, but it won't hold as many people."

"One was impounded by the Canadians," Gabe Andreotti explained. "Canada has its own procedures for disposing of cars impounded in a crime. The other one's now in the custody of the U.S. government, probably somewhere in Virginia. From time to time, the government has an auction of impounded property, including vehicles. Sometimes the law enforcement agencies take the cars to use as unmarked vehicles."

"I know," Omar said smiling. "Agent Andrews had an old Mustang in Winston-Salem she was joking about."

"After we use them," Gabe Andreotti continued, "we usually sell them. Let me check into things."

"That still leaves lots of money," Omar continued, "and likely some of Kamal's money as well. It'd be great if they had a proper mosque, not just that store front one. As it also turns out, there's an old abandoned church for sale. It's not in the greatest condition, but might possibly be bought in its current condition with the rest of Mohammad's money. The guys in the community could fix it up."

"What about the propriety of turning a church into a mosque?" Gabe Andreotti asked. "Wouldn't some Muslims object to such things?"

"No, not at all," Omar replied. "Some might even rejoice. History's full of churches becoming mosques."

"Oh, really?" Gabe Andreotti asked.

"Yes," Omar continued. "The most famous is probably the Hagia Sofia in Istanbul that's now a museum. It was a great Byzantine cathedral that was converted to a mosque when the Ottomans conquered Constantinople and renamed it Istanbul. One that's less well known but more magnificent is the Umayyad Mosque in the old walled city of Damascus. It was first a pagan temple, then a huge Christian cathedral. It was taken over by Muslims and made into a mosque way before the Hagia Sofia and is still being used as a mosque today. It's beautiful."

"You've been to these places?" Gabe Andreotti asked.

"Oh, no, but I wish," Omar answered. "If I had that kind of money, I wouldn't be here. We teach about them in Middle Eastern studies courses and sometimes comparative religion courses. There are plenty of pictures and videos. Some people in the town might object on religious grounds, Christians I mean, but it's an eyesore so most would probably welcome our fixing it up.

"The issue is that I can't just go out and spend $100,000 in cash and buy this old church," Omar continued. That'd really raise questions, but if you can get Mohammad to say that they'd been saving money to have a proper mosque some day, then there'd not be so many questions raised and people in the community wouldn't worry about having had a criminal for an imam."

"Ah" Gabe Andreotti began. "I see; get in touch with Jordan and get another unwilling statement out of Mohammad. I'll pass it along. But what about Kamal? We don't have that kind of leverage over Canadian authorities"

"I think I can handle that one," Omar said. "If we get Mohammad's statement that this money's for a new mosque, then I can hint that Kamal saved a small amount too."

"Anything else?" Gabe Andreotti asked. "Today I really do need to get back to the office, but of course, I don't want to leave you with unfinished things."

"No, I think that's it for now," Omar said.

NEW BEGINNINGS • CHAPTER 3

"OK," Gabe Andreotti said. "I'll be in touch. We'll meet again, if nothing else to say goodbye and thanks."

Gabe Andreotti left a tip and walked to the cash register to pay. As before, Omar deliberately dawdled so he could leave an additional one-dollar bill.

Chapter 4

Tuesday, August 1, 2006
Washington, DC, USA

Air Force General Stanley Sawyer stood before some ten people in a private room of the Boling Air Force Base officer's club wearing an impeccably tailored uniform, an equally impeccable hand-tailored shirt, starched and pressed to perfection, and shoes polished to a mirror shine.

His wife, Louise, had just pinned two bright new silver stars on each shoulder, and leaned to give him a kiss. She wobbled on spiked heels to give enough height to reach his shoulder showing red soles of Louboutin shoes. She wore a severely tailored cream-colored cotton and linen summer dress with jacket from the same material, matching color shoes, and gold jewelry; her brass-colored severely cropped hair was straight from the hairdresser's bottle that very morning in preparation for this event.

LOUBOUTIN RED SOLED SHOES

He began: "In life there's a time when people're put out to pasture, ready or not, and now's my time. The Air Force gave me shiny new stars to send me on my way into idleness called retirement after 30 years of dedicated loyal service. The world has changed, they say. The threat has changed. Fighter pilots are no longer kings of the sky. Now the golf courses and beaches of Hilton Head await us. Please have some more champagne and hors d'oeuvres."

Rhonda Philips moved away from the group. She was wearing a navy blue linen-cotton summer weight pants suit, a striped blue and light gray lady's business shirt, light tan leather sandals with wedge heels, and a carnelian pendant set in gold with smaller carnelian beads set in gold ear studs.

She said to Colonel Otis Granger standing alone nearby: "Good afternoon, Otis. I see you decided to come to his retirement and promotion party also."

"I'm his replacement so thought it appropriate," he replied.

"I'll go say thank you to Mrs. Sawyer and the General," Rhonda Philips said. "I don't want to stay longer."

"Likewise," Otis Granger said. "I'll congratulate the new General and let some glow from his stars fall on me."

A small group of women surrounded Louise Sawyer as Rhonda Philips walked up in mid-conversation and heard: "…just got back from Hilton Head. We found a townhouse to rent until we can settle and decide what we want and our house here sells. We think we'll like it there. There's one of our kind of churches there."

"What kind of church is that?" a woman asked."

"We're members of the Falls Church," Louise Sawyer answered. "You know the historic old church in the center of the city of Falls Church. Stanley's been a member of the council almost ever since we've been here."

"That's Episcopal," another woman commented.

HISTORIC FALLS CHURCH, FALLS CHURCH, VIRGINIA

"Well, nominally it is," Louise Sawyer replied. "The Episcopal symbol's still on the sign, but we've taken the name 'Episcopal' off. We pulled away from the Diocese of Virginia and are now only associated with the national church, for the moment that is."

"Oh, why's that?" the first woman asked?

"It's been going on for a long time," Louise Sawyer continued. "When the national church ordained that gay man as bishop, it was too much. That's when we began the process of separating ourselves; we and some other congregations like ours. Now that the national church has elected that woman as the head of the church, Stanley's pushing them to withdraw all the way. Go under the Anglican bishop of Rwanda."

"Oh, really?" One of the women commented.

"Yes," Louise Sawyer said. "Stanley wanted to stay at least until our house sold so he could push that one through, but in the end we decided to go ahead and move, especially when we found the right kind of church down there."

Rhonda Philips approached Louise Sawyer, offered her hand to shake, and said: "I'm Dr. Philips, Rhonda Philips. I've worked with your husband. Thank you for having me and I wish you well."

Louise Sawyer took Rhonda Philips's offered hand saying: "You're welcome, I'm sure. Good that you came." She abruptly dropped Rhonda Philips's hand and turned to the other women.

NEW BEGINNINGS • CHAPTER 4

Rhonda Philips walked to the group of men surrounding General Sawyer, which included Otis Granger, and again heard a conversation in progress: "… no, no real regrets, I suppose," General Sawyer said. "It's not the same Air Force. I need to get away from it before it gets me."

"Oh, how's that?" an Army colonel asked.

"Fighter pilots are obsolete," General Sawyer replied. "Now it's transport and logistics. Just you wait. When the enemy comes at us with fighters and we can't respond, then they'll realize."

"Oh, really?" the same Army colonel commented.

"Fighter planes are parked in the desert and we have no one to fly them," General Sawyer continued. "All they have are soft sissy cargo plane pilots, not real men like the fighter jockeys. Half of them are gay, I'll bet you, and now we can't even get rid of them. 'Don't ask; don't tell'. In the old days, we would've gotten rid of them for sure. It's the same thing with our church too. The homo perverts are taking over. Now it's time to go some place where decent people're left."

Rhonda Philips interrupted and said: "Thank you for inviting me, General. Best wishes on Hilton Head." *Or wherever you're going so long as it's far from us*, she said to herself. *Am I a hypocrite coming here? If he only knew what I did to engineer his involuntary retirement. Couldn't keep them from giving stars as an inducement; at least he's gone.*

"Please wait and I'll walk out with you," Otis Granger said to Rhonda Philips. "I need to go back to work too."

After Otis Granger shook hands and said good-byes, they walked in silence until they were out of the building and well out of earshot of anyone else.

"Have you ever heard such a self-serving, bitter speech?" he asked.

"No, I don't think so," she replied.

"Did you look at his record?" he asked.

"No," she replied. "I'm not sure I'd've had access, but I wouldn't have wanted to."

"All he did was fly planes," Otis Granger explained. "Even when he was promoted and given command assignments, he delegated administrative duties and flew as much as he could. Lots of people under him weren't happy, needless to say, but he kept polishing the top brass and managed to get his promotions. When his eyesight deteriorated to the point he couldn't fly any more, it was a cruel bitter blow. He even tried to manipulate things to keep flying. Finally, the Air Force assigned him to that position in the DoDIG to park him and get him out of their hair."

"I didn't know that," she said. To herself: *Now I know why I didn't have to work hard to get rid of him.*

"Do you need a ride back to the Pentagon?" he asked.

"No thanks, Otis," she replied. "I need to check on things with our operating people here at Boling. I might not even have come to this event were it not for that."

"OK," he said. "Nice to see you. No doubt we'll see each other again soon."

As he walked away, she thought: *Wonder how much he did to get rid of him. Maybe I wasn't the only one.*

Within 15 minutes, all guests had departed and General Sawyer said: "Hardly anyone showed up."

"Well, it is Tuesday," Louise Sawyer said. "People are busy during the week. Maybe if it were on a weekend."

"Yes, but today is the day the promotion and retirement are official; one August," General Sawyer stated. "I couldn't legitimately have had it this past weekend and I sure don't want to stay around to next weekend. I've had enough of the mamby pamby homo queer idiots."

"It's also August," Louise Sawyer continued. "Lots of people are on vacation."

"Yes, maybe," he replied. "It's a good thing we decided to have hors d'oeuvres instead of expensive food. We can sell the unopened champagne back to the club."

He started walking briskly out of the room while Louise struggled to keep up on her high spiked-heeled shoes.

CHAPTER 5

Saturday, August 5, 2006
Fairborn, Ohio, USA

Felicia was sitting in front of a mirror in the bride's room off the social hall of Mary Hope of Christians Roman Catholic Church, having just removed her pale blue wedding gown, reflecting: *Is that me so happy? Still can't believe it! Four months ago ready to kill myself. Now I want to live forever.*

Jack and Meredith almost forced me to go to Jack's promotion party at the officer's club. How could I say 'no'? Our best friends when Kevin was alive.

He was standing alone. Obviously Filipino: olive skin, black slightly wavy hair, Asian and Polynesian face with black eyes, but tall. Wore a Navy Captain's uniform. Manipulated someone to introduce me; I just wanted to slink away and hide. Spoke like an American. So sophisticated, suave, and distinguished. I was rude and indifferent. Can't believe he didn't just walk away.

Captain Peter Ramos, third generation Navy. Grandfather a Navy mess boy like Filipinos were over 100 years. Born in U.S., grew up on Navy bases, went to the Naval Academy. Now Academy chief of protocol. At Wright-Patt for a big conference.

He was persistent, thankfully. Recently widowed. I thought he could've wanted only one thing and I wasn't willing to give that! Finally, I agreed to meet for dinner. At the officers' club so I'd be comfortable around people I'd know. Found out I'm an officer's widow. He'll never know how close I came to standing him up.

Back in Annapolis he kept sending flowers; called; back to visit. Asked me to marry him. How could I? He doesn't know I was a poor Philippine whore who got pregnant and had to get married, and Muslim who pretended to be Catholic.

Told it all to the priest thinking he'd bar me from church forever. Was so kind, nice. 'God forgives all who truly repent'. Pray and he'd pray for me. Follow my heart. If God wants me to marry Pete, I'll know in my heart. Gave me private confirmation classes.

Kids and I went to Annapolis; announced engagement. He has two mixed-race children; two mixed-race stepchildren are just fine. He fell in love with them and they with him.

Daughter Christina just finished master's degree in software engineering; about to go to work in Northern Virginia. At first didn't like a little stepsister competing for Daddy's attention; soon took Denise under her wings teaching her to put on make-up highlighting Asian features.

David followed his father into the academy; graduates next year. Four generations Navy. Immediately adopted Timmy and started kicking the soccer ball around. Having a little sister and a big sister was cool, maybe better. Having only a big sister's a challenge, as Timmy knows.

He insisted we meet deceased wife's parents. Old-line Maryland family, Catholics back to colonial days. Came over with Lord Baltimore. They liked me!

When Catherine and Pete wanted to get married, they objected. Finally, accepted inevitable. At least Pete was a good Catholic; met at a church social. When Christina and David were born, Philippine ancestry didn't matter. Even after her tragic early death from cancer, Pete and the children remained part of the family and'll remain after we're married and I'm included!

Mrs. Peter Ramos. Felicia Ramos when I get name legally changed. Khadija'll soon be gone, not dead. Priest said to remember Khadija with pride, dignity, and respect; but confirmed me as Felicia.

NEW BEGINNINGS • CHAPTER 5

A proper wedding and beautiful one. Kevin and I got married quietly by a local priest. Today the old-fashioned American way. Full nuptial mass. Old-fashioned to a point. No one escorted me down the aisle. Simply beautiful when I walked down the aisle myself, Elsie and Christina following, Denise carrying flowers throwing petals. David was best man. Patrick perfect as head usher and groomsman. Timmy so perfect bringing rings on a little velvet pillow. Wasn't too happy escorting his big sister out of the church.

Frank came back from Maryland early just to be here. So nice of him to usher even though not in the formal wedding party 'cause he's not Catholic. Gracious of Jen to keep the guest register. Didn't get along at the office, but wouldn't exclude her. Looks so feminine and charming in her dress. At least no formal uniform like the men.

Meredith and Jack're here of course. Rushed away to get things set up for dinner and dancing. Give them a special hug later. Reception here so great; big beautiful wedding cake. Pete feeding me and me feeding him. Lots of pictures. Rigged garter-throwing so Elsie'd catch it.

Time to get dressed and say goodbye. Not everyone's invited to the dinner and reception.

She entered the social hall wearing a red satin summer party dress, red high-heeled shoes complimented with a ruby necklace and dangling ruby earrings both set in gold, a wedding gift form Pete. Elsie rushed up wearing her maid-of-honor gown, gave her a big hug, and said with a big smile: "Felicia, you look stunning!"

"Thanks," Felicia said beaming: "I feel stunning."

"I should change now if you're through," Elsie said.

Christina also came rushing up in her bride's-maid dress giving Felicia a hug and kiss on the cheek saying: "You look wonderful. Should I introduce you as my big step-sister? You're so young and beautiful no one'll believe you're my step-mother." To Elsie: "Felicia's so fortunate to have friends like you and Patrick. It's an honor to be in the wedding party with you."

Mr. and Mrs. Cavanaugh walked up when Christina went to greet and say goodbye to guests.

Mrs. Cavanaugh took Felicia's hand, gave her a perfunctory kiss on the cheek, and said: "We're going now. It's a long drive to Louisville and we want to be back by bedtime."

"Oh, you're not going to the reception at the club?" Felicia asked surprised. "I thought we made a hotel reservation for you."

"No, dear," Mr. Cavanaugh said as he too gave Felicia a perfunctory kiss on the cheek. "We're old fuddy-duds. The reception is for you young people. Besides, we have the dogs and couldn't find anyone to feed and walk them."

"Also, to be honest," Mrs. Cavanaugh said hesitatingly, "this's the first time we've been here since Kevin was taken from us. The memories are very painful. We don't want to spoil your party. We decided to cancel the hotel and just go home. Please understand."

Felicia replied softly: "Yes, I think I understand. Thank you two so much for coming."

"All the very best for your happiness," Mrs. Cavanaugh said squeezing Felicia's hand. "We've already said goodbye to the children."

"Yes, all the best," Mr. Cavanaugh said and they walked quickly to the exit.

Felicia thought: *They didn't say they'd see me later, keep in touch, or anything like that. It was so final.*

David came rushing up with a big grin, laughing, and said: "Hey, everyone. This's my new step-mom. Look at her, the most beautiful woman in the room. I can't wait to introduce her to all my friends at the academy."

Felicia blushed, a big smile returned to her face, and she stood on tip toes while David bent down so she could kiss him on the cheek. Together they greeted guests and said goodbye to those leaving.

Chapter 6

Saturday, August 5, 2006
Fairborn, Ohio, USA

While Felicia was speaking with others, Patrick and Frank were standing to one side in tuxedo-type military uniforms, Patrick saying: "Looks like you just got back in town. Couldn't talk much at the rehearsal dinner last night."

"Yeah, got in late yesterday morning," Frank replied.

"So did Elsie," Patrick said. "At least it wasn't a long transatlantic flight. When's your move?"

"Moving van's coming Monday morning and then I'll start," Frank answered. "Probably stop somewhere in Pennsylvania. No need to rush to an empty house."

"Oh, you got a place," Patrick said.

"Rented a town house in Laurel," Frank said. "I'll look for something to buy when my house here sells, if it sells. I'm sure you know about the depressed housing market, but falling prices make it easier for me to buy something around DC or Baltimore."

"Speaking of selling your house," Patrick said, "you heard the big news, I guess. Now I don't feel so bad about saying we couldn't buy your house."

"No, what big news is that?" Frank asked.

"I thought Jen would've told you," Patrick replied. "The office is being shut down. We're all being transferred, or Jen and me. We're the only two left after you got reassigned and Felicia resigned."

"I didn't talk to Jen," Frank said. "She left me a voice mail saying she had news and would see me last night, but after the rehearsal dinner, I was exhausted and went straight home. We agreed to talk later. Where're you going?" *I can't tell him Paco came for the night*, he said to himself.

Seems Frank and Jen aren't together any more, if they ever were, Patrick thought. He answered: "Jen'll likely tell you more; she's going to San Diego. I'm going to a NATO weapons system acquisition office near Brussels."

"Great!" Frank exclaimed. "Brussels; Nice city."

"You've been there?" Patrick asked.

"Just to visit," Frank replied.

"We're excited," Patrick exclaimed. "Elsie flies transatlantic a lot so we'll live together over there. We'll be getting married sometime soon. She can keep on working after we get married and officially live there with me. She may have a small apartment in Philadelphia, which is their base, but she can start from Paris, Munich, or wherever just as easily as she can from here."

"Hey, great," Frank exclaimed. *I wish Paco and I had could do something like that*, he thought

"We won't buy houses any time soon," Patrick said. "It's military quarters for a while. Hope you understand."

"Yeah, sure," Frank said. "Say, how's this war in Lebanon affecting you and your family?" Frank asked.

"Thanks for asking," Patrick said. "Folks're upset. It's their country and they love it. Their families are OK."

"Good to hear," Frank said.

"My father's family village is in the far north, almost on the Syrian border," Patrick added. "Things're tense, but no Hizbollah there and Syria's not sending weapons across that part of the border. My mother's family and most of my father's these days live around Beirut; so far Christian areas around Beirut haven't been touched."

NEW BEGINNINGS • CHAPTER 6

"That's what I gathered from the news," Frank said. "Israelis're leaving the Christians alone."

"It's not because they're Christian," Patrick said forcefully. "Israelis've demonstrated they don't care who the hell they terrorize, Muslim or Christian. They've certainly targeted plenty of Christians in the past both in Lebanon and especially in Palestine. This time they're only going after Shia and especially Hizbollah strongholds. Sunni and Druze areas aren't being hit either."

After a short pause Frank said: "I hope we can keep in touch. I'd like to go to your wedding. I have friends here; I'll be visiting from time to time."

"Yeah, sure," Patrick replied. "It'll be in Columbus most likely. That's where Elsie's from. We're in no rush, especially since Elsie can keep on living with me. Don't misunderstand. We're committed; we're going to get married. Just want to take our time to make sure we do it right. I don't know if any relatives from Lebanon will want to come over or not. I'm not close to them, but Lebanese have big extended families who feel obligated. I'll let my folks worry about that so long as it doesn't overload Elsie's family's budget. Elsie and I're willing to pay for the wedding ourselves, but Polish families have their notions of what's right and proper. For sure you'll be invited. It's been great working with you, especially these last few months."

"I'll be there," Frank said. "I've been in the military longer than you. Great friendships become great memories fast. You think someone's your best buddy forever, but then you drift apart when you go on to other assignments, maybe meet again, maybe not. Here almost all of my close friends are civilians. We'll see how we keep in touch. ... I'd like to get together with you before I take off; there's something I want to talk to you about."

"Yeah, I know what you're saying," Patrick said. "I've noticed that from university and my other assignments." *Interesting Jen doesn't seem to fit into anything with him,* Patrick thought. *Maybe they've broken it off or maybe we assumed too much was going on between them.*

"There's Elsie," Patrick said. "I should join her now. See you at the reception at the club. Give me a call and we'll do something before you take off. I'm not just being polite. I'd like to visit with you some more before you leave."

"Yes, me too," Frank said. "Can I call tomorrow? Sunday's the last day I'll be here and be free.

Patrick walked away thinking: *I thought they'd split and tomorrow he wants to talk to me about something, privately. He wouldn't have to be so private to say he and Jen have called it off. ... Wait. I think I got it. If I'm right, lots of things fall in place. Let's see if he calls. I should wait for him to call, though, and not call him.*

Chapter 7

Sunday, August 6, 2006
Fairborn, Ohio, USA

Patrick was sitting in his back yard in the afternoon in cut-offs and a sweat-drenched t-shirt drinking Snapple iced tea, having mowed and trimmed both lawns.

Hearing his cell phone ring inside, he jumped, rushed, then slowed saying to himself: *Let it ring; I can call back.* A few moments later he said into the phone: "Hi, Frank. I was outside; sorry I didn't get to the phone in time."
pause

"Yeah, sure," he replied. "Why don't you come over here? Elsie's visiting her folks for the day. Come for supper. I don't like eating alone; do it enough when she's gone. I'm not much of a cook and not in the mood to cook anyway; we can get something and bring it back."
pause

"That'd work," he continued. "We've got stuff here in the house to go with it."
pause

"Whatever you feel like," he replied. "I'll eat anything. Hey, our neighbors gave us fresh corn on the cob from their garden. I can do corn on the cob."

THREE KISSES

pause

"No," he replied again. "There's beer in the fridge and some wine Elsie brought from Germany. Don't know if I want to drink too much; I kind of overdid it last night."

pause

"Any time you like," he said. "Right now if you want to. Give me a few minutes to hit the shower. If I don't answer the doorbell, just come inside."

About 30 minutes later, he answered the door wearing blue athletic shorts and a red tank top saying: "Hey, bud."

Frank, dressed in jeans and sport shirt, carried two bags saying: "I got a grilled chicken at the Kroger deli and some coleslaw. There were some nice grapes and peaches are just now coming into season."

Patrick put the food in the refrigerator and said: "What can I get you to drink while I'm here?"

"What do you have?" Frank asked.

"Beer, Pepsi, and Seven-Up; iced tea's what I've been drinking. Here's the German wine I mentioned; we can open it now, if you like, or maybe have it later with the chicken."

"Later with the chicken sounds good," Frank replied. "Maybe I'll go for iced tea for now."

Patrick took two bottles of Snapple and asked: "You want to sit outside? It's not so hot in the shade on the patio or do you want to stay inside in the AC?"

"Let's see what it's like on the patio," Frank replied. "I've been inside in air conditioning all day."

Once seated, Patrick asked: "You ready for the move? It must be a chore. Up 'til now, I've just had myself to move with a few personal things when I was transferred. We don't know what we'll do when Elsie moves to Brussels now that we have furniture."

"It wasn't that bad," Frank commented. "Movers're coming first thing tomorrow morning. Good thing about the military, Uncle Sam pays to pack and move. I just packed some stuff to have the minimum to survive a few days until movers arrive plus personal stuff I don't trust to them. Mostly I've been sorting and throwing things away."

NEW BEGINNINGS • CHAPTER 7

"How do you feel about leaving your house behind?" Patrick asked. "You were talking a little about it last night. I'm sort of new to this moving around bit. You're older and have more experience."

Frank replied: "I'm pretty well immune. Growing up as a Marine Corps brat, we moved every few years and I've done it myself since I've been in the Marine Corps. This's the first time I've owned a house. Growing up, we always lived in base quarters. My parents bought their first house when they retired."

"You said last night most of your friends here're civilians," Patrick continued. "What's it like to leave them? I'm asking because Elsie and I mostly have civilian friends, people she works with."

I hope he doesn't think I'm getting too personal, Patrick thought. *Since Easter, he's become a lot easier to talk to; like someone I can open up with a little.*

Frank thought: *How can I tell him it hurts like hell? I never had feelings before; wasn't allowed to feel. Now they're intense, too intense at times. I'd better change the subject, maybe make a joke of it.* "Well, one thing about moving near DC," he said, "everyone wants to come visit and be a tourist. Maybe it'll be like running a bed and breakfast. You and Elsie want to come?"

Patrick replied: "Might be the same for us in Brussels."

Frank abruptly said: "Say, there's something I've wanted to ask you. You got an MBA. What's it like? What did it do for you? I need more education for another career after I get out of the Marine Corps."

Patrick began: "It kind of opened up my mind to other things, other ways of looking at things, not just technical stuff. It didn't help too much for what I've done in the Army. It's all private sector, profit making, free markets, and all that. It might be more useful if I were working more directly with military contractors, but was good for me."

"If I could do what I want and not worry about a job," Frank said, "I'd study foreign affairs, foreign policy. DC'd be the place for that, Georgetown or George Washington."

"Yeah, for sure," Patrick agreed.

"Last night you were talking about the Middle East and the war in Lebanon," Frank continued. "I really eat that stuff up. Not war stuff even if I am a Marine. I changed the subject last night because I didn't want to get involved in a discussion and have to stop in the middle."

"I thought maybe you were upset because I was criticizing Israel," Patrick said.

"Not at all," Frank said.

"I'm usually more cautious," Patrick said, "but last night maybe it was champagne or being tired. I'm careful what I say about Israel because so many people in the military think Israel is a great friend of the U.S. Kerry said at least twice that Israel's the best ally the U.S. has ever had. I've been to Lebanon and seen and heard first hand what Israel's done to Lebanon even before this latest conflict."

"I imagine," Frank said. "Your family's from there."

Patrick continued: "Lebanon isn't MY country; I'm American and proud of it, but, yes, my parents are from there. There're extended family there. I've been there. What works me up is how Israel's viewed as a poor aggrieved country of innocents that's just defending itself. Sure, Hizbollah started this latest war and sure Israel's justified in trying to wipe it off the face of the Earth and isn't doing a good job of it. What most people don't realize, don't think they're capable of realizing, is Israelis are as much of terrorists as Hizbollah. Imagine if you can al Qaeda and the Nazis going at it."

"But Israel has an elected government and treats its people decently," Frank argued back.

"Some democracy," Patrick responded. "A good third of the population are disenfranchised. Hizbollah's never going to be accused of being a democracy, but it provides good social services for its people. How do you think it gets as much support from the population as it does?"

"Never thought of it that way," Frank said. "Now that you mention it, Nazis were elected too. Like I said, I can eat this kind of stuff up and keep on forever."

"For me, it's pretty much limited to Lebanon," Patrick said "but I can get passionate. Say, what's this about getting out of the Marine Corps? Aren't you in for life?"

"No way!" Frank exclaimed. "I've got about five and a half years to retire. I'll try to stick it out until then. I'll be in my early 40s so I definitely need something else to do."

"Gee, I'd have never thought that," Patrick said. "What about your family? You're third generation Marine Corps."

"Fuck my family! Fuck the Marine Corps!" Frank almost shouted sitting up in his chair.

"Geez!" Patrick exclaimed.

"Sorry," Frank said. "I'm tired too; drank too much last night. I got carried away."

"No need to be sorry," Patrick said, "but I sure wouldn't've expected that reaction from you."

"The Reynolds dynasty in the Marine Corps is coming to an end," Frank continued. "I'd get out now if I wouldn't be throwing away so much money, half my salary for the rest of my life. I've got to live and pay for more education."

"Yea, for sure," Patrick said. "I've been thinking about that myself. If I don't do something pretty soon, I'll be too far along in the Army to give up retirement, but Elsie and I do want this Brussels assignment so guess we'll decide after that. What happened? Something must've made you want to break family tradition."

"You said I'm older and have more experience," Frank began. "Not sure I do have more experience. You've been exposed to different things in life. I've only been associated with the Marine Corps for all of my 35 years, almost 36. Even schools I went to were next to the base and most of the kids were Marine brats too. Then I went to The Citadel, an all male military academy. We were talking earlier about civilian friends; for the first time I have civilian friends. I've been exposed to other aspects of life and learned a few things."

"Oh, what sort of things?" Patrick asked, thinking: *I'm pretty sure I know, but let's see what he says.*

Frank replied: "Let's just say they have different viewpoints about some things. You just heard me say I don't approve of war much. I've not become a pacifist, but thanks to these guys, I've learned that decent and respectable people can have different viewpoints and lifestyles that many in the Marine Corps would find unacceptable." *Oops, I just said guys.* Frank thought.

Patrick said: "Frank, I've been baiting you a little, sorry, but I wanted to hear what you'd say first. I'm aware of the military's 'don't ask; don't tell' policy. I'm not asking, but not telling either. I know 'don't ask, don't tell' means something different in 'don't tell', but still I'm not telling.

Frank turned pale sinking low in his chair and got tense thinking: *How dare he!*

Chapter 8

Sunday, August 6, 2006
Fairborn, Ohio, USA

Frank sat dumbfounded, then blurted out: "I suppose you've set me up to tell me privately I'm not invited to your wedding after I pushed you publicly last night."

"Hell yes!" Patrick exclaimed, sitting up in his chair. "Or hell no I'm not setting you up. Of course you're invited! Why shouldn't you be?"

"And a boyfriend too?" Frank asked.

Patrick replied: "Haven't thought about it, but, yeah, it's normal for wedding invitations to include a significant other. Plenty of Elsie's co-workers are gay and have partners or boyfriends. We haven't talked about it, but I'm sure she'd want to include them. We'll invite who we want to and not worry about who might be upset at seeing you with a boyfriend or Elsie's co-workers and their boyfriends."

Both sat tense until Frank said: "This time it was me who was baiting you. Maybe looking for a reason to feel sorry for myself and be a martyr. Sorry."

"Look, Frank," Patrick said, "you said I probably have more different experiences than you do. I've been associated with gay people before. One guy in particular was in the MBA program at Bama. His name is Greg. We weren't close buddy-buddies, but we had classes together, worked on projects together, made presentations together. We'd go out for coffee and beers. He'd sometimes open up and talk about what it's like to be gay. He'd make comments about the good looking guys, especially when he caught me looking at the girls and wanted to tease me.

"Elsie works with lots of gay guys. You've flown enough to know what I mean. They're just like any kind of coworkers; they're just people. Some you just work with, others you become friends with, and some in between. Whether they're gay or not has nothing to do with it.

"I haven't had gay buddies in the military, until now that is. Elsie and I're developing civilian friends and that's including gay men. Who gives a rat's ass?

"Frank, once I figured out, I wanted to tell you it's fine with me, especially now that we've become closer these past few months and you're leaving. When you said you wanted to get together before you left, I figured this was the opportunity, but wasn't going to blurt it out first thing through the door."

Frank replied: "The reason I wanted to get together is to say 'thank you'. You've been a big help to me on the job; better'n anyone I ever worked with."

"You're welcome," Patrick replied. "Helped you in what way? I wasn't aware I did anything special."

"But you did," Frank continued. "I studied engineering, but, my education was ten years out of date. I hardly knew shit about computers. You helped me with that. Jen helped too, but mostly it was you.

"Hey, bud, lighten up on yourself," Patrick said. "You must've had some hard knocks in the Marine Corps and not for things we just talked about. I'm pleased you want to thank me. I'll gladly accept your thanks, but it was nothing really. We all help each other. Maybe I don't get anything directly back, but like old timers in Alabama'd say: what goes around comes around."

Frank's smiled: "I just appreciate your help and appreciate your accepting my thanks."

Patrick added: "You asked about my MBA program. They're damned competitive. Some assholes'd try to get an advantage by hiding things in the library; tearing pages out of journals so others wouldn't find the same hot article.

NEW BEGINNINGS • CHAPTER 8

"I told you about Greg. He's bright, sharp, and a damned hard worker. In all modesty, I did pretty good myself, but he's a little better. Some tried to sabotage him. Yes, a few did it because he's gay, but mostly they were jealous. I didn't realize this at first; I was just a small-town boy from the sticks who'd just come from Auburn.

"Those business students at Bama are a different breed. I naïvely asked Greg something; did something for him too. He's from Atlanta; big city boy. He wanted to get out of the rat race and come to Tuscaloosa, and he'd just had a big bust up with a boyfriend in undergrad school

"I'm kind of rambling here. When he could see I was genuine, about as bright as he is, not trying to screw him over, he did things for me too. Now that I think about it, Greg really expressed appreciation like you've done. Our skills complimented each other. I was technical, math, and problem solving; he was great in organization theory and human relations stuff. I wonder whatever became of him. I'll have to look him up."

Frank said: "Part of the Marine Corps shit's not being able to express feelings. These civilian friends, one in particular, made me realize that and not in a gentle manner. I'm still taking baby steps, but as part of my training, so to speak, I was determined not to leave here without telling you I appreciate what you did."

Patrick replied: "There's something I've been really curious about. Your attitude towards me changed a lot right after Easter. What happened? Before, you went out of your way to avoid me except at work, especially at the gym. When by chance we met in the shower or locker room, you'd go out of your way to avoid me and turn your back to me. When we were both at the club or some place like that, it wasn't so bad, but still it seemed like you were just being polite and not really wanting to be sociable. What happened? Was it something to do with that day you brought me home and put me to bed?"

Frank began: "I was afraid; afraid you'd notice some things and get upset. You were really nice and helpful at work. I really like you and respect you. I didn't want to risk something happening you'd misinterpret."

"Oh, you were lusting after me but didn't want me to notice," Patrick stated.

"No!" Frank said. "Well, there's a tiny bit of truth there, but not what you're thinking."

"How the hell can you know what I'm thinking?" Patrick exclaimed.

"Look at it this way, Patrick," Frank said with sudden inspiration. "You went to co-ed schools, didn't you? Let's say that for some reason you're assigned to live in a co-ed dorm and society's values have all changed.

"No, bring it closer to home. You're in a weird military assignment where you're the only guy assigned to live in the WAC barracks. Society's values are different. You have to take a shower with these girls and they think nothing of it. So far as they're concerned, you're just like one of the girls. You're the one uncomfortable, even ashamed. On a man's body, not on a woman's, certain things happen involuntarily; nature takes over and you can't control it and can't really hide unless you turn the other way or stand in the corner.

"Let's say one girl in particular is being nice to you, not in a romantic or sexual way, just nice and pleasant and helpful. You like this girl too, but not in a sexual way. You know she has a boyfriend and you have, well you have things in your life too. Still if you're in the shower with her, some things can happen that you don't want to happen. So what do you do? Avoid shower situations as much as possible? Are you getting the drift?"

Patrick, anger subsiding, said: "I haven't thought of things that way. I need time to think about this more. Things I wish I'd talked about more with Greg. I worked out in the gym there and he didn't. Maybe next time we're with one of Elsie's friends I'll ask him. You sure had me confused, even hurt that you're avoiding me except in the office when you wanted me to do something for you."

"Gee, I'm sorry about that," Frank said, "but I'd rather have you confused and hurt than have you really upset if you saw me in the shower, you know, aroused."

"Yeah, I guess," Patrick said, "but also I hadn't figured out that you are, er, you're the way you are."

"What the hell, Patrick," Frank said. "Go ahead and say it, I'm gay. Use the 'G' word. I'm having problems making my mouth and tongue actually form the word, but I'd better get used to it. Now that I think about it, this's the first time I've actually said the word 'gay' to anyone except my close circle of friends. Let me pinch myself and see if I am still alive or if it killed me."

Patrick said: "I think Greg used humor to deal with things, too. Sometimes, I got the sense things were really churning deep inside of him and he was feeling pain. I just liked him and respected him for who he was and he knew that. The feeling was obviously mutual. Now that I think about it, maybe he was avoiding going to the gym with me. He had a pretty decent body and was fit. But what happened after Easter? You changed almost over night."

Oh, God, here we go again, Frank thought then said: "I guess just a coincidence of timing. There were other things going on in my life then. Things were accelerating with one person in particular. You remember Easter weekend I made a trip to Texas ostensibly alone. Then the next weekend I took a week's leave to go visit my parents. I did visit my parents, but that wasn't all. That sort of brought things to a head."

"Oh," Patrick said. "Like maybe the weekend that Elsie and I decided we're going to be committed to each other. I'm not going to give you details, but maybe I understand."

"No, unfortunately," Frank replied. "Not committed, but some things happened. Like you, I'm not going to give details. I'm just now starting to feel feelings and am awkward at knowing how to respond to them. Let's just say that the process began then."

"How does this affect your change in attitude towards me, though?" Patrick asked. "No details, but something must've made you change your attitude towards me."

"Well, to tell you the truth," Frank said, "I've been asking myself the same questions. I can't really tell you, Patrick. I certainly started seeing you in a different way. For lack of a better word, maybe kind of like a brother. I don't want to carry that analogy very far. I never had a brother and have no idea what it's like, but even gay guys don't get aroused around brothers, or so they say. Maybe it was developing feelings and realizing that when I can feel, I can relate to people differently, each one in a different way."

"I don't have a brother, either," Patrick said, "but I do have a little sister; you've heard me talk about Anna Marie, only she isn't little any more. I don't get aroused around her, but I care for her very much. Maybe I can sort of identify. Now that I think of it, there've been a couple of women who've sort of become sister-like for me, like Felicia. I wouldn't have lusted after them after I got to know them."

Oh, like a sister with Felicia, Frank thought.

Both sat for few moments exhausted from the intensity of the conversation.

Chapter 9

Sunday, August 6, 2006
Fairborn, Ohio, USA

After a pause in conversation, Patrick said: "Hey, bud, this has been intense. I'm glad, really glad, we talked like this, but what say we give it a rest for a while? Let's get the wine and I'll start cooking the corn."

He put his hand on Frank's shoulder, guided him to the kitchen, handed him the wine, and said: "Maybe you open this while I tend to the corn. Here's the corkscrew; glasses are in that cupboard."

"Interesting," Frank said, "all written in German."

"Yeah," Patrick answered. "Comes from an area called Franconia known for its white wines."

"Maybe I need to learn German," Frank said. "For sure I need to learn foreign languages if I'm going into foreign things. Maybe I should learn Arabic. You speak Arabic?"

"Nah," Patrick replied preparing the corn. "When I was a kid, I spoke Arabic with my grandmother, but she died, bless her soul, when I was pretty young. My parents also spoke Arabic with me and Anna Marie when my grandmother was around. She also spoke French with my folks so we kids wouldn't understand. After she passed, we spoke English at home. Easier. Both my parents are fluent and spoke English in the store so natural to speak it at home.

"I don't know if you know, but in Lebanon a large portion of the population is educated in either French or English, sometimes both, but not Arabic. Kids grow up speaking English at school then on the playground and the television is mostly in English so many of them automatically speak English to each other. Lebanese aren't hung up on their language like in other countries. It's not part of their cultural identity so growing up not speaking Arabic's no big deal.

"All of that's a long-winded way of saying 'no', I don't speak Arabic. When I was there a couple of years ago, some words came back, but I never learned to read the characters. But, yeah, learn Arabic. Other Arab countries aren't like Lebanon. When I was in Syria, there was only Arabic, definitely not French, and not much English."

Frank sipped the wine saying: "Nice. Not too dry; not too sweet. Wonder if I can get something like this in DC."

"Yeah, it's good," Patrick said, "and Elsie says it costs less than two euros."

"That's about what?" Frank asked. "If I'm going into foreign stuff, I need to know things like that."

"About $2.50," Patrick answered. "She buys it at a regular supermarket in Munich."

Sitting opposite Frank ready to eat, Patrick raised his wine glass and said: "Sakhtain, That's one of the few Arabic words I remember. That's how Lebanese begin their meals."

"Sakhtain," Frank responded raising his wine glass.

During a pause in eating Patrick said: "You've mentioned a boyfriend or a special someone a couple of times. Care to tell me more about him? If you don't want to tell, that's OK but I'm curious who might have caught the fancy of a Marine Corps major."

"Oh, you touched a sensitive nerve, there," Frank smiled and chuckled. "There was a big blow up during that weekend in Florida. He said I was too much Marine, like a robot with a switch on my back I think were his words. I can turn it on when, er, doing it, but go back to stiff and formal, insensitive, not feeling, otherwise."

Patrick commented: "Now I see why you emphasize he's a civilian. He must not know much about the military."

"That's the rub," Frank continued. "He does. He works in a VA nursing home. He's around veterans all the time. Knows a lot about military, he never stops reminding me."

Patrick asked: "He from around here? Must be."

"Works in Cincinnati," Frank replied, "but lives between here and there, in Hamilton."

"What's he do at the VA place?" Patrick asked.

"He's a nurse," Frank answered.

"Where'd you two meet?" Patrick asked.

Frank blushed and smiled: "Well, let's just say at a certain type of bar in Cincinnati."

"Oh," Patrick blushed. "I'll stop the interrogation."

"No problem," Frank replied. "You're the first person outside a small group I've felt comfortable telling. It's awkward, but feels good to be able to tell someone about my personal life just like you and Felicia do."

Patrick said: "Elsie's gay friends are all out so they don't mind talking about their social life. I've never thought about what it'd be like for others. You said a big blow-up in Florida, but you also talk like something's still going on. Are you still together? What will moving to DC do?"

"We're patching it up," Frank replied. "Neither of us wants to break it off completely. We're talking about ways to keep it going once I move. Can't talk too much about it now."

"Oh, sorry if I asked the wrong question" Patrick said.

"Oh, nothing secret," Frank said. "It's just too soon. Some things might be in the works; just don't want to talk too much and get hopes up too high. He's Mexican by the way; been in this country since he was a baby. Everything's legal. He can move and work wherever he pleases, but Mexican families and especially Mexican mothers want their children around close and usually living with them. She's a dear soul. Maybe you have some idea what I'm talking about."

"Yes I sure do," Patrick replied. "Elsie's dealing with that with her parents. They didn't like her moving to Dayton in the first place. She might move back with them once I move to Brussels until she can move.

"I'd be dealing with this too if I weren't in the Army and had to move; Lebanese kids live with their parents until they get married. Anna Marie and I both moved away so my parents are adapting; besides they're pretty much Americanized by now. Mexicans don't have anything on Polish and Lebanese when it comes to dealing with their children. Maybe it's Americans who're out of step."

"I didn't have to deal with that," Frank said. "My parents were happy to have me out of the house. Say, Paco's cousin owns a bakery in Hamilton that makes fabulous Polish pastries including those special angel wing cookies they serve at weddings. If you and Elsie need them for your wedding, he can make them."

"That's something, a Mexican baker making Polish pastries in Ohio," Patrick chuckled. "Elsie's parents may have a Polish bakery they buy from in Columbus, but thanks for the tip. Might come in useful some day. You want anything else?"

"No, thanks," Frank said. "Enough for me."

"I'm in no mood to do the dishes now," Patrick said as he got up and started clearing off the table. "Elsie'll be pissed off if she comes home and sees dirty dishes, but I can deal with them later."

"I can help you." Frank said.

"Nah. It's me who's not in the mood," Patrick said. "Thanks for the offer. I'm not shy about accepting help. You must've figured that out when I apparently let you bring me home and put me to bed. You can do as many dishes as you want when you visit us in Brussels. Let's go watch TV. There should be some pre-season football games on."

"Yeah, sure," Frank said.

"You want coffee or something?" Patrick asked.

"No," Frank said. "Thanks. I'll let my stomach rest."

After a couple of hours when the game was over, Frank stood and said: "I need to use your facilities, if I may."

"Yeah, sure," Patrick said. "Down the hall by the bedrooms or there's one off the utility room as you know."

Frank smiled and chuckled also: "I'll use that one since I know it well. Then I need to go."

When Frank re-entered the room, Patrick stood and joined Frank near the door.

Frank said: "Thanks again for everything. I'm still not good at goodbyes."

"I'm not all that great either," Patrick said, "but I'm **really** glad you called and came over. Here, let me show you how Lebanese say goodbye. I wouldn't do this out on the street though."

He put his arms around Frank's chest and kissed him three times on the cheeks, first left, then right, then left again, followed by a big squeeze.

Frank, put his arms around Patrick and returned the hug. He turned to wave at Patrick as he got into his car and brushed tears away from his eyes as he drove away.

Chapter 10

Wednesday, August 2, 2006
Washington, DC, USA

"You don't need to pay for me," Joe Shaito said as he followed Roger Chen down the lunch line in the Department of Justice cafeteria.

"My pleasure," Roger Chen said. "I invited you."

When both were eating, Roger Chen said: "It's been obvious the past couple of weeks that you're preoccupied, not always present. It seems you're not getting enough sleep either. Don't misunderstand; the quality of your work hasn't declined, but I'm concerned it might. This is strictly personal and if you don't want to talk about it, that's OK. It's the war in Lebanon, isn't it?"

"Yes," Joe Shaito said."

Roger Chen asked? "Do you have family there who've been hurt or killed or are at risk?"

"No, not really" Joe Shaito replied, "but Lebanese have big extended families, and yes, some are in danger. We're Shia. Did I tell you?"

"No, or I don't remember," Roger Chen answered.

"I don't tell many people," Joe Shaito continued. "People automatically assume I'm Hizbollah or a sympathizer and avoid me. In large Shia extended families in Lebanon there're bound to be Hizbollah or sympathizers, and yes some distant family members live in South Beirut where the bombing is going on."

"Oh," Roger Chen said.

"My family moved here to get away from factional politics. Hizbollah hadn't been organized then, but there were noises it would. They just joined the exodus to the U.S. Like many Lebanese Shia, they settled in Dearborn."

"Why don't you take off and go home for a few days," Roger Chen said. "I am sure I could arrange it."

"No!" Joe Shaito almost shouted in anguish. "That'd be the worst thing I could do."

"Oh? Why if I may ask?" Roger Chen said surprised.

"Lebanese politics are spilling over into Dearborn whether my family likes it or not," He began. "Hizbollah sympathizers there view me working for the U.S. government as selling out to the enemy and are telling my family how terrible it is and I am."

"Oh," Roger Chen said startled.

"First my family was proud of me being a lawyer working here in the highest office in Washington," Joe Shaito continued. "Now suddenly I'm a disgrace. In the Lebanese culture, standing in the community is more important than almost anything, so now I'm the black sheep, I think you say."

"Oh, gee. What can I say?" Roger Chen said. "I'd have never thought anything like that."

Joe Shaito added: "They want me to get married, too."

"Oh?" Roger Chen said. "I didn't know you have a girlfriend or at least you haven't mentioned one."

"I don't," Joe Shaito said bitterly. "That's the point. They want me to marry someone in Lebanon so I can bring her here and all of her family as soon as it can be arranged."

"Ohhh," Roger Chen said. "That. It used to happen all the time with immigrant groups including Chinese. Now there're limits, but you surely know that."

"Yes, I know, but they don't understand or don't want to understand," Joe Shaito replied. "They know plenty of people who've done that including my sister. Besides, I'm working here at the top level in Washington.

I'm expected to use my influence to arrange it. That's why they supported me to go to law school in the first place so I could get this job and do things for them, so they say.

"My mother sort of half-way understands I want to meet the right girl, fall in love, and marry; it didn't happen that way for her, but she watches enough American television now. My father is totally beyond reasoning. First I'm disgracing them in the eyes of some people for working here and then I fail to use my position to do what I'm supposed to do. I am failing totally in my duty as a son."

"Oh, my God," Roger Chen exclaimed. "What about their duty to you to support your choices for your life?"

"Lebanese don't see it that way," Joe Shaito continued. "Lebanese parents own their children about like people used to own slaves. Oh, they love their children too; sometimes love them too much. Still it's the duty of the children to serve their parents."

"Serve them in what way?" Roger Chen continued.

"Making them look good." Joe Shaito began. "Parents select the career the children should follow so that they can do things for the rest of the family and make the parents look good by having a child in a prestigious position. It makes no difference whether the child wants to do this. I was lucky; they were pleased to have a lawyer in the family so when I said I wanted to be a lawyer, it was just fine.

"Also marry the right kind of person. It applies to both the boy and the girl. The right kind of spouse makes both sets of parents look good. The girl's expected to get pregnant within a year, or two at the most, or else someone is failing in duties to produce grandchildren. The vicious cycle starts all over again."

"I've heard about Muslim families and their arranged marriages," Roger Chen commented.

"Also back in Lebanon the children are expected to live with their parents until they get married no matter how old the children are or how well-off they are," Joe Shaito continued. "In our community in Dearborn, it's much the same. When I moved to Washington, I disgraced them in the eyes of some."

"In Lebanon don't people move to the city to get better jobs?" Roger Chen interjected.

"Yes," Joe Shaito replied, "but Lebanon's a small country. It's not unusual for someone to move from the South to Beirut, but if they do, it's only on work days, and siblings share an apartment, or they share with cousins, or stay with relatives, but they still **live** with their parents and go home every non-working day.

"My parents were cool with my moving to Washington for a good job and have some sense of how far away it is so I'm not expected to go back every weekend. Not everyone in Dearborn's as enlightened and now that other issues have come up, I'm triply disgracing them in the view of many."

"Whew! For sure you don't want to go home under these circumstances," Roger Chen said. "What can we do for you then to help the situation?"

"Nothing I can think of at the moment," Joe Shaito replied. "Just continue understanding."

"There's one thing I intend to do, although not immediately," Roger Chen said. "You were great in dealing with those two Arab-American guys at Guantanamo. We have lots of task forces. This issue of phony marriage to immigrate to the U.S. is one that's been plaguing us for decades. Part of the problem is we don't understand all the nuances of all the local cultures. I'm going to arrange for you to be on the task force to deal with legal issues, develop policy, and all that. You can bring a lot of insight about Arab societies."

"Er, OK," Joe Shaito gulped. "If you say so, but that might also make it even worse with the family if they see me as really selling out and being responsible for stopping the flow of relatives and friends into the U.S."

"Oh, I guess there's that to think about too," Roger Chen said. "As I said, not right away."

Both sat quietly for a moment when suddenly Roger Chen said: "Hey, we've got joint activities going on with the British, some of it related to the marriage issue and other more pressing issues of joint interest like terrorism. I'll see if I can't get you an assignment over there. I bet you could add a lot of insight with your knowledge of Arab ways. When you come back maybe there'd be less hostility at home."

"Well, er, thanks," Joe Shaito said. "Of course I'd like to go to London, but why me? There're plenty of Arabs in Britain; they could be as good or better than I am."

"You're one of us," Roger Chen replied. "The Americans on the task force will listen to you rather than the British. Even though we are basically together on these issues, in a task force there's always a bit of taking sides. Each side needs its own Arab expert so to speak. Do you have a current passport? We can get one on short notice?"

"Gee, now I don't know what to say," Joe Shaito said.

"Say why don't you come over to our house for dinner some time during the weekend?" Roger Chen said. "I'll bet you could stand a nice family environment for a change. My kids are like lots of kids, not that well behaved. We're not the greatest example of family congeniality on Earth, but we try," Roger Chen smiled.

"Gee, thanks again," Joe Shaito said. "I'm free all weekend. As I said, I'm laying low socially these days."

"I can't make plans without consulting with my wife," Roger Chen said. "I'll get back with you with a specific time and location. Don't worry, it won't be Chinese food."

"I wouldn't care if it is," Joe Shaito said with a smile. "I love the stuff. That's what kept me going through law school. Just so long as it's not sweet and sour pork."

"Oh, right," Roger Chen said smiling. "You don't eat pork. Guess we won't have Virginia ham either. We live in Virginia, you know. It's time to get back to work."

Chapter 11

Thursday, August 24, 2006
Duluth, Minnesota, USA

"I wonder who's coming to visit," Boudi said to Brahim as they waited in the visiting room of the U.S. federal minimum security prison camp wearing standard prison-issue clothes of blue jeans and light-weight blue denim shirts. They had bandages on their faces from recent surgery and a week's growth of beard.

"Beat's me," Brahim said. "Who knows we're here?"

U.S. FEDERAL PRISON CAMP, DULUTH, MINNESOTA

A guard ushered in a woman in her early 30s who had an average figure and stood 5 feet 8 inches. Her hair was so blonde it looked fresh out of the bottle until one looked at the roots to see it was natural; her blue eyes matched two of the 10,000 lakes of Minnesota and had sparkling friendliness that belied the otherwise stoic composure on her slightly rounded, expressionless face, typical of her Finnish ancestry.

As Brahim and Boudi stood, she offered her hand saying: "Hello, I'm Anja Ruusulaakso, case officer for your work-study release. Please let's sit. You are, please?"

Brahim replied: "Ibrahim al Asadi" thinking: *Her face is blank. We have to deal with her for the next five years?*

She then said: "You must be Abdullah Zakawi."

He meekly said: "Yes," thinking: *Is she out to get us? What's with her face with no expression.*

"Your names are almost as difficult to pronounce as mine," she said. "It's Anja, **AHN**-yah and then **ROO**-ooh-sule-ah .., oh forget it. Call me Anja; everyone does. It's Finnish. My grandparents immigrated; lots of Finns here. Your names sound Arabic. What country if I may ask?"

"Yemen," Boudi said.

"Our parents immigrated from there," Brahim clarified. "We were born here." He said to himself: *Just as I thought. We're Arabs so they're suspicious and we'll get bashed.*

"Yes, I see you're U.S. citizens," she continued. "We don't see many Arabs here. There're Iraqis who I'll talk about in a moment, but no Yemenis that I've come across. You boys're giving us a challenge."

"Oh, how's that?" Boudi asked timidly.

Brahim said to himself: *Here it is– 'we don't trust you'.*

"Don't worry," she said reassuringly. "It's a nice and interesting challenge. Almost all persons here are older men who've committed white collar crimes. About all we can do is put them in some dead-end job like janitorial work for their work-release and most of them were well educated professionals. We can get you started in school and in new directions in your life. That's a fun kind of challenge; I just haven't done it before. Before we get to that, let's cover preliminaries. You returned a week ago from cosmetic surgery, part of the witness protection program."

"Yes, ma'am," Boudi said thinking: *Is she being nice?*

"We didn't agree to change our names," Brahim added.

"I'm with you there," she said "My father refused to change his name and with a name like Ruusulaakso you can imagine he had a lot of pressure to change it. My grandfather refused to change his at Ellis Island and even insisted the immigration official spell it correctly, but he was showing off to prove he could read and write. I didn't change my name either when I got married. Are things OK? Healing well?"

"Yes, ma'am," Boudi answered.

"We're supposed to see doctors here for follow-up care," Brahim said. He thought: *Likely some local yokel doctor'll remove the bandages so he can collect money from the government and send us on our way.*

"Oh, good," she said. "We have really good doctors here in Duluth. We attract some of the best because the quality of life is good here and they get good patients. When I come back I hope I can see your full nice new handsome faces."

Boudi thought: *She's being sort of nice, but why's her face so blank?*

Brahim thought: *Cut the crap lady. What're you trying to do? Soften us up and then screw us?*

"It says both of you have prison jobs," she continued. "Ibrahim, you're working in the library. Do you like that?"

He replied: "Yes, I like it a lot. I've always liked books and reading things. Sometimes I have good conversations about books with other prisoners. Maybe I should become a librarian when I get out of here."

"It says here you want to study history and government and maybe become a teacher or a lawyer," she continued. "If you want to study to be a librarian, we can arrange that but don't give up on your dreams, either."

Brahim said to himself: *What? Don't give up on my dreams? She's sounding like that nice lady, Ms. Rhonda, and I was mean to her.*

"And Abdullah," she continued, "You're working in the gym and doing fitness training."

"Yes, ma'am," he answered. "People call me Boudi, short for Abdullah. I've always liked sports and been good at it. I've got some other prisoners organized into softball games, but some of them just like to work out and keep fit."

"That sounds good, too," she said. "It says here you want to be involved in sports in some way."

"Yes, ma'am," he replied.

"I have things to talk to you about your education now, Ibrahim," she said, "but for you, Booty, I need time to work and explore; there's no urgency for you."

"Thanks, ma'am," he said. "And, er, it's Boudi."

"Oh, sorry, Boo-dee?" Is that right?" she asked

"Yes, ma'am," he answered.

"Another thing," she continued, "both of you are Muslim. Is everything OK so far as your religious beliefs?"

"Oh, er, yes," Boudi replied thinking: *She's actually asking about our beliefs.*

"So far no problem," Brahim added. "They asked us about food. They have Jewish prisoners occasionally so they're used to preparing food without pork. I don't think it's kosher, though."

"I'd guess it's not halal either," she commented.

"Oh, you know what halal is?" Brahim asked.

"Yes," she answered "We're exposed to such things up here in the Northlands. We'll get to that point later."

"Er, you could call me Brahim if you like," he said. "That's the name most Arabs use for someone named Ibrahim. Really close friends and family say Bob."

"Ok, Brahim," she continued. "Now let's see what we can do for you guys' education.

Chapter 12

Thursday, August 24, 2006
Duluth, Minnesota, USA

After talking about general conditions of their imprisonment, Anja Ruusulaakso continued: "Ok, Brahim, now let's see what we can do for your education.

"At first I thought we might get you started at UMD, that's the University of Minnesota - Duluth, this semester that starts next week, but there wasn't enough time to get the admissions process completed. Besides, until your release in December, you'd have to go under guard; it could've been a hassle for the staff here, not to mention reactions from your fellow students at seeing guards, not being able to go have coffee with them, and study together."

What the hell? Brahim thought. *She was actually thinking of starting university now? Thought she was just going to tell us it wouldn't work out.*

"All's not lost," she continued, "We can get you into distance education, but we'll get to that in a minute. Now we need to start the process of getting you admitted to UMD in January. You've caused them a challenge too; they're not used to having prisoners apply."

"Oh?" Brahim said thinking: *Here it comes.*

"Don't worry," she said. "You won't have any problems. It's just that it's a new situation for them. Dealing with your fellow students might be a bit of a challenge if you tell them you're on work-study release from the prison, but I'm sure you can handle that. Minnesotans are tolerant and accepting unless you give them a reason not to be. We call it 'Minnesota Nice.'"

"Er, OK," Brahim said saying to himself: *Gee, she really does seem like she's trying to help me.*

"Here're application forms and lots of information," she continued. "Look them over and fill them out the best you can. I'll be back next week. If you have any questions, you can call me. I'll leave my phone number and instructions that you're allowed to call. Normally, you'd call the university direct but the prison won't allow that. We can make an appointment or I'll just come when I can."

"Whatever works for you, ma'am," Brahim said. "We won't go anywhere except to see a doctor."

She said: "I'll check when that's scheduled."

"Thanks," Brahim said overwhelmed.

"Now we need to deal with high school transcripts and SATs," she said. "You did take the SAT, didn't you?"

"Er, yes," Brahim answered.

"Do you remember your score?" she asked.

"No," Brahim replied. "They told me it was good. Maybe 1,300 or 1,400 sticks in my mind."

"That's under the old scale and plenty good," she said. "Here's the form to order a copy of your test results to be sent to the university. Fill it out quickly. I need to see other prisoners and I can pick it up before I leave for today. I've drafted a letter for you to sign asking your high school transcript be sent directly to the university. That means someone at the high school will know you're here. We can request the transcript be sent to some other address and then forwarded up here, but that takes more time."

"Oh, it won't matter, I'm sure," Brahim said. "Sooner or later they'll figure out we're here."

"That's probably right," she said. "Look this letter over and sign it; I'll pick it up today also."

NEW BEGINNINGS • CHAPTER 12

"Thanks!" Brahim exclaimed thinking: *I can't believe she's doing all this.*

She continued: "Don't get spoiled now. You're supposed to do things for yourself, learning to do things on your own so you can survive once you get out of here. I just did these things to get the process started because deadlines are close and you were away. Next steps are up to you.

"We're not using the prison address; we're using our office address, but not identifying it as such. When we get you a place to live later, it's easy to change addresses. College students change addresses all the time. The form asks parents' names, addresses, and permanent addresses. You can leave that blank for now. The system is set up for kids who're applying directly out of high school, but UMD has enough older persons applying they know how to deal with people like you. SOTA, students older than average, they call them. There're even clubs for older students. Gee, did you know that at 24 you'd be considered an old man?"

"Er, no," Brahim replied, "I don't know what to say." To himself: *Something I'd given up on, not even in dreams.*

"We try to help," she replied. "Now let's look at what we can do right now. There're community colleges that provide distance learning. I'm trying to arrange for you to take basic courses starting very soon. It's a little tricky because a lot's handled by video and computer. This prison's never had this situation and isn't set up for it. It shouldn't be that difficult. All you need is a computer that's connected to the internet. There're computers around here and space to do it. They might even use this room so long as it's under supervision.

"You have to figure out what courses from those available. They'll be basic ones like English, math, history, and the like. Did you have any advanced placement classes in high school? If so, you wouldn't take the courses here."

"Yes, I had some," Brahim answered. "So few students at our high school went to university they had trouble filling the AP classes. Counselors leaned on me to take them so they'd get enough. I don't remember what they were."

"We can look on your high school transcript when we get it," she said. "We can surely find something like a literature course or maybe a foreign language. Did you study a foreign language or speak one?"

"No, no foreign languages," Brahim replied. "We speak Arabic with our families, but English is our language."

"Maybe get you into a Spanish class then," she said.

"No, not Spanish!" Brahim blurted out.

She said: "Oh, you had bad experiences with Spanish."

"Yes," Brahim answered. "Central American students in our town spoke Spanish. Let's say we didn't like them and I wouldn't be motivated to learn their language." He thought: *Whew, thought of a reason without mentioning 'down there'.*

She said to herself: *That's a strong reaction. No need to go there now, but need to be cautious.* To Brahim: "Here's the brochure with the courses they offer and an application form. Look that over and fill it out. We can make a plan next week."

"Thanks." Brahim said thinking: *Wait. If I know Spanish, then if I ever come across those mother fuckin' asshole queer perverts who did that to us in Cuba, I can not only tell them what I think of them in their own language, but do it while I'm hurting them so they can never do anything like that again.*

"Now, Mr. Athlete," she said. "You **are** a challenge. Looking at your file I don't see any career goals we can aim you except something to do with sports. Nothing wrong with that; there's plenty of demand for sports managers, recreation managers, things like that. With all the gyms and health spas opening up, we've got to have someone to work in them and manage them, but you don't seem to have specific goals like your buddy here."

Boudi answered. "I never thought too much about it; I just liked to play sports and am good at it."

"Well, there're lots of ways we could go," she continued. "There're university programs. I think there's one at UMD and I'm pretty sure there's a good one at UWS, that's University of Wisconsin-Superior just across the bridge. St. Scholastica here in Duluth has something. That's a private

Roman Catholic University. I don't know if their being Roman Catholic would appeal to you. You'd need the SAT too. I don't guess you have that, do you."

"No," Boudi answered. "Bob has the brains in the family and took AP courses, the SAT, and things like that. I just sort of went along. I did OK in high school, but nothing special. And, no, Roman Catholics don't bother me. There're plenty of 'em back home."

"We can see about you taking the SAT," she said. *Be careful,* she thought. *They're vulnerable and may just do anything I tell them. I don't want to push him too hard and have him embarrass himself by making too low of a score, especially compared to his buddy who's way up there.*

"Brahim," she continued, "when you go back to the library, look to see if there're SAT preparation books. You can tell me when I come back next week. If not, we can get some. Then Boudi can start looking them over and see if that's something he wants to pursue."

"Yes, ma'am," Brahim said.

"There're community college programs in recreation. I can check on some and tell you when I come next week. Look at that list of distance education courses I just gave Brahim. There're courses on there just for fun. Might be something you'd enjoy and contribute towards sports or recreation. Here's an application form for you and we need your high school transcript too. Here's a letter I drafted."

"Gee, thanks, Ms. Anja," Boudi said "I just don't know what to think or say."

"Yeah, thanks, again," Brahim said. "But one question. Someone's got to pay for this. Did they tell you we're absolutely penniless and can't ask our parents for anything?"

Chapter 13

Thursday, August 24, 2006
Duluth, Minnesota, USA

When Brahim and Boudi asked Anja Ruusulaakso who would pay for their education, she replied: "The government provides released prisoners with a small amount of money, but, more than that, your former employer just sent your pay here where it's being held for you when you get out. I'm sure we can convince them you can use it to pay for application fees, tuition, and things like that."

Boudi and Brahim sat up startled as Brahim almost screamed: "What?!" How's that?!" saying to himself: *Mohammad does business under the table.*

"Don't ask me," she replied. "I figured you'd know. All they did is show me the documents; there're payroll forms and receipts waiting for you showing amounts taken out for taxes and the amount paid."

"Do you know how much it is?" Boudi asked.

"I guess it's all right to tell you," she said. "I thought you'd know. It's something over $2,000 from the best of my recollection. Don't hold me to it if it's less. I just remember thinking to myself it's plenty to cover what you need now for ordering SATs and transcripts, paying application fees, distance learning fees, etc."

Brahim thought: *They must've really gotten in there to find out what Mohammad was up to.*

NEW BEGINNINGS • CHAPTER 13

She continued: "As you know this is a work release program. You have to work and your pay from that can pay for education. We try to find you jobs. You've got one good thing going for you because you're Arabs"

Again surprised, Brahim asked "How's that?"

"There's an Iraqi guy in town," she began. "Rami, a refugee from the first Gulf war. Maybe you know the government spreads refugees all over the country; Rami ended up here. You can imagine that Duluth, Minnesota, is about as far apart from the South of Iraq as the sun is from the moon, and not because of geography."

"Yeah, I guess," Brahim replied. "We've never been to the Middle East; just heard about it."

"Back in Iraq he had a kebab place in a good sized town. For lack of anything better, he got seed money and opened a fast-food type restaurant here featuring kebab and other Middle Eastern food. Rami's Mesopotamian Delights he calls it. The name has a ring to it, certainly more than if he'd called it Iraqi Delights. It was an instant success. It's on Woodland Avenue by the university in sort of a commercial area. Gets lots of business. He also makes a point of serving only halal meat, which is also kosher, and attracts some customers for that reason alone. Those who don't care if it's halal or kosher like it too. I go there a lot.

"Now he wants to expand. He found a place in Canal Park. It's the trendy place to go; restaurants, cafes, and upscale shops. He just finalized the lease and is starting to remodel it. He hires only Middle Eastern people to work for him; has to for the atmosphere, he says. He hopes to open the new place before Christmas to get some of the Christmas crowd. That should be just about the time you're released.

"Not knowing you, but having had a good thorough look at your record, talking to the marshals who brought you here, and talking to the people in Roanoke, I decided to take a chance and tell him about you. He's taking most of the experienced staff to the new place and could use new guys and trainees at the university location.

"Absolutely nothing's guaranteed until he meets and interviews you. He's especially pleased you're English-speaking. Some of his employees are other refugees and don't speak English very well. Are you interested?"

Boudi said eagerly: "Sure I'm interested. I've always thought working in a restaurant could be fun, especially if lots of good looking girls come in."

Anja Ruusulaakso smiled and said: "Well there are pretty girls here in Duluth."

Brahim thought: *Oh she does smile and her face shows expression* and said: "Yeah, I'm interested. I never thought I'd like working in a restaurant, but it doesn't seem bad. I'd rather work in a bookstore, but as you say in this country 'beggars can't be choosers.'"

"Well, it's close to the university and there're plenty of nice places to live around there," she said. "You can walk to work and school and not have to worry about buses or getting a car. Besides, it's not forever."

"Yes, Thanks," Brahim said; "I appreciate it."

She took a quick glance at her watch and said: "That's all for today. I'll be back in a few minutes to pick up the signed letters and next week to pick up your completed forms. Remember you can call me if you have questions even if it's not a designated calling time."

"Thanks, again, Ms. Anja," Boudi said.

"Yes, thanks a lot, Brahim said.

"There's another person waiting to see you," she said. "I hope I haven't kept him waiting too long. He wanted to meet prison officials first. He's the new imam in town. I found out about him from Rami. I met him and talked to him briefly; in fact, we had lunch today at Rami's. This's his first week in town. He's nice." *And cute too*, she thought.

"Can you believe this?!" Boudi said when she left.

"I'm still skeptical," Brahim said. "So far everyone's treated us decently. Maybe not all as nice as her, but no one's been bad to us. I still can't get past stories we've heard about how Arabs and Muslims are so badly mistreated."

CHAPTER 14

Thursday, August 24, 2006
Duluth, Minnesota, USA

A young man entered dressed in well pressed olive-drab Dockers pants, a stylish sporty plaid shirt, a solid dark red tie that matched the colors of the shirt, and shiny new brown loafers with socks to match the trousers, all obviously recently purchased from a good quality clothing store. He wore new frameless glasses.

Boudi and Brahim stood nonchalantly seeing a young person about their age as they each thought: *Gee, I thought it'd be someone older, not our age.*

"*Marhaba*, Omar Abu Deeb," he said offering his hand while they exchanged names and greetings,

Omar thought: *Those names sound familiar, but Abdullah and Ibrahim are among the most common names in the Arabic language. Al Asadi; Zakawi. There're families back in Yemen with those names.*

He began speaking Arabic: "Good afternoon, how are you? Fine?" Then in slightly accented fluent English: "Or would you rather speak English?"

"We're English speaking," Brahim answered. "We speak enough Arabic to get by, but English is the language we use. You sound Yemeni?"

"I am Yemeni," Omar replied then thought: *It can't be. They're Bob and Boudi! Their families don't know where they are, only some place in the Midwest. This is too much of a coincidence. Do I dare let on? No, not now.* He continued: "I'm getting to the point where I speak English better than Arabic. Shall I call you Boudi and Brahim? I suppose you don't have children so I wouldn't call you Abou something."

"Not that we know of," Boudi replied grinning. "Yes, I'm Boudi and he's Brahim or Bob, I guess you know."

"Let's get the official stuff out of the way first," Omar said, "then we can visit a while. I'm the new imam in Duluth. I'm starting the process to get myself designated as the official Islamic chaplain for this prison. It seems they've not had Islamic guests before."

"Yes, that's what they told us," Brahim said.

"As the chaplain and as your imam, the rules of clergy confidentiality apply and from everything I know they're strictly adhered to," Omar continued. "Anything you say to me is in strict confidence unless you specifically say otherwise. I can't be forced to reveal anything you say to me. Are you aware of that?"

"They didn't tell us that; I guess they wait for you to tell us," Brahim said. "It's well known Christian chaplains and clergy have immunity. It'd only be fair and constitutional that Islamic chaplains would have the same."

Gee, this guy's well informed, Omar said to himself and continued: "The reason I said 'unless you specifically state otherwise' is that I can take messages from you and deliver them to the prison staff. I could even appeal to the Justice Department or the President himself if there's something serious enough. Are you aware of that?"

"No," Boudi replied, "but there's no problem."

"I'm just speaking for the record," Omar said. "So far these people seem very reasonable. I should also emphasize this immunity's limited to broad personal issues. You can't use me as a conduit to carry messages about illegal activities outside the prison. Besides, my ethics as an imam will not allow me to do that. Do you understand that?"

"Yes, we understand," Brahim said.

"OK, that's the official part," Omar stated. "How're you two getting along in here?"

NEW BEGINNINGS • CHAPTER 14

"Fine," Brahim said tersely, "considering we're in prison," thinking: *I shouldn't tell him we don't bother with Friday prayers, or other prayers for that matter.*

"I think they're treating us kind of nice," Boudi said. "But, yeah, we're in prison."

"They tell chaplains when we arrive about things that might be helpful for us to know, but they don't attempt to use us as go-betweens; but here I'm getting official again. They're pleased you've adapted well and working well in the library and in athletics"

"Oh they told you that?" Boudi asked.

"Yes, Omar replied. "They said you returned from the hospital about a week ago. Cosmetic surgery; part of the witness protection program."

"Well, sort of," Brahim said. "They put it under the witness protection program. That way we're not supposed to tell anyone anytime anywhere what actually happened. I suppose we could tell you, but for now I don't think I want to. Let's just say that some filthy mother fuckin' pervert bastards beat us up bad."

"That was before we got into custody," Boudi added. "No one in prison did it to us, but they wanted to get us fixed up before we're released in December."

"Sometimes Allah works in ways we don't understand to make amends for other persons' sins," Omar added.

"One good thing did happen today," Boudi said. "Was that Allah working in ways we don't understand?"

"What's that?" Omar asked.

"The lady who was just here, Ms. Anja, said we got about $2,000 back pay from our former boss," Boudi said.

"It was all official like," Brahim said. "Deductions for taxes and all that."

Omar thought: *Good. So Gabe did see to it that the money was delivered.* He replied: "Allah does work through other people. I'm sure it was Allah's doing even if other human beings were actually responsible for the payment and delivery. How's the food situation?"

"OK," Brahim answered. "Prison food's not going to be great. They said they wouldn't serve pork or use pork things. Won't be halal, though."

"Muslims have to do without halal most of the time in this country," Omar said. "I don't eat halal when I'm at school and traveling. Ramadan's coming up in October. They hadn't heard about it and didn't know what to do. I explained and they said they'd try to be accommodating. They can't keep the kitchen open all night so you can eat at bedtime and have an early breakfast before daylight. I'll help come up with a plan. Maybe they can make some food and set it aside for you, like a picnic basket."

Brahim and Boudi nodded and muttered: "OK."

"I'll try to get out here at least a couple of times for iftar when I'm in town," Omar continued. "For the Eid al Fitr, I'm working with them for something special. It may be just you two and me, but we'll do something. I explained that Eid al Fitr is as special to Muslims as Christmas is to Christians and I pointedly reminded them they have special events for Christmas and ease the rules so they need to do the same for you two. They agreed in principle, but need to know what I have in mind."

Gee, Boudi thought. *He's being nice too.*

Where's this guy coming from? Brahim said to himself. *I've never known an imam to talk like this and do things like this, but then Mohammad was the only imam we knew.*

"Maybe you guys'd like to know more about me," Omar offered. "I'm not going to take time to tell you everything; we can get acquainted over time as I stop by.

"I'm from Yemen, you know. I've been working on a PhD at the University of Minnesota; that's in the twin cities maybe you know. This is my last year. They got me a part-time job teaching here at UMD and also as part-time imam for the Islamic community here. I hear you two guys'll stay here in Duluth after you're released. I hope you can get involved in the mosque. Now it's your turn."

Brahim thought: *He's getting a PhD. In my dreams I thought I wanted a PhD.*

Boudi thought: *He seems like a cool, really nice guy. Not athletic looking, but bet he could kick a soccer ball.* He said: "Right now I just can't think of anything, er, Omar. You said you're coming back?"

"Yeah, sure," Omar replied. You didn't think so?"

"Well, you are awfully busy," Boudi said.

"An imam's never too busy to tend to his people," Omar said. "I admit, I'm not here every day and may not be as attentive as I'd like. I do have to teach and finish that dissertation, but I'll be back."

Brahim finally said: "I don't know what to think and what to believe. Since nine-eleven, all we've heard is how Muslims, and Arabs in particular, are being screwed over in this country and we've both experienced it. Now everything seems to be turning around for us."

Omar said: "Don't kid yourself. This's a great country, but it's not paradise on Earth. There's still bad stuff going on and there'll continue to be. This country's had lots of immigrants from lots of places. Lots of them have gotten screwed over. Now, unfortunately, it's the turn for Arabs. Even so, it's not as bad as the Japanese who were put in internment camps during World War II.

"There're some damned good things in this country too. That doesn't mean that they can't get better, but take the good while you can get it. Allah never promised we'd have a perfect existence. Instead, we have the blessed guidance of the Prophet and the beautiful Q'ran to give us inner peace even though we're facing turmoil outside. Somehow I think we're going to have great discussions over time, but maybe this's enough for today. What do you think?"

"Yeah," Brahim replied. "I need time to think."

"Yes, I guess so," Boudi said thinking: *just as I was getting to feel good about things, he's going. He'll be back he says. I hope he means it.*

"Let me guide you in afternoon prayer," Omar said. "It's not exactly the right time, but that's OK. I'm sure they don't have any prayer rugs here. Maybe I need to get some if I can. Let's move the table out of the way and the chairs. Wait a second; I'll go tell the guard what we're doing."

After leading them in prayers, Omar offered goodbyes and left giving them three Arabic kisses on the cheeks.

Chapter 15

Tuesday, August 29, 2006
Baghdad International Airport, Iraq

Jimmy said cheerfully as Ali approached: "Hey, Doc."

"Hello," Ali said. "I was told to see Colonel Jones."

Hearing voices, Colonel Jones went to the door and said: "Please come in. I've been expecting you. Please take a chair around the table; others'll be here soon."

Others? Ali asked himself.

Colonel Jones asked: "Something to drink? I'm having iced tea. Please join me. We finally convinced the kitchen to start brewing the iced tea instead of serving it out of a can or bottle. You've probably had some."

"Er, yes sir," Ali said. "They usually bring me a glass when they bring my food."

"You can have anything you like now, though," Colonel Jones said and asked Jimmy to bring the tea and something for him and Carrie. He said: "I'm so sorry about the loss of your friend Viktor. It must've been a big blow for you."

Ali replied: "Thanks. I appreciate your concern."

"We really appreciate the help you've given us," Colonel Jones continued. "Dr. Bob says you've done really good things to deal with unruly detainees."

NEW BEGINNINGS • CHAPTER 15

"Er, thanks," Ali said thinking: *Why's he saying that to me now? It's a month until they go.*

"So far I haven't had a chance to find out much about you other than you're a medical doctor and from Syria," Colonel Jones said. "You speak perfect English, just like an American. Where'd you learn?"

Ali described briefly his early years in New York and the international school in Damascus; his explanation was interrupted when they heard Jimmy say: "Please go on in. The colonel's expecting you."

Carrie arrived the same moment with four glasses of iced tea offering two to the newcomers saying she would get more for herself and Jimmy.

Major Armstrong introduced U.S. Army Lieutenant Colonel George Baba, deputy in charge of administration and personnel for U. S. forces in Iraq who shook hands with Colonel Jones and Ali: saying "*Marhaba. George Baba.*"

Colonel Jones began: "Josh, good to see you. You asked for the meeting; maybe tell us what's on your mind."

Major Armstrong replied: "Thanks. It's a pleasure to be in good company." To Ali: "Thank you for the good things you've been doing here. Not only do we hear good things about your medical skills, our interpreters tell us how good you are in deflecting detainees' attempts to get you involved in their issues, but calming them down."

"Er, thanks," Ali said. "Sometimes they just want someone to listen to them and talk to them." He said to himself: *He's the second person to thank me. It's like they're about to say good bye.*

"Also, you've done minor surgery that makes detainees more comfortable," Major Armstrong continued.

"Yes," Ali replied. "Some have injuries in places that can be uncomfortable and often takes very little to help them."

"I'm sure you know this unit goes home in a month," Major Armstrong continued. "We need to do something with you so that's why we're here."

Ali thought: *Yes, just as I thought. Where'm I being shunted off to next?* Then said: "Yes, I know something else'd have to happen soon."

"There'll be another Reserve unit coming to this prison," Major Armstrong continued. "We don't know yet what type of medical staff it'd have. We could keep you with them in much the same status you are now, but we think we have a better plan. There's a new prison here at the airport that's just opened and we can use you there."

Ali's face brightened as he asked: "As a doctor?"

"Sort of," Major Armstrong answered. "We'll get to that in a moment."

"But will I still be a detainee?" Ali asked interrupting.

"Technically, yes," Major Armstrong replied. "We're evaluating detainees to see which ones are a continued threat to our operations and the Iraqi government. Those who aren't are being released. You're clearly not a threat so you'll no doubt be released when we evaluate you. That's why Colonel Baba's here. George."

Lieutenant Colonel Baba said: "We've realized we need locally-hired longer-term medical personnel in the prisons. There's a risk we'll get too many like Dr. Sensenberg who're not always qualified to deal with situations that arise."

Noting Colonel Jones's displeasure, Major Armstrong interrupted: "Don't misunderstand, sir, Dr. Bob's a fine man and a fine pediatrician. He's done wonders to earn goodwill with the local people when he treats the children."

"We were going to tell you later, but we can tell you now," Lieutenant Colonel Baba added. "We're recommending him for a commendation medal for his work in the communities with local children and helping with children in local hospitals."

"Ah, OK," Colonel Jones commented, pleased.

Lieutenant Colonel Baba continued: "We now have authority to hire locally. The position can't be called a medical doctor unless he, it has to be a 'he' working with male detainees, is recognized as such in the United States. It can be a physician's assistant or some title we'll create for someone with Iraqi medical certification. We've gotten an OK to explore hiring you. The most significant obstacle is the lack of an Iraqi medical certificate. We've approached Iraqi authorities about getting you one; they've agreed in principle, but they want to see your credentials from Syria. For that, we need your cooperation.

NEW BEGINNINGS • CHAPTER 15

"You may have noticed I speak Arabic which'll make it easier. It may be easier yet because it's likely Syria and Iraq will establish diplomatic relations soon making contacts among government agencies easier. The question is are you interested? Shall we pursue this?"

"Er, yes, I guess," Ali stammered. "It's been good working with you Americans; you treated me nice with respect as a person and as a doctor. It'd be good to know what may happen over the long run. Being in this state of limbo has been terrible, emotionally, psychologically."

Lieutenant Colonel Baba continued: "You asked about the long run. Hiring a Syrian national could have repercussions as I'm sure you can figure out with the current state of relations between the U.S. and Syria. We've also approached Iraqi authorities about your obtaining Iraqi nationality. Again, they're willing to consider it in principle. The fact that your name is Ali makes the Shia majority more willing to entertain the notion and the fact your family name is associated with a minority group, the Alawites, who have no issues with the competing groups in Iraq, also works in your favor. Also having your skills as a cosmetic surgeon is appealing to them. What do you think about this prospect?"

Ali again was visibly shaken by the question and said: "Gee, er, I don't know about that. That's something I'd've never thought of. I guess I'm open to the possibility, but this's a lot for me to absorb all at once."

"Fortunately you don't need to make that decision immediately," Lieutenant Colonel Baba continued. "We've considered options for what we might do that'd be in your best interests and ours too and this is the best one we came up with for now. It's difficult to know what's in another's best interests. You don't want to go back to Syria and we concur for our own reasons. There're countries that'll accept refugees under some circumstances, but in view of your recent past, things that can't be easily reversed, that's not an option. Plus, it's not in our interest to reveal certain things to other governments about you right now." Colonel Jones interjected: "Ali, would you like to go back to your room and think about this for a while? These gentlemen can wait for an answer."

"Yes for sure," Lieutenant Colonel Baba interjected. "Things happen slowly in Iraq. That's why we approached you as early as we could. Maybe if we know by Friday, the Iraqi weekend, we can begin pursing the medical thing on Sunday when they're back to work."

Colonel Jones suggested: "Tomorrow before you go to the clinic, come here and let's talk. I can't give you advice, but I'm a good listener."

He walked to Ali's chair and gently put his arm on his arm just below his shoulder to guide him out.

Ali left saying: "Thanks. I appreciate your interest. Thanks for the iced tea."

When Ali left, Colonel Jones said softly: "Sorry if I overruled you. Call it a funeral director's intuition. We have to be able to detect when someone's too overwhelmed to make a good decision. The more unscrupulous of our profession take that opportunity to sell lots of things clients don't need or want, but Lincoln's a small city and we have a good reputation. You'll get what you want. When he comes to see me tomorrow morning, and I'll see that he does come, I'll just listen. If by some chance something goes totally and completely wrong in his head, I can deal with that too."

"You're right," Major Armstrong commented. "I've been working with you enough to trust your judgment."

"I have to trust yours and Josh's judgment," Lieutenant Colonel Baba said. "I'm sure you're right."

Later Ali lay tossing and turning thinking: *Me an Iraqi? Can I do that? All my life I wanted to go back to America, be like an American, like when I was a kid. Sure blew that when I let them change me. Can never go back.*

OK. So I stay in Iraq. Become Iraqi. Can't be worse than being Syrian.

What'll I tell the colonel tomorrow morning? He's nice to me. This's too much. Somehow got to turn my brain off. Stop these thoughts racing through my brain.

Finally, he fell into a fitful sleep.

CHAPTER 16

Monday, September 4, 2006
Baltimore, Maryland, USA

Frank walked north on Charles Street thinking: *Hope this place's worth the walk in humidity and hot sun. Baltimore gay website said it's bar of the year, whole complex of places, and a restaurant. With mobs at the Inner Harbor, couldn't eat there any time soon.*

Never felt lonely before when I moved. Now that I have feelings, loneliness hurts, bad. Damn I miss Paco! Somehow, someway has to work out for him to move here. ... Hey, that looks like it and there's the restaurant. More like a café, maybe Italian, but hey, if it serves food.

He entered a smallish dining area with tasteful décor and about ten simple wooden tables. A waiter who was about five feet nine inches with spiked coal black hair like it was fresh out of a bottle, green eyes, dressed in very tight fitting blue jeans and a sleeveless t-shirt with psychedelic designs said to sit where he liked and asked with a flirtatious smile if he would like a menu?"

"Yes, please," Frank said as masculine as he could, saying to himself: *He's so gay he flames.*

The waiter brought a menu and asked flirtatiously: "May I get you something to drink now?"

Frank thought: *Bud Light's not macho enough,* then asked: "You have Samuel Adams?"

"Sure do," the waiter replied.

THREE KISSES

GRAND CENTRAL GAY ENTERTAINMENT COMPLEX, BALTIMORE, MARYLAND.

Frank read the menu thinking: *in this heat nothing heavy, no pizza or pasta, not even pasta salad; that California Italian chicken Caesar salad isn't macho enough. Roast beef sandwich's good. This's a good time to go pee. Hey, I recognize that guy sitting over there; I see him at the NSA. Let me slip past him quickly; maybe he won't see me.*

Brad Spencer, wearing khaki Bermuda shorts, a blue t-shirt that read 'Abercrombie & Fitch' in white letters, and brown deck shoes without socks, looked up from his California Italian chicken Caesar salad to take a drink of a draft beer and said to himself: *I know that guy from somewhere.* After a moment: *Work! Wears a uniform. He's a marine, but not one of the cute young guard hunks. That's him coming back by now.*

He put down his fork, stood to shake hands, and said: "Hello. I think we work at the same place. Brad Spencer."

Frank, startled, muttered: "Hello," thinking: *I'll keep on walking, but not so fast as to be rude. Can't just say nothing; we do work at the same place. Maybe he'll get the hint I don't want to be sociable.*

"Frank," he said shaking hands half-heartedly.

"You're with the Marine guards, aren't you?" Brad asked. "I'm in the Arabic language section."

"Yes," Frank replied thinking: *Is he trying to come onto me or something?*

The waiter came from behind with Frank's beer and said: "Oh, there you are. You want me to set the beer here with Brad? I can get your glasses. You want the menu too?"

Frank said "No," which the waiter interpreted as not the menu, set the beer down and went for the glasses.

"Oh, please join me," Brad said. "I'd love company. I've been alone all weekend. My boyfriend's away and I don't want to go out hunting, if you know what I mean."

Frank muttered: "OK, thanks," saying to himself: *A boyfriend. Maybe he's not trying to come on to me.*

The waiter returned and asked: "Ready to order?"

"Yes, roast beef sandwich," Frank said.

"Comes with potato chips and pickles," the waiter continued. "Something else? A side of coleslaw?"

"No that's enough," Frank replied.

"What about you, Brad? Anything else?" he asked.

"No, thanks, Robbie," Brad answered.

When the waiter was out of ear shot, Frank asked: "You know him?"

"Yes, a little," Brad answered. "He goes to the church sometimes and Jason, that's my boyfriend, and I come in here a fair amount when we're in Baltimore clubbing."

"The church?" Frank asked.

"Yes, the MCC, Metropolitan Community Church," Brad replied. "You heard of it?"

Frank replied: "Some guys in Cincinnati talked about it. Didn't know it was all over. I'm not a church person."

"Oh, it's all over, including in Europe," Brad continued. "Jason and I just started going regularly."

"Please go ahead and eat," Frank said saying to himself: *I can be polite; no need to avoid conversation.*

"Thanks," Brad said and asked: "You're from Cincinnati?"

"I'm not from anywhere," Frank replied. "I'm a Marine Corps brat who moved around. The nearest thing to a home is Ohio where I just moved from, but not Cincinnati. I lived there longer than anywhere else; own a house."

"Oh, where in Ohio?" Brad asked.

"Around Dayton," Frank answered. "I was at Wright-Patterson Air Force Base."

"I'm from Minnesota, the twin cities," Brad added. "Jason's from Southside Virginia. He's there for a big family reunion; always held Labor Day weekend."

Robbie brought the roast beef sandwich along with an assortment of steak sauce, Tabasco sauce, and a homemade horseradish sauce asking: "Anything else you'd like now?"

"No, thanks," Frank replied.

"You, Brad?" he asked. "Dessert? Another beer?"

"No, thanks," he said, "gotta watch my girlish figure."

As Robbie took Brad's dishes away, Frank sprinkled Tabasco sauce on the meat, put a generous amount of horseradish on his plate, and began eating.

"You like it hot," Brad said smiling. "How butch. What brings you here today?"

Frank replied. "I'm new here; thought I'd check out Baltimore. I was at the Inner Harbor but it was too crowded so I walked this direction to see what I could find."

"Maybe a little like me," Brad said. "I've been alone all weekend and I'm going stir crazy. The only time I've been out of the apartment was to go grocery shopping and to church yesterday. I just had to get out today. I want to go to the bookstore so I thought I'd stop here for lunch."

"The bookstore?" Frank asked.

"Yeah, the gay bookstore, Lambda Rising," Brad said. "There's one here and the big one in DC at Du Pont Circle. I want to look for books on gay Christianity."

Frank muttered: "Oh," while Brad thought: *Maybe he isn't gay. Maybe that's why he's stand-offish. Doesn't know about the church and the bookstore.* "Say, you are gay, aren't you?" he asked. "I just assumed you are if you're in here. Sorry if I misjudged. Hope you're not offended."

Frank said: "You know I am a Marine Corps officer."

"Yes," Brad replied, "but that doesn't mean anything. There're plenty of military guys at the gay places here and especially in DC. They keep a low profile, but hey, sorry if I said something wrong."

Frank said: "It's OK. Believe it or not, I'm just now coming out at my age. It's taking a little getting used to say I'm gay."

"Oh, cool," Brad said relieved. "Lots of guys come out at all ages; some of them old enough to be my father or even grandfather. Plenty of 'em have kids or even grandkids."

"Oh, OK," Frank mumbled with his mouth full.

"You have a partner or boyfriend?" Brad asked.

Frank replied: "Partner, no; boyfriend, well, sort of."

"Back in Ohio?" Brad continued asking.

"Yeah," Frank said chewing.

"It must be sad leaving him behind," Brad said. "I don't want to think about what'd happen if Jason or I got another job and had to move. Are you going to try to keep it going now that you're here?"

"Yeah," Frank said. "He might get a job transfer here.

"Oh, good," Brad offered. "What work does he do?"

"Nurse," Frank answered with his mouth full again.

"Oh, work in a hospital here?" Brad asked.

Frank replied: "He works in a Veterans' Administration nursing home. There's a VA nursing home in Baltimore. He might get a transfer. They want male nurses. If there's an opening here, he could get it."

"That sounds good," Brad continued.

"Yeah," Frank said smiling. "One reason I came to Baltimore today is to see where it's located and what kind of housing there might be."

"Oh, you're going to live in Baltimore," Brad offered.

"No," Frank replied: "We won't live together."

"Jason and I don't live together, either," Brad continued. "Our work's too far apart. He works way out by Manassas in Prince William County in Virginia. He lives closer in to DC, but wouldn't think of living as far away as Maryland; he'd have to commute two hours every day each way and I'd have to do the same if I lived over there. We spend just about every weekend together. He almost always comes here. One reason is to go to church, but his apartment's always cluttered. He wants to be an artist and has his painting stuff all over the place. His day job's a graphic designer."

Robbie saw Frank was finished, sauntered over to the table, smiled, and asked: "May I get you anything else?"

"No, thanks," Frank answered.

"How was it?" Robbie asked grinning. "Roast beef's what the butch guys order. Twinks like Brad get salads."

"It was good," Frank answered smiling. "Really was."

"I'll get your checks then?" Robbie asked.

Brad said: "Say, I'm going to the bookstore next. You want to go with me, see where it is, and what's there? It's just a couple of blocks away; I can show you other gay spots too. They're all here within a couple of blocks of each other, all but one; the Eagle's about 10 blocks further up. You interested in the Eagle? It's an S&M place."

"I might be," Frank replied. "Yeah, sure I'd be glad to see other places too."

Chapter 17

Monday, September 4, 2006
Baltimore, Maryland, USA

Brad and Frank left Lambda Rising bookstore each carrying a bag; Brad commented: "There's Club Hippo; that's the other big gay club here. My car's parked near there."

HIPPO GAY CLUB, BALTIMORE, MARYLAND

"Thanks," Frank said. "That's nice of you."

Frank got in and said: "These little cars really have a lot of room inside."

"Yeah, that's one reason I bought it," Brad said. "A gay magazine recommended a Mini Cooper as the perfect twink car. It is, don't you think?"

"Yeah," Frank chuckled saying to himself: *He even calls himself a twink. Been hanging out with tough guys at the Serpent too much. More to gay life than I imagined. Seems like this's going to be a good move.*

Driving away, Brad asked: "Where do you live?"

"Laurel," Frank answered.

"Hey, that's where I live," Brad said. "Say, why don't you come to my place. We can hang out, maybe go to the pool. I'm a good cook, if I do say so myself."

Frank, surprised, said to himself: *Here I didn't think he was coming onto me. How can I tell him I'm not into twinks without hurting his feelings? Besides, I'm not ready to be with anyone else but Paco.*

Brad noticing Frank's hesitation added: "Hey, sorry if I came on too strong with my 'Minnesota Nice'. Back home when we're with someone whose company we like, we just keep inviting them. Don't misunderstand; I'm not inviting you to stay the night or even to the bedroom."

Whew, Frank thought. *No hurt feelings, but what excuse can I give? Wait. Wouldn't hurt to go. I'm lonely and he's nice.* He said: "I've never experienced 'Minnesota Nice', but, yeah, I can come. What should I bring?"

"Nothing," Brad replied, "not this time. I'm not shy; bring something next time or invite me to your place."

He drove down Charles Street then to the Eagle saying: "Jason and I went there once to see what it's like; guess we're not butch enough. Where's your car parked?"

"Down by the Inner Harbor," Frank replied. "Just off of a street called Gay Street, believe it or not."

NEW BEGINNINGS • CHAPTER 17

BALTIMORE EAGLE GAY LEATHER BAR

"Everyone knows where that is," Brad grinned.

After a couple moments, Frank said: "There, that cream colored Mountaineer with Florida plates."

"Oh, a Mountaineer. Gee, how butch," Brad giggled. "I take the Baltimore-Washington Parkway and the Laurel Fort Meade exit, then right again at the Knight's Inn and Bob Evans. You know where that is?"

"Hey, that's where I turn to get to my place." Frank replied. "We must live really close."

Laurel, Maryland, USA

Several minutes later, Brad opened the door to his apartment saying: "Welcome; look how clean and orderly it is. You won't see that much more. Not that I'm a bad housekeeper, but I'm not always this neat either. Being bored with Jason away, I really cleaned and organized. I almost said **straight**end," laughing.

THREE KISSES

BRAD'S APARTMENT, LAUREL, MARYLAND

"Thanks." Frank replied as he spotted colorful modern-art-type paintings on the walls with bright colors and almost psychedelic designs.

Brad said: "Those are Jason's. Nice, aren't they?"

Frank thought: *They do add color and brighten up the room, but wouldn't want them on my walls.* He said: "Yes, they add lots of color and excitement"

"Can I get you something?" Brad asked. "Beer, soft drinks, iced tea, something else?"

"Water'd be great hot as it is outside," Frank replied.

Brad said: "We can have wine later; you like wine?"

"Oh, yes," Frank answered and chuckled.

"I've got Lebanese wine," Brad said. "I got hooked on it when I was in Jordan. Sometimes I make an Arabian Nights dinner for Jason and serve it, but don't think I am in the mood now. Thought I'd just grill lamb chops."

"Fine with me," Frank replied. "Lebanese wine you say? I worked with a Lebanese guy at Wright-Patt, or his parents are from there. He said how good Lebanese wine is."

"There're at least a couple of shops in DC that sell it," Brad added. "In DC you can get almost anything from anywhere in the world. You should check it out sometime."

"I will," Frank said. "I'll tell him if I see him again."

After pouring water, Brad said: "Say, you want to go for a swim? We have a nice pool and there're usually a lot of nice hunks there."

Frank replied: "I don't have a swim suit. I could go get one. I live less than a mile away."

Brad said. "Bet Jason's'd fit you. He's skinny like you. Let's go see. I said you're not invited to the bedroom. I'm sure you know that was just a figure of speech."

Frank smiled: "Yeah, I know what you meant."

In the bedroom, his eyes immediately went to drawings on the wall that looked like charcoal and chalk, a couple of different colors. They were not life-like, not caricatures, but some recognizable as Brad. Others a slender man with a longish pony tail and goatee. Two were obviously nude but not full frontal and revealing.

"Those are more of Jason's art," Brad said. "That's him; self-portrait in front of a mirror. Good, aren't they?"

Frank muttered: "Yeah, interesting."

Brad handed a pair of royal blue swim trunks saying: "Try these. You can change in the bathroom if you like."

Frank closed the bathroom door thinking: *At least he isn't expecting to undress in front of each other.*

He returned to the bedroom wearing the swimming trunks and noticed Brad wearing red boxer-type ones and brown plastic-rim faux tortoise shell glasses rather than his usual contact lenses.

Brad gave Frank a large towel and a pair of flip-flops saying: "I'm going to go set the lamb chops out to thaw; meet you by the front door."

During the next hour and a half, they splashed in the water, lay in the sun, lay in the shade, exchanged glances when a particularly attractive man walked by, and in general relaxed without much direct communication.

Frank took the opportunity for serious lap swimming which caused Brad to comment: "Gee, how butch."

While lying in the shade, he asked: "What's your boyfriend like? You've seen pictures of Jason and heard me talk about him, but I don't know much about your man. You may've told me his name, but I don't remember."

"Paco," Frank replied.

"Oh, his name must be Francisco," Brad said. "I remember from high school Spanish that someone with the name Francisco has the nickname Paco."

"Yes," Frank said. "He's big and husky, not really fat; about six-two with broad shoulders. No one'd accuse him of being soft and tender, except his eyes. He has soft green eyes that really get to you. His hair's brown and short; he keeps it that way so it doesn't get in his way at work. People say he doesn't look Mexican as if there's a way a Mexican's supposed to look.

"He can be both sweet and gentle and strict and tough at the same time. They love him at the nursing home for that. He can lift and carry old guys who can't make it on their own, intimidate the old farts who still think they're tough, but his sweet gentle side soothes and calms the ones who're just plain scared." *Whew*, he thought. *That's the first time I've described him to anyone. Feels good.*

"He sounds nice," Brad said. "How'd you two meet?"

"At a bar in Cincinnati," Frank answered.

"S&M place like the Eagle?" Brad asked.

"Yes, exactly," Frank said thinking: *Might as well go ahead and talk about it; no need to keep it secret.* "It started with me and another guy. We were just, er, buddies, if you know what I mean. Then we hooked up with two Mexican cousins who'd been getting it on since puberty. For a while it was mostly foursome. None of us lived in Cincinnati so we'd meet weekends. About a year ago, we paired off more, me and Paco, and the other two."

"Sounds good," Brad commented.

"What about you and Jason?" Frank asked.

"Ran into him a couple of times at the Nation, a dance club in DC," Brad began. "At first he didn't appeal to me. Kind of a mixture of a long-hair hippie and country red neck and he smoked, but was trying to stop. I provided the final push to get him to stop because I told him there's no way I can be around a smoker. He kept dogging me every time we'd be there at the same time. I liked the attention and began to realize he's nice after all.

"One night, he suggested we go to another place nearby and I went along. It had a dark room and he sort of hinted, well more than hinted, we should go to the dark room. I told him dark rooms are not my style. To cut the story short, we ended up here at my place. Turns out he's really fun and nice to be with, in every way."

"Oh, nice, interesting," Frank said.

Chapter 18

Monday, September 4, 2006
Laurel, Maryland, USA

After an afternoon at the pool, Frank and Brad went back to Brad's apartment where he said "You can shower first while I start the charcoal. I'll get you a fresh towel."

When Frank came out of the bathroom with a towel wrapped around him, Brad was standing with only a towel over his shoulder causing Frank to say to himself: *So much for his modesty.* Once dressed, he went to the living room, looked at Jason's paintings again saying to himself: *Not bad after all.*

Brad came in wearing the same shorts and a navy blue t-shirt with light blue letters 'Polo Club', saying: "Seems you're kind of drawn to them."

"Yeah," Frank replied.

"Come keep me company while I start the lamb chops and rice cooking and make a salad," Brad said handing a bottle of wine to Frank saying: "You want to open this?"

"Chateau Ksara Cabernet Sauvignon," Frank read. "My co-worker said there's lots of French influence in Lebanon."

"Yes, it was a French colony," Brad said. "Lots of things in French there; not like Jordan where everything's English or Arabic. Jordan was a British colony."

"I don't know much about that part of the world," Frank commented. "My co-worker went there once to look up family and explore his roots."

Frank poured wine for him and Brad and held up his glass for a toast; Brad said: "Akhlan. That means 'welcome' in Arabic. Glad you could come over."

"Thanks," Frank said taking a sip. "This's good wine."

"That's 'shouqran' in Arabic," Brad added. "Means thank you. Excuse me a sec while I put the meat on the grill.

When Brad returned, Frank said: "Say, this IS good wine. If Patrick ever comes to visit, I'll make sure I get some for him. You ever been to Lebanon?"

"I was there a few days when I was in Jordan," Brad replied as he started the rice. "Say, let's go sit on the balcony. It'll take the rice about 20 minutes to cook and I need to watch the lamb chops. Lebanon's a nice country; most advanced and tolerant one there. Even has a couple of gay bars. Can't imagine what it's like now after the fuckin' Israeli's bombed the shit out of it, pardon my language."

"You don't approve of Israel either," Frank said.

"Well, it's more complicated than just approving or not," Brad began. "Sure Hizbollah began this war and needs to be stopped, but the Israelis are as much of terrorists and bullies as Hizbollah and always have been. The naïve people here don't realize it."

"You're the second person in a month who's told me that," Frank said. "My co-worker said the same thing. If both of you say that and you've both been there, there must be some truth to it."

Brad continued: "The things the Israelis did to the Palestinians who were forced to take refuge in Jordan is pathetic. And towards Christians and Muslims alike. The fuckin' Israelis don't care what religion the Arabs are. They just want to get rid of 'em.

"Christian groups in this country are so damned naïve. They think there's some special bond between Jews and Christians. Even at the MCC, many think because both gays and Jews were persecuted in the holocaust they have something in common. Some of them even still subscribe to the wacko fundamentalist notion that Jesus will come again when the Jews take over Israel again. The Palestinians bring it on themselves too. Hamas and Fattah are not any better and all Middle Easterners, Christians, Muslims, and Jews alike, are as homophobic as they come in this world."

"I'm getting an idea of that," Frank replied.

"Sorry if I'm getting so worked up," Brad said.

"Oh, no problem," Frank replied. "I eat this stuff up. I could go on and on, but I don't have much formal education in the subject like you must have."

"Oh, I just studied the Arabic language at the University of Minnesota," Brad continued. "That doesn't constitute much formal education. Sometime soon I want to go back to school; maybe get a master's degree in Middle Eastern studies or foreign affairs."

"Oh, really?" Frank stated. "I've been thinking about the same thing when I get out of the Marine Corps in about five years. I need to do something for the rest of my life. With only an outdated bachelor's degree, I'm not qualified for much of anything and the Marine Corps hasn't given me experience I can develop into a second career. If you have information about good masters programs, please let me know."

Brad continued: "Almost ready. Yes, I've been checking them out. The University of Maryland isn't half bad and it's just right here nearby; 20 minute drive. The two biggies are George Washington and Georgetown in DC. If I find something out, I'll definitely let you know. Here let me rinse this plate off and check on the rice."

While putting meat on the clean plate he asked: "What kind of undergraduate degree do you have and from where?"

"Engineering from the Citadel," Frank answered."

"I've heard about that place," Brad said as he motioned Frank to follow him inside. "I read about it in Pat Conroy's book, *Lords of Discipline*. Sure wasn't a good place for gays. Isn't that where a guy threw himself in front of a train rather than admit he's gay?"

NEW BEGINNINGS • CHAPTER 18

Frank followed him inside saying: "There was more to it than just being gay, but yeah, that's the book. I wasn't gay back then, so I couldn't identify with it."

"Oh?" Brad said skeptically. "I'll make the salad; go ahead and tell me more about the Citadel if you like."

"You want me to set the table?" Frank asked as he thought: *That sounded silly saying I wasn't gay back then.* Frank continued as he set the table: "Of course I was gay back then. I was born gay. I know that now, but I was like a zombie back then. Not gay; not straight; just going through the motions, doing what was expected of me. If that meant making fun of gays, of course I did it."

"Yeah, I know what you're saying," Brad added. "Jason says it was that way for him in high school and that fundamentalist church his family attended, but then he went to VCU, that's Virginia Commonwealth University in case you haven't heard about it, to study art and graphics and really got an awakening."

Frank thought as he sat the table: *Gee, the more I talk to this guy, the more I learn and realize I'm not all that different after all. The only other gay guys I've talked to are Paco, Luie, and Fred, and they're not a cross section of the gay world for sure. It's good I ran into him.*

"You want more wine?" Brad asked as he brought food to the table. "I'd like more, but I can't drink a whole bottle by myself and don't want to be drinking alone."

"Oh, don't know," Frank said. "I have to drive home."

Brad said. "I sure don't want you to get into trouble. 'Minnesota Nice' wouldn't let me send you out the door with too much to drink if you have to drive. I'd have to invite you to stay over, but only on the couch. Seriously, it's up to you."

"Oh, what the hell," Frank said. It's less than a mile and I can walk if need be, even if it is hot and humid. Go ahead and bring the bottle."

Chapter 19

Monday, September 4, 2006
Laurel, Maryland, USA

At the dinner table with wine glasses filled, Brad lifted his and said: "Sakhtain. That's Arabic."

"Yeah, 'To your health,'" Frank said smugly. "That's what my colleague said when I had dinner with him."

Brad giggled feeling the effects of the wine, raised his glass again, and said: "Here's to a good life in Maryland with Paco and a future in foreign affairs."

Frank raised his glass, smiled, and said: "Thanks. Here's to you and Jason and a future in foreign affairs."

While eating, Frank asked: "Just what is it you do? Something to do with the Arabic language, but seems to be quiet. The mission of the NSA is cryptography and breaking codes. They told me I should read Dan Brown's book *The Fortress*. Nothing about Arabic language stuff in there."

"It keeps a low profile, but isn't secret," Brad said. "Haven't you been reading and hearing about the fuss over eavesdropping on private cell phone conversations?"

"Yes," Frank replied, "but didn't know it was at the NSA. Is that what you do?"

"Yes, if in the Arabic language," Brad continued. "We listen to Arabic language conversations coming into the U.S. The vast majority

NEW BEGINNINGS • CHAPTER 19

are family so we click off after a few moments. Others we listen to and record if there's something of intelligence value. We're trained not to make judgments; if something's even remotely out of the routine, we record it and turn it over to be evaluated. Actually, kind of boring, but a job and lets me use my Arabic language skills until I can get more education and do something else."

"I thought the big scandal was over domestic eavesdropping, not overseas calls," Frank commented.

"It is, but sometimes it all gets tied up together," Brad said. "Say, you might appreciate this. It was sort of funny. Won't hurt to tell you; not classified. Besides, you're a military officer and have clearances out the wazoo."

"There's 'need to know'," Frank said. "Don't tell me if it compromises something."

"Nah," Brad said. "You might find it funny too. Was Good Friday; I remember because I decided not to go to church; had a date that night with Jason. I work with a couple of straight guys on my shift, at least I think they're straight.

"One of them started laughing and said: 'hey listen to this,' and turned on the loudspeaker; 'Couple of Arab queers', or something like that. The call was from Syria and now that I think about it, going somewhere in Ohio.

"The voice in Arabic from Syria told the person at the other end to check some guy's dick to see if it was cut or uncut and how big it was. My co-worker was laughing about gay Arabs. At first I didn't say anything because I'm not out to them. Then I realized they were talking in clinical terms, not like gay guys would talk, not like the ones I knew in Jordan."

Frank put down his fork and listened intently.

Brad continued: "I told him to start recording. He didn't want to, saying it was just a couple of gays having fun. When I told him it was clinical, he kind of woke up and did it. Now get this, the guy who got the call called another guy in the U.S. speaking perfect English like you and me; he had been talking in a strange Arabic dialect before. The guy he was talking to spoke English, but with an accent. The caller said he needed to check some guy to see if he is cut and how big he was, only he said 'circumcised'. But, get this. The guy receiving the call didn't even know what it meant and couldn't understand why anyone would be uncircumcised."

Frank thought: *Oh, my god. This's too much. Too bizarre. Too much of a coincidence. Better force myself to eat something or else he's going to notice.* He muttered something like: "Interesting."

Brad continued: "We marked the phone numbers to set off an alarm if there was another call and sure enough in a few moments the sequence of calls came back in reverse saying some guy had a big uncut dick. The guy in Syria got all upset and panicky."

"Weird," Frank said with his mouth half full beginning to panic himself.

"Yeah, for sure," Brad said. "One of the guys I work with wanted to erase the recordings that were in the U.S. because we've been warned not be caught recording domestic conversations. We convinced him the international calls didn't make sense without the domestic ones; keep the recordings filed away, but not do anything unless something else happened."

"Oh," Frank mumbled and thought: *Maybe this didn't get reported. Maybe a bizarre fucked up weird coincidence.*

"That's not all," Brad continued. "A couple of weeks later, we were sitting bored when the alarms went off. The phones we'd recorded were being used again. Some government agency with blocked numbers. We're guessing it's the FBI. We just heard bits of the conversation because they weren't talking directly into the phones, just dialing them to see what the numbers were. They said something about a package coming from Atlanta. We thought this was too weird and decided to report it, half expecting to get our wrists slapped for recording the domestic conversations. We didn't hear another word. Hey, you don't look good. Something wrong with the food? Too much wine?"

"No," Frank replied. "Weird story. Got me thinking about something that happened way back; can't tell you about it though. I never heard how that turned out either."

"At first I was scared they'd figure out I'm gay and I'd be outted over this," Brad continued, "but nothing happened. I also realized if I did get outted, it wouldn't be that big of a deal. I might lose my job; I might not. This country's so desperate for Arabic speaking people, I'd find something. I'm sure it'd be OK with my family too."

"Yeah," was all that Frank could say and thought: *Just like I realized it's no tragedy if I get outted. But, damn it, how could we've been so stupid about those phones? Thought it was clever to mail them to tweak their noses. Better get back into the conversation or he'll really get suspicious.*

"Hard to believe, too, there's someone in the world who doesn't know some guys are uncircumcised," Brad said. "Must've been some really weird Arab guy who's never been exposed to anything. Like sure, almost everyone in this country's cut. But not in other places. Even in Jordan, the Christians are uncut."

"Yeah," is all that Frank could think to say.

"You want dessert?" Brad asked. "I've got ice cream and some really nice cookies from the bakery."

"No," Frank answered almost instinctively then thought: *Wait. If I turn down his offer now, he might really get suspicious.* He said: "Wait. Yeah, why not. Sure, some ice cream and cookies sounds good."

"I got vanilla chocolate fudge strawberry twirl," Brad said. "That OK?"

"Oh, yeah," Frank said faking enthusiasm as he drained his wine glass.

Brad asked: "Coffee too? You know every gay household has to have an espresso machine."

Well, mine doesn't, Frank thought and said: "Sounds good if you're having some," and thought: *Strong coffee might settle me down or give me a good excuse to be rattled.*

"Coming right up," Brad said. "I'll take the dishes."

Frank leaped from his chair saying: "Here, let me help you," saying to himself: *Anything to distract us from that topic.* "It might be 'Minnesota

THREE KISSES

Nice' for you to invite me, but I can clear the table while you dish up the ice cream. You want help with the dishes, too?"

Brad replied: "No, no need. There's a dishwasher. I have only one pot I cooked the rice in. That's the beauty of grilling outside. Sugar? Milk?"

"No, just black," Frank answered.

After he brought coffee, Brad asked: "You want to watch a movie? I got a couple of new ones. I thought I'd be home alone tonight and I'm tired of reading."

Frank thought: *Damn. Staying to watch a movie's the last thing I want to do. I just want to get away from here and think over what I've just learned. But damn it, if I just get up and go he might get suspicious. Let me think.*

After sitting to drink coffee, he said: "Thanks a lot. It's been a long day. Those laps kind of wore me out. I haven't had a chance to get real exercise in a long time. I've got to get back into the routine of going to the gym. I'm sure they've got one on Fort Meade somewhere."

"Oh, yes, somewhere," Brad said. "We civilians aren't allowed to use it. Maybe ask some of your guards."

"Good idea," he said sipping the last of his coffee.

"There're some private gyms around here too," Brad continued. "I've been planning to check them out, but so far, haven't done anything."

"I need to use your facilities again and then I'll go, if that's OK with you," Frank said.

"OK," Brad replied. "Thanks for spending time. I really enjoyed being with you and that isn't just 'Minnesota Nice.'"

Frank said. "I appreciate your hospitality, really. It's been a great day for me." *Except for the startling revelation of how I got found out*, he said to himself.

He returned to the living room where Brad was still standing, walked toward the front door, and said: "This was fun; hope we can do this again. Maybe at my place next."

Brad said: "Here let me show you how they say good bye in the Middle East."

"Like this?" Frank said as he put his arms around him and kissed him three times on each cheek, left, right, left.

548

NEW BEGINNINGS • CHAPTER 19

BRAD AND FRANK SAY GOODBYE ARAB STYLE

"Yes," Brad exclaimed with a big smile." Where'd you learn that?

"From my straight-as-an-arrow Lebanese-American co-worker," Frank said as he walked out, turning to smile at Brad as the door was closed behind him.

Afterword

Welcome to the part of the book where I explain choices, make apologies, give thanks, and say what's on my mind.

The basic plot germinated ten years ago. It is even more relevant today with war in Syria, Yemen and Iraq in crisis, migrant crises, immigration issues in the US, gay lesbian issues, and many more issues of the mid twenty-teens.

This is a revised edition. Like many first-time authors, I learned from mistakes in the first edition. There would be no peace until I revised the book to make it more reader-friendly and remove other flaws. All the delightful characters and intriguing plot are still here.

This revision was set to be published in 2013. Here it is 2016. Unanticipated events delayed the process including two major international moves and an accident breaking bones that kept me from typing on a keyboard almost a year.

This delay was perhaps providential. Many fictional events and situations in this book created ten years ago have come to pass, maybe not exactly like in the book, but close enough. These include civil war in Syria and desperate attempts to escape the country; internal discord in Yemen and interference from Saudi Arabia; instability in Iraq and the difficulties of the U.S. government in dealing with the government and extricating itself. Especially disaffection of young Muslim Arab-American men in the U.S. and their radicalization. At the same time Muslims are increasingly integrated into U.S. society, especially at higher socio-economic levels, and on average have achieved education levels and income levels greater than the U.S. population as a whole. There have been significant advances in rights of homosexuals and their integration into society including the right to serve openly in the armed forces, the right to marry, emergence of predominantly homosexual churches, as well open acceptance of homosexuals in many mainstream religious groups. At the same time, there is an intensified anti-homosexual backlash that is hinted at in the book. Further, issues of immigration, especially by Hispanics, intensified.

This is a work of fiction. Many events actually occurred, but I had no idea they were going to occur when I started writing. The amount of serendipity, maybe providence, was utterly amazing; I want to tell you about some.

Some 30 or more years ago, when the cold war was at its height, I happened to watch an hour-long spy story on television in which the old Soviet Union created an exact double of a male U.S. military officer in order to infiltrate him into the U.S. for some nefarious purpose. The actual plot was soon forgotten, but it did occur to me that there's one part of a man's body that can't be easily duplicated. Then I thought what would happen if there were a closeted gay male military officer who works with the duplicated officer, who discovers the duplicate, and agonizes over what to do? This was the 1980s before 'don't ask don't tell'.

A few fanciful thoughts popped into my head that this would make a good story for a book and that I should write it. Because I was busy with my professional and personal life, raising a family, and all sorts of things, nothing was written. On a very few occasions, I shared thoughts with friends and acquaintances who gave occasional suggestions.

Soon the cold war was over and the basis for a book was gone. I forgot about it, or thought I had. To my surprise, the idea lingered in my subconscious. In very late 2005, four years after nine-eleven, al Qaeda had matured and grown more sophisticated. The idea I thought was gone, resurfaced. The story could be written with al Qaeda as perpetrators. Al Qaeda would have no difficulty obtaining access to Soviet, now Russian, medical technology. The idea kept kicking and screaming in my head and I would have no peace until I started writing, which I did in early 2006.

Even though inability to duplicate parts of a man's body was the initial impetus, other inspirations came strongly to develop the plot. The original impetus merely provided a thread to move the plot along. Inspirations came to focus on current events, lives and culture of Arab and Muslim Americans, issues of homosexuals. Little could I have anticipated that now in 2016 these issues are even more relevant and that the Islamic State would essentially supplant al Qaeda.

The skeleton of the plot took form readily. Because al Qaeda would almost certainly use an Arab for the duplicate, the duplicated military officer in the U.S. must be Arab-American. One immigrant group is obvious: Lebanese have migrated to the U.S. in fairly large numbers for at least 100 years and Lebanese-Americans, now into the second and third generations, have risen to high levels of U.S. politics and government, business, entertainment, and likewise in the U.S. armed forces. Identifying an Arab-American military officer to be duplicated would not be a challenge so I didn't bother to describe how it happened.

Al Qaeda would have difficulty operating in Lebanon, especially with access to medical facilities. The neighboring country of Syria presents no difficulty: Syrians are identical to Lebanese ethnically, especially physical features. It is well reported in news media that terrorist groups such as Hamas and Hizbollah operate openly in Syria with the support and blessing of the Syrian government; it is widely speculated that al Qaeda also operates in Syria. It has been reported that many Iraqi Sunnis have fallen under the influence of al Qaeda when they fled to Syria.

Syria was essentially a Soviet satellite for many years and lingering Russian influence is apparent; a Russian medical doctor in Syria would not be unusual. Lattakia, a city on the coast of Syria, provided an ideal and plausible location with its proximity to Lebanon and its university medical school and hospital.

In an early element of serendipity, in late 2005 while the idea was still kicking and screaming in my head, by chance I read a newspaper article about a community of Yemeni immigrants in Lackawanna, New York, a Buffalo suburb, that was struggling to keep a low profile and get on with their lives despite a split in sentiment towards al Qaeda. It has been widely reported that many founders of al Qaeda, including Osama bin Laden, have Yemeni roots and some in Lackawanna were in sympathy. At the same time, many Yemenis are upset at al Qaeda's dirty work in their country as was Omar. Lackawanna became an ideal place to develop a story.

Early in 2006 within days of writing about the smuggling activity, news media announced a major FBI raid and bust of cigarette and other smuggling activities to Canada from Dearborn, Michigan, involving Arab immigrants supporting Arab terrorist groups. If it could happen in Dearborn, it could happen in Lackawanna. I had no direct knowledge or suspicion of such activity in Lackawanna by Arabs or anyone else. Activities described here in Lackawanna are completely fictional. At the same time, it is well known that a community of Lebanese Shia settled in Dearborn thus inspiring the character of Joe Shaito.

It is fairly common for Arab immigrant shopkeepers all over the U.S. to sell food and other products made in the Middle East as sidelines to their regular businesses. Most products do come from Lebanon where there is a food processing industry and Lebanese have been global traders for thousands of years, at least since the days of the ancient Phoenicians. It is realistic for Baria to have such products in her shop and for Mohammad to be a distributor to shops along the highways through Appalachia. The use of a distribution activity for an extortion and protection racket is entirely fictional inspiration.

At an early point, I had the inspiration that one of the characters would be arrested in Canada for involvement in smuggling which would be connected to a major breakthrough in the plot.

On almost the exact day I was writing this part of the story, the largest item of serendipity occurred when the Royal Canadian Mounted Police (RCMP) made a *major* bust of an al Qaeda terrorist cell in Mississauga, Ontario, near Toronto, barely 100 miles from Lackawanna. This cell planned to bomb highly visible targets in the Toronto area. I had no inclination that such a bust would occur, but it enhanced the credibility of the plot considerably.

The storyline had already mentioned Yemenis in Lackawanna regularly traveled to Mississauga, a place with a catchy name selected merely by glancing at a map. It fit perfectly; there was no need to change the name of the city where the bust occurred. The only small literary license was to move the date of the arrest forward a few days from the actual date of June 2, 2006, to fit the timeline. Let me state I have no knowledge of the operations of the RCMP; everything comes from news media and inspired imagination.

Similarly, early in the writing process, the inspiration came for a major part of the plot to move through Guantanamo Bay Naval Station. In another major item of serendipity, at the exact time I was writing this part of the plot, three detainees at Guantanamo committed suicide and the base commander made his well-publicized comment about 'asymmetric acts of aggression'.

In early summer of 2006, in a chance encounter at a sidewalk café in a foreign capital city, I had a long discussion with a member of the Falls Church in Falls Church, Virginia, in which I heard about this congregation's dissatisfaction with the Episcopal Church of the U.S. and its likely withdrawal and affiliation with the Anglican Bishop of Rwanda as a protest against gay bishops, women's roles in the church, and related issues. Instantly, I knew it would fit the storyline, but would be several chapters later.

In November, 2006, I actually wrote the first draft of the chapter where this bit of serendipity fits the plot. In December, 2006, the Falls Church and others announced their withdrawal from the Episcopal Church and affiliation with an Anglican bishop in Nigeria. Apparently the congregation had decided to affiliate with Nigeria, not Rwanda. I did not change what I had written because the person actually said it was the bishop of Rwanda. Much later, in 2013, I learned that the attempt to pull away from the Episcopal Church failed and split the congregation.

In a tragic and sad element of serendipity, in July 2006, a war began between Hizbollah in Lebanon and Israel. It was exactly at the point where this war fit the story line and I readily incorporated it. Failure to do so would seriously detract from the story. Timing was so fortuitous I did not need to rewrite anything nor take license with dates.

Yet another item of serendipity was the location of Adnan's sleeper cell in Mesquite, Texas. Mesquite was a random choice from glancing at a map and choosing among the many possible suburbs of Dallas. In late

THREE KISSES

summer of 2006, after I had written this part of the story, news media reported local police and the FBI had intercepted a group of Arab immigrants operating out of Mesquite, Texas, in an alleged scheme to transport a huge amount of cell phones to be used to detonate bombs. I had no prior knowledge of any actual al Qaeda or other Arab terrorist activity in Mesquite, Texas, but the story was given instant credibility.

In the fall of 2006, news media reported the unfortunate event in which a group of imams were required to leave an airplane in Denver, Colorado, for the sole reason they were Muslim imams. The imams were on their way home from a conference of imams in Minneapolis at the University of Minnesota. This unfortunate event confirms Minneapolis and the University of Minnesota are indeed places where Islamic-Americans feel comfortable conducting high-level professional scholarly conferences validating Omar's decision to obtain a PhD there.

Another small item of serendipity and coincidence: the CIA did indeed have a new director on the exact date I had in the time line; I discovered this fact the day I wrote it.

All characters are entirely fictional and figments of inspirations. There are no thin disguises or composites. Names are actual commonplace given names and surnames in the U.S. and other countries. Failure to use common names would result in a story that would sound contrived. There are no actual given-name and surname combinations known to me. Nonetheless, because these are common names, there are bound to be plenty of people with these names. To all the persons named Martha Bishop, Frederick Watson, Luis Mendoza, etc., this is NOT *you*.

There is one way where I used actual persons. Early in the writing, a dear trusted friend read chapters one by one. This person told me that I had not described persons' physical appearance and that I really must do so. I became much more observant of persons I saw walking down the street, sitting in eating places, riding on public transport, etc. Often I would be startled saying to myself: That's exactly who I picture as Rhonda Philips, Paco, Frank, etc. If by chance you noticed me looking at you intently, you might be in this book. Thanks for lending me your appearances.

In even more bizarre coincidences, characters who I created and described in this book came into my life and became good friends six or more years later with different names of course. No names, but you know who you are.

Some persons mentioned, though not characters, are obviously well-known public figures, mostly prominent political figures. It would be contrived not to use actual names. Please let me emphasize the opinions expressed about these public figures are entirely those of Brahim, Patrick, Omar, etc., and are used to develop the storyline. They are not my opinions nor those of the publishers of this book. It would be incorrect to say these opinions are fictional because there are indeed persons who hold them; such opinions have more than just a few adherents. Still these opinions expressed in this book are entirely in a fictional context. The same thing can be said about Patrick's, Brad's, and others' opinions about events and circumstances.

Geographic locations were inspired lots of ways. Some like Russelville, Alabama, Mesquite, Texas, and Lincoln, Nebraska, were random choices looking at maps. Others are obvious, like Lattakia and Lackawanna, for reasons explained in the story. Wright-Patterson Air Force Base was selected because activities that occur there are well known. The office where Felicia, Frank, Patrick, and Jen work is a fictional inspiration. Yet similar type activities do exist there.

The choice of Minneapolis as Brad's hometown was not entirely random. It is common knowledge that the twin cities area of Minnesota has a strong presence of the United Church of Christ with a focus on its open and acceptance policy towards homosexuals. Other locations could have been selected, but the inspiration for Minneapolis stuck.

Later, using an online search similar to that described as being used by Omar, the University of Minnesota and the University of North Carolina at Chapel Hill emerged as number one and two locations in the U.S. to obtain a PhD in Islamic theology. Both fit the story line, but Minnesota became Omar's choice. Then much later following the procedure Roger Chen described, Duluth, Minnesota, emerged as the most logical location for Brahim's and Boudi's incarceration. The serendipitous connection between Omar's studies in Minneapolis and his work in Duluth became apparent.

Other locations like Baltimore, Cincinnati, Hamilton, and Lovington followed logically from the story line. As indicated by the photos included, I actually visited some of these places. Some photographs were taken from the internet and are in the public domain. Apologies if I failed to acknowledge copyrights and I will rectify such failures in later printings.

Information about these locations is readily obtained from public-domain sources like the internet. Wherever feasible, I used actual names for streets and roads. In a bizarre coincidence, I made a random choice of the Germanton Road exit off U.S. Highway 52 for the seemingly fictional location of a Days Inn in Winston-Salem based on a glance at a Rand-McNally map of the area. Later when I used software that gave more detailed information (this was in the days before Google Maps), you guessed it, there actually is a Days Inn at that location.

North Carolina is a natural location for the southern end of Mohammad's extortion and protection racket because it is well known state tax on cigarettes is low and many persons travel there to buy them. Tobacco-vending establishments such as the one in the story are visible on major highways near state lines. The business in Winston-Salem in the story is fictional. Winston-Salem is well known as a center of cigarette manufacturing. It is also well known that agents from other states observe purchases of cigarettes in North Carolina. The scene here is fictional inspiration. I have no knowledge how Virginia State Police actually operate.

The choice of Florida as the home of Frank's ancestors was quirky inspired by the rarity of native Floridians.

Early in the plot I realized that I needed a location for Adnan's sleeper cell. Because he had an Hispanic false identity, his cell needed to be located in a place with a large Hispanic population and in a large metropolitan area where cell members could blend in. Several cities including Denver, Los Angeles, Houston, Phoenix, Chicago, and New York were possibilities. I was drawn to the Southwest U.S. and for a moment seriously considered

NEW BEGINNINGS • AFTERWORD

Phoenix. For reasons I cannot describe, the inspiration for Dallas kept coming into my mind; the suburb of Mesquite as the actual location was a random choice. The choice of the Dallas metropolitan area was serendipitous. Luie, Paco, *et al.* would pass though Dallas on their way to Mexico and Frank could readily fly from there.

Locations in Mexico actually exist also and were selected mostly by looking at a map.

Government agencies in the U.S. and Mexico actually exist and their operations are generally as described on their web sites. I have no direct knowledge of their specific operations nor do I know anyone who works at any of them. In particular, I have no knowledge about intelligence gathering and investigative activities in Mexico and the U.S. I only hope that my fictional representations have not done a serious disservice.

Activities of the Moukhabarat in Syria can be discovered fairly easily if one is attentive. I have no direct knowledge; it is indeed a secret police force.

Mary Help of Christians Roman Catholic Church actually exists in Fairborn, Ohio, and has an interesting, appealing web site.

Reference to the website of the Metropolitan Community Church (MCC) indicates that it does have a congregation in Laurel, Maryland.

Brand names, Nike, Dockers, etc., are well known icons of American retail and are used to add authenticity. Did I receive commercial representation payment? Absolutely not.

Similarly, actual names of commercial establishments were used to provide authenticity. J.C. Penney, Walmart, Wendy's, Golden Corral, etc. are well known. Grand Central actually exists in Baltimore at the location mentioned as does Inn Leather in Fort Lauderdale. The Serpent actually exists in Cincinnati and has an interesting web site. I have not been there except to make photographs and have no idea how it actually operates. Again, I can only hope that my fictional description does not do a great disservice.

Gino's Diner in Buffalo is fictional although similar diners exist throughout the area. 'Gino's' is a common name for eating establishments, especially in the Northeast U.S. If such a place exists, I hope it is as good as I have described.

Similarly, the Elite Bakery in Hamilton is fictional. Similar bakeries do exist in Midwestern county seat towns so the description is not completely far-fetched.

The Hispanic bakery in Lovington, New Mexico, does exist, or at least it did some 40 years ago when I passed through there on a cross-country trip in the days before there were many interstates. The apple fritters were so yummy I still remember them vividly. Continuing along the same highway westward from Lovington about 100 miles, one passes through an apple growing region and indeed New Mexico apples are the best, or so claims the New Mexico Apple Growers' Association.

Felicia's ethnicity is yet additional fortunate serendipity. From the outset, I realized I needed someone on the inside working with Patrick to help al Qaeda and a female would fit the story line better. In order for such a person to be controllable by al Qaeda, she would almost certainly need to have a Muslim heritage. While pondering and waiting for inspiration, I read a news article about the Philippine army's having attacked a suspected al Qaeda terrorist group in the Muslim area of the southern island of Mindanao. Bingo.

Filipinos, especially women, often have married U.S. armed forces personnel stationed in the Philippines and have then moved to the U.S. Many other Filipinos have immigrated through the years when the Philippines was a U.S. territory. Also, I recall having read a feature story about the early tendency of the U.S. Navy to recruit Philippine men to be their mess stewards and these recruits became U.S. citizens and settled in the U.S. Maryland, perhaps because of the Naval Academy, and Baltimore is an area with a relatively large Philippine population.

I have no legal knowledge and training and no medical knowledge and training. I only know what I read, hear on the radio, or see on television. I can only hope I have done no great violence to reality.

Many dear friends and some casual acquaintances, have contributed greatly to my writing this story and the revision. Sone of them would not want to be identified by name, so I will not identify any. You know who you are. Great hugs and kisses where appropriate, and eternal thanks and gratitude.

The sequel, *Day of Judgment* is now ready. Please read and see which of your favorite characters are involved in new exciting intrigues.

Heath Daniels is a semi-retired consultant on various topics involving international activities. He was born and grew up in the U.S. where he worked for many years, moving often to different locations within the country. He now lives wherever his clothes are hung in a closet, recently outside the U.S. His work allows him to travel extensively. In the process he has developed a large network of colleagues and friends who have contributed directly and indirectly to insights and knowledge brought into this book. When he is not busy thinking of ways to spoil his grandchildren, he writes, reads, and travels. Throughout his life, he has been a keen observer of current events with special interests in culture and language, history, and spirituality, and reads extensively on the subjects. He has written and published extensively on professional topics. This is his first novel.

This book is dedicated to my Muslim friends and acquaintances, most of whom are Arabs. They have indeed made significant contributions to society and culture in the U.S. and other countries. One inspiration was to show them in both positive and negative ways. Like all human beings they have their upsides and downsides.

It is also dedicated to gay friends and acquaintances who represent many walks of society and demonstrate that gay men and women are like all other variations in society and the only thing is common is an affectional orientation for the same sex. In particular, this book was inspired to show that gay men can be involved in international intrigue in many different ways and that stereotypes do not apply.

Made in the USA
Columbia, SC
19 December 2017